THE PROMISE

L. M. AFFROSSMAN

SPARSILE BOOKS LTD

*To my mother who
said I would
and
To Jim (Bear) Campbell who
said I should
and
To Tom for being one of the good guys*

And this I believe: that the free, exploring mind of the
individual human is the most valuable thing in the world.
And this I would fight for: the freedom of the mind to
take any direction it wished, undirected.

John Steinbeck, East of Eden

Contents

Chapter 1

'HOW d'ye know when you're dead?'

The voice in Mags' ear was so sudden and so urgent that it was all she could do to prevent herself from glancing round to face her small interrogator. Instead, she put her pen down, and staring directly at the wall opposite, answered, 'I don't know. You just do.'

'But you must find out somehow. Mibbe when you've no skin left. Or when your fingers all drop off? Or mibbe when your eyeballs explode?'

'No. Nothing like that.'

'Then how?'

Still staring at the wall, Mags swallowed once then answered carefully. 'When you get to heaven, that's when you find out.'

For a while there was silence, and she might almost have believed that he'd left the room, when he asked, 'What's it like?'

'What's what like?'

'Heaven.'

Mags sighed. 'What do you mean, what is it like?'

'What colour is it?'

Another conundrum. Mags picked up her pen and dragged it across the top of her exercise book. It left a thin, straggling trail of ink, like a child's impression of the sky. 'Blue,' she said at last. 'Heaven is blue. Just like the sky or the sea.'

'The sea's not blue. It's grey.'

'Only in the rain.'

'I've only seen it in the rain.'

'Well, it's as blue as the sky when the sun shines. Like it is in hot countries.'

'Is it as blue as your ring?'

'Like sapphires? Yes, that kind of blue.'

As she said these things, Mags kept her head bent over the untidy pile of books and papers she'd been studying before Daniel entered the room. She was working on an essay that had to be handed in by lunchtime and she was running out of time. She gave him a pleading look. 'One more page then we'll talk. All right? Just one more.'

He gave a small shrug that might have been, yes, and she turned back to her work. To one side of the ancient kitchen table, which she always referred to as 'my desk', was a paperweight made from a painted egg box, given to her by Daniel last Christmas, her discarded glasses, a filled ashtray, and four cups of cold, half-drunk instant coffee. The rest of the table was covered in lecture notes, dog-eared books from the library and scrunched up balls of paper, bearing a strong resemblance to the droppings of some voracious, but nonetheless literary, beast. At her feet, was a parcel wrapped up in brown paper. She knew what it contained, but from time to time her toe would nudge against it curiously, like a small animal sniffing out its quarry.

She worked, marooned by the dingy yellow glow of a solitary lamp, the rest of the room still lost in the grey, cobwebby light of morning. Mags preferred it that way. The shadows hid the cramped corners, with their mottle of damp patches inexpertly concealed behind cheap prints. It gave the illusion of spaciousness. And besides it saved on electricity if you only burned one lamp.

Beyond the window was the sound of the street stretching itself to wakefulness. Children's voices rising, harsh as smoke, above the faint rumble of the traffic.

He shoved me.

No, he didnae.

Aye he did.

Mags rubbed the tip of her forefinger along one temple. Just a little longer. But it was no use. The noise of their ball thudding against the tenement wall, thump, thump, thump, had started up. She knew they would stay there all day kicking it, over and over, like a machine's mindless mechanism, until her nerves frayed and her temper flared. I shouldn't complain, she chided herself. At least they can't reach us up here. Not less than three times in the last month, she had passed by the shattered remains of her less elevated neighbours' windows. The police had been called. But nothing had been done and still they came back.

It was why Mags chose to work in the twilit hours of the morning when all was still. And even on Daniel's worst nights, the dawn would see him succumb to a fitful sleep. The morning was her time when she could look past the damp patches on the walls and beyond the window frames that rattled when cars drove past. A time when she could see into a different world. Hidden between the musty covers of her books, this world did not really exist for Mags, but she liked to peep into it, as though, by doing so, she was breaking some unwritten taboo. She read:

Freedom is always and exclusively freedom for the one who thinks differently

It was a feeling she enjoyed, the thrill of breaking the mould into which she'd been set.

'Is it cold in heaven?'

The question caught her off guard and she had to force herself not to look up. 'No. No, why should it be cold?'

'I thought it might be blue, like ice.'

'No. Heaven's a lovely warm blue.' She turned the page of her textbook with great deliberation. 'Like those flowers, we found in the park in the summer.'

'What were they called?'

'Forget-me-nots.'

'I knew that.'

She read again. Freedom is always and exclusively freedom for the one who thinks differently. But it had lost its meaning. It hummed inside her head, like a persistent and aggravating fly. The fly buzzed that the pursuit of Freedom was meaningless to someone like her, a woman who could never step into the light because she found it cheaper to live in the dark. And the more she read, the more the fly buzzed, and she might have given up on Rosa Luxemburg and her visions of liberty altogether had circumstances been otherwise.

As it was, she picked up another pen and slashed a vicious stroke of red through the last paragraph of her essay. And keeping her voice steady, went on describing the colour of heaven, as though merely voicing her own thoughts to an empty room. Because that was important. It was how you played the game.

Eventually, when she could think of no more ways to describe the loveliness of blue to a little boy, she paused and stole a sidelong look at Daniel. He was leaning on the edge of her chair, brows furrowed in concentration. He's looking better today, she thought. Very nearly pink. Her eye fell on the gap at his waistband. Thinner? Was he thinner? But he's growing. Little boys always go skinny before they grow.

But then he began to cough. A dry, wheezing cough that cracked out of him, like dead wood snapping under foot. She watched in terror as his lips turned blue.

Dear God, don't take him. Please. Not now.

She could see clearly the tracery of blue veins standing out on his forehead, and she wanted desperately to reach over and draw him to her. But he hated that. A little soldier must stand alone. And with difficulty she held herself in check.

He stopped coughing, and looking up, caught her anxious gaze. Guilty, she looked away. He waited, watching sternly by her side until he was sure she was bent over her work once more, then asked, 'Is there a big light in Heaven, like the sun?'

'Yes. A huge light.'

'Just like the sun?'

'No, bigger, much bigger. And brighter too. Everything's bigger and brighter in Heaven.'

Daniel considered this revelation for a moment before asking, 'Then do people get sunburnt a lot?'

A smile broke out on Mags' lips, and she had to catch her breath to keep it there. 'No, sweetheart,' she said carefully. 'In heaven, the light can't hurt you.'

'Not even to look at?'

'Not even to look at.'

She'd been about to say more, but a slight cough caught her attention and she whirled round.

'Ewan?'

Ewan. It still seemed strange to call him by his first name. Like that other world, there was something forbidden about such familiarity.

'I didn't hear the front door.' She glanced down at her watch. It had stopped again and she pretended to read its immobile face. 'It's later than I thought.'

He smiled, fleetingly. His mouth a crooked lightening streak illuminating the angular set of his features. Then the smile was gone and his expression resumed its usual solemn contours. She saw that he was dressed for lecturing, grey woollen trousers, and a jacket of olive green tweed, a little past its best. The sombre shades of a man, who wore his clothes always a little self-consciously, as though it was somehow surprising to find himself in them. Aristotle waking up in modern dress. Under his arm was a newspaper with a headline about John Major, something about a Conservative government leading the economy from strength to strength.

She considered practicing her ironic tone by making a comment, but Ewan was looking at Daniel over the top of little, half-moon spectacles. The ones he wore for driving or whenever he'd been holed up to in the library for hours. Mags had noticed that he often forgot to remove them, so that he carried his look of professorial distraction out into the world with him. And this little trace of conceit always gave her a pang of unexpected tenderness towards him. It was the bridge she used to cross into his world. But finding him standing there, intruding into the precious moments of her time with Daniel, she suddenly felt resentful, and found herself thinking, He shouldn't come here. He doesn't belong.

Then she felt guilty at her lack of charity. Ewan was a good man. And, if he wasn't always there, wasn't that partially her fault?

I need time, see? To prove I can go it alone.

And she was lucky Ewan had been so understanding, never pushing her for more commitment. She forced a smile. 'Going to the library?'

He glanced with deliberate slowness at the books under the crook of his arm then up to meet her eyes, and Mags felt some of her indignation coming back. The little ironic gestures, so charming at first, sometimes made her want to yell and smash things. She bit her lip. Maybe that's what he expects of me. Screaming and ranting, like a fishwife. Showing my true colours.

He was looking round, searching out the parcel wrapped in brown paper. 'Have you had a chance to start—'

'No.' She cut him short. 'I've an essay to finish.'

'I see.' He nodded absently, but she felt his disappointment. She had let him down. 'I'll start it tonight,' she said quickly. 'I wanted to give it time.'

But his eyes were on Daniel again. 'I think we need to talk.'

'O?' The blood was rising to her cheeks.

And the anger. The anger that sprang out of nowhere, that welled up at the least provocation these days, exploding, like fireworks and spilling uncontrollably over her lips. Ewan was looking at her, examining her actions with academic calm, and she had to breathe hard to stop herself from telling him to get out. None of his business. Judging me when he can walk away whenever he pleases. Men can do that. Never the women. Never the mothers. She was caught, trapped in the fine print of motherhood. No get out clause.

She glanced over to see if Daniel had sensed her sudden tension, but with that strange, little old man manner of his, he was already heading towards the door.

'I want to do a painting in my room,' he said.

Mags nodded and produced one of her bright, false smiles of encouragement. 'Don't take too long. You've got school in half an hour.'

'It's all right. I done some of it yesterday.'

'Did some,' she corrected automatically, but Daniel was speaking to Ewan now.

'It's going to be about heaven,' he said, emphasising the last word deliberately. 'I'm going to do it blue with a big light.'

Ewan frowned slightly, then offered, 'I'll come through later and take a look.'

'You can't,' Daniel stated emphatically. 'I have to go to school.'

Mags was torn between the urge to admonish Daniel for being rude and the pride she felt in the way Daniel spoke to the older man as an equal. 'Don't get paint all over your clothes,' she said at last, trying to sound stern. Daniel nodded vaguely at some spot above her head then left, shutting the door after him. As always, Mags felt a wrench whenever he disappeared from view. 'Don't forget to take your pills,' she called. 'Remember what Dr Collins said.'

She was smiling again. But like the sun in heaven, her smile had no warmth.

Chapter 2

THE patchwork of dream and sleep, which had held Sadie so snugly during the uncertain hours of night, was suddenly torn away, plunging her headfirst into the icy depths of consciousness. She awoke violently, and spluttering and gasping, hauled herself up the bed to a sitting position, trying vainly to recall where she was.

For a moment, her dreaming mind refused to accept the coarse outlines of the bedroom as real, transforming the mirrored dresser and the tall, Louis XIV armoire into towering, leafless oaks. The swirls and whorls of the carpet's pattern formed a brackeny undergrowth, and the chill in the air held the promise of snow.

But slowly and painfully things settled back into their familiar shapes and she began to accept the grey shadows for what they were and to put the tremulous Kodachrome of her dreams aside.

With difficulty, she flicked the switch of her bedside lamp and looked round the room. Something had wakened her. But what? Everything seemed the same. The coverlet on the bed was undisturbed. She had always been a more peaceful sleeper than Isaac. The big, heavy furniture stood as solidly as ever, and the lined velvet curtains were pulled so tight that not even the tiniest chink of light could escape them. She shook her head, trying to discard the cobwebs. If it wasn't something in the room that had wakened her, then what could it be?

A cog in her brain turned. She'd been dreaming. Of escape.

A long time since I've had that dream, she thought A life time almost. Was there something different this time? Something about the end? She snapped her fingers with recollection. It was something important. Only trouble was, now she couldn't remember what the important thing was.

For a while she struggled to bring it to the surface, but eventually fell back on the pillows, exhausted. Her eyes felt gritty, and she rubbed them with the back of her hand. Overslept again. Always a bad thing. You sleep too long in the morning then you spend the night counting the stars. That's what Isaac always said, and bless him, if he hadn't always been right. She felt a pang at the thought of Isaac. It didn't matter how long he'd been dead, just the thought of him always sent a poignant ripple through her. Not that Sammy understood. 'Dad's been dead twenty years, ma,' he said. 'It's time to move on.' But Sammy was young, and what do the young know?

Thinking about Sammy made Sadie suddenly wonder if his wife had received the present she'd sent. It wasn't much. Just a bottle of eau de cologne She wasn't even sure if what's-her-name — *what was her name? Sammy said she forgot on purpose, but it wasn't true. It just wouldn't stick. Jodie or Codie? One of those unlikely American names.*— Anyway, she didn't even know if what's-her-name liked perfume. But what could you do on a pension? If Isaac had been alive things would have been different, but as it was. Well, there was no point in dwelling on as it was. The thought of the present suddenly brought to mind the important thing she'd forgotten, and it wasn't so important after all. Today was her birthday.

Sadie heaved herself out of bed and shuffled over to the dresser. She inspected her face in the mirror. The glass had turned greenish over the years and it was hard to make anything out. Last time he'd been over, Sammy had said she should get a new one, offered to buy it himself. But Sadie was fond of that mirror. It had been a wedding present or anniversary present from Isaac or was it his mother? Anyway, what do the young know about the value of things? The minute a thing gets a little chip or a tiny scratch they're all for throwing it out and buying a new one. You tried to tell them, but who listens?

Sadie leaned forward and squinted at the greenish reflection. The reflection squinted back. 'Sadie,' she said out loud to herself. 'At eighty-one, birthdays are not what you most need.'

Daniel was listening. His small, tense body pressed against the door of his bedroom, straining to hear every word. His mother was angry. He could tell by the crash, clatter of dirty plates being thrown into the sink. Mags always tidied when she was angry. Not that the place would look any cleaner when she had finished. It was too small and they had too many things. Even when Mags had time to do the dishes there were always clothes hanging up to dry, and toys and games he'd played before bedtime but grown bored with, and piles of books and papers stuck through with pens and pencils, like huge, unsteady porcupines. When she was in a good mood, his mother used to joke that somewhere underneath it all there must be a carpet. But when she was in a bad mood, like now, she stirred things about and threw things in the sink, as though she could impose order simply by moving everything round.

'You don't know what it's like,' she was saying. 'You can't know.'

Ewan's voice was a growl, low and rumbling, but Daniel heard him say,

'I just think you're on dangerous ground.'

'Do you now?'

Mags voice was brittle, and she sounded as though she was throwing words when she would have preferred to throw plates.

Daniel couldn't see Ewan, but he imagined him standing as he usually did during arguments, with his feet apart, hands in pockets, an unreadable expression on his face. The immovable object against the unstoppable force.

'I'm just saying,' he said slowly, 'that it's dangerous to start discussing heaven with him.'

'It wasn't a discussion,' she snapped defensively. 'He just wanted to ask a few questions.'

'But why on earth tell him it's blue?'

'Because,' she replied ferociously, 'it was the furthest thing I could think of from red. You know how he hates red. And you know why.'

Daniel stiffened. Blood. Don't think about blood.

'I still think it was a mistake.'

'Why? Do you think he'll be upset if he finds out I'm wrong?' There was a catch in Mags' voice, but Daniel didn't hear it. His hands had suddenly balled into fists and his eyes had grown dark with pain.

If he finds out I'm wrong.

The words swam in his head. Dangerous words, words whose meaning he didn't want to catch.

Finds out I'm wrong.

She doesn't know. His brows drew down against his thoughts. But he couldn't stop them, and they came tumbling out, forming a dreadful kind of reason out of his confusion. Heaven is blue, that's what she'd said. But now she was saying that she might be wrong. It was the most important, most special question in the whole wide world and she'd lied. She'd told him lies.

Ewan's voice had risen a little, as though he was getting impatient. 'No, of course I don't mean that. All I'm saying is, that when you start lying, it's too easy to contradict yourself. What if, tomorrow you said the colour of heaven was pink. Children are very sensitive to that sort of thing.'

'And you'd know all about that, would you?' Mags sneered then regretted it the moment she'd said it. Ewan coloured, a deep, unflattering shade 'I don't pretend to be any expert on children,' he said quietly. 'But I am fond of Daniel, and I wish you'd see sometimes that you aren't the only one who cares.'

Mags didn't answer. She swirled the dishes round in the sink, oblivious to how little affect the tepid water was having. She wanted to say she was sorry for the low blow. But she was also angry at him for patronising her. And, at the same time, she was afraid he might be right. Eventually, she said, 'I'd better check Daniel puts his coat on. I think it's going to rain.'

'Daniel. Danny. It's time for school.' She opened the door to his room, but there was no sign of him. His paints were strewn about the floor, and he seemed barely to have started on the picture of heaven. Mags was disappointed. She liked to see him to the school gate, then stand, feigning disinterest, as he gave her a perfunctory wave and ran off to join his classmates. And this morning she had hoped Ewan would offer a lift, letting them play at being a family for a little while. A chance to see what it would be like when they were finally together. But, then again, maybe it was for the best. At least Daniel had gone out without hearing any of her outburst. Unconsciously, she ran the nails of her left hand down the wrist of her right. Stupid. Stupid, she said aloud. 'When will you learn to keep your mouth shut?'

She picked the still damp painting up, and studied it. The top half of the picture was filled in with a block navy blue. Below the skyline was the outline of an angel. Mags could tell it was an angel because it had giant, improbable-looking wings coming out of its back, like the plastic angel they placed on top of the Christmas tree each year. It seemed to be carrying something in its hands, an oblong shape that could have been a cake or possibly even the console of a computer. Below the angel, a small boy with a disproportionately wide smile was reaching up to accept the heavenly gift. Looking at it, made Mags' heart constrict, and she placed it hastily on the unmade bed and hurried from the room.

And in her haste, she quite failed to notice Daniel's school bag lying in the far corner of the room, where it had been thrown. It was lying helplessly upside down, like an overturned turtle, its innards spilling across the carpet; his homework from the night before, the clumsy sandwiches she had lovingly made for his lunch; the pills that Dr Collins had prescribed.

Chapter 3

SADIE put down her needles and looked inside her knitting bag. There was a skein of grey wool and she lifted it out and matched it to the incomplete sleeve hanging from one needle. It might do. In this light the shade seemed identical. But it was too hard to tell. And what if it was worn outside? Even the tiniest differences became obvious when you saw things in daylight. She peered closely at the wool, trying to detect a change in shade. But the light in the lounge was so dim first thing in the morning. You couldn't tell a colour in amongst all these shadows. She tried not to glance at the doorway. But there was no denying that the light was better in the hall. She could see it peeping round the door, like a beckoning finger. And it would only take a minute. She got to her feet, and trying not to walk too hastily, hurried out.

Once there, she made a great show of examining the wool, attempting to fool an audience made up only of herself. But, no matter how hard she tried, her eyes kept falling on the mat beneath the letterbox, registering that it was empty.

It was still empty when she came out to check if the soil around the potted geranium was moist, and later when she decided the banister couldn't go another day without dusting.

Eventually, when the grandfather clock in the dining room wheezed out an asthmatic quarter hour chime, she had to admit that it was well past time for the morning post. Was there a second post on a Friday? She couldn't remember. But surely a person couldn't spend all day making excuses to enter the hall.

Why not? Asked a voice in her head. What have you to be so busy with?

Stop being an old fool, she told herself sternly. You were the one who said at eighty-one birthdays are not what you most need.

But it was strange and sad not to have anyone remember your birthday, and a little dejected, she turned back towards the kitchen to make herself a cup of tea. On either side of the plaster archway that led to the kitchen were pictures of Sammy. Black and white images of a snub-nosed, velvet-headed infant in gilded frames. Starched, stiff school portraits. The rebellious teenage years. And finally, her favourite, the one of him on his graduation day, a proud, dark-eyed, young man ready to fly the nest.

It was this image of Sammy that stuck in Sadie's mind, and it was how she pictured him whenever he entered her thoughts. And so the last time he'd come over on a visit, she'd been mildly shocked to discover he had a beard.

'Why should you have noticed, Ma?' he'd said. I only grew it twelve years ago.'

But that was Sammy. Always quick with the answers.

No, he hasn't forgotten, she decided. Such a thoughtful boy. Phones regularly. Not like Ruth's eldest, and she's only on the other side of the country. Now Sammy, we've got the entire Atlantic Ocean separating us.

Sammy had always been such a good boy. Only he'd been so busy lately. Pressures of work, he'd said. So maybe he was a little late this year. It wasn't the end of the world. And who ever died because their birthday card was late?

Her eyes settled on a baby photo. Sammy swaddled in a white lace-work shawl. The shawl that Isaac had managed to ruin by putting it in the loft when she'd told him there were moths the size of bats up there. But that was men. You couldn't tell them anything. The pattern of the shawl was still quite clear even if the picture was —*how old was it? nearly forty years surely.*— Still, it was a beautiful shawl, delicate as a cobweb, but snug. A baby could feel protected in a shawl like that.

'Don't open your eyes.'

The words were so clear, that for a moment, Sadie thought that they'd been said out loud. But it was just memory playing tricks on her again. Sounds and scenes from the past had been seeping out into the present a lot recently, enveloping her when she least expected it. That was the trouble with getting old, she supposed. And then she remembered that this wasn't the first time she'd supposed that, and reckoned that was part of getting old too.

She went into the kitchen, and ignoring the jar of decaffeinated granules Sammy had brought during his last visit, got out a packet of Earl Grey tea. The aroma of scented leaves filled the air as soon as she opened the packet, soothing her disappointment, and hinting that a little something to sweeten their flavour wouldn't be such a tragedy in the circumstances. She put down the packet and went to the cupboard to fetch the sugar.

'Don't open your eyes.'

Her mother's hands were over her eyes, hiding the light. She was giggling as much from fear of falling as from excitement, but her mother guided her steadily twisting this way and that and turning her in circles until she had no idea where she was.

'Look now.' She took her hands from her eyes and all Sadie could see were dazzling stars of light. But, after a moment, the stars solidified and she found herself swaying on the ship's deck looking down into a world of grey. Grey buildings, rising sombre as giants to meet skies, greyer still. A drab world of lead and ash. Hung from the walls were monstrous portraits of stern-looking men, and banners proclaiming: Long Live The Communist Party and Life To Our Proletarian Brothers. It seemed that they had been painted in red, but the pigment had bled away so that now they were the dirty pink of soiled bandages.

Sadie's bewildered eyes sought her mother out. She was gazing over the rail, her eyes black and unreadable. 'This is Russia,' she said softly, almost as though she couldn't believe it. 'Our new home.'

Fearfully, Sadie glanced behind her, looking back the way they had come. There was nothing to see, only miles and miles of grey water reaching all the way back to meet a pewter sky. She might have dreamed that there was a world beyond there. Her mother's hand was on her shoulder and she tilted her head towards her.

'Are we ever going back to Glasgow?' she asked in a frightened voice. And her mother answered,
'Never.'

As the memory faded, Sadie found herself holding the door to the cupboard, eyes misted with the resinous passage of time. She wrenched herself back to the present with difficulty, mentally scolding herself for drifting off again.

Old fool, she chided. You've got to find something to do with yourself. That's what Sammy would say. She glanced guiltily at a large, metal biscuit tin lying on top of one of the counters. The archive. She hadn't touched it in months. Sammy would be cross.

She pulled over a stool to sit down on, then gingerly reached out and prised open the lid, disturbing a layer of dust as she did so. It was all as she remembered, yellowing pages, their edges curling, faded photographs forgetting their images. An old woman's memories. A box of dried leaves.

She lifted out the sheet at the top. It was newer than the rest and bore the motto of Glasgow University in a tiny scroll along the top, *Via Vertias Vita*. She placed it face-down on the counter wanting to avoid the polite reproach in its content. *I would be grateful if you would contact me with the final draft by …*

She shut the words out and began to turn out the photographs, one by one.

Rivka Lazareva
Dead.
Mikhail Leskov
Dead.
Leib Kagan? Haven't heard from him in years. She put it with the others.

Probably dead.

The heap of the deceased grew, staring out of their frames with blank, indifferent eyes, as if to remind her that they were gone. And in their going she was forgotten, vanishing a little more from living memory with each passing year. Abruptly, she swept the photos back into the tin. 'My God,' she thought. 'I'm disappearing.'

Somehow the tea didn't seem so inviting any more. And, come to think of it, since Sammy had cleared out her cupboards on Dr Farmer's orders, there was nothing to help the tea go down. And how could you drink good strong tea without a little cake or even a sweet biscuit? That did it. She got to her feet, and, mind made up, fetched her hat and coat, and hurried out of the house.

Daniel hadn't meant to get on the bus. He had left the flat blindly, like a sleepwalker negotiating a strange country. *Heaven is blue.* She hadn't understood. All that time he had been asking questions about heaven, bursting with the need to know what lay ahead of him, she'd been treating him like a little kid playing a game of let's pretend.

Nothing changes.

He'd heard his mother say that to Maureen, the woman who sometimes took care of him in the evenings.

'Did you hear? There was a fire at your old place.'

'In the kitchen?'

'Aye. Faulty wiring. They'd reported it. But nothing was done.'

'Nothing changes.'

But everything had changed. His mother's lie had toppled the world. If heaven wasn't blue, nothing was certain. Nothing could be the same. Ever again.

He felt as though he was floating in space unable to find his feet. For a time, blind instinct led him in the direction of school. But then a car overtook him, a blue Rover with his mother in the passenger seat, her anxious eyes scanning the pavement, and he dived for cover into the grimy confines of a bus shelter.

He stood there for a long time in amongst the fag ends, the smell of stale urine making him feel sick, unable to move forwards or to turn and go back. Then it happened.

An orange single-decker bus drew up and a couple of dowdy, grim-faced women climbed down. Daniel took a step towards the bus then stopped. What would he say if his mother asked him what he had done at school today? He took hold of the rail and hoisted himself on board. He could lie too.

'A thirty-five? Are ye sure, son?' The bus driver looked doubtful. But Daniel nodded and pushed a pound coin into his hand. The driver still did nothing, and Daniel had the terrible feeling that he was going to order him off the bus. *Away home to yer mammie.* With more bravery than he felt, he pulled himself up to his not very great height and said clearly. 'A thirty-five single, please.'

The driver continued to stare at him and Daniel fought the urge to bolt, then suddenly the man sighed and his shoulders sagged forward. Grudgingly, he began to count out the change. As soon as he had his ticket, Daniel hurried to the back of the bus where he would be less conspicuous. Avoiding being noticed was a trait he'd picked up from his mother. He wedged himself against the emergency-exit and slouched down so that he could rest his knobbly knees against the metal back of the seat in front. He added the coins in the change to his *please-like-me* fund from Ewan. He thought of the money this way because Ewan always forced his mouth into a dreadful contortion of complicity as he slipped the pound coins into Daniel's pocket. The grin, that was supposed to make them co-conspirators, didn't make Daniel like him, but it didn't make him refuse the money either.

The bus gave a strangled gasp and began to inch forward. The sudden motion brought home to Daniel the enormity of what he had done, and he almost reached for the handle on the emergency-exit ready to make a break for it. But no. He wasn't going to give up. Not today. He made himself sit still, listening to the raspy sound of his breath, just as his mother made him do when he was having a bad night, and gradually he felt calmer. He knew this bus, the 23B.

During the summer his mother took him on it as often as she could afford. She liked to show him the university where she went every weekday. Holding his hand, she'd point up at windows made of many little squares of glass that you couldn't see into. 'That's where I'm getting an education,' she'd tell him. And Daniel would look up at the windows that you couldn't see through and wonder if you could see through them from the other side, and if you couldn't, what was the point in having them.

And afterwards they'd take their sandwiches, and the lemonade they kept in an ancient, leaky thermos, and sit in the park, watching the astonishing feats of boys on skateboards. And it wouldn't be until they got home that his mother's face would close up again, and she would stop telling jokes and he would know to leave her to her thoughts.

From his vantagepoint, he watched warily each new traveller that mounted the bus, and was filled with dread if they walked down the aisle towards the back. But no-one noticed him, and the bus creaked on until it reached the side of town where the houses no longer huddled defensively together and there were huge trees lining the pavements, like guards on watch.

He kept his mind as blank as possible, not letting his thoughts out. But once the bus stopped, and he spotted a woman, who looked like his mother standing outside the shelter. He looked away quickly, screwing his eyes tight shut.

What if tomorrow, you said the colour of heaven was pink?

He kept them shut until the bus moved off.

Fear made the journey seem twice as long as it normally did, but suddenly, without warning, his stop was upon him. And recognising the busy junction only at the last moment, he was forced to run the length of the aisle and stand clinging on to the central pole that divided the doors. For a moment, he was afraid that the driver wasn't going to stop, but a strangely dressed girl with a silver ring through her nose appeared by his side and reluctantly the bus slowed to a halt.

He jumped down as soon as the door opened and stood breathlessly on the pavement overwhelmed with the enormity of his adventure. An explorer. Just like dad. He was proud of himself for negotiating the trip, even getting off at the right stop. He was certain this was the right stop. What he wasn't ready for was a terrible sense of disorientation that made all the usual landmarks seem distant and unfamiliar.

If his mother had been with him they would have set off at once in a particular direction, first to the university then to the park. It was perfectly straightforward and they did it every time. But now, alone, things seemed quite different. He wasn't sure if the great sandstone church behind him shouldn't have been on his left, and he could see the gates to the park over the road, only that seemed much too soon. Nothing was in the right place, and it was so busy, that the more he looked the more confused he became.

After a while he sought refuge beside one of the huge oaks and tried to think what to do. He considered asking someone for directions, but everyone seemed to be in such a hurry that he was afraid to make an approach. It wasn't at all like the times he remembered coming. Then, everyone had seemed carefree and relaxed, taking their time as they wandered from shop to shop. Men on bicycles weaving through the near stationary lines of cars, and girls in the strangest clothes sauntering past, making his mother grin and nudge him. But now, in the grey light of morning, everything seemed bleak and forbidding. All he could see were the sombre blacks and browns of business suits marching past him in grim silence.

For a moment, he felt like crying. But he was an explorer and explorers don't cry, so he dabbed at his eyes with the cuff of his jacket, careful to make it seem as though he was only wiping his nose, and came to an important decision. He wanted to go to the park and he could see the gates on the other side of the road. Why not cross the road and take a peep through those gates? A great explorer never flinches in the face of adventure.

Chapter 4

THEY had reached Byres Road. Ewan was talking, as he had been for most of the journey, about the manuscript. Mags had heard it all before, but she didn't mind. He needs this time, she thought. Helen doesn't listen to him. Not the way I do. The thought gave her a delicious *frisson* of intimacy, and she turned to him, smiling. He glanced back a little anxiously.

'I'm boring you.'

'No. Not at all. I love to hear about your work.'

He smiled then. 'It'll be better when you've had time to read it yourself.'

Mags nodded, but she was thinking, I'll make a chilli tonight. He likes that. The mince isn't too old and I can spice it up with a lot of peppers. Her brow creased. But then Daniel won't eat it. He could have fish fingers. But he had fish fingers last night. It won't kill him. Not this once. But she could see his face, brows drawn down, accusing her. *You made him mince.* Maybe I should make mince and potatoes. Daniel will want those little dough-balls though. She glanced furtively at Ewan. He was frowning disdainfully at the cars in front of him, as though they had no right to be there. Not the type of man to find little dough-balls charming.

I'll make the chilli, she decided. But her fingers played remorsefully with the clasp of her bag, while she fought the urge to take her purse out and count the coins inside. I've got my bus fare. I can put it towards Daniel's birthday present. Seventy pence can go a long way if you know how to stretch it. And, if Ewan could give me a lift, — she paused, her mind doing arithmetical leaps of faith— even once a week, it would add up in no time. Surely a bigger birthday present is worth fishfingers two nights in a row. She sat back in her chair and sighed. If only she could explain it to Daniel.

They pulled up at the lights, where a newspaper bulletin board announced Princess Diana's return to public life after the scandalous publication, *Princess in Love*. How easily we fall from grace, Mags thought. Not that anyone would write a book about me. But they don't like us, women who break the rules. She glanced towards Ewan and saw his eyes making uneasy, darting motions towards the university. She knew what he was thinking. It didn't look right. Not the two of them together this early in the morning. She fingered the buckle of her seatbelt. *Perhaps I should offer to get out.*

Leaning forward slightly, she followed his eyes. The streets were busy, grey suits and scarecrow students hurrying about their business. She studied them gravely until a thought made her want to laugh. *Who exactly are we looking out for?* She turned, grinning, to Ewan, but her eyes fell on a group of people standing on the far side of the road waiting for the traffic lights to change.

Her heart missed a beat. At their centre, half hidden in amongst the grey wool and torn denim stood a small boy. His back was to her, but she could see that he was very small and lost looking, turning his head from side to side, as though uncertain which way to go. *Daniel.* The windscreen drew her fingers and she leaned forward mouthing his name.

'Do you?'

'What?' She started round to find Ewan's eyes upon her. He was looking at her coldly. 'I was saying I think it may be better to even up the two halves of the book.' He drew the words out deliberately. 'Do you?'

But she hadn't time for his games. She was unclipping her belt. 'Look I've got to get out. It's—' She broke off. A middle-aged woman had pushed her way through the throng. Mags watched the scene unfold, like a street-performer's eerie mime. The woman taking hold of the boy's shoulder. Turning him to face her. A freckle-faced, snub-nosed face. Another woman's child. Mags watched as he burst into noiseless tears and his mother enfolded him in one arm, pointing wildly at a shop doorway with the other.

Ewan's arm gripped her hand. 'Mags, what is it? Have you seen someone?'

She slumped back in her seat, shaking her head. 'No. I was mistaken.'

'Ah.' He let her go. 'Probably best let you out here, though.'

As she stumbled on to the pavement, the lights changed and Ewan's car sped away. Mags took an involuntary step towards it. *Wait. You didn't say what time you're coming tonight.* But he was gone leaving her behind, abandoned by the roadside, like the little, freckle-faced boy.

The sun came out as Daniel walked through the wrought iron gates, a huge, overripe autumnal sun that cast its mellow light, like Midas, turning everything to gold. It was warm for the time of year. An Indian summer his mother had called it. He took off his jacket and tied it round his waist in exactly the way Mags disapproved of. And keeping a weather eye out for any Indians that might be lurking in the bushes, he started up the tarmac path.

But soon he came to a fork, and stood uncertain which direction to take. To one side was a huge glass hot house, its Victorian roof rising, pagoda-like, to a point. He pushed his face against a pane of glass and could see a marvellous jungle of trees and creepers, the perfect place to hide. But when he tried the door he found that it was locked, and there was no-one to ask when it opened.

There seemed nothing for it but to continue his adventure, so he took the path's right fork and continued on his way. He was certain now that this was not Kelvingrove Park, but it seemed to have a special kind of magic all its own. And, what was more, he'd discovered it all by himself, like a real adventurer. He wondered if his mother knew about it. Maybe one day, when his dad was back, they'd come here, just the three of them, to see his discovery.

The path became gravelly beneath his feet and overhung with trees, like a jungle. Perhaps it was a jungle, a secret jungle that he had stumbled upon. He stopped to listen for animal cries, but a sudden chittering in the branches directly above him made him break into a run. He wasn't frightened, of course. It was just that he couldn't be standing around all day when there were more important discoveries to be made further along the path.

He descended a steep slope and came out on a bridge suspended over a wide shallow river. It was peaceful here, and attracted by the water's greenish depths, he stretched out on his stomach to watch the lazy current drifting by. Spindly-legged insects skittered across the shallows, and from time to time, he saw a tiny fish pop up to bite at them. Perhaps, if he could find a stick long enough, he could get the fish to bite at him too?

'Water boatmen.'

Daniel scrambled to his feet. He hadn't heard anyone approach, but now a man in a park keeper's uniform was standing a little distance from him, gazing down at the river. 'Water boatmen,' the man repeated, pointing a bony finger at the water's surface. 'That's the name for those wee bugs.'

Daniel said nothing, not daring to take his eyes from the man's shadowed profile.

'They're out late this year,' he continued conversationally. Then, still, without looking at Daniel, he glanced at his watch. 'Mind you, you seem out awful late too. On a school day.'

Daniel needed no second warning. Before the keeper had finished speaking, he was already over the bridge and heading into the unknown. He ran down a sandy path, past a crumbling play park, and scrambled up a narrow dusty track that led the way along the river's opposite bank.

Not until he reached a great archway of marble spanning the path did he stop running. The sound of his echoing footsteps slowed his feet. And thoughts of the park keeper forgotten, he leaned against the cool walls and panted for breath. When he felt a little better, he called out his name and heard the bridge catch the sound and toss it back and forth, higher and higher, until it vanished in the shadows far above him. Stone that carried words. A kind of magic. Perhaps the stone could pass on his words to other stones, on and on, until his message was carried right to the other side of the world.

He called out, 'Dad,' then waited. The echoes died. 'Dad. It's me. Daniel.' Still nothing. 'Is heaven blue?' Maybe the transmitter only worked one way. 'We moved house again. We're in Cliftondale Street now. Number sixty-seven. Don't forget, dad. Number sixty-seven.' He wondered whether to warn his father about Ewan's blue Rover being parked outside then decided against it. After a moment, he added. 'I have to go now. I'm having an adventure.'

The path grew rougher now, bare earth trodden by occasional travellers, and began to ascend. Daniel felt his legs growing weary and he knew he needed to pee. He considered doing it on the edge of the path. But his senses were heightened with the strangeness of everything, and he was afraid of being caught.

He was contemplating the feasibility of doing it behind a large elm somewhat off the path and further up the slope, when he noticed a brick wall further up the slope still. It had partially collapsed along the East side, and he could make out rose bushes hidden within its confines. Intrigued, he scrambled up the slope and squeezed through the gap.

It was obvious as soon as he was inside, that it wasn't part of the rambling park. A neat Victorian townhouse stood at the top of an orderly lawn, and at regular intervals there were flowerbeds, rectangular or oval in shape. Daniel almost turned and ran there and then. But the windows were so dark and still that it seemed impossible that anyone was home. Besides, his need to pee was quite urgent now, and throwing caution to the winds, he unzipped his trousers and relieved himself on a compost heap near the gap in the wall.

It was only as he zipped himself up again, tingling with the contentment of release, that he saw it. The most beautiful thing he'd ever seen. A single rose, standing out above all the others. Perhaps it was the shadows in the garden playing tricks on his eyes after he'd been squinting in the sun, or perhaps it was something his mind saw that was not truly there, but it seemed that the rose was bluer than anything he'd ever seen. Bluer than a summer sky, as blue as heaven should have been if his mother hadn't lied.

And then all the anger that he'd used the adventure to divert himself from, all the anger he'd hidden, came bubbling up from deep down in the depths of him, pouring out of his eyes and nose in a molten rage, making him run at the treacherous object, and start to kick and tear at it so that the petals fell, like his tears, on to the moist earth below.

And so engrossed was he with the task of destroying the rose that he quite failed to hear the garden gate being opened at the front of the house.

Chapter 5

THE secretary was a square, solid woman somewhere in the region of fifty-five. She wore too much makeup to be flattering, but not so much that a discerning eye might consider it vulgar. For several long seconds, she'd been staring down at Mags' outstretched hands, a sour, doubtful expression playing about the thin line of her lips. At last she gave the deep sigh of one whose burden is about to be unbearably increased, and asked, 'How can I help you?'

Mags nodded towards the paper-clipped sheets in her hands and said pointedly, 'My essay.'

A faintly malicious smile played about the secretary's lips. 'The deadline was lunchtime.'

Mags swallowed. 'It's only five past two.' She was trying to beg, but only succeeded in sounding sullen. Her voice had a flat, dull sound to it, the beat of a drum when the skin has been stretched too far.

In an exaggerated manner, the secretary looked up at the clock above the doorway. Mags followed her gaze. It read two ten. Mags looked back at her essay and saw the pristine sheets contort under the pressure of her grip. What did it matter if her essay was forty minutes late? Over by the desk, she'd seen a pile of essays handed in by other students. They'd not been picked up yet, but it was obvious that the old biddy was enjoying the chance to execute the letter of the law and wasn't prepared to budge. In other circumstances Mags would have told her what she could do with her deadlines. But she'd been late before and she needed this essay to be considered if she was to pass.

She looked back into the intractable lines of the secretary's face. She wants me to beg, Mags thought. She knows I can't do it without her and she wants me to beg. Colour rose in her cheeks and she lowered the essay to hide her trembling hands. What can I do? She looked round wildly. What can I do? There was only one thing she could do. She blotted out the secretary's look and forced herself to conjure up an image of Daniel. She saw him, small and afraid. A pinched, white face, calling out to her in the middle of the night. She, stumbling into the bedroom, eyes refusing to open, ready to reassure him because the pain was bad or because he was frightened and needed to know about heaven. 'Tell me what colour heaven is. Is it blue? Tell me. Please.'

'Please,' said Mags.

The secretary interrupted. 'I really don't feel that I can. All the other students went to the trouble of getting their essays in on time.'

And all the other students don't have a sick child, who gets them up night after night to change the soiled bedsheets and fetch his medicine and coax him back to sleep. Mags wanted to say this aloud, to shout it out and make the old crone sit up and take notice. But she couldn't. Couldn't make Daniel a pawn in her life, not even when he wasn't there. Defeated, she was about to turn around and go back the way she'd come when a voice said,

'Ah Mags. I hope I didn't keep you from handing your essay in.'

She could have wept with relief, but she answered as coolly as she could, 'A little, I'm afraid. I'm just handing it in now.'

Ewan smiled down at the secretary from the doorway and the secretary blinked back at him then gave the obsequious smile of the underling. 'Better give that to me, dear,' she said grabbing the essay from Mags hands. 'You're lucky Dr Johnstone hasn't been in to collect them yet.'

Ewan appeared to follow none of this exchange, but simply took his letters from the pigeon hole in the wall and headed off down the stairs. As she picked up her books, Mags caught the secretary's eyes on him, narrowed and suspicious, and she couldn't resist the temptation to wink at her as she went out.

Once on the stairwell Mags was overcome with guilt at her indiscretion and didn't allow herself to catch up with Ewan until he'd almost reached the East quad. There she could fall into step beside him without it seeming odd.

'Thanks,' she said, a little breathless with hurrying after him. 'You didn't need to do that.'

'Not at all.' His face was serious again. 'I do little enough for you.'

She found herself blushing, like a girl and hugged her books closer to her chest to divert herself. It was such a rare experience to feel girlish that she wanted to hold on to it. She stole a sideways glance. The university makes a good backdrop for him, she thought. He looks like a scholar here. Ageless.

His hair was still dark and, now she came to think of it, his face had fewer lines than her own. But then, Ewan had never been through what she had. As soon as she thought that, she felt guilty. Ewan had problems of his own. That was her trouble, she decided. Always measuring others against the yardstick of her own pain.

At the door of the East tower he stopped and whispered, 'Come and see me after my lecture finishes.'

She nodded eagerly, and at the same time, felt a faint resentment that he should see how vulnerable she was.

Sadie stood for a long while wondering whether there was more fat in a slice of strawberry cheesecake than in a slice of Dutch apple pie. She thought of asking Michael, but looking at his rotund frame reaching over the counter to give Mr Silver his change, she decided that the fat content of his food wasn't something he gave overly much consideration.

She turned back to the cakes. If Isaac had been there, he'd have told her to take both. A body needs all the fuel it can get. But then Sammy would have shaken his head and led her towards the health food shop on the corner. 'What you need is a diet, ma. Why not think about going vegetarian? Macrobiotic even?'

'Sammy! You want I should become like a robot?'

'That's bionic, ma.'

She had almost made up her mind to take the cheesecake when a voice called,

'Sadie, is that you?'

Sadie turned and there was Etta, a neighbour from the days when Sammy was small, a tiny, bony woman with the bright-eyed, slightly manic expression of a fox terrier on the scent. Before Sadie could reply Etta was at her side.

'Well, look at you,' she said. 'The picture of health and not a sign of you for weeks?'

Sadie looked apologetic. 'My back,' she explained. 'Sometimes it gives me trouble still.'

'Ach,' said Etta. 'Don't I know it.' She patted her hip vigorously. 'Never the same since they replaced it.'

'You are going back to the hospital soon?'

'Hah! Hospitals,' Etta snorted. She laid a confiding hand on Sadie's shoulder 'You'll be as good as new, Etta, Dr Cowden told me. Etta he called me, like he didn't look like he was just out of wetting his pants. But what do doctors care? I'm no sooner in hospital than I'm out. And it's don't just sit around Etta. You've got to keep on the move.' Her grip on Sadie's arm tightened and she lowered her voice to a whisper. 'On the move, I say? You said that to Tommy Liebermann after you fiddled with his heart, and the poor man winds up dead within a week.'

Sadie was trying to recall exactly who Tommy Liebermann was, when Etta leaned over the counter and called to Michael. 'Hey, Michael, you got any of that Taiglach in yet.'

'No.' Michael was cutting thin slices of salami and didn't look up.

'What about fresh lox?'

'No.'

'Latkes? You must have latkes by now.'

'Nope.'

Etta turned back to Sadie, saying loudly, 'A person could starve from buying in this shop.'

Michael kept cutting.

'That reminds me,' Etta said, poking a bony finger into Sadie's chest. 'Did you hear about Miriam Alexander?'

'No. I was thinking that maybe I should call...'

Etta held up a hand to silence her. 'Found dead in her lounge last week.'

'No.' Sadie was shocked. 'Her brother. He lived with her?'

'That's right,' Etta beamed. 'Found with her.'

'Is he?'

Etta nodded vigorously. 'Dead as a doornail.'

Sadie's eyes were wide with dismay. 'How could this happen?'

Etta leaned over and dropped her voice to stage whisper again. 'Gas.'

'But they lived in a sheltered home, no?'

'Pah!' Etta waved a disdainful hand. 'Those places are death traps. I tell you, once they have your money they lose interest.'

'You think so?'

'I know it.' Etta's eyes rolled heavenwards. 'My daughter wanted me to go into one. Ma, she said, You're not getting any younger.' Her eyes rolled back towards Sadie. 'Do you know what I said to her? Do you?'

Sadie did, but she obediently shook her head.

'I said, what's wrong, Jacqueline? Am I not dying quick enough for you?'

Sadie shook her head again, but Etta was looking at Michael. 'How much is the chopped herring these days?'

'89p a quarter,' he said, without looking up.

'Robbery,' Etta squealed. 'Don't you know that your customers are on pensions?'

When Michael chose to ignore this rebuke, she turned back to Sadie. 'Not like his father,' she said loudly. 'Now there was a *mensch*. Always had a full shop. And at his prices you could buy. Mind you,' she added ruminatively. 'He came to a terrible end.'

Sadie was wondering how she might hint that it wasn't in the best of taste to discuss Michael's father's demise in front of him, when Etta spotted an elderly, sweet-faced man passing by in the street.

'Sadie dear, that's Mr Armstrong.' Etta's eyes glittered. 'Poor old soul just had a heart bypass. I should go out and have a word with him. Just to cheer him up.' So saying, she gave Sadie's arm a quick pat, and headed for the door, throwing over her shoulder, 'Remember now. Don't be a stranger.'

'Goodbye,' Sadie called, but the shop door had already swung shut.

Sadie turned back to Michael. He raised wary eyes above the tray of pastrami he was laying out. 'What can I get you, Mrs Gordon?'

Sadie smiled, a little embarrassed. 'A slice of the strawberry cheesecake, please,' she said. And then, because that didn't seem quite enough to make up for Etta's rudeness, she added, 'And a slice of the Dutch apple pie.'

'This much?' He indicated an enormous slice with the blade of his knife.

'Oh no.' Sadie felt the need to protest. 'That is too much for an old lady like me, no?'

Michael's face remained impassive. He moved the knife a fraction. 'How about this?'

'Yes, that is good,' she said quickly, then added guiltily, 'My birthday is today.'

Michael was still cutting the cake. 'Congratulations.'

'Thank you.' She handed over a five pound note and he gave her a paper bag containing the cakes. He turned to the till and Sadie couldn't stop herself from saying, 'I am eighty-one, you know.'

'Really?' He handed her back her change. 'Many happy returns.'

'Thank you,' said Sadie again. She put the paper bag in her shopper then hung around a little in case Michael wanted to say something else. When it became evident he didn't, she mumbled her goodbyes and hurried out.

There was a metal banister on the staircase outside Ewan's office. Mags paused several stairs from the top and studied her distorted image in it, critically. The reflected face blinked back at her and narrowed its eyes. But it wasn't her face. It belonged to a stranger now.

She stared at it, trying to force it into some semblance of familiarity. But the cheeks remained hollow, the mouth unsmiling, and the eyes, grey and sad, looked back at her with an expression so haunted and so full of pain that she was forced to look away.

Hard, she thought. That's what people think when they see me.

She straightened, and pulling a cheap, elasticated band from her bag, scraped her hair into a pony tail, quickly smoothing back the dark tendrils that escaped behind her ears.

Three paces took her to Ewan's door, and she hesitated, fist raised to knock. The denim cuff of her jacket had begun to fray. She folded it over, angry with herself for noticing, angrier for caring, then knocked twice, sharply enough to hurt her knuckles.

'Come.' Ewan's deep voice penetrated the thick layer of wood that separated them. Mags opened the door, and almost furtively, slipped inside. In contrast with her flat, Ewan's office was as spotless and fastidiously arranged as the man himself. The walls were lined with books, heavy tomes too precious to be lent out to students. The desk and chair were cheap, but the carpet was of better quality than the one in Mags' flat. Behind Ewan was a framed quotation by Guedalla: *History repeats itself. Historians repeat each other.*

Ewan's serious, ascetic face broke into a smile when he saw her enter. 'Mags. Glad you could make it.'

She wished he wouldn't make her appearance sound so humdrum, almost as though he was afraid of spy cameras in the books, but she returned his smile. It was difficult for her. As the day wore on, her mouth seemed set in a permanent droop. 'You're not going to give me a hard time over that essay, are you?' It was meant to be teasing, but her words came out a little anxiously.

He was still smiling, but his eyes had grown serious. 'It's me that needs to be given the hard time, I'm afraid,' he said apologetically.

'O?' Even knowing what was coming, she couldn't stop herself from forcing the inevitable. 'What's on your mind?'

Ewan glanced away from her, scanning the rows of periodicals, as though searching them for an answer. 'I can't make tomorrow night,' he said at last.

'O.' The sound escaped again, like a balloon deflating. 'I see.' She tried to keep the smile, nodding vaguely into the space between them, but she was defeated by his rejection. It shattered her illusions, setting her firmly back in her place. He was everything. She was nothing.

He got up from his desk and came to join her, standing in front of her, so close that she could smell the musty scent of his tweed jacket and the faint aroma of aftershave from his skin. But he didn't touch her, and she felt the space that separated them as acutely as a wall of stone.

'Mags, please. I didn't plan this.'

'It doesn't matter,' she said stiffly. 'I've got a lot of studying to catch up with.'

His eyes searched across her in the same way they had searched his books. 'It's Helen.'

Helen. Of course Helen. Always Helen. She should be angry. Show him that she couldn't be picked up then dropped at a minute's notice. She opened her mouth, but he was still speaking.

'She's making things very difficult just now.' He was looking for understanding, and she let her gaze fall to the floor, thinking all the time, Don't give in. Make a stand. Helen or me. Make him choose.

'Don't be angry, Mags. You know I wouldn't have agreed if I thought there was any way I could get out of it.'

She looked up then, eyes blank and disbelieving. But he looked so sad, as though she was the one thing in the world that was left to him and now even she was turning away. And, despite herself, she felt ashamed. 'I should be going. I have a lecture.'

He didn't try to stop her, but at the door he reached down and took her hands in his. 'Don't give up on us, Mags. It's times like these I need your strength. It's what I love about you. It's what makes you special.'

But she couldn't resist hurting him. 'Do I have something to give up?'

She let the door shut before he could answer.

She had almost reached the West quad before she began to feel guilty. Leaving Helen was never going to be an easy option for Ewan. His integrity fought against the betrayal. And wasn't it his integrity that she loved? Ewan was battling against himself. And, God knew, she understood what that was like, to fight the command of 'thou shalt' with the hopelessness of 'I must'. It had taken her long enough. She should have been more understanding.

She glanced at her watch, and realised, horrified, that she hadn't phoned up about Daniel's results yet. Stupid, she cursed herself. Always trying to do too many things. She tried to form a plan. The bell had sounded as she came down the stairs. That meant she had five minutes. And Dr Storrie was nearly always a minute late and another minute sorting through his papers. She glanced over at the McIntyre building where the public phones were held. She could make it if she ran.

Sadie heard the noise as soon as she opened her garden gate. At eighty-one you couldn't expect your hearing to be what it once was, but it was quiet at this time of day and sounds carried. The street she lived in was inhabited only on one side. Her house, the exception, stood opposite a row of sandstone terraces. The occupants of the terraces tended to work long hours to pay for their beautiful old homes, and consequently were rarely there to disturb the sleepy hours of the afternoon.

Sadie stood, listening. Could it be burglars, she wondered. If so they were not very professional, making enough noise so the whole street could hear. And it didn't sound as though they were breaking into the house. I should phone the police, she thought. But what if it was only cats or squirrels? Another silly, old woman bothering them. And you were always reading about how busy they were.

She stood undecided, then took a hesitant step towards the sound. Etta's voice boomed in her head.

'So they found her. What was left of her. An axeman no less. A tragedy. And all she ever wanted was to die in her own bed.'

Sadie screwed up her eyes, interrupting the mental image. 'I'll only take a peep.'

'A peep,' Etta's voice came back. 'That's what they told her son. She was just going to take a peep, then—' The imaginary Etta drew a finger across her throat.

Sadie paused afraid to go on. She'd call the police, that's what she'd do. But the sound came again, and this time she realised what it was.

Isaac's roses!

Fear forgotten, she dropped her shopper and started to run.

Her heart was sending out warning signals long before she'd run the length of the house. Not at your age. Slow down. But she ignored them, pushing stiff legs across the lawn. Thinking only of the roses.

She couldn't make it. Too old. Too fat. Her body was betraying her. Sadie gasped. The ghost escaping the machine.

Then she was on him, drawing herself up in a trembling, outraged halt, just inches from his back. And he, whirling round to face her. Caught in the act.

But it wasn't what she'd been expecting. No, not at all.

To find herself looking down into the tear-stained, snotty-nosed face of an angel.

He had black curls. A dark halo surrounding a face too fragile to belong to a boy. He was looking up at her through tear-sparkling lashes. Huge eyes. Luminous with the wonders of a child's universe. The ikon of a Christ-child on the lap of a Mantenga Madonna. The Cupid's lips parted.

'I hate it.' he sobbed. 'I HATE IT!'

Chapter 6

CONTRARY to its fragile appearance, the rose took a long time to die, and Daniel wept blind tears of fury as he kicked and tore at it. The death of the rose intoxicated his mind, so that his whole world became nothing more than force and action and brutality. A man's world, where pain and suffering were refused entry. Even when the woody trunk of the rose finally yielded, falling to the earth, like a wounded soldier, he continued, grinding the petals into the soil with the heel of his trainers. And it wasn't until there wasn't a scrap of blue to be seen, and the bush lay in pieces, that he realised someone was thundering over the lawn towards him.

For an instant, he almost bolted. But the long walk and the destruction of the rose and the crying and the terrible anger had left him spent, and he stood staring up at the stranger, panting and weeping, unable to take another step.

Her image was smudged by his tears, but he could see that she was very old. She wore a heavy grey raincoat, though the day was warm, and a brown fur beret pulled down over her ears. The face beneath the beret was very ugly, lined and leathery. A hobgoblin's face with pointed chin and long nose, and on one cheek there was a mole, the same colour as her hat, from which two black, insect-like hairs protruded. She was studying him with grey, hooded eyes, unblinking, like a bird's.

He was afraid of this face and fear made him fierce. 'I hate it' he cried.

Sadie didn't answer immediately. She was agog with conflicting thoughts. Such eyes. Still wet with tears. Not the eyes of a child at all. And such a complexion. Flawless. Like a statue, Michaelangelo's David in miniature. Could this be the face of a thug? And how old can he be? Five? Six at most. So young to feel such rage. He was cheaply dressed in polyester trousers and shirt, a thin nylon anorak around his waist. No way to dress a child when the weather could turn any minute. What was his mother thinking of?

'I hate it!' he cried again. The angel with a dock-worker's voice.

'What is this you mean,' she answered sternly, 'breaking into people's homes and knocking down their roses?'

Daniel looked up at her, puzzled. Her accent was strange, like nothing he'd ever heard before. He didn't answer the question, but stood staring blankly up at her, as though he hadn't understood. Exasperated, Sadie pointed towards the remnants of the rose. Daniel followed the direction of her finger and was awe-struck by the power of his rage. He turned bewildered eyes towards her, then hung his head and began scrubbing at the soil with a toe. But that revealed torn scraps of petal and he quickly stopped.

'Why is it you break my rose?' Sadie asked. Still Daniel didn't reply and Sadie began to wonder if he might not be an imbecile. But the truth was much simpler. Daniel no longer understood the reason for his actions. All he could remember was the blind fury he'd been hiding deep inside him, and that somehow it had been unleashed out into the world.

He shook his head slowly, as though denial would be answer enough. But she was still staring at him, her witch's eyes holding him in her thrall, and he began to feel afraid. 'I was angry,' he said in a small, toneless voice.

Sadie considered asking him what his mother would say if she knew. But then, the kind of mother who would let a small boy run around on his own in such a thin jacket wasn't the type to care what he got up to. Instead, she asked, 'What is your name?'

He seemed reluctant to tell her, but eventually he said. 'DnlGalher.'

'What is that?' asked Sadie.

He looked up at her and grimaced, but said slowly and clearly, 'Daniel Gallagher.'

'Good,' said Sadie. 'Now we have something.'

He looked frightened on hearing that, and Sadie decided to play on it. 'So, Daniel Gallagher, what will you do about my rose?'

He stared at her, uncomprehending, then wiped his nose on the back of his sleeve. Unable to bear this, Sadie reached into her pocket and fetched out a hanky. 'Use this,' she commanded.

As he wiped clumsily at his eyes and nose, another thought occurred to her. What if this child was even younger than she'd thought? His mother might be frantically searching for him. 'How old are you?' she asked.

Daniel stopped wiping his face and drew himself up to his full height. 'Eight,' he said. And then, when she looked at him, disbelievingly, he added, 'Nearly Nine.'

'I see,' said Sadie, astonished. 'Then you should be in school, no?'

'It's a holiday.' The falsehood fell easily from Daniel's lips. Lies were easy. It was the truth he couldn't explain.

Sadie frowned. She had lost touch with the school calendar long ago. She thought of challenging him, but it seemed pointless as he was already standing in the middle of her garden. 'So Daniel,' she said at last. 'Are you going to pay for my rose?'

He blanched at the mention of money, and she noticed that one of his trainers had a hole in the toe. She tried a little experiment. 'That was a very special rose,' she explained. 'My husband bred it and there is not another one like it. To buy it would be very costly.'

The news of the rose's value brought on a fresh bout of weeping from the angelic face. Sadie steeled herself against pity. 'It's well to be sorry after you've done a bad thing,' she began. But then she realised he was saying something, and stopped to listen. Over and over, he was sobbing,

'Don't put my mum in jail. Don't put my mum in jail.'

Sadie was taken aback. 'What is this you are saying?' she demanded.

The huge eyes were upon her once more. 'Please don't put my mum in jail.'

Sadie was perplexed. Jail? No-one had mentioned jail. She studied his face wondering if he was trying to deceive her, but the sobs sounded heartfelt. After a while, in which she watched her lace handkerchief turn into a sodden, snotty rag, she asked, 'You think your mother would go to jail because of what you did?'

Gulping, Daniel nodded. Sadie was more perplexed than ever. She wanted to ask why his mother should have told him such a thing, but it was obvious that Daniel believed it and to question it would cast doubt on his mother's wisdom. Instead, she said carefully, 'Mothers have to pay for what little boys get up to.' She said it half as a question, but Daniel began to cry harder. His words came out thick and disjointed, difficult for Sadie to make out.

'Goes out an leaves me … big boys … trouble … go to jail.'

Somewhere in the muddled mess of it, Sadie got the impression of a mother who left her child alone at home for long periods with dire warnings about parental incarceration should he fall foul of the law. She was at loss as to what to think. What kind of mother leaves such a young child alone? She wants to teach him right from wrong. But how can she do that by telling him such a silly lie?

She looked down at him wondering what to do. Badly brought up, she thought. Tell him to go. He's had a fright. He won't come back. Give him a warning and tell him to go. No fuss. No bother. His mother won't cause trouble if you don't follow it up. Just tell him to go home. She bent down and retrieved her handkerchief. 'Do you like cake?' she asked.

The phone booth smelled unpleasant from too much use. Mags had been standing there longer than she dared think about, letting it ring, knowing it was better to let it ring for a long time than to try ringing in short, frustrated bursts. She felt frustrated nonetheless, and kept checking her watch. She had three minutes.

Opposite her, within earshot, was a small, huddled group of students, four boys and a girl. Three of the boys were dressed in faded denims, the kind of denims that suggested a lifestyle of intrepid defiance somewhat at odds with the pink, bland faces of their owners. The fourth boy wore glasses and a wool sports jacket, and around his neck was a red silk cravat, which he kept pulling at, as though it was too tight. The girl was taller than two of the boys and terribly thin. She wore a bulky leather jacket, a tiny, black bubble skirt and thick black tights, whose feet were lost inside heavy, workman's boots. To Mags' eyes she looked like one of the characters from Daniel's set of *Pick and Mix* people; a call girl on top and a navvy on the bottom. She had a thin, shrieking voice that Mags couldn't ignore. She was saying,

'Sartre, yes. But to me, Kierkegaard will always be the first existentialist.'

One of the boys in denim seemed outraged by this remark and launched into a fierce attack.'

But the boy in the sports jacket interrupted. 'It's all ballocks to me.' He pulled at his cravat. 'I say we go to the Beer Bar and drown our sorrows.'

'And you pretend to be such an intellectual, Duncan,' the girl sneered.

Duncan smiled amiably at her. 'I pretend because life is pretence.' He waved an arm in a grand manner. 'It's all false,' he said. 'But after a few drinks you don't mind so much.' He turned tail and led the denim-clad three to the door.

'Morons,' the girl called. But, after a moment, she followed them in the direction of the students' union. Mags watched them with a mixture of amusement and envy. They were filled with the directionless passion that only youth enjoys, and she felt an aching regret never to have experienced it herself.

'Park Street Medical Centre, how may I help you?'

Mags jumped and nearly let go the receiver. She had felt so distanced from the world she was witnessing that it was hard to believe she was still a part of it. The voice in the receiver seemed to come from a long way away.

'How may I help you?' the voice said more sharply.

Mags found her tongue. 'I'm calling about Daniel Gallagher's test results.'

She went through the usual routine of giving his date of birth, his address, the date the results were supposed to have arrived. There was a long silence then the voice said. 'Mr Wilson asked for a word when you called in.'

'Daniel's consultant.' Mag's heart lurched.

'I'll just page him now,' the voice said.

Mags waited while the phone on the other end clicked into silence. It was a long wait and she watched the coin slot gobbling up most of the change in her purse while she stood waiting numbly for Mr Wilson to be found. Several times she thought she'd been cut off, and when she began to run out of money, she panicked. She called down the receiver and slapped the round mouthpiece with her hand.

'Hello. Can anybody hear me? Hello.'

Eventually a voice said, 'Park Street Medical Centre, how may I help you?'

'I'm waiting for Mr Wilson.'

The voice on the other side gave an irritated sigh. 'Mr Wilson is coming as fast as he can.'

'But I can't wait.' The anger was rising again.

'I'm afraid Mr Wilson is a very busy man.'

Mags didn't answer. She was mentally wrapping the phone cord around the neck of the stupid woman on the other side and pulling it until her eyes bulged. She breathed deeply, trying to keep control, but before she could say anything a male voice broke through.

'Mrs Gallagher?'

Mags had long ago given up correcting him. 'Yes.'

'I have Daniel's results here with me now.' There was a rustling of paper and Mags fed her last twenty pence into the slot.

'Now then, what have we here?' There was a longer silence and Mags watched the twenty pence being eaten away.

Nineteen.

Eighteen.

Seventeen.

She wanted to shout at him to hurry, that not everyone had time to meander through life at his pace, but he had an educated, authoritative tone that intimidated her, so she said nothing and watched her pennies ticking away.

Sixteen.

Fifteen.

'Ah yes.' More rustling. 'Not good. Not good at all.'

Mags wanted to scream. She stared ahead, mouth set in a straight, hard line. 'Could you tell me what's wrong?'

There was a surprised pause, as though she'd committed an inadvertent breach of etiquette. 'It's very simple, Mrs Gallagher.' The authoritative voice was now also cold. 'Daniel's cell count is down.'

'I see.' Mags felt the muscles in her abdomen constricting. She stared blindly at the LCD panel.

Twelve.

Eleven.

'What does it mean?' she asked.

Her question was not put medically and therefore was ignored.

'Has he had an infection lately?'

'Just the diarrhoea. Dr Collins, our GP, has been treating it. He said it wasn't anything to worry about.'

The consultant tutted, and Mags wasn't sure if it was because the situation was more serious than she'd thought or because she'd taken the word of a GP.

'And how is he treating the diarrhoea?'

'With *Imodium*. Three times a day.'

There was a grunt from the end of the line. Mags felt her heart lurch.

'Isn't that right?'

'Oh, it'll do,' the grudging tone came back. 'But I'd like to see him sometime in the next fortnight.'

Mags breathed out, surprised to find she'd been holding her breath.

'The receptionist will give you a date.'

But Mags looked at the LCD. There was only a penny left. 'That's all right,' she said quickly. 'I don't know exactly when we can come. I'll phone back for an appointment.'

'See that you do,' the consultant said and hung up just before the pips sounded. Left holding a dead phone, Mags hung the receiver back on its hook. He thinks I don't care, she thought despondently. Then she grew angry. So what? He doesn't have to worry how much a phone call costs. But she did care and she felt a tension at her temples that would doubtless lead to a headache later that evening. She groped in her bag for her cigarettes. There was a no smoking sign outside, but she didn't care. The packet was empty anyway.

She checked her watch. The lecture had started ten minutes ago. Not worth going now. She'd go to her tutorial then leave. Pulling her bus fare from her pocket, she did some calculations. If she got off at High street she could walk the rest of the way and still be home before Daniel, and she would save money. Then the consultant's hateful tone came back into her head. *See that you do*. Not a fit mother. Doesn't care about her own child. She balled her hand into a fist until the money inside cut into the flesh of her palm. I'll buy Daniel some sweets with the money I save, she decided.

Chapter 7

HAVING unlocked the back door, Sadie now stood inside the kitchen, beckoning him to enter. But Daniel hung back. Did the caution, not to follow strangers, apply here? Sadie was certainly a stranger, and a terrifying one at that. A face like a witch and a strange, foreign-sounding voice. But then he had gone into her garden uninvited, and there was also the matter of the rose. Uncertainly, Daniel took a step backwards.

Sadie watched him, saw the looks flitting across his face, distrusting, suspicious. His eyes were narrowed, darting from side to side. Trying to decide.

A young animal, that is what he is, she thought. What got into me? Asking him in. They stared at each other for a long, unblinking moment. Then, abruptly, she turned her back on him, as though, unobserved, he might vanish, dissolving into the clouded realms of hallucination.

She tried to unthink him by concentrating on the solid tools of tea-making. Warm the pot. Fetch the tea. Almost at once, she felt better. Perhaps he wasn't there at all. Never had been. She, an old fool, dreaming up catastrophes to fill the lonely hours. Didn't Etta say something of the sort about that Mrs Harris who lived down in Clouston Street? Screaming and raving at the end. Something about wild beasts. Lions. That was it. Daniel in the lion's den. Sadie looked round. He was still there, watching her. Head cocked to one side.

Daniel saw her turn to look at him, felt the grey, hawk's eyes paralysing him, like a small animal caught in the downward swoop of the predator. But then she moved away again, busying herself with making a cup of tea, and curiosity got the better of him. He took a tentative step forward, placing him back on the threshold, and peered inside.

The kitchen was like nothing he'd ever seen before. Instead of being a mere galley appending one end of the living room, this kitchen had an entire room to itself. It was surrounded on three sides with wooden cupboards and dressers groaning under a huge weight of pickle jars and jams and bowls of apples and pears picked from the garden, somewhat brownish. These, in turn, sat on crocheted mats, marooned like little lacy islands floating between the eddies and currents of the oak surface beneath them. And on the wall, was a cork board covered in faded postcards and envelopes, exotically stamped, all held in place by coloured pins, like the arrangement of an eccentric lepidopterist.

In the middle of the room sat a large table, covered in two embroidered cloths set at jaunty angles to one another, and guarded by four thick-set chairs standing in solemn silence, one to each side. At the far end of the room was a Welsh dresser, adorned with a rose-patterned tea set, clearly fashioned from good-quality china, but missing a saucer and the handle off one of the cups. There were windows, set too high to see out of, on the same side as the door, and through them streamed the yellow, opalescent light of day, gilding everything inside in the fool's-gold of autumn. It didn't seem much like a witch's den, and, uncertainly, Daniel stepped inside.

Busy with filling a large, silver teapot, Sadie seemed to have forgotten all about him. But, as she crossed the room to fetch the milk, she stopped to pull out the chair nearest him, so that it stood apart from the others half facing him, in bashful welcome. He waited until she had retreated to the far side of the room, then careful to leave the door open behind him, scuttled across the tiled floor to find refuge in its solid frame.

Seemingly preoccupied, Sadie placed the teapot on a cross-stitched doily in the centre of the table. Then, reaching into her shopper, brought out the bag of cakes and laid them near the end of the table where Daniel was sitting, half-crouched ready to run. There was a teacup already on the table opposite him, so it seemed only natural that Sadie should choose to sit there.

With no particular sense of urgency, Sadie reached for the pot and filled two aromatic cups of rich tea. She pushed one towards Daniel. 'Be careful,' she warned. 'It's hot.' She stirred her own cup lovingly with a long-handled teaspoon, then reaching out for the sugar bowl, popped a cube into her mouth and began to sip the tea through it. Much fascinated, Daniel scraped his chair closer, balancing on the edge and gripping the table for support.

'Why are you drinking it like that?' he asked.

Sadie looked up, and seemed surprised to find him opposite. 'Like what?'

'With the sugar in your mouth.'

'That is the way I have always drunk it.'

He thought about this for a time, then said, 'You're not from round here, are you?'

Sadie smiled and shook her head. 'No. Not from round here.'

'From far away?' Daniel ventured.

Sadie nodded. 'Yes. Quite far.'

'London?' he suggested doubtfully.

'A little further than that.'

Daniel was about to ask another question, but Sadie nodded towards the bag of cakes. 'Aren't you going to open that?'

For a split second, he stared at the bag, as though fearing it wasn't real, then reaching forward so that he almost fell off the chair, pulled it towards him and ripped it apart.

She was surprised to see his face fall. 'Daniel, what is the matter?'

He turned disappointed eyes towards her. 'No chocolate.'

'Ah.' She had forgotten how it was to have a greedy, little boy in her kitchen. She racked her brains. There was no chocolate in the house. Sammy had made her promise. Not a promise easily extracted. But one she'd kept to nonetheless. Daniel was still looking up at her. Think of something else.

'You like strawberries?' she said coaxingly.

Daniel shrugged. 'Mibbe.'

She slipped the cheesecake out of the bag and on to a plate. 'Try a little. You'll enjoy.'

He didn't move. She tried again. 'My little boy used to like strawberries.'

There was no response.

'Of course, he was a much bigger boy than you.'

His eyes flickered towards the cake and doubtfully he reached out for it. Hastily Sadie pushed a fork towards him, which he accepted seemingly without noticing.

Slowly, reluctantly, he scooped off a generous chunk of the topping on to his fork then held it hesitantly before his mouth. Sadie waited patiently while he exposed the tip of his tongue and took a tiny, almost imperceptible, lick. He withdrew his tongue and ran the taste around his palate for several moments before venturing a second and larger lick. Sadie waited until the contents of the fork were gone, before asking, 'How is the cake, Daniel?'

'S'alright,' was the crumb-muffled reply.

Sadie took another sip of tea, letting it glide down her throat and warm her stomach. It was funny how tea always tasted better when you drank it in company.

Mags stood with her tutorial group in an awkward, broken line outside Ewan's office, aware as always of that faint, imperceptible barrier that separated her from the others. There was no evident difference in the distance between herself and them, but something set her apart. A sense of not quite fitting in. Perhaps it was because she was older. What age were they anyway? Nineteen? Twenty? Just kids. Perhaps it was something else that differentiated her. She preferred to think it was her age.

Today, there were four of them, two girls and two boys. One of the boys seemed in a state of perpetual, motion, continuously glancing at the door, as though half expecting it to open, fumbling in his bag yet never removing anything, then glancing back at the door. Next to him, slouched the other boy, shoulders sagging against the wall. He seemed tired or bored or sleepy, and his only action was to roll a dead match continuously between his two forefingers, as though trying to create a spark.

The girls stood opposite. The smaller of the two had a mousy, forgettable arrangement of features, while the taller girl, though not beautiful, had a dramatic, striking face and tangled, cascading auburn hair that made her conspicuous amongst the others. Mags had never seen her before, and wondered why she was there. She was already engrossed in conversation with the mouse, and Mags overheard her replying to a question that the mouse had put to her.

'Not really. It was such a bore getting out of bed every morning for that nine-o clock lecture that I hardly ever went.'

She had a low, educated voice that echoed in the dusty angles of the corridors. The mouse said something more that Mags couldn't hear and the girl replied, 'Why worry? I mean, an exemption is nice, but what does it matter if you have to sit the degree exam? It's just a few extra weeks on to the end of term.' She laughed and for a moment her eyes fell on Mags, stayed an indifferent instant, then returned to the mouse.

What does it matter? Mags could feel the pressure of her fingers biting into her canvas bag. An exemption meant precious weeks when you could work full time, a chance to set up financial stores for the rest of the year. An exemption wasn't a luxury. It was a terrible goal that you struggled towards every spare moment, poring over textbooks and cramming in facts until your eyes blurred and your head swam. Don't get angry, a voice in her head was screaming. She doesn't know. It's not her fault.

'So what's this Dr MacLeod like?' the girl was asking.

'He's okay,' the nervous boy replied. 'Pretty much like the rest of them.' He didn't notice Mags' look of disdain. His eyes flitted to the closed door. 'A bit martyred if he thinks you're not a hundred percent devoted to his subject.'

The girl laughed, and the sound seemed simpering and contemptuous and sexy to Mags' ears. 'What I wanted to know is,' she said, 'did I finally land a good-looking one?'

There was a dull thud, and Mags became aware that they were staring at her. She followed their gaze to her feet and saw that she'd dropped her bag and that the contents had spilled out creating a shabby clutter on the floor, crumpled papers, a comb with broken teeth, and a purse that had opened to reveal it was almost empty. Automatically, she fell to her knees and began pushing everything out of sight. But it was too late. She had been exposed.

'Can I help?' The girl was crouching beside her, a hand manacled in expensive rings, reaching out to take hold of her things.

'No.' Mags snatched the bag away. She knew they were watching her, waiting for an explanation, but suddenly the air was stifling. She scrambled to her feet, and mumbling some incoherent excuse, fled down the corridor. Get away. Go home. Wait for Daniel. Surprise him. As she rounded the corner, she could hear laughter following her down the stairs.

With each mouthful of cake, Daniel relaxed a little more visibly. He leaned against the chair-back now, and his legs swung back and forth in lazy arcs beneath the table. At one point, he leaned his elbows on the table's edge and felt it give a little beneath his weight. He turned puzzled eyes to Sadie. 'What's wrong with the table?'

'One of the legs,' Sadie explained. 'It had to be replaced and it doesn't work so well.'

'Why don't you fix it?'

Sadie blinked. The childish simplicity of the question threw her off balance. 'I don't know how,' she admitted.

'My dad would know what to do,' Daniel said. He knocked some crumbs off his plate and began to pick them up, surreptitiously.

Sadie felt slightly alarmed at the thought of having an unknown adult appearing on her doorstep. 'You will mention this to your father?' she asked tentatively.

Daniel looked at her with wide-eyed amazement. 'My dad?'

She was puzzled by his reaction, but felt compelled to elaborate. 'When you get home, you will ask him?'

He leaned back in his chair, and head cocked to one side, studied her for some moments. She had the impression that he was trying to make up his mind about something, then he said sadly, 'My dad hasn't been around since I was a wee baby.'

'O.' She felt foolish, as though somehow, she should have known. Then a dreadful thought occurred to her. 'Your father, he is not dead?'

To her relief, Daniel seemed even more surprised by this question. 'Dead? No.' He shook his head emphatically. 'My dad's just lost.'

'Lost?' It was Sadie's turn to be surprised. What manner of adult is 'just lost'?

Daniel smiled, a wonderful, cherubic smile that lit up his face, and he wrapped his arms about himself, as though hugging his secret in closer. 'He's lost in Africa,' he explained.

'Africa?'

Daniel laughed. 'You keep saying the last word I say.' And he said, 'Africa?' several times to demonstrate. Sadie shook a finger at him to make him stop. Trying to make sense of the conversation, she suggested, 'Your father, he works in Africa?'

'No,' Daniel shook his head again. 'I told you. He's lost. He crashed his plane when I was a wee baby.'

Sadie frowned. 'But Africa is not so far away. He would be home by now, no?'

'They couldn't find the body.' He made this statement in a matter-of-fact voice and began chasing crumbs around his plate with one finger.

Sadie on the point of saying, 'Body?' thought better of it, and asked very gently, 'You think he is still looking for you?'

Daniel had caught the crumb and was crushing it unmercifully. 'He's lost his memory. That's why he hasn't found us. But he will one day.' A cloud passed across his eyes and he set the crumb at liberty. 'Only it has to be soon.'

Chapter 8

BOOKS and papers under one arm, a bag of liquorice *Allsorts* in her teeth, Mags manoeuvred the front door key into the lock and jiggled it up and down trying to get it to catch. It didn't, of course. It never did first time, but she rattled it angrily knowing all the time that it wouldn't work. Not until she had gone through the ritual of dropping her books and almost losing her grip on the sweets did it finally yield to her shoulder-assisted push.

It was cold inside. Even on the hottest days it was cold. The landlady had told her, when she'd come to view it, that it caught the light in the evenings. A lie. But then she'd found out it was only one of many lies. Mags dumped her notes on the desk and threw her jacket over the back of the sofa. As she placed the bag of *Allsorts* on the mantelpiece, her eyes fell on the gas fire. The thought of switching it on was tempting. Just one bar to heat the room. Her brow crinkled, and she went into the kitchen and opened a scarred tin marked *Abernethy* biscuits in orange scroll across the top. Inside was a card for the electricity meter, but that was all. She hadn't budgeted to buy another one for the gas until Monday and that was three days away. But the flat was cold, a dank coldness that infested the air with a musty, neglected smell that clung to her clothes and hair.

Daniel would feel the cold as soon as he came home. But she needed the card to last until Monday. Mags tried to weigh the moral dilemma objectively, but the day had been long and fruitless and she felt beyond dealing with it. She lifted an old woollen cardigan from where she had dropped it earlier that morning and draped it around her shoulders. That would do the trick for now. She needn't worry about the fire until Daniel got home. He was looking so much better today. And, the room'll heat up in no time. It was a lie, but no worse than those of the landlady.

Daniel watched while Sadie opened her mouth and swallowed a large, bullet-shaped pill.

'Are you not well?' he asked curiously.

Sadie waited a moment for the drug to take affect before answering. She'd felt the pain as she'd reached over to fill a second cup. 'Too much caffeine, Mrs Gordon,' Dr Farmer would have said, shaking his head in a world-weary way, as though he alone was a preacher of old wise secrets, and she an idolater at the honeyed feet of her god, Cholesterol.

'You looked funny,' Daniel added when she didn't reply.

'I'm not ill,' she explained, touched by his concern. 'It's just high blood pressure. At my age your body doesn't work so good any more.'

'How old are you?' Daniel's eyes searched the lined face for a clue. Sadie was mildly shocked by the question. 'That is not a question for small boys to be asking,' she said.

Daniel was put out by the reference to small boys and felt it was time to redress the balance. 'I take pills,' he said, looking down as he said it, studying the crumbs on his plate.

'Pills?'

He was pleased to see that she was impressed.

'What kind of pills are these, Daniel?'

'Red ones,' he explained. 'I take those twice a day when I get up and again when I go to bed. And white ones for pain that you put in water and they go fizzy. And green and brown ones. They're for diarrhoea,' he added with pride.

Sadie opened her mouth to ask a question, but at that moment the shrill tones of the telephone interrupted her. They turned towards the hall then stared back at one another, as though the sound had reached them from another world. Then, without speaking, Sadie heaved herself up and hurried out of the room.

The line was crackley against her ear, like an old 78, scratched and hissing. But she made out Sammy's voice and called out to him. 'Sammy. Is that you? What time is it over there?'

'Ma,' the receiver crackled. 'Many happy returns.'

Sadie's heart swelled with pride. He'd phoned. A good son. Not like Ruth's eldest. And her only on the other side of the city.

'Sammy,' she shouted above the interference. 'How are you? Are you eating well?'

There was a hiss on the line that might have been a sigh of exasperation, but Sadie didn't notice, then Sammy said. 'Jamie sends her love.'

Sadie was on the point of asking, who, when she remembered just in time. 'Did she like the Eau de Cologne?'

There was a hesitant silence then he said quickly, 'Yes. Of course, she did, ma. She loved it.'

Sammy, a good boy, would lie to save his mother's feelings.

'How's Etta?'

'O never happy, but she is *kvetching* about something.' Then because she felt disloyal, she asked quickly, 'How is your job?'

'Good. They keep me busy, though. You know how it is.'

She felt alarmed by this admission and worriedly admonished him, 'Don't do too much. You need your rest.'

Sammy laughed. 'My bosses don't see it that way.'

Sadie was shocked. 'Sammy, you lose your health, you lose everything. That's what your father would say.'

'Ma, I'm a big boy.'

She wasn't sure if he sounded annoyed or amused. Either way he wasn't listening to her advice. But children only learn through their mistakes? Isaac would have said that too.

'Who did you celebrate with?' Sammy was firmly changing the subject. 'Ida MacIntosh? Did she come round?'

'No. Don't you remember. She moved away to be with her son.'

'O yes.' Sammy clearly didn't remember. 'What about the Greens? Didn't you have tea with them last year?'

'Sammy, they're dead.'

'O.' There was a silence then he said. 'Ma, you're not alone, are you?'

Sadie was touched. 'No. I'm fine.' She glanced in the direction of the kitchen. 'Daniel Gallagher is celebrating with me.'

'Who?' Sammy was interested. 'Do I know him?'

'No. We met only recently.'

'Do you know much about him?'

Sadie thought for a minute. How much should she say? 'He likes gardening and he has a taste for strawberry cheesecake.'

'Well,' Sammy said. 'Who'd have thought?' Something occurred to him and his voice changed. 'You do know his background, don't you, ma? He's not just someone you met in the park.'

'Sammy, he is eight years old.'

'Eight?'

'Nearly nine. Or so he tells me. Looks more like six.'

She expected Sammy to laugh. Instead he asked worriedly, 'Is he the son of someone you know?'

'No,' Sadie admitted. 'I met him...' Her voice trailed off. Sadie always tried to be scrupulous with the truth, but at the same time, she didn't want Sammy to worry. And she couldn't very well tell him that she'd come across a young tearaway destroying his father's roses. 'I met him near the park,' she said at last.

'Ma,' Sammy sounded worried now. 'I don't think you should have him in the house. He could be up to anything.'

'But Sammy, he's so little. He won't cause me any bother.'

'Did it occur to you that he might steal from you?'

'Of course,' insisted Sadie for whom it hadn't.

Sammy sighed. She could tell he would have liked to get on a plane and rescue her from the threat of the delinquent infant loose in her home. She was proud of him. A good, loving boy. But three thousand miles was three thousand miles, so he said, 'You're sure you know what you're doing?'

'I'm sure.'

He laughed. 'From my memories, you're more than a match for small boys.'

Sadie beamed with pride. 'I'll be fine,' she assured him. There was a short awkward silence between them, two people losing contact with each other's lives, then Sammy said, 'I'd better go now. We've got the move tomorrow.'

'The move?'

'Yes. Remember I told you last time. The job's moving up to New York.'

'New York?'

'So good they named it twice,' he chuckled.

'You know, Sammy, I never understood why they did that.'

'Ma, you're one in a million,' Sammy said. But the line had begun to crackle and she only just had time to hear him call, many happy returns, before it went dead.

There was a sound by her side. Daniel was standing next to her, though she hadn't noticed him enter. She wondered how long he'd been standing there, listening to her conversation, and she shivered, suddenly a little afraid.

Chapter 9

MAGS looked up at the clock on the mantelpiece. Three fifty. Daniel should be home in another forty minutes. Mags took off her glasses and pinched the bridge of her nose between thumb and forefinger, trying to concentrate her mind. But it wouldn't be held and fluttered away from her, flighty and disobedient, throwing images and memories in her path distracting her every time she was near to catching it.

The crisp white sheets of Ewan's manuscript were before her, the brown wrapping eviscerated and discarded at her feet. She had looked forward to this moment for so long that it was almost an anti-climax to find herself finally at it. She glanced again at the clock. Forty minutes. Time enough to begin.

Placing her glasses back on she read the front page. The Shadow In Our Wake, a personal account of revolutionary Russia. There was a disclaimer at the bottom of the page. The facts herein are true, but certain names and dates have been changed to protect the identity of contributors. Mags traced a finger over the disclaimer. She had a great longing to devour those facts, even if they were wearing false faces. Ewan had seen that curiosity in her, had recognised that she alone, out of all his students, would reach beyond the words on the page into the minds of those who wrote. Hadn't he said as much? 'I need someone like you, Mags. Someone who understands.'

She wondered if he would have an opportunity to phone. Phone. Ewan's phone. He ought to phone. He paid for it after all. For Daniel, he'd said. In case of an emergency. And how could she refuse? But he hardly seemed to use it. Helen doesn't let me out of her sight. Perhaps he would get the chance if Helen took one of her sleeping pills. There was so much she wanted to say to him, things that took time to express. But that was the one thing they didn't have. Time. Snatched moments. Desperate fumbling in the dark, one eye on the door. And always the fear of being caught before … . Caught before what? He hadn't made any promises. The future was blank, unknown.

Mags began to scratch at her left wrist. What if she was making a terrible mistake? What if Ewan had no intention of leaving his comfortable home with his comfortable wife and their nice, respectable lifestyle? What if he'd been stringing her along all this time?

She saw it now. She had been easy. Lonely. Fooling herself into thinking that she was aloof. But all too easily taken in. And she'd thought he'd seen something else in her, something special. A rose blooming behind the plain façade. But all the time she'd just been a warm place to lie, a place to slum it, roughing it with the have-nots before returning to the haves.

She stopped scratching. Her hands were sweating. Hadn't he been cooler lately? Perhaps it wasn't Helen. Never had been. Perhaps he was looking for a way out. But, how could he? Turn his back on a sick child. She'd trapped him. And maybe there was more to it. She was his student. The scandal if she talked. She tried to cram her doubts back down, into the black recesses of her subconscious, but they kept popping up, like malevolent jack-in-the-boxes, chanting a saying from her childhood. *No ring, no man. No ring, no man.*

It was a relief when the doorbell went, and she jumped up and ran across the room to get it.

Her relief soured when she saw an elderly man standing on the threshold. He was dressed in a charcoal grey suit, the white of his shirt showing at the collar and cuffs. His back was to her, as though she'd caught him in the act of changing his mind. He turned when he heard the door opening, and she saw a face in which time had mapped itself in deep gouges about the mouth and eyes. This is what my face will look like in a few years, she thought, but she held the door open a little wider, and said, 'Dad, what are you doing here?'

He didn't answer her, but stepped past her into the living room. 'Where's ma wee grandson?'

'At school.' She nodded awkwardly towards the sofa, but he stayed in the middle of the room, hands in pockets, looking up at the ceiling, as though she'd invited him to inspect the plasterwork.

'Would you like a cup of tea?'

'Aye. All right.' He accepted with clumsy graciousness.

'I've no biscuits.'

'I'm not the queen, Mags.'

As she put the kettle on, she saw him walk over to her desk and riffle through the pages of her book, losing her place. 'Dad, don't,' she called out sharply and he let the book go as though burned. She regretted it as soon as she'd said it, but it was too late. He'd gone back to the middle of the room.

When the kettle had boiled, she filled two cups, though she didn't really want one, and crossed the room holding them gingerly in each hand. She handed him one and he took it without looking at her. Mags wanted to sit down, but she remained standing, leaning against the back of her chair. They stood without speaking, as though mutually obedient to a vow of silence. Eventually, he said, 'Cold in here.'

'I don't notice it,' she lied.

'For the wee one I meant.'

She stiffened. 'I put the fire on when he's home.'

'Even so.'

'He's fine, Dad.'

They fell back into their hostile silence. The tea finished, he placed the cup on the mantelpiece. 'Well I'd better be off.' Reaching into his pocket, he extracted a handful of coins. He examined them then placed a fifty pence piece next to the paper bag of *AllSorts*. 'Tell Danny his grandpa was asking for him.'

'I will, Dad.'

Mags put her cup down to follow him to the door and open it for him. They hesitated at the threshold, both feeling there was more to be said. 'Your maw's asking for you,' he said, looking away from her, again.

Mags bit down hard on her bottom lip. 'She knows where I am, Dad.'

He was looking down into the stairwell. 'Are ye still seeing that man?'

'His name's Ewan.'

He shrugged, wrinkling the shoulders of his suit. 'I'll tell your maw you were asking for her.'

'Aye. You do that, Dad.'

He walked away and Mags watched him, with an odd, dislocated feeling of loss, as though something indefinable had been snatched away from her.

Looking down into the angelic face, Sadie saw that there was no sign of the earlier tears. Only a child could weep like that, she thought, with no more sign of it than a cloud passing the sun. She looked at him questioningly, and he said, 'I've got to go now. My mum will want me in for dinner.'

She hid her relief by asking, 'Where do you live, Daniel?'

He seemed surprised by the question and a little reluctant to answer, but nodded to a vague location over his right shoulder. 'Over that way.'

'I see.' Hillhead Street? Woodlands Road perhaps? She decided not to pry. Perhaps Sammy was right. She shouldn't get involved. She waited, but Daniel seemed in no hurry to move, and, at last, she asked, 'Is something the matter?'

He looked at his shoes and drew an arc in the carpet with the toe of one. 'It isn't like I'm a baby,' he explained. 'It's just that she'll worry.'

Ah, was that all? His pride. She understood. For a moment, another small boy appeared in her head.

He was taller than she was, but smaller than the boys around him. That didn't matter. He had the unmistakable authority of the unquestioned leader. He was regarding her through metal-framed glasses, behind which his eyes were dark and fierce. Two pinpoints of light lit the centres, like cold stars.

'Go away. You're just a baby.'

'Am not.'

'Run along and play with your mother's apron strings.'

'I want to come with you.'

Then another boy, taking her defence. 'Let her come, Piotr. What harm can it do?'

The dark eyes flashing. 'What do you know of the Communist Manifesto?'

'Nothing.'

'Have you read Marx?'

'No.'

'Engels?'

A shake of the head.

A laugh as cold as the eyes. 'Well, when you can tell me what the relationship between Marx and Engels is, then you can come.'

White anger. A rage, greater than anything she has ever felt, filling her. 'I hate you, Piotr Shamilyevich. I hate you.'

'Who's Pee otter?'

Sadie blinked unfocused eyes at the boy in front of her. The pale, serious visage was replaced by a thinner, grubbier one. 'Who's Pee otter?'

She rubbed a hand over her eyes. So real. Just for a moment. Then she shook herself because Daniel was still watching her, and she didn't want to frighten him. 'Piotr,' she began, forcing her lips into a smile, 'was a boy. Very much like you. A little older, eleven I think.'

She hoped that was explanation enough, but Daniel was interested. 'Does he live here?'

For an instant Sadie's smile flickered into life then faded again. 'No, he doesn't live here.'

'Then where is he?'

She reached down and stroked Daniel's cheek, watching him instinctively recoil, as all little boys do. 'Piotr is dead,' she said gently. 'A long time ago.'

As she turned away, to fetch her hat and coat from the coat stand, she thought Daniel had said something, but when she looked back down at him he was staring ahead, his lips closed back into their cupid's pout. She was about to turn away again, but her subconscious was fitting together the jigsaw of fragmented sound, and she found herself asking, 'What is this you say?'

Daniel didn't answer for a long time. He was still staring ahead, perhaps at the picture, perhaps at nothing at all.

'I'm going to die.'

Chapter 10

THE page Mags was staring at was from a yellowed, musty-smelling textbook. She had borrowed it from the medical department of the university library earlier in the day. And, unable to believe that such an ancient looking tome could possibly provide the information she needed, she had checked with the librarian at the desk.

The librarian, a man about fifty with a rim of grey hair neatly bisecting his head, looked up, as she approached. He didn't ask what she wanted, and as he was staring at her with the air of a surgeon needlessly interrupted during a delicate operation, Mags was forced to ask, 'Is this book up to date?' She placed it awkwardly on the counter and it landed with a dull thump that echoed incongruously in the unnatural silence.

He took it from her and examined the cover in a manner that suggested that he suspected her of stealing it, then, without opening it, said calmly, 'I think you'll find it will do.'

'But how do you know?' Mags blurted, awed by the authority in his tone.

He looked back up at her, as though surprised to find that she was still there, and said, not unkindly, 'This is an anatomy textbook. I don't think you'll find much has changed about the human body over the last few thousand years.'

He offered her the book, and humbled, Mags took it and hurried off, colliding clumsily into the door jam in her haste to get away.

But now she stared at the yellowed page and wondered how it was human anatomy had survived unchanged down through the millennia. The page was mostly taken up by a diagram of the human heart, a great, ugly, pulsing monster drawn in lurid, childish pinks and yellows. It didn't look like the emblem of love. But then, Ewan had laughed when she'd said that, insisting that the lovers' heart was no more than a representation of female buttocks presented for male use. And she'd blushed at this revelation because it excited her, then grown angry when he laughed at her for her proletarian prudishness.

The heart on the page didn't excite her. It filled her with fear. Auricle. Atrium, Vena Cava. They were mystical words on which so much depended and so little was understood. She read,

Ventricular fibrillation is considered a life-threatening condition because no blood is pumped into the arteries. This is the cause of death in approximately one out of every four persons.

One out of every four. She reached out and traced the outline of the diagram. Pulmonary. Coronary. Musuli Pectinati. Words. Words. Words. Words without meaning. Words without hope.

She began to scratch the inside of her left wrist with the fingernails of the right, but she was wearing her watch and it got in the way. Impatiently, she began to pull it off, but she caught sight of the round, frozen face and that made her glance at the clock on the mantelpiece. It was quarter to five. Daniel should have been back by half past.

It was only quarter of an hour, she told herself. Fifteen minutes. Nothing. But her mouth went dry and her heart, her real heart, the mucus covered, blood-filled pump which knew nothing of love, began to pound against her ribcage as though it was trying to break free. Leaping to her feet, she dragged on her jacket and ran to the door.

Outside, she took the stairs in twos, one hand on the rickety banister for balance, a voice in her head screeching frantic reassurances. He's playing with friends. He's been kept back at school. He's looking in shops. But images danced before her eyes, of malevolent strangers and drunken drivers and ¾ *dear God, no* ¾ Lying there. 'What's wrong? Is this child ill?' Lips blue. 'Call an ambulance. Is he alone? Where's his mother?'

Her head filled with Daniel, she didn't see the woman come out of her front door, and stand, waiting for her on the first landing. And she might have missed her completely if the handle of a mop hadn't been thrust into her face.

'I want a word with you.'

Mags looked up into a broad, red face surrounded by a halo of little, yellow curls too blond to belong to the ruddy face beneath them. A monstrous cherub in a cheap, polyester blouse buttoned loosely over a skirt belonging to an entirely different outfit.

'I havenae time, Mrs McKellor.'

'Ye havenae time no to listen. Ye havenae done the close for weeks. Did ye think we wouldnae notice?'

'Later, all right.' Mags tried to push past the woman, but she blocked her way. 'Wee Moira's been doin your share.'

For a moment, Mags couldn't recollect who wee Moira was, and seeing her confusion, Mrs McKellor seized on it. 'Aye, wee Moira that's no well. And she was right good to ye, when ye moved in without a man to help you an' all.'

Mags tried to interject something in her defence, but Mrs McKellor knew she had right on her side and was determined to have her say. 'A disgrace that's what it is. This is a decent close and we all take our turn.' She leaned down so that her face was close against Mags'. She smelled of harsh, antiseptic chemicals, a legacy of her job as a cleaner. 'We all know you go flouncin' off to the university, leaving yer wee laddie sitting waitin' for his tea. But just because yer above the rest of us now, don't think ye can get away with leavin' the place like a midden.' And so saying, she thrust the mop handle into Mags' hands, and with a final. 'Ye dirty besom,' thrown over her shoulder as if in farewell, she went back in her front door, slamming it hard enough to rattle the frame.

Trembling from rage and fear and guilt, because she'd forgotten all about wee Moira and mopping up the close, Mags had to lean against the mop handle to steady herself. But then she heard someone come out on to the landing above, and she threw down the mop and ran down the last flight of steps out into the street.

Daniel and Sadie were standing only inches apart, but it was as though miles separated them. Since Daniel's confession there had been an appalling, charged silence in the air that made it impossible to draw breath, let alone speak. He hadn't explained what he meant or asked if she understood, but waited, with his head lowered, avoiding her eye.

At last Sadie ventured, 'We all die, Daniel.'

He still wouldn't look at her and his face had grown closed and mistrusting again. Sammy's words floated back. *He could be up to anything.* But she detected a tremor in his shoulders, and saw that he was struggling to hold something in that desperately needed to be released. She wanted to put her arm around him, but was too wise to do so.

'Dying?' she said at last 'This is something your mother has told you?'

'I hear them arguing,' he said flatly. 'They think I don't hear them, but I do.' His hands had balled into fists, and he no longer attempted to conceal the trembling in his shoulders.

Sadie opened her mouth to ask another question, but Daniel began again.

'I've got a thing,' he said earnestly. Sadie shook her head. 'A thing?'

'Inside me,' he explained. 'In my heart. It means that I won't live as long as other boys and girls.'

Sadie could feel the creeping paralysis of shock stiffening her facial muscles, and she struggled to control herself, seeing him glance up to see if she'd understood. But all she could do was to repeat,

'A thing?'

'Yes. I hear my mum crying about it sometimes. When I've gone to bed, I hear her. And sometimes she talks to him about me.'

'To your father?'

'No.' His face twisted. 'Just someone my mum sees. He told her that no-one knows anything about being dead. That we just make things up to tell little children.' He emphasised the word, *little*, with such disdain that in other circumstances it might have been comical.

As it was, Sadie could feel the paralysis reaching her legs, making them go weak. 'Daniel,' she interrupted. 'This is too big to tell me here. Let's go back into the kitchen. You can tell me properly.'

She had led the way, and he'd followed, meekly, taking his chair at the end of the table and waiting while she settled herself opposite. As she poured the dregs of the tea into her cup, she noticed that he hadn't finished the cheesecake. She took a swift gulp to steady herself. But it didn't perform its magic, and she felt just as cold as before. Daniel was watching her, waiting for her to speak.

'Tell me more about this thing inside you,' she prompted. He shrugged, bringing bony shoulders up to meet the pointed chin. And, suddenly Sadie could see that this wasn't a well child. He was too small, too thin. His eyes seemed so huge because the rest of his face was so gaunt, and the clothes he wore were not baggy because his mother didn't care, but because they hung on limbs too slender to fill them.

Daniel had not elaborated, so Sadie tried again. 'Are you ill?'

He brightened a little, feeling she understood. 'Yes.'

'What kind of illness?'

He shook his head unwilling to tell. But Sadie needed to know more. 'Has it a name?'

'My heart is all wonky and doesn't work right.' He spoke flatly and quickly, as though afraid of sound of his own voice. Sadie understood. She didn't need Etta to see the fear behind those words.

They sat in silence, as though the speaking of it had separated them on either side of a huge, terrible chasm. At last Sadie said timidly, 'Not everyone dies of an illness nowadays. There are special medicines.'

Daniel speared her adult rationalisation with childish logic. 'Then why does my mum cry at night when she thinks I'm asleep, "Don't take him away from me." She says it over and over.'

Sadie was about to offer trite reassurances about hope and the future and not looking on the black side of things, when it occurred to her that this was the response Daniel must hear from all adults. Is he telling me for a different reason? She looked over at him wondering how to ask, but his mind was momentarily distracted.

'Can I go to your toilet, please?'

Sadie smiled, relieved to have such a simple question to answer. 'Of course.' She pointed into the hall. 'Use the one under the stairs. It's the last door.'

Daniel's eyes widened. 'You've got other toilets?'

Sadie was amused. 'Only one. Upstairs in the bathroom.' He frowned and she could tell he was impressed and puzzled. 'Why do you need two toilets?'

It was a good question, and Sadie, on the point of answering, suddenly couldn't think of a reason. 'I suppose it was useful when we were still a family here,' she said lamely.

'Are you all alone?'

Sadie nodded. 'I am now.'

Daniel looked into the hall, and she saw his eyes surveying the towering, Victorian dimensions, seeing it, as it was, a vast empty space too large for one old lady.

'I have a son,' she added, feeling an inexplicable need to account for her extra plumbing. Daniel turned towards her. 'Does he come to stay?'

'Sometimes.' Then she added a little pridefully. 'He lives in New York.'

'New York?'

'So good they named it twice.'

Daniel stared at her. 'Why?'

Sadie spread her hands. 'I don't know.'

He cocked his head to one side, unsure whether she was laughing at him then, unable to decide, turned and ran towards the toilet. The one under the stairs.

When he returned, Sadie had laid out a large, ceramic mixing bowl, flour, butter, eggs, and a pound bar of cooking chocolate. Daniel stared at her, wide-eyed, as though he'd caught her performing some strange cabalistic rite. She smiled when she saw his expression. 'Daniel, look what I've found.' She pointed at the chocolate bar. 'Sammy didn't find this one.'

Daniel hadn't moved from the doorway. 'Are you making a cake?' he asked uncertainly.

'A chocolate cake,' Sadie announced, tipping flour out of the bag on to a plastic scale. Daniel's face grew pink, the first colour she had seen in it, then his eyes grew doubtful and he asked in a small voice, 'Who's it for?'

'For my guest, of course,' said Sadie, not looking up, but carefully breaking the shell of an egg on the side of the bowl. Daniel looked round, as though there might have been someone else in the room all the time that he'd accidentally overlooked. But when realisation dawned, he grew pinker still and crept into the room to stand by Sadie's side.

He watched with a connoisseur's interest as she blended the ingredients together and poured them into a greased baking tin.

'My mother, she used to buy chocolate for cooking from a shop near the top of Byres Road,' she said conversationally. 'But it isn't there anymore. Nor the toy shop or the stationers.' She smiled at the memory. 'Do you know, when I was a little girl, the post box outside the post office was so tall that children couldn't reach it unless they were lifted up.'

Daniel looked up with interest. 'I thought you lived somewhere far away.'

'I did,' Sadie agreed. 'I lived in Russia for many, many years. But not till later. Glasgow was my home as a very little girl. Then my father, he died, and my mother decided to go back to her parents.'

'Then why d'ye sound so funny?'

Sadie was taken aback. It had never occurred to her that she sounded funny. 'I was away for a very long time,' she said at last. 'I forgot most of my English. And when I relearned it, it was never quite the same.'

'You forgot how to speak?' Daniel was impressed.

'Glasgow seemed so far away sometimes that I began to think I'd dreamed it.' She looked dreamy for a moment. 'And when I came back, everything was changed.'

'Where did you live?' he wanted to know. 'Was it here?'

Sadie laughed. 'No.' She pointed back towards the park. 'It wasn't far from here. A street called Bower Street. Isn't that a pretty name?'

Daniel shrugged. Pretty names were not the sort of thing he gave much thought to, but Sadie didn't notice. 'Such a beautiful place,' she was saying. 'It was a part of a tenement, but we had two floors and a front door. The family had the upstairs and cook and the maid had downstairs. There was a big washroom downstairs, and I used to go there to see the women scrubbing the clothes in big tubs filled with soapy bubbles.' She blinked rapidly once or twice, as though trying to shake off the memory. 'I went there once, you know,' she confided. 'A few years ago. I could never look at it after I came back. But then I thought I would just go, why not.'

Did you go in?' Daniel's eyes never left the mixing bowl.

'No.' She shook her head sadly. 'I thought of it. But just as I got there, the door opened and a huge, hairy man with a grey beard was standing there. And behind him I could see a motorcycle parked in the hall.' Her hand flew to her face at the memory. 'A motorcycle. My mother would have turned in her grave to see such a thing.'

She stopped mixing and poured the contents of the bowl into a greaseproof tray. As she popped it into the oven, she asked, 'Do you want to lick the bowl?' He didn't answer, and she turned to find him staring at her with a look of disgust evident on his small features. 'Don't you want to?' she asked again, puzzled by his expression. Her memory was full of Sammy watching anxiously as she scooped the cake mixture on to the greaseproof paper, his spoon at the ready. *Leave some for me, Ma.'*

Daniel wouldn't meet her eye, evidently uncomfortable with something. She waited, and at last he said in a small voice. 'In our house, we usually wash them.'

They went through to the lounge to await the cake, and Daniel perched on the edge of the sofa, like a tiny emperor, ruling from a throne of crocheted cushions and embroidered seatbacks. Sadie busied herself with putting her knitting away in her bag because she wasn't certain what to say. After a minute, he asked, 'Will the cake be long?'

Sadie opened her mouth to answer, but just at that moment she heard the familiar creak of the letterbox being lifted, and the gentle thump of envelopes landing on the mat beneath. 'That's the post,' she beamed. 'Wait a moment, while I get it.'

When she returned, clutching to her chest two white envelopes, and a pink one with a foreign postmark, she found Daniel slumped over to one side, his head resting on an unsteady tower of appliquéd cushions. He was snoring, the gentle susurration of dreamless sleep. She regarded him tenderly for a few moments then settled down in her seat and took out her knitting. Now that she had them, she would save her cards for later. She looked over at the sleeping figure. Perhaps this isn't such a bad birthday after all.

She must have dosed off, because, when she awoke, the light had dimmed and the shadows had inverted themselves. She stared over at the sofa trying to remember something, and it wasn't until one of the appliqué cushions stirred itself and sat up that she recalled what it was.

'You are awake?' she whispered, only to be sure that he wasn't a dream.

He nodded sleepily. 'Is the cake ready?'

The cake! Thank God she'd set the timer. A new cooker. Sammy's idea after she burnt the Sunday roast. 'Before you incinerate yourself, Ma.'

'But who am I going to cook for?' she'd protested wanting him to feel a little guilty. 'And you know I don't understand these new-fangled things.' But he'd only answered, 'You never know, and I'd rather you didn't cook the guests along with the dinner.' And, as always, he'd been right. When all was said and done, you never knew.

Daniel greeted the chocolate cake with more relish than the cheesecake, but still did not eat much. A sick child's appetite, she thought. His poor mother. And she felt a sudden pang for the suffering that woman must have faced and the suffering she was still to face, and, knowing her feelings were written on her face, she got up to make a pot of tea.

Still playing with the remains of the cake on his plate, Daniel asked suddenly, 'You're very old, aren't you?'

Sadie coughed and put down the kettle. 'I suppose so. Yes.'

'A lot older than my mum.'

Sadie lifted the kettle and resumed the task of filling it. 'Yes.'

He thought about this for some time then asked suddenly, 'Do you believe in heaven?'

'Of course.' Sadie was surprised, but she tried to answer casually, understanding as she did that children are often wise enough to suspect too much enthusiasm. 'Don't you?'

But he didn't answer. At last he said, in the very quiet voice she'd noticed he used for important questions. 'You'll be going there soon? To heaven.'

'I hope so,' Sadie answered carefully, her back still to him. Daniel put down his fork and leaned his head on one hand. 'Does your son live in New York all the time?'

The conversation had changed tack again, and Sadie returned to the table to fill the teapot. 'He visits,' she explained. 'But he is very busy and cannot come often.'

Daniel thought about this then asked casually, 'You're all alone most of the time.'

Sadie frowned, puzzled, but nodded. 'Yes. Most of the time.' She wondered where the conversation was leading, but then it occurred to her that he must be angling for another invitation to see her, or rather her larder, and she smiled, satisfied to have the measure of him.

'So, when you go to heaven, you'll be all alone?'

She nodded again, and he looked away, considering something. 'Do you like being alone?'

'Nobody likes being alone, Daniel.' She thought how true that was and a little of the day's sadness returned.

'Then mibbe someone could go with you. Like a friend?'

Sadie was touched, a considerate boy, so like her Sammy. His face was still turned away from her, and she couldn't see the poignant expression that clouded his eyes.

'Why yes, Daniel,' she said. 'I think that is a very nice thought.

He turned to her then, beaming. 'You mean that?'

Flattered that her chocolate cake could be such an attraction, Sadie answered, 'Yes, of course I do.'

He leaned over the table towards her, and she was taken aback to see the intensity in his eyes. 'You promise?'

She didn't answer and she saw a glaze of fear turn his eyes opaque. 'Promise!' The word trembled out over his bottom lip. Sadie nodded, mesmerised by the urgency in his voice. 'I promise.'

He slumped back in his chair, as though a great bargain had been made, and smiled at her with the satisfaction of accomplishment. How different he looks when he smiles, she thought. You can't see the shadow of his illness. But before she could follow her train of thought, Daniel pushed his chair back and jumped down from the table. 'I have to go now,' he announced.

Sadie nodded. 'Your mother will be missing you.'

'She'll be back from the university.'

Sadie was taken aback. This didn't fit the picture of Daniel's mother she'd imagined. 'She is a teacher?'

Daniel laughed as though he'd been asked this question before. 'No.'

'Then why is she at university?'

'To get an education.'

Sadie was impressed. 'That is a lot of work, to get an education while you have a child.'

Daniel shrugged. 'It's just something she does.'

Sensing that his feelings were ambivalent towards his mother's achievements, Sadie got up and opened the back door for him. He pulled his jacket on and joined her on the threshold. 'G'bye,' he said.

Sadie was surprised to feel a genuine pang of disappointment that found her asking, 'You will be coming back?'

Daniel gave a perfunctory nod. 'Got to,' he said. 'Now that I'm going to heaven with you.'

Sadie shook her head. 'Heaven?'

But Daniel was out of the door, running across the garden towards the gap. She watched him, the lines in her face deepening as she puzzled over what he'd said. *So, you'll be all alone even when you go to heaven?* And she had nodded, told him, yes. And she hadn't seen what he was really asking. *Then mibbe someone could go with you. Like a friend?* Sadie's eyebrows rose, like two exclamation marks of alarm across her brow. Dear God, he wants me to take him to heaven. 'Daniel, no. Wait!'

He was already out of sight. But she couldn't let him leave, not with such a dreadful misunderstanding between them. She replayed the morning's scene, running across the lawn in pursuit of him. She was gasping long before she reached the gap, and by the time she got there, and stood panting and coughing, holding on to the brickwork to support her trembling legs, Daniel was almost at the bottom of the hill. She waved frantically, willing him to stop. 'Daniel, don't go.'

He paused at the bottom of the slope and stood there a long, hesitant moment, as though uncertain which way to turn.

'Daniel.' But her voice was a hoarse whisper lost in the rustling, groan of trees. She drew in a sharp breath as he took a step forward. But then he turned, and was looking back up at her. She waved, beckoning him back up the hill, and he smiled and took a step towards her. Thank heaven, she thought, unaware of the irony. But his hands formed a cup round his mouth, and he called, 'Don't forget, you promised.' Then he was gone, a will o the wisp lost amongst the autumn leaves.

Chapter 11

RISING as high as the dark recesses of the Victorian ceiling, wraiths of steam whirled and eddied, their long fingers clawing at the black window panes before vanishing through the cracks in the wooden frame. Blind to their tragic beauty, Mags poured some bubble bath into the running water then thumped the bottle down on the ledge under the windowsill. But it was made of plastic and provided only a dull, unsatisfactory accompaniment to her anger. Daniel was already in the bath, his legs drawn up underneath his chin, watching her with huge eyes filled with reproach. Mags didn't care.

It was almost five o clock before she'd found him sauntering up the street, and by that time she'd run all the way to the school, finding no-one who could help her. *I'm afraid Mrs Ferguson has gone home for the evening. The headmaster? O, he's away today. A conference. On safety standards.*

Then she'd run up and down the streets, like a madwoman, calling his name, blindly, helplessly, barely hearing the well-meaning questions that stabbed at her from all sides. *What's wrong, missus? A wee boy? Naw. He'll be with his friends. Don't greet, hen. We'll keep a look out.*

She'd even tried to phone the police from a callbox, but found it vandalised when she entered. Eventually, in despair and out of breath she forced her oxygen-starved limbs to run back in the direction of home where there was a phone.

She didn't see the number 23B pull up on the other side of the street or the small boy get down from its platform. Even when she caught sight of him as he drew level, she dismissed it as one of the shadows that kept turning around with other children's faces. And it wasn't until he called, mum, and gave a cheery wave that she stopped and stood there, grateful, sweating, angry, trembling.

She hadn't struck him. She never struck him, but she took him by one shoulder and dragged him up the street, letting him yelp and whine and twist against the cord that bound mother with son. Son with mother. She who gave him life, who stretched and tore and bled beneath a stranger's hands so that he might breathe the sweet, foetid, antiseptic air of the world she'd brought him into.

When they reached their front door, they found a mop propped up against it. Mags let him go, and taking hold of it with both hands, like a quarterstaff, threw it down the stairwell. It made a lot of noise, clattering against the banisters as it fell, but no-one came running out to see, and Mags opened her front door and pushed him inside.

Only then had she begun to shout, a strange, high-pitched wail in her voice, which frightened him more than the pain in his shoulder.

'Where have you been? Do you know what a fright you gave me? Do you know?' She was shaking him now, not letting him speak, and he saw suddenly that she was frightened, and that was even more frightening than discovering that she didn't know what heaven was like, and he burst into tears.

She hadn't dried his tears, but said in a slightly gentler voice. 'It's time you had a bath.'

As he followed her out of the lounge, he'd noticed a paper bag or sweets and a fifty pence piece on the mantelpiece, but had been afraid to inquire after them.

Only when the bath was full and she was roughly soaping his back, did Mags ask, 'So where were you?'

'At a friend's house,' he answered carefully. With his hands, he was busy building a castle out of soapsuds. His face was in shadow.

'Friend? What friend is this?' But she sounded pleased. He hadn't made any friends since the move. She'd been worried.

'I only met her today,' he explained.

A girl. Mags was surprised. Girls were the objects of disdain to eight-year-old boys, not friends. But then, she reflected, a girl would be gentler. She wouldn't have to worry about him over tiring himself. And it's good if he's making friends. She felt a thrill of hope. Perhaps everything was going to be fine. Perhaps their future was bright after all.

'What's your new friend's name,' she asked, starting to massage the soap into his hair.

Daniel shrugged. 'I don't know.'

Mags hands stopped. 'You don't know?'

His soap castle was beginning to dissolve due to the unsuitability of its foundations and, absorbed in trying to shore it up, he did not immediately answer.

'How come you don't know her name?' Mags asked. She was still waiting, her soap-covered hands poised in mid-air.

'Forgot to ask,' he said at last, trying to persuade a stray island of soap, floating dangerously near the drain, to return to the fold. 'She's Russian.'

Mags shook her head. 'Russian? What makes you say that?'

Daniel brought a bony shoulder up to meet his ear, and Mags watched anxiously the way the shoulder blade stood out against the thin covering of flesh.

'She said so. Anyway, she sounds Russian. She's got a funny voice.'

'Does she live near here?' If Mags had still been soaping his back, she might have noticed his shoulders tense. As it was, he pointed vaguely in the direction of the door and said, 'Over that way.' Then hearing his mother's intake of breath, as though she was about to ask another question, added a bigger lie. 'Near the bus stop. The 23B.'

'Well, I hope you weren't any bother to her mum,' Mags said, but there was no real doubt in her voice. She had brought him up well. 'Tell me about what you did,' she suggested. This would be good for both of them. There was never enough time together. But Daniel seemed disinterested, telling her only small, disconnected details of his day, focusing a little reproachfully, she felt, on the apparent abundance of cakes at his new friend's house. But she gathered these scraps eagerly to her and drew comfort from the magnificently ordinary sound of them. A normal child enjoying a normal life.

Treading a dangerous path through fact and fiction, Daniel was wondering what else he could safely divulge when he remembered the echoing bridge and calling out his new address to his father. He wanted to ask if echoes carried messages, but that seemed risky. Instead, he asked, 'How will dad find us now we've moved?'

He felt Mags hands freeze on his scalp, two tense spiders clinging to the sides of his head. 'That's a funny thing to ask.' But Mags' voice suggested that she didn't find it funny at all.

Daniel gave up trying to save the castle and began to actively participate in its destruction. He gave a funny, little sigh, as though trying to express something that he didn't have the words for, then said very quietly, 'He might get his memory back and go looking for us.'

He heard Mags swallow and she didn't answer him for a long time, then she said in a strange, flat voice. 'Danny, your dad's been gone a long time.'

He was awed to hear her call him, Danny. She only did that when she was in a very good mood or, during the night if he was in a lot of pain. But he still needed to know, so he said loyally, 'He'll be home when he gets his memory back.' Then as an inspired afterthought, 'Mibbe he hasn't got his plane fixed yet.'

'*Maybe* he hasn't,' Mags corrected. She picked up the plastic measuring jug beside the bath and began rinsing his hair. As usual, he squealed and tried to wriggle away, not noticing that she hadn't answered his question

'Grampa left you fifty pence,' she said.

'I saw it,' he admitted.

'And I suppose you saw the sweets.'

He grinned then spluttered as he swallowed a mouthful of soap. 'Can I have the sweets now?'

Mags twisted his hair between her fingers to wring out the water. 'After tea. And I think you should have an early night. You've been overdoing it with your wee Russian friend. You've no colour.'

'But mum, I'm not tired. Not even a bit.' But he was yawning and trying to conceal it from her behind his hand. She pulled the plug and reached over for a dry bath towel. That was the trouble of being eight, she thought fondly. You hadn't any guile.

Sadie sat with the biscuit tin of memories in front of her on the kitchen table. Strewn around, as though a frenzy of wind had whipped them up, were the faces of the dead. She would pick them up later. For now, she was staring down at one particular image. A photograph, so worn and creased that its hues had faded in nicotine stains of sepia. But still he was there, a boy staring out through metal rimmed lenses, with eyes so dark and fierce, that even now, they seemed to be looking directly at her. She didn't miss their reproach.

How had this image been saved when so many others were lost? Had she had it on her, tucked inside her blouse, even at the end? Sadie searched for a memory of discovering the photograph concealed amongst her belongings, some tingle of shock or relief, or perhaps a shudder of remorse that had followed her down through the years. But there was nothing. 'Nothing.' She said it aloud, as if to trick her brain into answering. But her thoughts remained silent, holding their secret close. And it suddenly seemed that this silver-plate image, that stared at her so sternly and sadly from its world of fading pigments, might have come into existence only now to haunt her. And she snatched it up and flung it, face down, on to the table, so that her lap was empty, save for her hands, which trembled with the memory of what they had held.

At seven fifteen, Daniel's babysitter arrived. She was ten minutes late and Mags was pacing the floor in a frenzy of impatience. She couldn't leave Daniel alone. Not at night. It was bad enough to do it during the day. But if she was late again, she'd lose the job altogether. Mind you, he was so sound asleep. Maybe she could just…. No. No. She couldn't.

When at last, the bell rang she called a curt, 'Maureen, come in. It's not on the snib.'

A scrawny woman somewhere in her late thirties, though she appeared older, hurried through the door. 'I'm really sorry, Mags,' she apologised, dragging off a worn raincoat and throwing it over the back of a chair. 'Archie was late again.'

'You should have called.'

Maureen's eyes widened, and Mags knew what she was thinking. Who does she think she is, giving orders out like the boss? She felt an angry blush creep along edge of her jawline. She understood that she was paying the piper. But what kind of tune could you expect when you only paid pennies? 'It's just that I'll lose my job if I'm late again,' she explained lamely.

Maureen nodded, but her eyes said she didn't see, not a bit of it. If Mags was one of the workers, why was she handing out orders? 'Can I have my money tonight?' she asked suddenly.

It was Mags' turn to be taken aback. 'Tonight? But it's not due till Monday.'

Maureen shrugged. 'Archie's a bit short this month.' Then she added quickly. 'I need it for my bus fare to get here.'

Mags swallowed. She couldn't argue with that, but she had no money in the house. 'I'll have to ask Alec if he'll give me an advance.'

'Aye, you do that.' Maureen's tone told Mags that she didn't believe her, but then, Mags was the boss. It was up to her to sort it out.

She ran all the way, holding her watch up in front of her face from time to time, forgetting it had stopped. At the door to the off-license, she halted, panting, and peered through the glass to see the round-faced clock that hung above the counter. Seven twenty-nine. Everyone knew it was a couple of minutes slow. But she'd made it.

Trying not to gasp for air, she pushed open the heavy, grilled door and stepped inside. The harsh, fluorescent light assaulted her eyes, and she saw the blinking eye of the security camera recording her every move as she crossed the floor towards the cash register. Big Betty, a woman so named for the striking similarity between her girth and height was sitting behind it. She didn't look up when Mags entered, and only grunted in response to Mags' gasped greeting. Mags frowned. What's wrong with her?

'Do you want me to take over?' she offered.

'No.' Big Betty was counting notes, her small eyes, lost within their folds of flesh, concentrating wholly on the task. Mags watched her for a moment. 'Is there a stock take on tonight?'

'No.'

Puzzled, Mags opened her mouth to ask another question when the door behind big Betty opened. A young man appeared. He was dressed in a sand-coloured suit that matched the band of his narrowing hairline. 'Mags, can I have a word?'

Mags turned frightened eyes towards him. Had he noticed she was still in her jacket? Late again. He's caught me. She tried not to look at the expensive watch on his wrist. Was it two minutes slow, like the clock? Silently she followed him into the office at the back. It was not really an office at all; some of the stockroom had been boarded off with plywood. But the large, leather-topped desk in the centre and the heavily padded chair behind it gave the place an air of authority.

Mags waited meekly while Alec squeezed himself round the desk and settled into his chair. He let the silence between them grow for several seconds, as though trying to reach a decision, then, belatedly, gestured to her to take a seat. Mags sat in a straight-backed, armless chair of orange plastic. 'Is there a problem?' she asked at last. Why? Why had she done that? Never give an opening. Let him do the talking. Stupid. Never keeping your mouth shut when you should. But it was too late. Alec's eyes were glinting. 'Well, now that you mention it, there is a wee bit of a problem.'

'O?' Mags could feel the muscles in her face grow taut. Alec saw it too. 'Now, no need to get on your high horse, everyone has to work together here, and it's as well to nip problems in the bud.'

Mags forced herself to give a jerky nod of assent. 'What's up?'

Alec laced his fingers together into an arthritic weave and stared down at them. 'You did the stock take last Wednesday.'

Mags frowned. 'Yes.' Then, because he seemed to be waiting for her to give more of an explanation she added helplessly, 'Tuesdays and Wednesdays are always quiet. There was nothing much going on, and I thought I'd do it.'

'But it's Betty's job.'

Her mind, which had been running round in panicked circles came screeching to a halt. It was ridiculous. She wanted to laugh. Instead, she closed her eyes and breathed out hard through her nose. 'I thought I was helping.'

'Betty doesn't see it that way. The stock take is her responsibility, and she thinks you're muscling in.'

Mags threw her hands wide. 'For God's sake, I was only trying to help. I don't want her job.'

It was the wrong thing to say. She saw the laced fingers tighten their grip and knew she'd made a mistake. Doesn't want the job. Too good for the job. Wanted to give Betty a showing up. Maybe too good to work here?

She ran a hand threw her hair. 'I didn't mean any offence.'

'Betty doesn't see it that way.'

The fingernails of her right-hand bit down deep into the wrist of her left. 'I won't do it again.'

Alec relaxed. His fingers untwined and he cushioned the back of his head on them. 'No problem there then.'

His smile was almost more than Mags could take. Without waiting to be asked, she got up and headed for the door.

'Mags.' He restrained her as she reached for the handle, and she turned slowly knowing that she must, and hating herself for doing so. 'Yes?'

'If you're going to try anything else, make sure you clear it with me first.'

She was on the other side of the door, not certain how she got there or how she had answered. She leant against it, breathing hard. Big Betty's crafty eyes were watching her. 'What did Alec want?'

Mags shrugged. 'To discuss the stock take.'

'Ah.'

Betty's satisfied expression told Mags more than she wanted to know.

Chapter 12

'BUT I wanted some chicken.'

Irina Derzhavina's expression became exasperated. 'You can't. There was chicken in the soup at lunchtime.'

'Hardly any.' Sadie's eyes grew round with pleading. 'I don't think I got any.'

Irina Derzhavina snorted her disbelief and ran a hand through her hair. Three months ago, that hand had been white, a pale petal of her vanity. Now it had become the raw and reddened flag of their Soviet lifestyle. 'You know we observe the six-hour rule now,' she snapped. 'Why must I keep repeating myself?'

Sadie slumped into her seat, her bottom lip pouting. 'Piotr Shamilyevich's family don't observe the six-hour rule. They have milk and butter at the table when they eat meat. At the same time,' she added to emphasise her point.

Her mother waved the reddened hand dismissively. 'That is because they are communists.'

'I want to be a communist too.'

'Hush.' Irina's face grew taut. 'Do you want your grandfather should hear you? Do you know how lucky we are to be here? Hmmm?' She went on listing the advantages of the strange, new world they found themselves in. But Sadie wasn't listening. She was remembering home, with its filigreed papered walls and its smiling maid. And the food. The wonderful food that spilled in rich overabundance over Royal Doulton tureens and servers on to the spotless expanses of a white damask tablecloth. 'Were we communists in Glasgow?' she asked.

Her mother's eyebrows lifted heavenwards. 'No, of course not. Whatever makes you ask such a thing?'

'We didn't have the six-hour rule there.'

'No.' Her mother's eyes became distant. 'Your father was not observing.'

'Then I don't want to observe either.'

'Nonsense.' Irina Derzhavina's hand slapped the table. 'Enough of this talk. We are not in Glasgow now.'

'I want to go back.'

'We are never going back.' Irina Derzhavina's voice was hard and cold and desperate. 'There is nothing there for us now.'

Sadie's pouted lip began to tremble and her small hands clenched into tight fists. 'We had chicken there.'

Irina Derzhavina drew in a long breath then let it out in one long shuddering exhalation. 'Sadie, I know this is hard for you to understand, but we are never returning. You must put Glasgow from your mind and not think of it again.' She turned away. 'And besides, your grandfather ate all the chicken.'

The glass hit her head squarely between the brows, and for a moment Sadie was filled with confusion. Glass, dirty glass, and outside hurtling, grey buildings that ran away from her with the sound of screaming metal. But no, the motion was hers. It was she who moved. Bus pass shown to driver. Pushing her way to the back. A young man giving up his seat. Sadie glanced nervously up and saw a girl staring down, her face a kaleidoscope of distrust and curiosity and concern. She thinks I'm senile, she thought, and felt a rush of indignation and shame that made her turn back to the dirty window.

The world outside the streaked glass looked as dark and unreal as the blurred, family daguerreotypes that had sat astride her mother's grand piano. My God, she thought. My memories are starting to be more vivid than the present. How was it that recollections three quarters of a century old could still come out of their wrappings crisp and lavender-scented, while the memories of last week or yesterday, or even this morning, were grey and eaten away, like rags?

Pondering this, she kept her face turned to the window until the bus pulled into London road then hastily gathered up her bag and her umbrella, nearly forgetting the roses lying by her side, and shuffled off her seat, head down. But it was all for nothing because the girl with the kaleidoscope eyes had gone.

It wasn't raining when she stepped off the bus, but the sky was black and threatening, a winter sky encroaching on autumn. She paused a moment on the pavement, looking up at it, then checking that her coat was buttoned right to the collar, pulled her brown woollen hat further down over her ears. As she walked, the hat insulated her from sound, muffling her footsteps so that they no longer seemed to belong to her and she felt herself slipping back into a twilight of events long gone and words lost to the distant drum of decades.

Her mother pointing at an unset blancmange. 'A delicacy is what I asked for. This would turn the stomach of the bravest amongst us.' Cook weeping into her apron, her chin wobbling like the blancmange.

Then later, when her father arrived. 'No, Sadie. You're mother worries too much.' A shake of his great bearded head. 'Business is fine. Everything is fine.'

A row of tenements overlooked the cemetery. They were modern, roughcast with neat, symmetrical windows turned black in the light. They stared down at Sadie with the vacant, disinterested stare of the imbecile. The caretaker opened the gate, and recognising Sadie gave her a small, solemn bow and let her through. On another day, she might have stopped to talk to the caretaker, to ask how his family were doing, but today her mind was preoccupied with the task ahead and she walked purposefully up the aisles of plain headstones to the place of Isaac's burial, roses held a little in front of her, like a bride's bouquet.

She stood a moment in the awed silence of the cemetery, thinking back to the bleak day of the funeral. Sammy so upset he could barely say the Kaddish. Then later, the sad ceremony to raise the stone. And how she'd thought she'd feel better by that time, more able to cope, but the tears had come all the same, and she'd stood there, insisting the others leave her, wondering what it would be like when Sammy went back to America, and how it was going to be now that she was all alone.

She did not visit often. It was a long ride and involves changes. But today she had come with a purpose, so after a moment she glanced from side to side to see that no-one was there, then shrugging a little self-consciously said, 'Surprised to see me?'

Her voice echoed in the silence. An old woman talking to herself. For a moment, her courage nearly left her, then she said determinedly, 'Look, Isaac, I know you're not still here and you know you're not still here, but I need to talk to someone, and you're the only one who'll understand.' She remembered the roses and laid them gently in front of the stone. 'I brought you some flowers. Roses, your favourite.'

It was probably imagination, but Sadie sensed an accusation in the air. She raised her eyes heavenwards. 'All right. I know. Flowers only for the living, but I thought you would want to see how they were doing this year. I even remembered to prune everything on time.' She didn't mention the rose Daniel had destroyed. There was no point in upsetting him. She recalled something. 'And the lilac. You should see it. Growing faster than Sammy did when he hit twelve. You remember. The year we visited your Aunt Irma when she moved to Southport.' She stopped talking. Nothing stirred. She glanced round and saw the caretaker pulling weeds from around a grave near the entrance. His back was to her, and for the moment he was too far away to hear. Reluctantly, she turned back to the stone. 'I know,' she said tiredly. 'I should get to the point.'

But it wasn't easy, and she heaved a great sigh, before saying all in a rush, 'Isaac, I don't even know why I came. We both know you're not here anymore, but … ' She swallowed hard, and her voice dropped to a whisper. 'But I've done a terrible thing, and I need to talk to you.' She waited to see if there might be some sign that he was listening, a tremor in the earth or a crack of thunder overhead. But there was nothing, not even the merest rustle of wind, and she went on, hopelessly, 'I've made a terrible promise to a little boy. A little boy who's dying. I've promised to take him to heaven with me.'

Then, despite the stillness, she felt a terrible tension in the air, as though, all around, the dead had gasped. Tears sprang to her eyes. 'What should I do, Isaac?' she begged. 'I can't make good on this promise, I know that. But how can I go back on my word?' She shook her head despairingly. 'What should I do? Tell me what to do.'

But the graves remained hushed, unmoved.

Back at the gate the caretaker let her out. 'Not such a nice day as yesterday,' he said.

Sadie nodded absently. 'Rain later, I should think.'

He looked up at the sky, as though examining it for the first time. 'Still, good for the garden,' he said. 'Been too dry lately.'

Sadie didn't answer. She heard him locking the gate behind her, keeping the dead in.

But there's no-one there, she thought sadly.

She retraced her steps back to the bus stop, and had very nearly reached it before the rain began.

It was raining when Mags hurried across the West Quad. The leaf-choked puddles, that had formed amongst the worn stone slabs, exploded, like miniature cloudbursts, as she ran through them. The water came in through the split in her left sole, but she was in too much of a hurry to notice. She was late. Again. As she'd run in through the main gate, the old clock had chimed the hour; lectures had started.

She was late because she had called the hospital to make an appointment for Daniel, and the receptionist had taken her usual ponderous time to offer a suitable date. Mags made several attempts to explain that certain days were out of the question, but the receptionist offered them anyway. And by the time they'd come to a mutual agreement, the first strokes of the hour had already slid away.

Head down, she charged through the West door, her feet resounding on the worn stairs as she took them two at a time. At the top, she hesitated only long enough to catch her breath, then slowly, cautiously opened the door to the lecture hall.

The lecture theatres in the West Quad were unchanged since their original construction in the eighteen nineties, tall, many-paned windows, hard-wooden benches and a dais for the lecturer to give his oration. The door was old too, and as Mags opened it, the hinges groaned loudly and wearily in protest at the inconvenience.

Dr Johnstone, a small, rotund man, with Mephistophelean beard and eyebrows, and the mannerisms of an orchestra conductor, was already giving his lecture. As the door creaked open, he stopped, chalk poised in mid-air, and turned to give the late-comer the full benefit of his stare. Behind him the class stopped writing, and pens and pencils suspended, like musicians during a pianissimo, turned to follow his gaze.

Caught in the act, Mags froze, fighting the desire to slam the door shut again. Her eyes searched desperately for a refuge, but all the benches, near the door, and therefore convenient for a quick getaway, were filled. Their occupants stared at her with vacant eyes. No-one moved. She glanced furtively at Dr Johnstone, taking in no more than the even shine of his shoes and the crease his trousers made at the knee, then slowly, eyes on the floor, she began to climb the steps to the top tier. Her footsteps echoing in the silence.

She was almost at the top when Dr Johnstone's booming voice addressed her,

'You, at the back.'

Aghast, she turned. He was smiling benignly up at her, and as though obeying some silent command, the class craned their heads round to watch. He said,

'Fugit inreparabile tempus.'

In the silence that followed, Mags' heart attempted to bang out a reply against her ribs in Morse, but she didn't speak. How can you answer someone who has spoken to you in a dead language?

'Do you know what that means?' he asked.

'No.' Her voice barely stirred the silence.

The hand holding the chalk flicked out, a conductor raising his baton. 'Time,' he translated, his eyes never leaving her, 'Irretrievable time is flying.' He waited for her to respond, and when the long seconds ticked by and she only stood there, shoulders hunched and defeated, he added, 'And if you want to know who said it, I suggest you make more of an effort to be on time for my classes in future.'

She said nothing, and losing interest, he turned back to the blackboard to proceed with the task of disseminating knowledge. The class continued to stare a half moment longer, then, as though waking out of a dream, returned their gaze to the front. There was the sound of pens and pencils whispering along paper.

Mags sank slowly down onto the back bench, making no attempt to open her notebook or lay out her pen. Her hands were trembling too much. He didn't have to do that, she thought. Then more fiercely, I should have stood up to him. Told him to talk English.' She looked down at the bent heads below. They'd have told him. Feeling humiliated and hopeless, she sat wondering what she was doing there.

Always the outsider, separated from their easy couples and cliques by the weight of her years, she would never fit in. He knew it, she thought bitterly. All her dreams of being a scholar suddenly seemed nothing more than that. Dreams. Illusions crumbling under the weight of reality.

It wasn't as she'd imagined, a bright new future in the hallowed halls of learning. Instead the corridors were dark and dusty, the truth she sought, a phantom always beckoning around the next corner. What was it Ewan was always quoting? Achievement is ten per cent inspiration, ninety per cent perspiration.

With a pang, she realised that he hadn't phoned last night after all. And suddenly she felt angry, very angry indeed.

Chapter 13

THE shrill noise of the doorbell startled Sadie out of her seat, sending balls of wool scattering, like comets, across the lounge. Daniel. He's come back. Her legs had stiffened while she'd been sitting, and she made slow progress across the paisley carpet, half hoping he would be gone before she reached the door, and, at the same time, terrified that she wouldn't make it in time. The bell didn't ring again, and she was certain that the door-step would be empty by the time she got to it.

It wasn't. On it, stood a small, plainly dressed young woman. She blinked myopically at Sadie through a pair of enormous round glasses, like a nocturnal bird unused to daylight. In confusion, Sadie blinked back.

'Can I help you?'

The owl nodded, blinking a couple of times before saying, 'How are we today?'

'Well, thank you,' Sadie said cagily.

The owl hopped up onto the threshold. 'Today's the seventeenth. Did you forget I was coming?'

The penny dropped. 'Ah, Sheena, you're right. I had forgotten all about it.' Sadie held the door wider. 'Please come in.'

Sheena walked into the lounge, clutching an untidy folder of papers under her arm. She perched on the edge of the sofa and began ruffling them, like feathers.

'Shall I put the kettle on?' Sadie asked without enthusiasm. Sheena looked up from her papers. 'Not for me, thanks. Everyone feels obliged to make me a cup of tea and I end up running to the loo all day.'

Sadie nodded sympathetically. 'Unpleasant for you.' She was tempted to offer something stronger, but remembered just in time that it wasn't wise to joke with social workers. She had seen Sheena slyly noting things down on her forms while they talked, and while she was fairly sure that there wasn't a box, marked, dipsomaniac tendencies, it wasn't a risk she wanted to take. Sitting back down, she noted Sheena glancing at the spilt balls of wool.

If she would ask me, I could explain, thought Sadie. But if I mention them now, I'll sound as though I'm making excuses.

She watched nervously as Sheena found the papers she was looking for and held her pen poised and at the ready. 'And how have you been since I last saw you?' Sheena had a bright smile. Mrs Gordon could be a difficult customer, like so many of them once they reached their eighties. Out of touch really. But you had to try.

Sadie couldn't remember the last time Sheena had visited. Not that it mattered. She could hardly tell her that she'd taken a young vandal into her home, fed him chocolate cake, then, discovering he was dying, made him a promise she couldn't possibly keep.

'You've been okay, Sadie?' Sheena asked again when Sadie didn't answer. Her voice was unnaturally loud, due her misapprehension that she was not being heard when in fact she was being ignored.

'I am fine, thank you.'

Sheena gave an approving smile and noted something down on her form. 'And the back doorstep,' she asked without looking up. 'Have you had that fixed yet? Can't have you falling when the icy weather comes in.'

Sadie had no memory of having agreed to fix it or of it requiring fixing, and she'd been out that way only yesterday with Daniel. She considered telling Sheena that it was none of her business, but she was never entirely sure how far the extent of the Social Work department's powers went. Sammy seemed to think their visits were a good idea, and she could never quite get over her feelings of mistrust to him. 'Ma, they're there to help. Just let them.' But Sadie had lived too long not to treat all government establishments with equal suspicion.

At last, because Sheena was blinking expectantly at her, she said, 'I have not got around to it.'

Sheena seemed shocked. 'You really must attend to that soon, Sadie.'

Sadie wished this twenty-two-year-old girl would stop calling her, Sadie, but Sammy said that was how everyone was now, even the people who worked for him called him by his first name. She tried to remember what Daniel had called her, then realised, with surprise, that he hadn't asked her name. Then he isn't coming back, she thought darkly. Perhaps it was all just a trick to take my mind off the rose. A flush came to her cheeks. What if it had all been a trick? The cakes. The sickness. The promise. That could be why he'd disappeared when she called him. She was shocked by how much pain she felt at his deception.

'O Sadie, you old fool.'

A hand took hers and she looked up, startled to find Sheena kneeling by her side. Horrified, she realised that she'd spoken aloud. She stared helplessly into Sheena's eyes, which had grown large and moist with professional compassion. 'You mustn't worry, Sadie. We can help you arrange to get it fixed.'

Sadie looked away. The girl thinks I want my step fixed. Does she think that's all you have to upset you when you reach my age? She fixed Sheena with her sweetest smile. 'You're right, my dear. I am a little overwrought. Perhaps you would fetch me a glass of water from the kitchen.'

Sheena was on her feet almost before Sadie had finished speaking. It was a real thrill to finally make some headway with these harder cases.

Sadie waited until the door was shut before heaving herself on to her feet once more. She crossed the room as quickly as she could, grateful to the thickness of the paisley carpet masking her footfalls. The archive was lying open on the sideboard, and it was only a matter of time before Sheena noticed it. She had been going through it in the hope of finding childhood memories to amuse Daniel. But the thought of Sheena poking and prying her way through them was almost unbearable. 'And who is this, Sadie?' Wink 'An old boyfriend, hmmm?'. No. Better to shut the lid on this box. She should never have let Sammy talk her into keeping it.

'Sadie, did you lose this?'

Guiltily, Sadie turned towards the door. She hadn't heard Sheena come in. 'What is that?'

Sheena held up a locket in her hand. It swung in delicate pendulum arcs catching the light and shadow in the room, alternately. Unconsciously, Sadie's hand reached for her neck. The familiar bump under her blouse was missing.

'I think one of the links has worn through,' Sheena said, advancing towards Sadie. She held up the chain to show her a break in the chain about an inch before the clasp. 'And the catch on the locket is damaged too. It won't close properly.' Sheena clicked the locket open and shut several times, like a small, golden mouth. 'Perhaps it was damaged in the fall.'

Sadie nodded vaguely. She had worn that locket so long that she she'd almost forgotten what was inside. Sheena was beside her now, pushing it into her hand. She gazed down at it, seeing the two faded photographs inside, as though for the first time. Sheena pointed to the one of an infant, swaddled in lace, still chubby with rolls of baby fat. 'Your son?' she asked.

Sadie nodded, recovering herself a little. 'A beautiful baby, no? The doctors said I was lucky to have such a beautiful baby so late in life.'

Sheena pointed to the second photo. It was of a young girl, dark, bobbed hair and a wide smile that contrasted with the watchful eyes above it. 'Who's this?'

'Ah.' Sadie was surprised. 'Do you not know?' And when Sheena went on staring blankly, she added hastily, 'That is me.'

'Weren't you a beauty?' Sheena said, and Sadie had the impression that she couldn't reconcile this young girl's image with the old woman at her side. Wispy white hair, colourless eyes, and a complexion creased and contoured, like the surface of an ancient and little referred to map. Perhaps sensing her indiscretion, Sheena asked hastily, 'Where was it taken?'

'In Russia.' Sadie frowned down at the picture trying to push away the sights and sounds of it. Sadie, don't look so solemn. It's bad enough when Piotr does it. You communists are so intense all the time? I thought you were in love.

Her frown deepened. 'I lived in Russia many years before returning to Glasgow. My mother took me there after my father died and we were in debt. It was a strange time. Difficult to explain' She was about to say more, but Sheena was gathering up her papers. 'That's fascinating,' she said without turning around. 'You really ought to write your story someday.' She swept her papers into her bag and turned to face Sadie. 'I'll have to fly. I'm running a little late.'

Sadie nodded. The young are always in a hurry.

Sheena adjusted her glasses and blinked several times to emphasise the importance of what she was about to say. 'You will have that step looked at, won't you?'

Sadie nodded again. 'I will do it today.'

'Good.' Another life saved. She pulled on her coat, not bothering to button it. The young don't feel the cold. 'I'll be off then.' She held up a hand. 'I'll see myself out. I know the way by now. Your next visit is in a fortnight.' She dropped a small rectangle of card on top of the closed biscuit tin. 'I've written it down on there. You won't forget about me this time, hmmm?'

'No.'

She was out the door and Sadie wasn't sure if they'd said goodbye or not. She turned to the sideboard, and flicking the reminder card disdainfully on to the floor, she placed the locket there and headed for the kitchen, leaving the child and the young woman to gaze out at the light.

'Mags.' It was the second time he had called, and on both occasions, she had ignored him. Let him run. Let him be the one sweating and out of breath, gasping out his words, like a landed fish. A light tap on her arm made her look up. He was at her side, seeming neither rumpled nor out of breath. 'Mags, didn't you hear me calling.'

'No.' She said it flatly so that the lie would be obvious.

She waited for him to mention Helen, to apologise for letting her down, again. But instead he said, 'I'm on my way to the staff club. Beckett has been hounding me for the questions again, as though he'd set the damned exam for tomorrow.'

Mags gave a non-committal nod. Normally, these small intimacies about academic life excited and pleased her, a hint of things to come. But not today. She wasn't to be so easily bribed.

Ewan had fallen silent, and she sensed he was frowning at her, but she offered no clue. Let him do the running.

'Mags, is something the matter?'

She shrugged. 'You tell me.'

She was looking up at him, seeing the frown crease his brow. He raised the papers in his hand. 'Come to the staff club with me. We can discuss this later.'

She made a show of glancing at her watch. 'All right. If it doesn't take too long.'

The staff club was a large, rectangular room, comfortably furnished with a well-stocked bar at one end and a dining room at the other. The floor was carpeted and there were curtains at the windows. Few of the tables were occupied, and those that were, mostly by drably dressed academics huddling over their drinks and talking in hushed voices. Here and there were students, who, discovering the little publicised fact that the staff club paid less tax because it claimed to be open to the student body, had come there in defiance of the normal protocols. They looked uncomfortable and stared sullen challenges at anyone who happened to glance in their direction.

Ewan turned to Mags. 'Do you want something to eat?'

She hadn't eaten since last night, but she shook her head. 'No thanks.'

'A drink?'

'I'm fine.'

'Ewan, my love.' A voice broke through their whispered tones. 'Is that you skulking there?' A large, woman, almost as tall as Ewan, her meaty proportions wrapped, like individual cutlets, in an expensive, tailored suit, tapped Ewan briskly on the shoulder. 'What are you up to hiding in the shadows like that?'

'Tonia.' Ewan's smile was one that a gracious father might bestow on a precocious child. 'How lovely to see you.' They exchanged a kiss that did not touch flesh. 'Is Alan here with you?'

Tonia waved a bored hand in the direction of the bar. 'Where else would Alan be at lunchtime? I only dropped by to dump my shopping on him. My car's gone in for a service.' She gave a shuddering, little sigh that shook her large shoulders. 'Another service. Can you believe it?'

'Awful for you.'

Mags heard the hint of irony in Ewan's tone and her lips curved up in a quick, unexpected smile.

'Of course, you have troubles of your own,' Tonia was saying. She laid the fingertips of a fleshy hand lightly on Ewan's breast. 'How is poor Helen these days?'

Ewan stiffened. Even behind him, Mags saw it. Is it because I'm here, she wondered.

Ewan spread his hands. 'Helen is just Helen. You know how it is.'

'O, I do,' Tonia sympathised. 'Still, it'll all work out, I'm sure.' Her eyes flicked over Ewan's shoulder. 'And who is this you have with you?'

Ewan stepped back and Mags had the unnerving sensation of having a flashlight turned upon her. 'This is Margaret Gallagher.'

'O?' Tonia didn't offer her hand, but her eyes crawled across Mags, examining every detail. 'And how do you know Ewan?'

'She's one of my students,' Ewan explained. Tonia was obviously waiting for more explanation, but Ewan was looking over in the direction of the bar. 'I really must give these to Alan. Mags and I have a tutorial next. She's helping me proof the book, you know, and has been kind enough to wait. So, if you'll excuse me.' He headed off without waiting for Tonia's permission.

Tonia didn't move, and caught between the indecision of whether to follow Ewan or stay where she was, Mags made no move either. Tonia, still studying Mags with narrowed, curious eyes, said suddenly, 'You seem a little old to be a student.' Then, seeing Mags' shocked look, added coolly. 'If you don't mind my saying so.'

'I'm a mature student,' Mags explained uneasily. Her voice suddenly sounded unnaturally harsh and deep to her ears. It made her stumble over her words.

'Still,' Tonia said doubtfully. 'Ewan must think a lot of you if he's letting you read his precious manuscript.'

Not knowing how to answer, Mags gave a little shrug. 'I hope so.'

'What's your opinion so far?'

Startled by the question, Mags could only mumble incoherently. 'There's a very interesting anecdote I'm reading just now about a man who still refuses to give his real name because he's afraid of being tracked down by the GPU. Well, I suppose we'd call them the KGB today. It seems that—'

'Yes. Yes,' Tonia interrupted impatiently. 'But what do you think of Ewan's writing?'

Mags stared at the older woman. What should she say? Was it a trick to see if she would wax lyrical, like some lovesick teenager or was Tonia hoping for some juicy scandal to entertain her friends with? 'I … I don't really know,' Mags began awkwardly. 'I haven't read much. I have a little boy, and … '

Tonia's eyebrows rose, as though she had discovered something very interesting at last. 'How old is he?'

'Eight. Nearly nine.'

'Goodness.' Tonia placed her hands at the base of her neck. 'How brave of you to take up full time education when you still have a child at home. I thought about it when the girls were small, but just the thought of organising nurseries and nannies and things gave me the absolute shivers.' She laughed in a way that Mags found impossible to join. She didn't belong to this world of options and choices. The walls of her world were made of bare necessities, stark and unavoidable.

Tonia seemed on the point of asking something more, and it was a great relief when Ewan reappeared, minus his sheaf of papers. He laid a hand on Mags' shoulder as if daring Tonia to read anything into it. 'Sorry to interrupt the gossip, but we really have to be getting along. I'm lecturing at two.'

'What a pity.' Tonia's eyes were still on Mags. 'We were starting to have the most interesting chat.'

Outside, Mags gulped fresh air into her lungs. And, noticing the action, Ewan said, 'Don't let Tonia get to you. She's a bit overpowering on a first meeting.'

'She wanted to know all about you,' Mags said grimly.

'And what did you tell her?'

Was she imagining it, or did he sound anxious? 'I told her I had more important things to think about.'

Ewan laughed. 'Was she ferreting about the book again?'

Mags gave a little shrug. 'She wanted to know what I thought.'

'And what do you think?'

Mags looked away, not certain she wanted to say. 'It frightens me.'

'Indeed?'

She still didn't look at him. Her mind was running across all that she had read so far, trying to put something into words that she didn't yet fully understand. 'All those people,' she began clumsily. 'All that belief in freedom. Sucked into the machine of the State until …' Her voice tailed off and her hands drew empty arcs in the air. She expected Ewan to finish the thought for her. Instead, he asked, 'Have you read *The Heart of a Dog* yet? It's in the recommended reading.'

'Bulgakov? Yes. I remember it. No, I haven't read it yet. I haven't had the time.' Some of her original anger was coming back.

'Do you know what it's about?'

'Something to do with the brain of a dog being transplanted into a human being?'

'Brain and sexual organs,' Ewan corrected. 'It was a satire of a supposed event that took place between Lenin and Pavlov.'

Mags shook her head. She didn't really care about dogs' brains in human bodies. She wanted to talk about their future. But Ewan had an infuriating habit of leading the conversation and she didn't know how to bring it back to where she wanted it.

Ewan took her silence for interest. 'Lenin wanted to find out if Pavlov's experiments in controlling dogs could be applied to human beings.'

'But why?' Mags was curious despite herself.

'That's simple. He wanted to control human behaviour so that the masses would follow his communistic plan for the future without question. To him, the individualism of Russia's past was a destructive, divisive force that drove the country to revolution.'

'But that's horrible.' The words spilled out before she had time to clad them in more detached terms. And knowing she had sounded foolish, she kept her eyes on the ground, afraid to see the mockery in his face. Speaking before thinking again. He's laughing at me now. Perhaps he'll share this little anecdote over drinks with Tonia. *And then she said, 'But that's horrible.'* Her cheeks were burning and for a moment she didn't realise that Ewan was speaking.

'Your view would have been thought to be very old fashioned at the time,' he was saying. 'Remember, this was an age of Utopian dreams. Anything was possible. The science of communism was going to make a new kind of man, rational, disciplined and bound to his fellow by a collective vision of the future.'

'You can't free a man by making him part of something else,' she interrupted. 'He has to be himself. At some level, at least.' She frowned. 'And you can't free people by telling them what to think.'

'You don't approve of the enlightenment of the masses?'

She glanced up sharply, annoyed with the tone in which he asked the question. 'Not at the expense of the enlightenment of the individual, no.'

He smiled. 'Neither do the contributors to my book. And that's why I wanted you to read it.'

She didn't answer. She was looking at his smile and wishing that it didn't charm her so magnificently, that it made her crave to find clever ways to please him just for the joy of seeing it again.

They were standing round him, barring his way. Five boys, older than he, brothers of his classmates. They were skinny, with narrow, wolverine faces and hungry eyes, and they made him feel afraid just looking at them.

'Hey, wee man,' said the largest boy. 'We want to talk to ye.' His tone wasn't altogether unkind, but Daniel felt his bladder growing taut as he answered, as bravely as he could, 'Aye.'

Two of the other boys started laughing and mimicking the way he had answered.

'Aye. Aye. Ai. I. I.' They drew the vowels out, growing louder and shriller. 'Aaaa Eeeee.'

Daniel felt the need to pee grow very bad.

'Are you a pouf?' one of the laughing boys asked.

Daniel bit his lower lip to stop it trembling and answered, 'No.'

'Ye sound like one,' the boy said. They laughed at him again and Daniel stared down at the tar macadam beneath his feet. Little white stars on a murky sky.

'Wee poufter,' the largest boy said.

Daniel looked up, and immediately one of the boys cried out, 'He is a pouf. He looked up when you called him a pouf.'

'I'm no a pouf,' Daniel said, drawing himself up with all the strength his trembling knees would allow.

'Then what are ye greetin' fer?' the boy said.

Daniel wanted to say he wasn't crying, but he was too near tears to be able to reply. The largest boy was speaking again. 'My wee brother says you've been telling him that your da's a pilot.' He took a step closer, his eyes daring Daniel to deny it.

Daniel didn't answer.

'A pilot in Africa,' one boy sneered.

'Wi' no memory,' said another. 'A big hero comin' tae get ye.'

'In his plane.'

'Aye he is,' Daniel said. 'He's comin'.'

He was crying now. The biggest boy poked a bony finger into his chest. It hurt his scar, but that wasn't why he was crying.

'Ma big sister knows your da,' the boy was saying. And, despite himself, Daniel whispered, 'Is she in Africa too?'

Their laughter rained down on him, hitting him, like hammer blows, crushing him. And over it he could hear the biggest boy saying, 'Your da's no in Africa. He's nothin' but a druggie that lives on the same estate as ma sister. And she says that the council's goin' tae evict him and his pals soon.'

'He flies a plane,' Daniel insisted. He wasn't looking at them anymore. His eyes were fixed on a patch of cloud-covered sky past the boy's head.

The boy pushed his face close to Daniel's. 'The only way your da flies is round in his heid.' Then suddenly they were all whirling around him, swooping and diving, their arms wide spread. 'Danny. Danny. It's Daddy comin' tae get ye.'

And Daniel stood, stiff and still, his shoulders hunched, but his eyes fixed on a patch of white cloud emerging from the leaden sky. It looked like a plane. A beautiful, white plane coming down from the skies. A biplane, like in *Raiders of the Lost Ark* The kind of plane his father piloted.

Chapter 14

IT was foolish to come out again for a long walk after exerting herself by going all the way out to see Isaac, but somehow, she felt stifled alone in the big house all by herself. She half thought of ringing Sammy, but she was never sure of the time differentials, and it was embarrassing to wake someone from a deep sleep just because you wanted a chat. And besides, the one thing she needed to talk about was the thing she couldn't tell anyone.

As the rain had stopped, she took the route through the park, descending the steps carefully, watching out for wet leaves and concealed roots, then made her way along the gravel paths into the park proper. What to do now, she wondered. It was a dull day for walking. In the grey light the autumn colours looked washed-out and drab. I need peace, she thought. Somewhere I can sit down and think. She shivered a little in the damp air. Somewhere warm.

There was the sound of a door opening and a man in a park keeper's uniform stepped out of one of the botanical greenhouses. He was nursing a tray of plants under a plastic sheet, and he hurried past Sadie, as though she was one of the small, drab, leafless bushes, not worth a second glance.

When he had disappeared from view, she turned towards the greenhouse and stepped inside the open door. The damp, stifling air surrounded her, like a blanket. It warmed her sufficiently so that she loosened the top button of her raincoat and took off her gloves. And, as she wanted to think, she followed the circular path around the exotic foliage to the quieter seats at the back. But when she got there she found she was not alone. Etta was holding court with three other ladies, who Sadie knew only as Mrs Ferguson, Mrs Easedale and Miss McKinley. They were hung on Etta's every word and bobbed their scrawny necks up and down, like pigeons, in time with Etta's remarks.

'Sadie.' Etta saw through Sadie's impression of an Angelica tree. 'Come join us.'

After a moment's hesitation, Sadie advanced upon the group, her smile fixed. She perched uncomfortably on the small space made for her on the end of the bench.

'You know I can't move up further, Sadie dear,' Etta said. She pointed at her hip. 'My arthritis.'

'O,' Miss McKinley, a thin woman with nervous, darting eyes, said, 'I thought that was the hip you had replaced in the operation.'

'It *is* the hip I had replaced,' Etta said with annoyance. 'It was the operation that gave me the arthritis.'

'O,' said Miss McKinley more faintly.

Mrs Ferguson, a jollier woman, obviously felt it was time to intervene. She turned to Sadie. 'Have you heard the news?'

Sadie glanced at Etta to see if she had, then said, 'No. I have not heard.'

'Elspeth Roberts is dead.'

'No.' Sadie was shocked. 'I spoke to her only last week.'

'Terrible,' ventured Miss McKinley, and all four heads bobbed.

'Of course,' said Etta raising a hand to interrupt. 'We don't know for sure that she's dead.'

Sadie's eyes widened. 'Then— What makes you say such a thing?'

'Well, it came from Alice McIlvanney.'

'O.'

Everyone nodded. 'And we know how wrong she was about Mrs Ramsay.'

'Mrs Ramsay's not dead?' Mrs Ferguson was surprised.

'No.' Etta waved a hand. 'The poor woman just got bored with hearing Alice's stories all over again and went to sleep. The next thing she knows, she's getting In Fondest Memory cards through the door.'

'So, we don't know if Elspeth is dead?' asked Sadie.

'O, I think we do, dear,' Mrs Easedale said comfortably. She patted Sadie's arm. 'I got it from Mr Brink at the newsagents.'

'No good,' Etta interrupted, shaking her head. 'I told him.'

There was a brief moment of silence in which Etta scrutinised Sadie's face then a triumphant smile began to curve the corners of her mouth. 'You know, you don't look so good.'

The pigeons had become crows. They searched Sadie's face for shadows of the other world. But Sadie shook her head. 'No, Etta. I'm fine. It's just that I went out to see Isaac today and I'm a little tired.'

Etta frowned. 'I thought you didn't like visiting the dead.'

Sadie didn't know what to say. Her mouth felt dry and incapable of forming a suitable explanation. She glanced at the others hoping for help, but they were lost to their own thoughts. At last Mrs Ferguson said thoughtfully, 'I went to visit Stewart's grave a few times, but I never really felt he was listening.'

'Well dear,' Mrs Easedale interjected. 'He was never really a man for listening in life either.'

Mrs Ferguson looked so shocked at this thought that Miss McKinley felt it necessary to say, 'I visit my mother's grave every week. After she died I missed our little chats so. And besides she was completely deaf towards the end and never answered me when I spoke, so when I talk to her gravestone it really isn't that different.' Miss McKinley had been looking into the distance with a dreamy expression as she spoke. Suddenly she became aware of the sceptical eyes surrounding her and became a little flustered. 'But I really do think she's listening. When I talk to her I feel as though I can sense her all round me.' She looked around quickly, as though hoping for an unexpected visitation then let her eyes fall on the ground. 'But, as they moved her grave to make way for that extra lane in the motorway, I suppose that's just me being silly.'

'Well,' said Etta briskly. 'I don't hold with graves. Never have. And neither did Oscar. When he was dying, he said to me, "Etta, promise me that you won't put me in the ground. I want a nice place, not fancy or anything. But somewhere I'd feel at home. Somewhere I could hear the birds sing." And I said, "Oscar, have you gone soft in the head? When you're dead, you're dead and listening to the birds is the least of your problems. Besides you've got to get buried. But he said, "Promise me, Etta." And a promise is a promise so I've got him in a casket on the mantelpiece. I open the window in the spring so he can hear the birds. Of course, he can also hear that Nicholson woman when she's been drinking, but I keep the window open anyway. You can only listen to so much bird song.'

'And you don't find it a terribly depressing thing to look at?' Mrs Ferguson asked. Etta looked surprised. 'No. Not at all. I always said that mantelpiece needed something. Anyway, it's a nice teak. They wanted to sell me this one in oak, but I took a look inside and saw straight away that it wasn't finished right. No workmanship. Would chip the first time it was dusted.' She looked over at Sadie. 'My cousin got me a good deal. Harry. You remember him. You met him at Oscar's funeral.'

Sadie nodded though she didn't recall Etta having a cousin let alone one called Harry. Etta was continuing her story. 'It was lucky Harry was there. I mean, I hadn't expected to arrange this side of things. So, anyway, Harry says to me, "Leave it to me, Etta. I know just the place to get your casket.". And he goes off to see his cousin Lena. You remember Lena. She was the one that married out.'

Sadie was nodding absently to this when Etta stopped her with a wave of her hand. 'No, of course you don't. You weren't at Lena's wedding.'

Sadie began shaking her head, and satisfied, Etta carried on. 'Well, Lena and Kevin ¾ was the one she married. ¾ ran a little funeral parlour over on the South side. Beautiful place. All wood panelling and sofas. Very tasteful. Made you feel like you were at home. Anyway, they'd had a bit of an accident. A burst pipe or something, so they were selling off a lot of stuff at discount.'

'And you got the casket there?' Miss McKinley asked timidly. Etta looked at her severely and Miss McKinley became absorbed in a stain on the hem of her coat.

'Of course, that's where I got it. Beautiful. Not a mark on it. And the finish inside? What can I say? A craftsman's work. The work of a man who takes pride in doing things right.' She leaned forward, pointedly ignoring Miss McKinley. 'I looked at that casket and I said to myself, "Etta, don't even ask what it costs. You could find peace next to such workmanship. You gave your word, and Oscar is going to be comfortable in there." She sat back. 'So, I took it and I've never regretted it. He sits on the mantelpiece now, no trouble at all. And I tell you this. It's the tidiest that man has ever been.'

'Except for the time that cat got in and knocked him over,' Mrs Easedale commented.

Sadie, who had heard this story several times, and found it longer each time it was retold, had not really been listening. But, now that some sixth sense, told her that the story was at an end, she came to a decision. Without looking at any of the others, she asked. 'Suppose you hadn't been able to find a casket?'

'Why wouldn't I be able to find a casket?' Etta wanted to know. 'If Harry couldn't help. Paul or Miriam's boy, Jonathan would have found me something.'

'You could have tried the Co-op,' Mrs Ferguson suggested.

'But supposing,' Sadie asked. 'You couldn't get a casket anywhere. No-one could.' They were staring at her, open-mouthed and she went on a little desperately. 'Perhaps if there had been a … a shortage.'

'A shortage of caskets?' Miss McKinley repeated, puzzled.

Sadie ignored her, and trying to keep the urgency out of her voice, asked, 'Suppose you couldn't keep your promise. What would you have done then?'

For once Etta looked non-plussed and Sadie pressed her point home. 'You would have broken your promise, no? You would have to break it because you had no choice.'

Etta frowned. 'Oscar used to say, promises were like his aunt Bella at a bar mitzvah, after she'd had one too many sherries.'

Sadie looked at her enquiringly.

'Best carried out quickly.'

'I don't think—'

But Miss McKinley added dreamily. 'My mother used to say "A promise is a cloud; fulfilment is rain." It's an Arabian proverb I think.' She frowned. 'Because it doesn't make a lot of sense in Scotland.' Then, when she realised no-one was listening to her, she said in a small voice. 'But I don't suppose it matters.'

Sadie was still looking at Etta. 'Wouldn't you have broken your promise? If there hadn't been any caskets.'

Etta's face was inscrutable. She's wondering why I'm asking this, Sadie thought worriedly. But it was too late to change the subject, and at last Etta heaved a sigh and shook her head. 'No. I wouldn't have broken it. You can't break a promise to a dying man.'

The others nodded in approval.

'But how could you … ,' Sadie began, but Etta interrupted her.

'I only promised to make him comfortable so that he could hear the birds,' she said thoughtfully. 'So, I suppose he would have been just as happy if I'd put him inside the birdhouse he built at the bottom of the garden.' Her eyes widened with sudden alarm. 'My god. What if that's where he meant me to put him all this time.' She looked at the others, a hand clasped to her heart.'

'Och no,' Mrs Ferguson said comfortingly. 'It would ruin the teak.'

Ewan's smile had gone by the time they reached his office. All the way up the four flights of steps, Mags had steeled herself to do what knew had to be done. But when Ewan closed the door and took a seat behind his desk, she suddenly experienced that vague nausea associated exclusively with points of no return. Her voice abandoned her and she found herself looking at him, willing him to understand, to make it easy for her, just this once. But he said nothing, and eventually she forced herself to speak. 'We need to talk. About us.'

'Ah.' He said it, as though she'd raised a point of particular gravity during a philosophical discussion, and turned away letting his face fall into shadow. She expected him to say more, but when he didn't she said as evenly as she could manage, 'We've been seeing each other for a year now.' Then she stopped, hoping that this would be enough to explain her feelings, to express the pain of all those lonely, unfulfilled nights sitting by a phone that never rang. Eventually, she added despairingly, 'I can't live in the present forever, Ewan. I need to know where we're going.'

She was about to say more, but the phone on the desk suddenly burst into shrill life and Ewan picked up the receiver. His face was still in shadow, but she saw him tense, the hand at his side curling into a fist. 'Thank you, Mrs Drysdale,' he said. 'Put her through.'

There was silence apart from a faint crackle from the phone. I should go, thought Mags. This is a private conversation. But when she went to stand up she found her legs felt too weak, and she sat there, staring ahead, trying to merge with the furniture. Ewan said,

'No, of course I haven't.' then 'Why would I? I have the Rover with me.' There was a prolonged series of crackles from the phone then he said, 'Now there's no need to upset yourself. Why don't you take a taxi? I'll look for them tonight. Yes. Yes, I promise.' There was another crackle followed by a silence in which his breathing increased, then he said, 'You too, darling,' and put down the phone.

He turned towards Mags giving a small, apologetic shrug. 'Helen lost her car keys again.'

Mags was still staring at the wall opposite, her face, like stone. He looked at her then sighed. 'You know I want to be with you, Mags,' he said, leaning down to take her hands. 'But Helen is still so …,' He searched for a word. 'So fragile. I need to give her time.'

He went on talking of Helen's mental state, describing it like the delicate parts of a machine that he was forced to tend, and couldn't abandon until he was certain it could run unaided. But Mags heard only Helen, Helen, Helen. A name from the classics. Suitable for the wife of an academic. Mrs Helen MacLeod. *We are delighted to invite Dr and Mrs Ewan and Helen MacLeod.* Mags MacLeod? Her name had a heavy, ugly sound to it. It clung to Ewan's, like a clod of mud, dragging it down.

Quite suddenly she was on her feet, her cheek pressed against his chest. There was the smell of musty tweed and the harsh, clean chemical odours of starch and deodorant and aftershave, and something salty on her upper lip, which she realised were her own tears. Embarrassed, she tried to pull back, but he wouldn't let her go, and held her firmly by the shoulders, whispering her name over and over, into her hair. 'Mags. Mags. Mags. Don't cry. It'll be all right.' And she didn't answer him, because there was so much she wanted to say and so much that she was afraid to say, that she just stood there letting him stroke her hair and wondering exactly what it was that would be all right.

After a moment, almost by accident, his hand slipped down and rested on the curve of her left breast. She felt its weight almost as an annoyance. Why do men associate comfort with sex? But it had been so long since they'd made love. How long had it been? She couldn't remember, and when he said her name it didn't sound ugly any more, but something precious and unobtainable, a gift only she could grant. And his hand was cupping her breast entirely now, a soft shell, grazing her nipple with the force of his palm. The nipple of her right breast began to strain in frustration against the worn fabric of her shirt, and quite spontaneously, she stood up on tiptoe, and bit down into the soft, exposed curve of his neck. He closed his eyes and gave a moan, so soft and so out of keeping with his character that she felt the need for security and promises melting away. Forget the future with all its worries and fears and unpaid bills. Forget responsibility. Forget anger. Forget guilt. All that mattered was the craving of the here and the heat of the now and the chance to seize the moment before it was lost. Carpe diem she thought, and almost wished Dr Johnstone was there to hear her.

There was a sharp rap at the door and they sprang back, as though the other had suddenly become red hot to the touch. 'Come,' Ewan called, and by the time the door opened he was standing by the bookcases, his hand resting lightly on one of the spines, while Mags stood, facing the desk, her face hidden in the shadows as Ewan's had been.

'Ah,' said Ewan heartily. 'Mrs Drysdale, what can I do for you?'

Mrs Drysdale was a small, brisk woman, plainly dressed with the evident intention of dispelling any notions that working for the Arts faculty was her personal choice, noted the unnatural distance between lecturer and student and allowed it to be seen that she noted it, before saying, 'I'm looking for one of the students, Dr MacLeod.' She glanced in Mags direction and sniffed slightly. 'Her tutor has been phoning round everywhere looking for her, and he thinks she may be in some of your classes.'

'There are a lot of people in my classes,' Ewan said doubtfully. 'I can't say I know all of them.'

Mrs Drysdale glanced over at Mags' back, holding her stare long enough to indicate that she recognised the posture was defensive, then turned back to Ewan, a thoughtful expression on her face.

'What name did you say?' he asked.

'I didn't,' she said pointedly. 'I believe it's a Margaret Gallagher Dr Lyons is looking for. It's quite urgent. Her little boy is ill.'

Chapter 15

SHORTLY after their last child had flown the nest, Mags' parents had moved to a four-in-a-block in Croftfoot. 'I've done my bit,' a tight-lipped Mrs Gallagher had said, surveying the tiny flat. 'Time for them to stand on their own feet.' She chose a house with only one bedroom.

It was situated in a neat, quiet street, where there wasn't enough provision for parking, so that the road was obstructed to a single lane by cars parked along either side. Mags barely remembered giving Ewan frantic, contradictory directions on how to get there, but she was vaguely relieved that there was nowhere for him to pull over and she could avoid refusing an offer to accompany her.

She had her seatbelt off and the door open almost before he'd stopped, but his words restrained her.

'Sure you don't want me to come with you?'

'Yes. I'll be fine.'

He frowned at her helplessly. 'I could find somewhere else to park and come back for you.'

'No.' She gave him a quick, strained smile that deepened the lines about her mouth. 'It's all right. You've got work to get back to.'

'I can phone in. Say it's an emergency.'

She shook her head, but he was about to protest, so she was forced to say, 'You never know, Helen might phone you again.'

'There's no reason for her to do that,' he said. He sounded as though he meant it, but she saw him slip the car into gear. Her glance went to the green door with a seventy-four hanging lop-sidedly next to the letterbox, and she nodded urgently towards it. 'I've got to go.'

He seemed torn. 'If you're sure?'

Her strained smile didn't waver. 'I'm sure.'

Her father answered the door to Mags' hammering. 'No need to break the door down,' he said. 'The worst is over.'

But Mags pushed past him and ran up the narrow staircase to the lounge. Daniel was lying on the sofa, wrapped in a pink Paisley patterned downy. Mags recognised it from her childhood bed. He was lying limply his eyes half shut, but he was less blue than she'd feared. He didn't smile when he saw her. Mrs Gallagher, a large woman with soft, shelf-like breasts and a hard, harsh

96

face, was perched on the edge of the sofa, holding one of Daniel's limp hands in her own.

She looked up as Mags entered the room, eyes accusing. 'You got here awful fast.'

Mags forced a smile. 'I got a lift.'

'O?'

Mags fell to her knees beside Daniel. 'What have you been up to, wee darling?' she asked. She reached out to stroke his hair. Mrs Gallagher didn't release her grip on his hand.

'Big boys,' he said hoarsely. 'Said things about my dad.'

'Boys?' Mags felt the blood rushing to her cheeks. She'd let Ewan run his hands over her, let him tug at her breast, when the only one who had any right to be there was surrounded by thugs and bullies without her protection. Suddenly, what she'd done with Ewan seemed sordid and cheap. 'Oh pet,' she said, her eyes filling. 'Do you know who they were?'

He opened his mouth, but his expression was vague. 'I saw Dad's plane.'

'He's not to talk,' Mrs Gallagher said severely. 'The doctor says he needs to rest.'

Mags bit back the desire to snap that she didn't need advice on handling her own child. Keeping her eyes on Daniel, she said, 'Well, you're safe here.'

'Aye, he is,' Mrs Gallagher said coldly. 'A good job one of us was here for the wean.'

'Would ye like a cup of tea, Mags?' Her father's interruption was clumsy and earned him a hard stare from his wife.

'No. Thanks, Dad.' Mags didn't look up. The pressure of the dark rage building in her chest was so great that it made her ribs ache. She kept her eyes on Daniel, stroking the hair back from his forehead. His eyes had closed. He was sleeping.

'Well,' said Mr Gallagher. Then again, a little later. 'Well.'

When it became obvious that repeating the word only made the atmosphere tenser, he went over to the television and began flicking through the channels. Mags said nothing until she was sure she could speak evenly, then she asked, 'What did Dr Collins say?'

Out the corner of her eye, she saw her mother open her mouth then snap it shut again, as though swallowing the impulse to lash out again. When she spoke, it was in a flat, controlled voice. 'He said what they always say, it's to be expected.' She let go Daniel's hand and straightened the downy round his chin. 'You should go back to that consultant that did the operation.'

'We're going next week,' Mags said grimly.

Her mother didn't acknowledge this in any way, but she added more gently. 'Dr Collins said it wasn't as bad as it looked. No need for the hospital this time.'

Mags nodded, not trusting herself to speak. Mrs Gallagher sighed, then letting go Daniel's hand, heaved herself out of the seat. 'You'll need to tell him. Those wee animals knew everything. But he needs to hear it from you.'

'Yes.' Mags' voice was defeated.

'You should have told him in the first place.' Mrs Gallagher was not finished. 'I always said it would end in trouble. You can't lie tae a wean.'

'Yes.'

'Well then.' Mrs Gallagher was clearly put out by Mags' resignation. 'I'd better see to the dinner. Gary's coming round tonight.' She nodded over at her husband. 'He plays darts with your Dad. They're on the team now.'

'Keeps him off the streets,' Mr Gallagher said without looking up, and Mags almost managed a smile. 'How's my little brother doing?'

Her mother's face softened. 'You know Gary. Always some cause or other.'

'What's he campaigning for this time? Longer holidays and less work hours?' She'd said it without thinking and saw her mother's face freeze.

'I'm sure it's a good cause,' she said lamely.

'It is.' Mrs Gallagher's expression was cold. 'He's trying to prevent the ones that leave the council for greater things, then try crawling back a couple of years later, from getting higher wages than people that were loyal and stuck things out.'

Mags frowned. 'But surely the ones that leave took all the risks. Maybe they're bringing new skills back with them.'

She'd got it wrong again. Mrs Gallagher's face closed, like a door. 'I suppose that's university thinking for you,' she said sarcastically. 'I'm afraid it's a bit too difficult for the likes of me.'

There was a groan from the sofa, and both women turned frightened eyes towards Daniel. He shifted uncomfortably, as though aware of the tension around him and his breathing sounded hoarse and laboured. Mags lifted the downy back to cover his arms where he had pushed it away. 'It's all right,' she crooned. 'All right. Mum's here.' She glanced round at her mother. 'We should be getting back.'

Mrs Gallagher's eyes were still on Daniel. 'We're having shepherd's pie tonight,' she said stiffly. 'You can stay for some if you'd like.'

'No,' Mags answered equally stiffly. 'I've got studying to do.'

'Your lift waited then?'

The air grew taut again.

'No.' Mags stood up. 'I'll get a taxi.'

'Students must be richer than I thought,' Mrs Gallagher said, and pursing her lips, turned and walked through to the kitchen.

The page in front of her remained determinedly and stubbornly blank, her pen hovering above it lifeless and inert. How did you explain to the young about a world that is almost gone? Even her living recollection was malleable, kneading the facts with hindsight and false recollection until they grew wet and pulpy. A putty of memories, soft to the touch. How do you explain? Everyone understood what had happened. But did anyone understand why? She put the pen down. He could have made them understand. Piotr Shamilyevich could make the atheists bow down before God.

'But I don't understand, Piotr.'

'Remember that Bogdanov is describing a futuristic world. He uses metaphor to make us see what we have yet to achieve.'

'But how will wearing the same clothing as each other make us more free?'

'Sadie. Sadie. Do you understand nothing? Individual liberation through the collective is fundamental to the whole ethos of the revolution. "Not I but we". Only when all men are equal can a man be part of the world's beauty and spirituality.'

'I still don't see—'

'You should read Gorky. No. Better still. I will read it to you.'

She wasn't a big woman. Mags thought that, catching sight of herself in the scarred, lopsided mirror hanging on the wall opposite Daniel's bed. She wasn't tall, and if her clothes were anything to go by, she'd lost weight again. But she had carried Daniel, a boy of nearly nine, without effort up to their flat and into his own bed without waking him. The knowledge of this made her cover her face with her hands. It's not right, she whispered brokenly into the gloom. It's not right.

Out in the living room, she stood staring down at the phone. She didn't have to do this. Maureen was coming. What difference did it make if she wasn't here? Maureen was a mother. She knew what to do. It was daft to get herself all worked up like this. The doctor had already said everything was going to be all right. Her hand darted out and snatched up the receiver. She began to dial.

It was Alec who answered. She'd hoped it would be Betty. Woman to woman, a special plea.

'I can't make tonight. My wee boy's not well.'

There was a silence then he asked, 'What about your babysitter?'

Mags cleared her throat. 'I don't feel I can leave him.'

There was another silence, longer this time, and Mags held her breath.

'I'm sorry Mags,' he said at last. 'But this is a business I'm running.

Everybody has to pull their weight if you understand what I'm saying?'

'He's sick, Alec.'

'I'm sorry Mags. You know I am. But, if you're not here tonight, we're going to have to call it a day.'

Her hand was trembling so much that the she dropped the receiver, and when she picked it up again the line was dead.

Comrade Lenin, the problem of lice has gotten out of control. Nothing we do stops them.

Hah, the solution is easy, comrade Trotsky. Turn them into a collective. Half of them will run away and the other half will starve.

Sadie blinked. She could still see Piotr's angry, ashen face, his finger pointing, like a weapon, at the boy who had told the joke. *There is no room in the new Russia for people like you.' And, ignoring the boy's embarrassed excuses, he'd taken her hand and led her away.* And what did I do? Sadie tried to remember. Did I stand up for the boy? Did I follow Piotr? All she could remember was that the joke had made her smile.

'Mum.' The sound buried into Mags' brain, hovering fretfully under her eyelids.

'Mum!'

She struggled to open her eyes. Blackness. Was she still sleeping? No. No. Phantoms of furniture were appearing out of the gloom, while needles of cold held her stiff and clenched under the thin protection of her covers. Why was she awake?

'Mum!'

Yes. Yes, of course.

Dragging herself to the edge of the bedcovers, she ventured a foot into the biting air. Her slippers were caught up in the tangle of her dressing gown. When will I learn, she thought grimly, trying to free them. By the time she had both feet encased, her eyes had closed again. She drove her fingertips under her eyebrows, forcing her lids up, and got unsteadily to her feet.

Even with her towelling dressing gown pulled tight at the neck, she couldn't stop shivering. She groped her way to Daniel's room, muttering words of comfort that he couldn't possibly hear.

'Put the light on,' he said when he saw her. And, too tired to argue, she flipped the switch of his bedside lamp. It cast a dull yellow light that did not hurt her sleep swollen eyes too badly and she fought to focus on him. He had the duvet and the extra blankets pulled up almost to his nose, so that he seemed to be nothing but an enormous pair of eyes staring up at her. 'What's up wee man?'

'Those boys. They said my dad was a druggie.'

'O.' Mags sat heavily down on the edge of the bed. She was still shivering, but it didn't seem so important now. 'Did they say anything else?'

'They said he was living on one of the estates and he was going to get evicted. One of the boys' big sisters knows him.'

'I see.'

He was watching her, eyes wide, eager to hear her deny it all as lies. 'That's what they said,' he ventured at last.

She turned to look at him. 'Daniel I …,' she began then stopped. But her face had said it all. He stared at her shocked. 'My dad's not in Africa?'

She shook her head. 'No, Danny. He's not.'

'But you said—'

'I know what I said.' She was angry to cover her guilt. 'You were so wee when he left. You kept asking for him and I didn't want to tell you what he was really like.'

'You're a liar,' Daniel interrupted venomously and Mags was startled into silence. She gazed down at her hands, knowing that she should rebuke him for speaking to her like that. Her mother would have said so. Never let a child talk to you as an equal. It'll lead to trouble. It always does. But, how could she? He was right. She was a liar.

'Danny?' She lifted her head with a great effort, but he had turned his back to her, his thin shoulder hunched defensively against his ear. It seemed so vulnerable that she reached out to touch it, but he flinched away, and she was forced to let her hand drop back into her lap.

After a long while she said into the darkness, 'I was going to tell you. One day.' Then she got slowly to her feet and left the room.

The light in the living room was grey. Not worth going back to bed. She stood in front of the telephone for a while wondering whether it was worth ringing a number that she could barely remember, and was probably disconnected by now. And what could she say? Come home. Daniel needs a father. And him answering, like he did on that last day, 'Just a wee bit space, Mags. A man needs that to sort out his head. A wee bit of time. I'll be back. I can handle it. Just need a wee bit space.' And all the time the red rims round his dazed eyes had told her that he'd left them long ago.

No. She wouldn't phone. She wouldn't put Daniel through that again. Deliberately, she turned from the phone and sat down at her desk. Ewan's manuscript was lying open. Outside, a drunk had begun to sing the same two lines of a song over and over, his voice strangling on the end of each note.

O flower of Sco-o-o-o-otla-a-a-nd

When will we see you likes agai-ai-ai-ai-n

She pressed a hand over one ear and flipped through the pages to a new chapter. It was entitled, Sergei's story. Mags read the opening lines.

It was not that we told lies. I do not ever remember being told to tell lies. But, at some point, I realised that we were no longer telling the truth, or anything remotely like it.

Mags put the paper down and buried her head in her hands.

Sadie woke with the sound of guns pounding in her head and the smell of snow in her nostrils. Can you smell snow? She blinked dazedly and rubbed her eyes. Her mind had wandered again. Where was she? Not in bed? No. Queuing. For what? Food. Yes. Did her mother send her? Piotr with her, waiting patiently, holding her hand.

'Don't pull at the old lady, you silly boy.' A woman's face appeared in front of Sadie. She wasn't young and she had a harassed, exhausted expression. 'Sorry. He's just at that age.' She pulled at a little boy, who was firmly tugging Sadie's sleeve. Sadie didn't answer, but looked down at her shopping basket to cover her confusion. Too old. At risk. A danger to herself.

Why had she come here? Looking down at the basket she could see a pint of milk, low fat, a cut of lean meat and a pound of milk cooking chocolate. For Daniel? But Daniel wasn't coming back. Sadie shook her head, trying to dislodge the cobwebs. But they clung to her thoughts winding around them and mixing them up. She'd been talking with Etta in the park. Yes. I must have decided to do some shopping. But that wasn't right either. Something was telling her that it wasn't right. And she glanced anxiously about, searching for a clue.

In front of her was the checkout. And a tired looking woman with a hard, closed face, her hair scraped back in a ponytail, was standing listlessly as the girl punched through her groceries. There was a newspaper near Sadie's end of the checkout that had not yet been rung through, and she took a step closer trying to read the date. She couldn't, of course. Without her reading glasses, fine print was nothing more than a grey smear across the page. But the headline didn't seem familiar, and now she was certain that it wasn't the same day as the one she'd spent in the park talking to Etta.

Where else have I been, she thought in panic. To Isaac's grave. To talk to him. Yes. She remembered the silent graves. All that way and he wasn't there. Saddened by the memory, she rubbed her forehead trying to even out her thoughts. Did I talk to him before or after I met Etta in the park? It was no use. Her memories were lost between the furrows of her brows, all disjointed and confused now, their delicate pattern never to be reconstituted, spider webs torn apart by careless children.

The woman with the tight, clenched face had packed her groceries and was arguing with the checkout girl.

'Where does it say, you can only use them one at a time.' She slammed a dog-eared bunch of grocery vouchers onto the counter. The checkout girl sighed. She had bored, sleepy eyes and she was tired of taking the blame for policies she neither made nor agreed with. 'It says here,' she explained politely, firmly. 'Near the bottom.' She turned one of the vouchers over and pointed to some tiny type. 'Not to be used with any other offers. It's the way we do it.' Then she added hastily as the queue was now agog and her supervisor was staring curiously over. 'All stores have the same policy. It's a very good deal, really.'

Mags bit down hard on her bottom lip. She'd only used the supermarket because she'd been saving the vouchers, snipping them out of newspapers left in the refectory. Daniel had pretended to be asleep that morning when she went in to say goodbye, and she had thought to make things right by making preparations for his birthday. And now that she'd thought of it, it was coming up faster than she'd bargained for. How was she going to be ready on time? The taxi ride home had taken all her spare cash and most of her lunch money for the next week, and she was still to pay the man who'd fixed the cooker and no-one cared. They were all watching her with weary, irritated expressions because they wanted to go home, and she was just another obstacle in the way.

'Which voucher do you want to use?' the cashier asked briskly.

Knowing she had to hurry made the decision suddenly seem insurmountable. Mags drew her top lip over her teeth and pointed to one with an orange slash that offered ten pence off peas. 'I'll use that one.'

'Right.'

The girl's face told Mags she thought she'd made the wrong decision, but she was past caring. All she wanted was to be out of the shop and away from the grim stares of the queue.

'That'll be twelve pounds sixty-five,' the girl said, reading the figures form a small panel at the top of the till. Mags knew before she opened her purse, but she opened it anyway so that she could look down as she said. 'I haven't enough. I'll have to put some back.'

The groan from the queue was audible. There was an immediate burst of angry whispers and a man's voice from near the back could be heard saying. 'Good God. It wasn't my idea to pick the slowest queue in the place.' The little boy, who had tugged at Sadie's sleeve, began to cry. Looking wearier than ever, the sleepy-eyed cashier asked, 'What do you want to take out?'

Cheeks burning, Mags began to unpack the plastic carrier bags of shopping, looking for things to give back. The most expensive things all seemed to be at the bottom of the bag, and she didn't want to give them up. Bread, milk, jam, sausages. All things Daniel needed.

'Keep his strength up,' Dr Collins had said, glancing over at the dirty dishes in the sink and the chipped *Baby Belling*. 'Strength is critical in keeping his immune system going.'

She put the items back in the bag. Coffee, she thought, taking out a small jar. I don't need coffee. But the thought of trying to study on a couple of hours sleep without stimulants was unbearable, and she put it back. There was an irritated sigh from the queue, and from the corner of her eye, she saw an old lady put down her basket and hurry out of the shop.

The walk through the park seemed to take Sadie longer than ever. Perhaps it was because she felt it had a surreal, dream-like quality that made her footsteps leaden and her progress slow. She couldn't help thinking it should be wet. Her last memory of the park was of grey, fading colours, dank clouds overhead and the feel of rain threatening in the air.

But now the sky was blue, a pale, pre-winter blue, and the clouds that scudded across it were white and fragile. The ground was covered in a thick layer of tarnished leaves that crunched beneath her feet, so that it seemed that she was walking over a ripe, rich earth beneath a firmament of Wedgwood blue. A day to be born on, that's what Isaac would've said. But she didn't revel in it, because it seemed somehow false, a gaudy overlay on the day she felt was somehow underneath it.

It would be a relief to get home, and to put the kettle on. She was almost sorry she'd left the milk behind in the supermarket. But the air had become so stifling, and that strange woman, with the face clenched like a fist, arguing with the checkout girl. She had to get away.

She went around the back because her shoes had picked up mud and leaves along the way, and fumbling in her bag for her keys, noticed it lying on the back step, the one Sheena insisted had to be fixed. She bent down and picked it up. It was a jotter. A plain, grey-covered jotter with the word, English, scored out and in large, uneven letters below was written,

PRIVIT

HIGHLY CONFDENSHAL

And beneath that a skull and crossbones had been drawn and something that might have been a radiation symbol.

She studied it while something nameless that might have been joy, but was more akin to pain, rose up in her breast, and she was just about to open it when a small voice said, 'Oh, there you are. I thought you were never coming back.'

Chapter 16

WHEN Sadie made the chocolate cake this time, Daniel helped by pouring the flour on to the scales and breaking the cooking chocolate into the bowl. Sadie noticed him stealing small squares and popping them into his mouth when he thought she wasn't looking, and she waited until he had swallowed them before asking, 'Why do you want to learn to make cake?'

Daniel looked up at her, his face guiless, except for a couple of chocolate smears around his mouth. 'I want to teach my mum to make them.'

Sadie's eyes widened. 'Your mother doesn't know how to make a cake?' This confirmed most of her preconceptions about Daniel's mother, but she said nothing. Daniel was putting the chocolate in a bowl and didn't see her frown, but he added, 'Things are going to be different when we move in with Ewan.'

'Ewan?' Had he mentioned the name before?

Daniel put the bowl on top of a pan of water and carried it over to the cooker. 'My mum's boyfriend.'

'Ah,' said Sadie. This information puzzled her somewhat. Hadn't he said his father was coming back? But nowadays, that didn't mean that he was coming back to the family home. She hoped her disapproval wouldn't be evident when she asked, 'When are you going to live with him?'

Daniel shrugged. 'Dunno. We can't do it until he sells his house.'

'He has a house.' This Ewan may not be an entirely bad prospect for the boy, she thought. And a boy needs a father.

'He has a house,' Daniel confirmed. 'But he can't sell it.'

'Why not?'

Daniel turned to face her, his smooth brow crinkled in concentration. 'He can't sell it,' he explained, 'because of the thing that lives there.'

Sadie's eyebrows rose in alarm. 'Thing? My goodness, child, what kind of thing?'

Daniel considered the question for a moment then said grandly, 'A Negative Entity.'

Sadie had never heard such a thing and her expression must have seemed doubtful for Daniel said quickly, 'I'm not making it up. I heard Ewan telling my mum all about it.' He drew his brows down and lowered his voice, trying to sound like Ewan. 'I can't sell the house because of the Negative Entity.'

'Well,' said Sadie impressed. 'Whatever will they come up with next?' She began breaking the eggs into the mixing bowl and made a mental note to ask Sammy to explain what exactly a Negative Entity was and what to do in the unlikely circumstances she ever came across one.

Once the cake was in the oven, she made Daniel wash his hands and would not accept his protests that he had already licked them clean. She watched fondly as he climbed up on to the little stool that Sammy had used at his age. Out on the back step, he'd told her that he'd been sick and that was why he hadn't come to visit sooner. She had sensed that there was something else, something he wasn't ready to tell her, but she'd been so pleased and delighted to see him that she'd had to hold back her joy by pretending to be busy with the lock. And she answered his hopeful, 'Are you going to be baking today?' with a casual, 'Why yes. I think today I shall be baking a chocolate cake.' and hadn't really cared whether he had been sick or not. But now, looking at the thin legs that balanced on the stool, she could see that he had lost weight from a little body that had been painfully thin to begin with.

As he splashed water on to his hands and arms, exclaiming with surprise that it was warm, she watched him and something tight clasped at her heart. In his absence, she'd begun to disbelieve him. How could such a little child be thinking of his own death? He was confused. That was it. Children today watched too much television. He'd picked some theme from a program and muddled it with his own life. And the promise? A joke, something that she would say a firm, no, to when the time came then console him with the offer of a jam sponge or some strawberry tarts. But now she could see the blue veins through his skin, and it seemed he was fading from this world even as she watched.

He seemed to sense she was watching him because he turned around, a questioning look crinkling his brow. 'What's wrong?'

Tell him now, she thought. Remind him of the silly promise and tell him you know it's a joke. He was still looking at her. 'I was wondering if you got home on time,' she began carefully. 'You left in such a hurry.'

A cloud passed over his face and he looked away, but he nodded. Sadie sensed there was something he wasn't telling her. 'Was your mother angry?'

He still didn't look at her, but shrugged, drawing up one shoulder and letting his head loll on to it. 'She was a bit angry.'

Sadie, who had been smiling in gentle encouragement, suddenly froze. What if he told his mother about the promise? What would she think of me? And a woman who can leave a sick child to roam the streets while she disappears off for hours is the sort of person who you don't want to have a grievance against you.

Her mother's face was pressed up against her, contempt twisting the familiar lines she'd grown up with out of all recognition.

'Look at me.' Zinaida's tongue was weighted down with vodka. —Her mother drinking.— 'Look what a good communist I am now. I work all day and I queue all night.' She swayed a little, but still did not let her daughter go. Her eyes were glassy, seeing things afresh in their alcohol clarified haze. 'A common labourer for the common cause,' she announced. 'A good proletarian giving her life to the People.' Suddenly her hands fell to her side and she slumped clumsily on to one of the kitchen chairs. 'And still they fire me because I don't know how many tractors they are making in the Volga region.'

She pointed a trembling finger at Sadie. 'You know why. You know what this great liberation is all about. Tell me.' Her eyes were red and swollen. 'In the name of liberty, are we to throw away our minds along with our chains?' She got up and advanced, stumbling towards her daughter.

Sadie backed away. 'Not in the 'I' but the 'we' do we find the emancipation of the individual,' she quoted. She had not meant to. The words just fell from her lips. Wide-eyed, she awaited her mother's wrath. But Zinaida stood straight suddenly, and flinging back her head began to laugh. And she laughed and she kept laughing great, soot-filled gobbets of laughter until Sadie fled the room, hands over ears.

Sadie suddenly felt her legs going weak and she sank down into one of the kitchen chairs. Daniel seemed to think this was an invitation because he jumped down from the sink and joined her in the chair opposite. 'What's your name?' he asked suddenly.

Sadie shook her head and the images of the past dissolved, as though she'd drawn her hand over a reflection in the water. 'Wh what is that?'

Daniel was smiling again, his face open and unguarded. 'What's your name?' he repeated. 'My mum wants to know.'

'Your mother.' Sadie was alarmed. She would want her address as well. I won't give it, she thought, then realised how ridiculous withholding it would be, when all his mother had to do was get Daniel to lead her right here to her house where she had no protection. Not even a neighbour. It was a stupid house. She'd said that to Isaac when he told her they were moving to it.

'Who am I going to talk to? And why do we need a house so big it could house a family of ten? And that roof, it doesn't look safe.'

'Now, Sadie, don't pretend. It's a beautiful house. You'll love it. And think of Sammy. He'll have the whole park to play in.'

But now she was trapped in it. And Sammy was three thousand miles away. And Daniel's mother was coming. And what if she had rough friends?

There was no escape.

Sadie clutched at her throat unable to breathe.

Daniel, who had waited for Sadie to reply, and watched her clutch her throat, wondered if she was ill. Maybe she needs her pills. He looked round to see if her handbag was nearby. It wasn't. Looking back, he was fairly sure now that she wasn't ill. Why's she not telling me her name, he wondered, and began to become anxious that he had done something wrong.

In the three whole days that he had waited to make another daring visit, he had worried that she wouldn't want to see him again or make cakes any more. Mags had insisted that he spend the time in bed. She had phoned the school and he'd heard her shouting in a way that frightened and intrigued him. 'You've no right to leave him alone.' Then 'I don't care who you are.' And most frighteningly 'Do you want to kill him? Will you take responsibility then?' She had slammed the phone down then and said that she'd swing for that old bastard that ran the school. He'd stared to hear his mother use such a bad word, but she'd come over to him and touched his face and said that he didn't need to worry because he'd be staying in bed for the next few days and she'd get something sorted out. Then he'd cried, and said he had to get up because his new pal was waiting for him. And, in her worry, Mags had offered to fetch his new friend for a visit, and that had only made him cry harder. And, when she couldn't console him, Mags had finally got to her feet, shrugging angrily, and saying, 'What is it you want? I'm not magic, Daniel. I can't look inside your head. You have to tell me.'

But then he'd been afraid that maybe she would look inside his head and know about the park that was his special secret that he'd discovered all by himself, and the old Russian lady with her son in New York and her cakes, who knew about heaven and going there. And so he'd turned his head away to face the back of the sofa with the towels from the bathroom and the dirty washing for the laundrette hanging on the back.

On the fourth day Mags had said, 'I have to go back. I can't miss four days and still get an exemption.'

He didn't know what an exemption was, but he knew by now that it was something important that his mother had to have. But then he'd thought of the boys who'd told him about his father, and he'd asked, 'Do I have to go back to school tomorrow?'

And Mags had smiled and shaken her head. 'No. No. You still need to rest. Dr Collins said so. You stay here and read your comics and I'll be back before you know it.'

He thought of how long she would be out of the house and that there was still some of Ewan's please-like-me money left and his granda's fifty pence. It was enough for another trip to see the old, Russian lady. But only enough for one more trip. He'd need more soon 'Will Ewan be coming to see us soon?' he asked.

Then Mags had smiled. A real smile. Not her anxious smile or the one she gave when she wanted him to think everything would be all right, but the kind of smile she gave only when he'd done something unexpected that was particularly amusing or clever.

'I'm sure he will,' she said then hurried into the kitchen to make him some sandwiches to leave for his lunch.

Sadie still hadn't spoken and he looked down at the floor sadly, and asked, 'D'ye not want me to know?'

Then Sadie had made a funny sound in her throat and he had looked up, surprised to see that she, too, looked sad.

'My mum says you can't really be pals with someone if you don't know their name,' he explained feeling a little bolder. And suddenly the old Russian lady smiled. 'Sadie,' she said. 'You can call me Sadie.' Didn't Sammy say that everyone called everyone by their first names these days.

Chapter 17

EWAN had not yet arrived, but the tutorial group was already seated. There had been a note on the door telling them to enter in his absence. But they had stood about, looking at each other uncertainly, as though afraid to discover it was an elaborate form of jest, until the auburn-haired girl shrugged and tried the handle. Then they had followed her inside taking their places silently in their mismatched chairs around the scarred, wooden desk, its polished surface worn away by generations of elbows rubbing across its surface.

Mags sat opposite the auburn-haired girl, staring stiffly into space, trying not to notice how brimful of life and energy and pent up sexuality her fellows were. She didn't want to hate them for treating their education as a kind of joke, but their bored comments and languorous postures made her feel older and greyer than ever. Their futures were infinite it seemed, while her future was mapped out before her, like a dark tunnel, growing narrower and dimmer as she slid inevitably down it.

She wondered how Daniel was doing. He hadn't mentioned his father again. And she'd been afraid to remind him. But, recently, she had found herself looking up from her studies to catch him staring at her. He'd looked away as soon as he realised she was watching him, but not quickly enough to hide the blank, angry expression of distrust that cut more keenly than any rebuke.

Perhaps she should phone. But he might be sleeping and he needed his rest. Maybe she could skip the three-o clock lecture. What was it? Leibnitz? The best of all possible worlds. That was a hard one to swallow. But she'd seen the past papers. Questions on Leibnitz came up again and again.

1. Does Leibniz's system leave room for free will?
2. How does Leibniz explain the goodness of God by showing things which are possible are not always compossible?

No, she would have to go. But afterwards she would rush straight home. If she ran she might make the four ten bus. No, that wouldn't be any use. A frown deepened the lines around her eyes. She wanted to slip into *Woolworths* to look at the toys. It was the last day of the sale, and with his birthday next week, she had to get something soon. She began to claw at the inside of her left wrist, wishing she had known Ewan was going to be late. She could have had a cigarette. Maybe not a whole one. But a few quick, puffs to calm her nerves. She felt resentful that she hadn't known that he was delayed. Surely she should know. If their relationship was to mean anything this was the kind of thing she had to know. She wondered if she'd mentioned that it was Daniel's birthday next week. What if there was nothing left in the sale? If only that taxi hadn't been so expensive. If only she had a few more days. If only this was the best of all possible worlds.

Ewan hurried into the room, breaking her train of thought, and silencing the chatter. 'Sorry to have kept you,' he said in a tone that left no doubt that his apology was merely a courtesy. He took his seat beside Mags and spread the tutorial papers out in front of him. She couldn't help feeling a little thrill at the nearness of him, and had to fight the temptation to comfort herself by leaning a little closer.

'I hope you weren't too bored without me,' he said, without looking up.

'That's all right,' said the girl with the tangled hair. 'Don't they say that history makes itself in the gaps between events.'

Ewan put down his pen and smiled directly at her. 'Very good,' he said in an absent almost dreamy way. 'Audrey, isn't it? Very good indeed.'

Mags watched his smile with a hard, clenched grimace of her own.

Quickly thumbing through the papers, he pulled one to the top of the pile. 'I have your essays here,' he announced. 'And I thought, as this is the first essay you've done for me, we would spend our time together going over them.' He paused briefly to allow for the suppressed groan and shuffling of feet to die down. Audrey gave a giggle that was nervous and simpering and sexy all at the same time. 'Be gentle with us,' she said.

Without directly acknowledging the comment, Ewan smiled. A very brief smile that only Audrey and Mags caught. Ewan picked up an essay and Mags' heart leapt to her throat. Was it hers? Wanting Ewan to like it, she had put so much work into it; so much of herself, but perhaps it would sound silly and naïve against the cool assessment of the others. She felt exposed, and glancing at Ewan, willed him not to choose her.

'Craig,' said Ewan looking at the sullen boy, making Mags relieved and perversely disappointed at the same time. 'I'd like to start with you.'

Craig shrugged slightly, as though speaking was beneath him. Ewan glanced down at the essay, scanning the first page, as if to remind himself what was written there. He had a neutral, slightly bemused expression, as though masking his true thoughts. 'This is a good essay,' he said thoughtfully. 'But it's not altogether clear whether you think independence is the same as freedom or not.'

Ewan looked up, but Craig's expression was stonily unresponsive. 'I think you need to indicate a little more analytically what you mean by parliamentary independence and devolution. And I think you need to increase the historical perspective. You sight the Highland clearances as a positive force towards independence, but nothing more recent.' Ewan stopped, raising a questioning eyebrow, but Craig remained stolidly silent. Mags regarded him with a growing mixture of embarrassment and awe. How could he remain silent through so many cues to speak? The underlying defiance in his reticence made her edgy and apologetic and she had to forcibly quell the urge to answer for him.

The silence continued until it was almost unbearable, then Ewan turned towards the nervous boy. 'Scott, do you believe that a Scottish parliament is the way forward?'

'Yes.'

'Yes?' Ewan repeated, his expression suggesting that he expected something more than a single word reply.

'Well,' the nervous boy began, glancing at the table then at the bookcases and back again. 'It seems to me.' He stopped, looked wildly round then back at the table. 'It seems to me that a Scottish parliament will give us the kind of freedom of choice we haven't had for years. Perhaps if we're in a position to make our own choices we might benefit from our natural resources such as oil or even water.' He looked round, flushed with the fervour of his argument. 'How long will it be before an English government pipes away our water to feed their dried-up reservoirs? And how much do you think we'll benefit from that?'

'You're missing the point.' Audrey interrupted. She was twisting a strand of auburn hair between two fingers, and Mags saw that she wasn't looking at Scott, who was now opening and shutting his mouth, like a fish, but at Ewan. There was a kind of insouciant challenge in her eyes as though she was teasing him. Mags felt palms of her hands grow sweaty.

'And what point would that be, Audrey?' Ewan asked.

Audrey threw Scot a pitying look. 'A Scottish parliament will never have the kind of power you want. It simply adds a layer of government without removing any. We'll have more taxes to pay, and it'll be used as a vehicle to buy votes.'

Mags stole a look at Ewan. He was resting his chin on one hand, his eyes narrowed and concentrated on Audrey.

'I agree,' Craig suddenly broke his silence. 'A Scottish parliament is a sop to the masses. If we're ever to distribute wealth equally we need total independence.'

'But given time that freedom would evolve naturally,' Scot argued. He looked over to the bookcases for support, and when they didn't give him any returned a brief glance in the direction of Craig. 'We once had one of the strongest education systems in the world. With a parliament of our own we could rebuild that kind of love for learning without the struggle for survival that total independence would bring about.'

'Rubbish,' said Craig.

Ewan didn't move his head. 'Audrey. You seem to agree with Craig,' he said. 'Perhaps you could elucidate his stance.'

Craig shot Ewan a filthy look, but Ewan seemed not to see it, and he waved a hand to encourage Audrey to speak.

Audrey gave her simpering, sexy giggle again then leaned forward and said, 'Independence is freedom. It's the only way forward because it's already a part of us.' She paused delicately to see if the impact of her words had sunk in then hurried on. 'We crave freedom. It's in our blood. You can see it personified in history over and over again, the way we rush into hopeless causes in its defence. As long as we're tied to another form of government, we'll suffer the silly snobberies of an aristocracy that gets its education in England then foists it on us. Freedom is about having the power to act autonomously, to be able to stand on our own two feet, to make our own decisions about the future. It lies with the ordinary men and women of this country.' She sat back with a satisfied grin. 'Freedom is the freedom to build a society of equals.'

'No, it isn't.'

For a moment, the words hung in the air, abandoned. Then, slowly, with terrible certainty, Mags realised it was she, who'd spoken them. They were staring at her with shocked, disbelieving faces, and she lowered her head, willing only to address the scarred surface of the table. Her mouth was so dry that she had to cough several times before blurting out, 'This idea that freedom is somehow wrapped up in ordinary people turns us into nothing more than the noble savages the media likes to portray us as.'

'Well that's a new one on me,' Audrey laughed. 'The Beeb want us to fool ourselves into thinking we're noble.' She had a tinkling, infectious laughter that affected the others. Mags felt her cheeks growing warm and she clenched her hands under the table to prevent them from shaking. 'It's not new,' she said angrily. Her words sounded clumsy and lumpen to her ears, but she had to explain. 'It's been going on for thousands of years.' She glanced at Ewan, hoping that he would help her out or at least grace her with the same approval she'd seen him give Audrey. But he was still leaning on one hand, staring thoughtfully into the distance, and she was forced to continue alone. 'The intelligentsia has been holding up the shortcomings of their own class by endowing ordinary men and women with almost mystical qualities for generations.' She could see that they didn't understand her and her voice grew thin and nervous as she struggled on. 'It's as though being ordinary made us purer in some way.'

'Can you give any sources to this historical perspective?' Ewan asked quietly, and Mags shot him a grateful look.

She thumbed hastily through her notes then pulled a few sheets of paper to the front. 'This kind of thinking drove the Russian intellectuals in the nineteenth century. Marxism has its roots in it. And it's the philosophy that underlies the whole Bolshevik movement in this century.'

'In fact,' interrupted Ewan, 'it has been going on a great deal longer than the last century. We can see its roots in Tacitus when he puts classical rhetoric into the mouth of a Caledonian chief to show him as a contrast to the corruption of Roman intellectualism.'

Mags was grinning despite herself. She dared an impish look at Audrey, only just managing to suppress the urge to mouth, I won.

'Of course,' Ewan was saying, 'we must ask ourselves, if freedom does not lie in the heart of the common man for Margaret, what alternative is she offering us?' He nodded at her to begin, but the grin had left Mags' face. She hadn't anticipated this and she had nothing to offer. 'I … ' she said into the expectant silence. 'I … '

'You sound like you don't like the idea of freedom,' Audrey interrupted. She was twisting a small, expensive ring round one finger and she looked from Mags to Ewan and back again. 'I mean what are you offering us? The dictatorship of the minority? Don't you consider men to be equals?'

Mags swallowed hard, forcing herself not to look to Ewan for help. 'Not entirely,' she admitted. They were staring at her, as though she'd said something unclean, and she wished she hadn't spoken. But it was too late. She had followed her gut feeling and now she had nothing to back it up with. Audrey's face was triumphant. 'It sounds as though you're advocating the rule of the Superman.' And before Ewan could ask her for her source, she quoted, 'Nietzsche. Didn't his so-called views on freedom eventually give rise to the Nazi party? Surely such a monstrous philosophy isn't what you're advocating?'

Mags couldn't meet Audrey's gaze any longer. Feeling sick to the stomach, she couldn't look at any of them. Are they right, she was thinking. Am I a monster? Daniel's mum, a monster. *You're a liar.* But what if I'm something worse? What will Ewan think of me now?

The bell rang, and Ewan said something about the next tutorial. She didn't hear, but followed blindly as the others scraped back their chairs and hurried from the room, scattering as freely as leaves in the wind.

'It's my birthday next week,' Daniel said through a mouth full of crumbs.

'I'm going to be nine.'

Sadie nodded to show she was impressed. 'That is a very important age for a boy,' she said.

'Is it?' Daniel was wide-eyed.

Sadie nodded then doing a quick calculation in her head said, 'It is nearly three quarters of the way to being a man.'

Daniel was even more impressed. 'When are you a man?'

Sadie saw him push his plate away the cake half eaten. Would this little boy ever be a man? 'At thirteen,' she said.

'O.' He looked crestfallen and Sadie wondered if she'd said something wrong.

'That's a very long time away,' he said wistfully.

Sadie smiled fondly at him. 'Not at all, my dear. It's less than the blink of a cat's eye.'

Daniel laughed. 'That's a funny thing to say.'

Sadie nodded at him. 'It is a funny thing,' she agreed. 'My uncle Max used to say it and he was a very funny man.'

'My uncle Gary isn't funny,' Daniel confided. He lifted his fork and began digging it into the remaining half of the cake. 'He never says anything funny. And he doesn't know anything about planes or computers or dinosaurs.'

He looked up at Sadie, his eyes wide and beguiling. 'Do you know about dinosaurs?'

Taken aback, Sadie shook her head. 'I know they lived a long time ago,' she offered lamely. Daniel's expression told her that he thought little of this. He went back to stirring the cake crumbs with his fork. 'There's a big exhibition about them at the Kelvingrove galleries next week,' he said casually. 'You could find out all about them there.'

On the point of saying she had no great desire to know more about the poor, dead creatures, Sadie suddenly changed her mind. 'You would like to see them?' she asked.

Daniel was using his fork to push the cake crumbs into the defensive wall of a fort and didn't look up. 'Mum says it's rude to ask people to take you places,' he said.

'I see.' Sadie drank the dregs of her tea. Daniel stole a look at her.

'Of course,' she said thoughtfully. 'I could not go alone.'

Daniel didn't look up, but his fork froze on the plate.

'I would need someone who could tell me about them. An expert.' She sat silently a moment, seeming to cast about to see who would come to mind. The fork trembled on the plate. At last she said, 'Daniel, would you come with me?'

He looked up at her then with the broadest most radiant smile she had ever seen him give. Then he shrugged, and said, "Suppose. If you want me to.'

Sadie hid her own smile behind a hand. Now was the time. 'Daniel,' she said gently. 'I want to talk to you about something important.'

But he jumped up staring at her with wild, excited eyes. 'I forgot to show you it,' he said. 'I forgot to show you.'

Before she could reply, he'd jumped down from his seat and fetched the jotter, marked, PRIVIT, HIGHLY CONFDENSHAL, from the countertop near the door. He held it up so that she could admire the front cover then dragged his chair over next to her and climbed on to it, setting the jotter down on the table between them. She felt his leg, warm and bony, against her thigh and something stirred in her. A feeling that, not even Sammy could stir these days, that she'd thought, like the dinosaurs, extinct long ago, but now made her look at Daniel and want to reach out and lift him onto her lap. She didn't, of course. You can't lift a boy who is three quarters the way to being a man on to your lap, so she shifted her gaze to the jotter and asked, 'What's this you have here?'

He looked up at her, his expression grave. But when he spoke, his words came out in a rushed jumble so that she had to concentrate just to make them out.

'When those boys came all round me I thought I was going to die. And then I saw a plane and I thought I was going to heaven. But I woke up in my gran's house. Then when mum made me stay at home she phoned the school, and said that they were going to kill me and it was their responsibility. And I had to be quiet a lot of the time because she was writing her essay.' He paused a moment to explain. 'That's not like a story. It's her work for the university. And I thought about going to heaven with you and what if I went first. And mibbe we should have an emergency plan.' He looked up, scanning her face to see if she'd understood. 'They have those in the council, where my Uncle Gary works. In case there's a big flood or a nuclear war.'

He could see that she didn't understand, so he opened the jotter at the first page. At the top in red pencil it read,

Special Important Emergancy Plan

Beneath it in black ink were the words,

Plans to help ¾ he'd left a gap for her name ¾ come to heaven with me if I go first.

Drowning. Falling in the sea or river or the swimming pool

Being eaten by a furoshous animal at the zoo

Eating some poisen My mum's cooking. Ha.

Falling off something very big

Not eating anything for a very long time

'The bit about my mum is just a joke,' he explained, as Sadie read the list, open-mouthed. She still didn't answer him and he looked at her anxiously. 'It's not a very good list,' he admitted, after a minute in which she still hadn't spoken. 'I don't think number one would work because someone would jump in and save you. And I don't think we can get near enough to the animals in a zoo to get eaten.' He drew his finger down the list. 'I don't know where to buy poison. And if you fell off something you might not be dead. And not eating for a very long time would take too long.'

He sighed. 'I thought mibbe you'd know a good way.'

'Daniel,' said Sadie. Then she said it again because her voice had been so hoarse the first time she'd barely heard it herself. 'Daniel, I …'

But he interrupted her. 'Grownups shouldn't tell lies, should they?' His eyes were on her, suspicious, accusing.

Sadie felt her chest grow tight. 'No,' she said uneasily. 'No-one should tell lies.'

He nodded, as though they had come to some mutual understanding. 'My mum tells lies.'

'Surely not.' Sadie felt she should take the side of the adult. But he looked at her contemptuously. 'She told me that my dad was lost in Africa. And he's not. He's a … ' His lip curled at the thought. 'He's a druggie. He takes drugs and he only lives a couple of miles away.'

Sadie kept her face very still, not certain what to say. 'Perhaps your mother did not want you to think badly of him.' Daniel's glower told her that this was the wrong thing to say. 'She told lies,' he said emphatically. 'I think she even told me lies about heaven. She said it was blue. Do you think it's blue?'

Sadie shifted in her seat. 'No-one knows for sure what colour it is.'

Daniel nodded grimly. 'We'll find out when we get there.'

Sadie gave herself a mental shake. This must stop. It's gone too far already. She forced herself to speak. 'Daniel, I think there has been a dreadful mistake.'

But he wasn't listening. He'd jumped up, clutching at his chest, and she saw, to her horror, that his lips had turned blue. He keeled against her, and instinctively she drew him down on to her lap to support him. He lolled against her chest, like a baby, strange, high-pitched wheezing sounds escaping his lips.

She knew she should get to a phone, call nine. An emergency service. Plans for an emergency. But she couldn't move. Her legs were paralysed, and she sat there, rocking him in her arms murmuring over and over, 'Daniel. Daniel. Daniel.'

After a while the high-pitched wheezing became less frantic and gradually gave way to ragged intakes of breath. He was still on her lap and made no effort to move. Eventually he said, 'I'm okay now.' into her breast. But he stayed where he was, letting her stroke his hair and rest her cheek on the top of his head. And, after a little, his breaths became regular and shallow and she knew he'd fallen asleep. She freed one hand and lifted the jotter, reading down the list one more time. A promise is a promise.

Chapter 18

S HE had wanted to walk home with him, but he had refused.
'I just get tired sometimes. You do that when you've got a funny heart.'

'Perhaps I should call your mother?'

'No.' He hadn't like the idea of that at all. And, if she was honest, Sadie had no great desire to meet Mrs Gallagher. When Daniel was near, the promise seemed the most natural thing in the world. How could you refuse a sick child? But when he was gone, the world of adult condemnation came crashing down upon her head. A sick child? How could you? And she would know what she was doing was wrong and be unable to excuse herself or offer the meagrest explanation to vindicate her actions. Better not to meet his mother. It would only make things more difficult.

But now that he was gone, she was worried that he would become ill on the way home. Why didn't I find out where he lived? I'm getting senile, she thought. Not capable of rational thought. They'll lock me away before I become a danger. She looked at the empty space on the table where the jotter had lain. *Being eaten by a furoshous animal at the zoo*
She shook her head. It's too late.

Without thinking about it, she went through the hall and picked up the receiver of the phone. She began to dial then remembering, put the receiver down and went into the lounge. Her birthday cards were still sitting on the mantelpiece, and she hurried over and lifted down the one from Sammy. It had a pink border, and on the front, were the words, *Mother, you're an angel.*

She opened it, and inside it read, *How else could you give birth to a cherub like me?* Underneath, Sammy had drawn a cartoon of himself as a cherub lying in a champagne glass smoking a cigar.

Sadie smiled. So like Sammy. Always the funny one. She could still remember him at three years old dancing round on his toes waving his chubby fingers in the air making Isaac and her laugh until their sides split. So long ago. Her smile faded and she looked back at the card. At the bottom was a telephone number. Sammy's apartment in New York.

It rang three times. At least she thought it was ringing. Foreign telephones never sounded right.

'Hi,' said a sleepy sounding American voice. 'Who's this?'

I've dialled wrong, she thought in panic and nearly dropped the phone then she enquired nervously, 'Is Samuel Gordon there?'

The American voice laughed and changed into something more familiar. 'Ma, is that you?'

'Did I call at a bad time, Sammy?'

'No. No. I was just getting up.'

She heard a suppressed yawn, and a great rush of love overwhelmed her. Would Sammy understand? It was the question that tortured her more than the promise itself. Sammy was a man. He had a life of his own. But what if he needed her? One last time. And she'd gone. Forever.

'Did I wake …,' She hesitated. 'Tonie?'

'It's Jamie, ma. No, you didn't. She's not here.'

Not in bed with her own husband? A thousand questions sprang to Sadie's lips but she couldn't think of a way of forming them. At last she asked, casually. 'She is taking a bath, perhaps?'

There was something of a snort from the other end. 'No. She's not here. She decided to stay back East until I get settled in a bit more.'

Sadie wanted to ask if that was any way to treat a husband who needed her support, but she confined herself to asking, 'How's the new job? Do they treat you well?'

'It's tiring,' he admitted. 'I think I'm getting too old for a young man's market.'

She was shocked by this confession. 'But Sammy. You're not even forty. In the prime of life.'

'Thirty-nine, ma. And if this is the prime, I'm not sure I want to see the rest.'

'Sammy,' she was alarmed. 'You're not well.'

He heard the panic in her voice and moved quickly to reassure her. 'No. No, ma. I'm fine. You just woke me up. You know I always look on the black side when I wake up.'

They were silent for a moment, he lost to his thoughts, she trying to work up the courage to tell him her plans. At last she said, 'Sammy, you are all right, aren't you?'

'Of course.' His voice was back to its normal light-hearted tone. But she wasn't reassured. 'You really are happy, aren't you? You have got a full life?'

It was his turn to be concerned. 'Ma, are you all right? Has something happened?'

'No. I'm fine.' She forced a careless laugh. 'Why Sammy, you sound like an old woman.'

He laughed, not entirely convinced. 'Is something wrong? Do you need me to come back?'

She did need him. More than anything in the world she needed him to come and tell her he loved her, that he understood, that she was doing the right thing. She needed him to come so that she could see his face one last time. But if he did come back and stand before her, warm and living, she might lose courage altogether. And she couldn't do that. She had made up her mind. 'No, Sammy. You don't have to come back. Everything is fine. Just fine.' Then, before her courage failed her completely, she said, 'You know I love you, don't you?' She heard his sharp intake of breath, but put the receiver down before he had time to reply.

Yorkhill hospital for sick children was part of the Queen Mother's maternity hospital, and, in common with all maternity hospitals, was built on one of the largest, steepest hills in the vicinity. Once, an exhausted and out of breath Mags had enquired why this was, to be told that it dated back to the times when the city was polluted and hills provided better air for new mothers and their infants. 'But how many women went into labour trying to get up the hill in the first place?' Mags had asked grimly, only to be met by the disinterested shrug of a staff nurse. 'You can be sure it wasn't enough to save the nursing staff any work,' she'd been told.

Mags wished she could afford a taxi, but ordering another one so soon was out of the question. They'd made their way up, taking frequent rests, hanging on to the railings and making wheezing noises, like asthmatic jungle animals at the traffic below. Daniel had done well, seeming almost cheerful as they finally reached the top and made their way to the main entrance. But once inside the doorway he froze, refusing to move.

Mags dropped to one knee beside him. 'What's wrong, wee one?' she whispered. Knowing how much he hated it, she had called him that on purpose, hoping it would make him angry enough to move. But he stood, stock still, staring up at the paper cut outs of animals and fantastical flowers that adorned the upper sections of the walls. She examined his face, and saw that his eyes had grown huge, the pupils eating away the irises, like pools of dark fear. And her heart had begun to knock against her chest, and she had to struggle to get her voice in control before speaking again. 'Danny,' she said gently. 'You're not going to stay. It's just to check everything's all right. You'll be coming home with me tonight, I promise.'

He stayed where he was, but she saw a flicker of doubt in his eyes. She took him by both shoulders, forcing him to look down at her. His eyes had an unfocused expression. Suffering and the fear of suffering. 'It's just a check-up. I promise.'

She stood up and took his hand. It lay in hers, insubstantial as a dream, but when she moved he went with her.

Mr Wilson was a rotund, jocular man of about fifty. His hair and beard was turning from black to grey, and he had a habit of hooking his thumbs into the belt of his trousers and leaning back so that his stomach was better exposed, rather like St Nicholas making an out of season appearance. He had a reputation for being good with children. 'Well, little fellow,' he said kindly, reaching out to pat Daniel on the head. 'Been in the wars again, I hear.'

Daniel flinched back, and was held in place only by Mags gripping his shoulders. 'He had another fainting fit in school,' Mags explained. Daniel noticed how his mother grew smaller in front of medical men, her voice humbler, as though she was secretly pleading with them. It frightened him.

'Uh huh.' Mr Wilson dismissed this information, as though Mags had commented on the weather. He turned to Daniel. 'And how have you been since? Any weakness? Feeling faint? Hmmm?'

Daniel thought of Sadie's kitchen and the terrible fear and dizziness flooding through him when he thought she was going to break her promise. 'No,' he said.

'Good. Good.' Mr Wilson seemed excessively pleased. He pointed to an examination table covered in coarse tissue paper. 'Let's have you up here for a quick look then.'

He lifted him onto the table and picked up a stethoscope from the desk. 'We'll have a look at that chest and back, eh. Best give Mum your shirt.' Daniel unbuttoned his shirt slowly. His fingers felt wooden and wouldn't work properly. He flinched when the cold disk of the stethoscope touched his skin.

'Good. Good,' Mr Wilson said again when he breathed in. 'Now pretend you're blowing up a balloon.'

Mags was sitting on a chair in front of the desk. Her brows had risen to form anxious wrinkled waves in her forehead, and she was leaning forward, as though straining to hear his heart without aid of the stethoscope. She caught him looking at her and gave a lopsided grin and a little wave of encouragement, so unlike her, that it frightened him all the more.

Mr Wilson put the stethoscope down on the desk and began tapping him on the back. He asked him to cough, and Daniel obeyed.

'Och, you're being very polite,' Mr Wilson said cheerfully. 'A big boy like you can do better than that. Try again. As hard as you can.'

Daniel coughed again. The sound came out a thin wheeze as before.

Mr Wilson stopped looking so cheerful. He put his arms round Daniel's waist and lifted him down. 'You go back to Mum and get your shirt on now,' he said. He turned to the desk and switched on the intercom. 'Staff Nurse Neil. I need a blood. Are you available now?'

Daniel was tucking his shirt into his trousers when Staff Nurse Neil entered. She was a plump woman of about thirty, her hair tied back in a ponytail, like his mother's.

'Is this the young man who needs to give a sample?' she said to Mr Wilson.

'That's right,' Mr Wilson agreed. He gave a him a pat on the back. 'You go with Staff Nurse Neil. And make sure you get her to tell you where the lollipops are kept. I heard a rumour that she's been eating them herself.'

Daniel glanced up at her, surprised, and Staff Nurse Neil shook her head and laughed. 'Come on now,' she said.

Mags stood up, but Mr Wilson held up a hand to restrain her. 'No. You stay here, Mum. We'll have a wee chat while Danny's busy. Isn't that right, Danny?'

Daniel nodded, briefly, twice.

'That's the ticket,' Mr Wilson beamed. 'Don't forget those lollipops.'

Mr Wilson's smile lasted until Daniel and Staff Nurse Neil were out of the room, then it vanished, guillotined by the shutting door. He walked over to the examining couch and leant against it, looking down at Mags. His silence unnerved her, and she said, 'I know he's still quite blue, but it's much better than it was last week. And before that …'

He still hadn't spoken and she looked away, the words dying on her lips. He waited until she had composed herself and looked back up at him before beginning. 'Mrs Gallagher, I believe I spoke to you about Daniel's last angiogram at the time.'

'You said his blood flow was down.'

Mr Wilson nodded. 'You can see for yourself that he's obviously cyanotic. And there were clear signs of dyspnoea even at rest.'

'We've just climbed that hill outside,' Mags explained. She gave a little laugh to show that it was easily explained.

Mr Wilson shook his head. 'The angiogram showed that your son's pulmonary blood flow is becoming progressively inadequate.'

He went over to the desk and pulled out the angiogram, placing it on the desk before her. She wouldn't look at it, unable to bring herself to see inside her son, to see the delicate mechanism of life, the ticking clock. Running down.

'Do you remember what I said to you after the test?' Mr Wilson asked.

Mags looked up at him, her eyes wide, pleading. In a small voice, she said, 'You wanted to discuss another operation with Professor Jacobson.'

He looked at her without speaking for a long moment then said very gently. 'I wanted to discuss the possibility of another operation.'

She didn't say anything. As long as she wasn't speaking nothing had changed. She was just another mother bringing her child in for a check-up. If she spoke, she'd be pushed through a terrible barrier of knowledge and trapped forever behind it, unable to get back to this moment through the inexorable barrier of time.

'Mrs Gallagher,' Mr Wilson said, his voice soft, but penetrating. 'I'm afraid Professor Jacobson concurs with my opinion that Daniel's heart is inoperable.'

She looked at him foolishly, as though he'd said something that made no sense. 'But you said … another shunt.'

He was shaking his head, a slow pendulum wiping out hope. 'You must understand that the abnormality of your son's heart is not an isolated condition which we can treat by repeating the operation.' He was speaking slowly and clearly, as if to a child, but still she couldn't understand.

'But there must be something …?' She was begging now. All pride lost. Forget pride. Forget dignity and never asking. She'd get down on her knees. She'd crawl. Just let him say there was a way. But his face was stone. She was begging a rock.

'Mrs Gallagher, it's a miracle that Daniel survived the first operation.'

A miracle? Her son's life wasn't a miracle. It was her right. She'd given him life. And now this man in his white coat and his antiseptic smell was telling her that the precious life she'd carried was a miracle. But miracles aren't real. Daniel's life. Not real.

Mr Wilson was speaking again. 'The operation is long and painful. Surely you wouldn't put him through that again?'

But she would. The dirty bastard was passing the buck. Putting the guilt back in her hands. But she would. She'd put Daniel through anything just to keep him. Just a bit longer. A little more life.

He saw it in her face and quickly added, 'The operation wouldn't save him. You might have a little longer with him.'

Hope flared in her eyes.

'Or he might die on the operating table and you'd lose what time you have left.'

For a fraction of a second, his words hung in the air. Meaningless. Then Slowly, without conscious effort, her head sank down towards her chest and her shoulders slumped. She'd failed. Daniel's champion and she'd let herself be beaten by the coarse blows of logic.

He'd beaten her.

He was still speaking. Saying something about understanding what he was saying, implications for the future. And she was answering, 'Yes' over and over in a flat monotonous voice, while she shook her head to and fro contradicting her words.

She was out in the corridor, walking towards reception, unable to remember how she got there. The corridor was painted pale green and a mural of Humpty Dumpty had been pasted along the top of the walls. She followed it blindly, knowing the nursery rhyme ended where Daniel was waiting with Staff Nurse Neil.

Humpty Dumpty sat on a wall

The corridor was empty. She could hear sounds coming from behind closed doors. Trolleys being wheeled, the clatter of equipment and nurses calling out in clipped, professional voices. They seemed very far away. Another world. A place she could never go back to. The brighter lights of the reception area were visible now.

Humpty Dumpty had a great fall

She couldn't go there. She couldn't face Daniel, knowing that she'd failed him, and unable to tell him. How could she keep the lies from sliding off her face? She couldn't do it. But she'd done it before.

'Mum, what colour is heaven?'

She stopped. He knew.

And all the king's horses and all the king's men

Couldn't put Humpty together again

No. He didn't know. It was nonsense. Children don't know about their own deaths. But what if he did? She pressed her fingers to her temples. I'm going mad. I've got to get out. She glanced wildly down the corridor looking for an exit. A place to run. Fresh air on her face. Turn back. Keep going.

'Mum.'

The word pierced her through the centre, pinning her to the spot. She kept still until he was almost upon her then she turned her face into a mask and bent towards him.

'What have we here?' she said, admiring the wad of cotton wool taped to his arm. 'Were you a brave boy?'

He was looking up at her, his head tilted to one side. 'Mum, have you been crying?'

She had to fight the impulse to jump back and cover her face. 'No, of course not.' And then, because she had said it much too quickly, she added. 'I got some dust in my eyes. That's all.'

She could feel the lie tightening her mouth and eyes, pulling her face into a ridiculous exaggeration, like a clown's mask. Daniel seemed about to say something else, but Staff Nurse Neil's voice cut in. 'He was such a brave boy, Mrs Gallagher that I felt he really had to have two lollipops.'

'Well,' said Mags, straightening. 'You must have been brave.' She knows, she thought looking into the smooth features of the other woman. Her face is a mask. Like mine. She gave him two lollipops because that's what you do with a dying child. You give them two of everything because they won't have time to wait for another one.

A white flash exploded in her head. And she looked angrily over at the staff nurse. She's written him off, she thought unreasonably. Like all the rest of them.

Like the first operation when she'd waited outside the doors of the lift, her last glimpse at his tiny body dressed in green. He'd waved sleepily, the premed taking affect. Then the doors shut. And he was gone. Leaving her to pace up and down, standing guard, like a demented sentry ready to challenge the shadow of death. They'd passed her then, some fresh and crisp beginning duty, others tired and crumpled, not wanting to know, thinking only of home. They'd thrown her pitying glances, offered cups of tea, and when she had turned away, refusing them, they'd whispered between themselves that she was Daniel Gallagher's mother and nodded to each other, knowing what that meant.

But she had defied them. He had lived. Mags looked coldly at Staff Nurse Neil's pitying face. 'We'll be going now.' She put her arm defensively around Daniel's shoulders and he winced slightly at the pressure. 'Don't mum, you're hurting me.'

But she didn't listen. She got him outside, out of the hospital grounds and down the hill. Back to the world where he belonged, then she fell on her knees and hugged him until he began wriggling with embarrassment and pushed her away. 'Mum, don't.'

And she saw then how very much alive he was, how grown up he had become, too old to be hugged by his mother in public. And suddenly she felt very powerful and calm. Science was against her. Logic was laughing in her face. But she had a mother's love, and that would be enough to beat the men in white coats. She'd show them. She glanced back up at the hospital. It's glassy, black windows didn't believe her. Mags took hold of Daniel's shoulder. She'd show them.

'Mum,' he said. 'You're crying again.'

Chapter 19

THE *shul* was very quiet. The last time Sadie had visited it had been during the Samuelsson's wedding. And that time, it had been bustling with excited guests, exchanging gossip and nudging each other about the mother of the bride's quite inappropriate outfit. But now the only other occupant was God, and she had never been the kind of person to make small talk with their deity.

'Mrs Gordon?'

She turned. She knew Rabbi Karpf was Rabbi Josefert's replacement, but she hadn't expected him to be so young. He had the looks of a young Paul Newman playing the ardent young Zionist, and she understood now, what had prompted a return of faith amongst so many of her contemporaries. He was looking down at her expectantly. 'You asked to see me, Mrs Gordon?'

'Yes.' She shook his proffered hand.

Now she was here her questions seemed impossible to put into words. She cast about for an opening, all the words she'd carefully rehearsed along the way dissolving uselessly on her tongue. It had been foolish to come, and more than anything she wanted to turn tail and run for the door. But he was still looking at her, his blue eyes crinkled at the corners with curiosity. 'What can I do for you, Mrs Gordon?'

She looked away from him, but it was worse to feel God's eyes upon her so she looked back. 'I need you to answer some questions for me,' she blurted unable to keep his gaze. 'I've tried to find a way round things. And now I think I have. But I need to know that I'm not doing something terribly wrong.'

She stole a glance at him and found him studying her curiously. She knew she was making no sense, but she couldn't go on. He seemed to sense that, because he led her over to a seat and stood in front of her. 'Perhaps if you started at the beginning,' he suggested.

He was so kind. She felt reassured. It was like being a little girl again able to ask an adult what to do. 'Suppose,' she began then stopped. Would he be shocked? Would he laugh? It had all seemed so simple when she'd first thought of coming. She looked desperately up at him.

'Suppose?' he prompted.

'Suppose a person is nearing the end of their life.'

He raised a questioning eyebrow and she felt certain he knew it was her.

Her words dried up, and for a moment she considered changing her mind. Asking some innocuous question then leaving. She glanced over at the door she'd come through, still lying open, offering an escape. But what of Daniel? If she didn't find out the answers she couldn't help him. And she had promised to help. She was committed.

She heaved a big sigh and said as quickly as she could manage. 'Suppose a person is nearing the end of their life and God has no more use for them?'

Rabbi Karpf's eyebrows rose simultaneously in surprise. 'Mrs Gordon, God's purpose is not always easy to see.' He waved his hand through the air to emphasise the mystery. 'But be certain that God always has a use for us, right up until the last moment we breathe. The *Midrash* tells us that from the moment of birth there is always the possibility of death.'

She hung her head. He didn't understand. But she had to make him. 'But what if that purpose was to go to heaven?' There. She had said it. No turning back now.

Rabbi Karpf's eyebrows collided with each other then sprang apart, repelled, like magnets. 'Heaven is something we all aspire to,' he said carefully.

'Yes. Yes.' Desperation had made her bold. 'But what if you had to take someone there?'

'To take someone?' he repeated her words in a whisper, as though echoing a blasphemy.

She'd got it all wrong. Everything she'd planned to ask was coming out mixed up and not at all what it had sounded like in her head. She wasn't up to the task. She looked up at Rabbi Karpf and noticed he seemed further away, as though he'd taken a step back. She had to make one last attempt.

'What I meant to ask,' she began slowly, still looking into his face. 'What I meant to ask was, if you know you're at the end of your life, might it not be okay to …' She searched for words. Rabbi Karpf was staring at her with round, saucer-like eyes, as though he expected that she might transform into demonic proportions should he let his gaze slip. Sadie frowned. This was hopeless. Worse than she'd feared. 'If you're sure,' she said pleadingly. 'If you've done all you might need to. If you've put everything in order and told everyone you love them, might it not be all right to speed things along a little.'

He didn't say anything for some time, but stood blinking at her, his eyes closing a little longer each time, as though he hoped, given the chance, she might vanish before he opened them again. When it became apparent she would not, he licked his lips and said uncertainly, 'Mrs Gordon, you're not talking of suicide?'

At last. She beamed at him and nodded vigorously. His face changed. This was a problem he knew how to handle. He sat down beside her and placed a comforting hand on her shoulder. 'This is a very serious matter,' he began, but she interrupted him. 'O yes, I understand.' Her face was earnest and he had the strangest impression that she was waiting for instructions.

Her eagerness was putting him off, and he coughed once or twice to clear his throat then said on a slightly sterner note, 'I'm afraid that on the possibility of self-harm leading to death, all teachers agree it's quite forbidden.'

'O.' She seemed crestfallen, and he watched her anxiously, feeling that he was somehow failing to get through. She wasn't familiar, but he knew the type. She was the kind for whom religion meant funerals and weddings and a nephew's *Bar Mitzvah*. A lip-service Jew, he thought of them. But to be considering suicide, she must be in some sort of trouble. He'd seen it before, these old ones. Near the end, no family, debts mounting up. The lure of heaven must be strong.

'Sadie,' he said very gently. 'Is something troubling you? Do you have problems at home?'

She studied his face, eyes darting back and forth, trying to read something there, then opened her mouth, and he was sure she was about to say something. But she closed it again, and sighing deeply, got to her feet. 'No. No problems.'

She began to walk towards the door and he followed her, suddenly fearful that he was letting her go without providing the reassurance that she needed. He stopped her at the threshold by offering her his hands. 'Don't forget that God is infinitely merciful,' he said.

But she seemed distracted, not meeting his eye. 'There is great comfort in prayer,' he added. 'Pray to Him for guidance.'

At last, she took his hands between the cracked palms of her own, and holding them very gently, looked up into his face. 'You are very young,' she said, and was gone.

Chapter 20

SHE slipped into Daniel's bedroom to make sure that he was still asleep. Daniel's room was light despite the hour, a wan shaft of moonlight stealing through the gap between curtains that never met. The model planes hanging from the roof were in silhouette, dark shadows guarding their charge. Daniel was sleeping on his side as usual, one bare leg resting on the writhing bedclothes, the other tucked under him. He'd thrown an arm above his head and his profile was delicately outlined against its curve. Looking down at him, Mags felt so much love that, for a moment, she could do nothing but stand, hardly daring to breathe, afraid that the slightest noise might disturb him.

But he was in a deep sleep. His skin had the waxy, translucent texture of dreamless slumber and his breathing was shallow, hardly perceptible at all. A sharp blade of fear stabbed at Mag's heart and she hurried to the bed and placed her hand just above his mouth. He seemed to sense her presence and moaned slightly, rolling over and spilling the blankets over the edge of the bed. Gratefully, Mags picked them up and tucked them over him. 'I love you, wee darling,' she whispered, but he didn't respond.

Back in the lounge, she went to her desk and thumbed through a textbook looking for her place. Earlier in the evening a row had broken out between the couple who lived directly above. Mags had been forced to put down her books and listen as a man hammered incessantly on the front door, his voice changing from rage one minute to an almost pitiable whine the next.

'Mary. Let me in. I'm the weans' Da. I've got the right.'

A muffled, shrieking sound indicated his wife's reply then more hammering on the door.

Pacing up and down in front of the phone, Mags had argued with herself over whether or not to call the police. In the end cowardice won over duty. She didn't want to get involved. And besides he'd gone away in the end.

Mags checked her watch. Enough time to take a look at the manuscript. It was lying open at the place she'd left it, Sergei's story, and she let her eyes skip over the first few accusing lines looking for a new place to start. Her eyes fell on a line at the bottom of the page. *A great man can inspire great love but it should never be forgotten that great love can engender great blindness.* Intrigued, she turned the page.

But, before she could read anything, the light went out, blinked back on again then went out for good. 'Damn.' Mags got to her feet and groped her way to the Abernethy tin again. She knew it was empty before she felt inside, but she couldn't help herself from running her hands round the metal lining just to be sure. It was past midnight. Nowhere to buy a card until morning. 'Damn,' she said again. And then she added a long list of words she could never repeat in front of Daniel. She put the tin down and kicked at a pile of dirty washing lying under the sink. Stupid. Stupid. Stupid. Why didn't I pick another one up? I passed the shop twice today. There was a scab on the inside of her left wrist and she picked it off, letting a tiny trickle of blood seep out. She felt better. Candles? Yes, there were some in the cupboard over the sink.

Relying on touch alone, she opened the cupboard door and felt inside. Her hands met only air. There was nothing there. She'd used the last one. No. Wait. There was a small one at the back. A scented candle, a present from someone last Christmas. She took it out and held it up in the dim light. Only two inches high. How long would it last? She shrugged. It didn't matter. It was all she had.

She carried it back to the desk, and removing the remains of a sandwich from a saucer lying next to her textbook, set it down in the centre. The light from the candle was yellow, flickering, not quite enough to read by comfortably, but she pushed her chair as close as it would get to the desk and leaned over the manuscript, poring over the words. The candle gave out a sweet, spiced scent that made her think of holly and marzipan and almonds, and she looked up from her work to gaze at its stubby form surrounded by a trembling pool of light. Just an hour, she thought, and she'd be finished. Then she'd have more time. Time to spend with Daniel. Time to plan his birthday.

She'd thought about it on the long walk back to the underground after they'd seen the consultant. She wanted to ask him what he would like, to tell him he could have anything he wanted. But it was their tradition that her present to him was always a surprise, a custom borne from her lack of finances and the fear of making promises she couldn't keep. Daniel had always accepted this way of doing things and to change it now might arouse his suspicions. She caught sight of herself in a shop window and frowned angrily at her reflection. Why shouldn't he have a surprise this year? Why should she act as though there wasn't going to be another year to celebrate? She shook herself mentally. I'm as bad as that nurse, she thought.

But still, the consultant's words had frightened her. She could still feel the after tremors of the shock rippling through her, making her agitated and uneasy. She had to do something to assuage the ugly, little voice of doubt niggling beneath her resolve.

'Danny?'

He looked up, surprised, wondering if she was about to start crying again, and wondering if he was the reason that she was crying. 'What?'

She smiled and he felt relief flood through him. Everything was going to be all right. He returned her smile and waited expectantly.

'Would you like to ask some friends round for your birthday?'

He stared at her, astonished. Birthdays were always a business carried out strictly between the two of them. 'Like a party?' he asked doubtfully.

She nodded, then added hurriedly, 'Not a lot, mind. But you could ask a few.'

He fell silent, thinking of the hungry, wolverine faces whirling round him. He looked up at his mother seeing only her jeans with the holes in the knees and her man's shirt poking out of the denim jacket with the frayed cuffs. She didn't look like other mothers, and he didn't want them taking this image of her back to the playground where they would tear and gore at it, spitting the bloody tatters back at him from their laughing mouths.

No, he didn't want them. But she was looking down at him, smiling, and he didn't want that smile to disappear. 'Can I ask Sadie?' he said at last.

'Sadie?' She looked puzzled. 'Is that your new friend's name?'

He nodded.

'I thought you didn't know her name.'

He'd forgotten. He hadn't mentioned his last visit. And inviting her to his birthday suddenly didn't seem to be such a good idea after all. What if they began talking? But it was too late. Mags' smile had grown wider than ever. 'Well you're an easy wee man to please.'

They began walking again.

Chapter 21

SHE laid the last page of the chapter to rest and stared off into space. Sergei's story was finished, and she felt somehow cheated to find herself back in her shabby room, straining her eyes by candlelight. Leaning back, she stretched her neck and arched her spine. It had been a long day. Sergei's story had gripped her long past the hour she had promised to herself and now she was tired. Go to bed, she thought. Get some sleep before Daniel wakes up. But the story had agitated her and she couldn't let go of it. If I could only talk about it with someone. She glanced wistfully at the phone. No. No. Don't think about it. Distract yourself.

She thought of starting a new chapter of the manuscript, but the candle had sunk down so low that it was no more than a tiny flame flickering on a sea of wax. Such a short life, she thought. Then she grew very cold and still and sat watching as the flame guttered and died leaving her in the darkness with only the after image of its light behind her eyelids.

Without thinking, she got to her feet and went to the phone. She dialled three digits.

'*Directory Enquiries*,', a polite voice said. What name please?'

'MacLeod,' she said in a whisper. 'Dr Ewan MacLeod.'

'Do you have the address?'

'Bearsden.'

'Do you have the street name?'

'No.' She felt panicky, as though the operator must guess what she was up to, and almost slammed the receiver down, but the voice at the other end said,

'Checking for you now.'

A metallic voice sounded, speaking digits that she didn't hear until the second repetition, then she pressed the cut off button with a trembling finger and dialled from memory, not caring that she forgot it again as soon as she'd finished. The phone gave three shrill rings and she held it pressed tight to her ear, listening to sound as though it was something completely foreign, like the distant roar of the sea inside a shell. She wasn't sure what she was going to say. She wasn't even sure if she would say anything, but she wanted to hear his voice. To know there was another world out there. Just for a moment.

'Hello. Zero five double seven,' a woman's voice said.

Mags froze. Stupid. Stupid. Stupid. She had never asked what Helen looked like because she didn't want her image haunting her with her existence at every idle moment of the day, but now she'd given her a voice.

'Hello,' the woman said again. 'Hello. Is anyone there?'

Mags wanted to put the receiver down, but her animal brain was convinced that, if she moved, she'd be seen.

'Hello,' the woman said uncertainly one more time.

Mags held her breath. The line went dead.

The elms lining Kelvin Way had lost most of their leaves, forming a thick, brittle carpet that Sadie and Daniel crunched through in the direction of the Kelvingrove art gallery.

'You've got the money for the tickets?' Daniel asked for the third time as they passed the gates of the park.

'Of course.' Sadie reassured him and she patted the front of her handbag where her purse was kept.

Daniel walked on in silence for a little then said a little uncomfortably, 'You don't have to buy me one.'

Sadie turned to look at him. 'And why is that?'

He frowned at her, as though he'd expected her to understand, then sighing explained. 'You can get in for free if you're under six.'

'But you're nearly nine,' she reminded him.

Daniel made a sound that reminded her strongly of Sammy when he was irritated. It sounded strange coming from such a small voice and she had to hide a smile so as not to hurt his feelings.

'But sometimes people think I'm only little.'

It had cost him to say that and she was moved, but she chided him gently. 'Daniel, that would be dishonest.'

He shrugged and looked up at her slyly. 'Only a little bit.'

'But Daniel, every time we do something dishonest the world becomes a sadder place.'

He considered this information for some moments, then asked, 'Does that mean if you do a good thing the world gets better?'

She nodded.

'Does it get better for you?'

She was astounded at his perception. Such a clever boy. Why is it always the gifted ones God chooses? Then she felt guilty for the thought, because, after all, Sammy was gifted, and God hadn't taken him. 'No,' she said in reply to Daniel's question. 'The world does not always get better for you.'

'But that's not fair!' Daniel was outraged. 'If you do a good thing, you should get a reward.'

Sadie studied the lines in his crinkled brow fondly. 'But that would be a terrible way to do things.'

Daniel stared. 'Why?'

She smiled. 'Because, if we got a reward every time we did good, everyone would only do good in the hope of a reward.' She struggled to put it into a child's terms, to remember how she'd explained it to Sammy. 'Being good would not be difficult any more. Anyone could do it, and we would not have to choose.'

'O.' He dropped his gaze. Something in Sadie's voice told him that she thought the argument was over, and he knew from experience that there was no point in trying to ask more. But, for the life of him, he couldn't see what would be bad about a world where everybody did good and was duly rewarded for it. Perhaps he would mention it to God when they got to heaven.

They walked through the autumn sunshine in companionable silence, and it was hard to believe that there was anything more sinister overshadowing them than a secret of a special outing. Sadie might have forgotten altogether until Daniel stopped suddenly and sat down on one of the rocks suddenly panting and pale.

'Daniel,' she said, alarmed. 'You are unwell again.'

'No.' He shook his head. 'No. I just get tired sometimes. Dr Collins said I wasn't to worry. Just sit down and not mind what anyone said.'

Sadie watched him anxiously. How did I get mixed up in this? Isaac would say I'm going *meshuga*.

'You are unwell again.' She did not mean it to be a question. Piotr sat opposite, his face drawn, the fierce eyes hidden under the shade of his hands. 'It's nothing. I am just a little tired.'

'Is it because of what happened in Kirsanov?' When he didn't answer, she leaned across the table and pulled at his elbow. 'I want to help.'

'They hate us,' he said simply.

'They don't understand you,' she soothed.

He looked at her contemptuously then. 'They understand that they have no food in their bellies and that their children are starving. I would say that is all the understanding that a man needs.'

They sat in silence for a time, as though waiting for something to happen. His face was hidden in his hands again and she couldn't see his expression. From time to time he gave a low moan. A man in pain too deep to articulate. Until, at last, she said, 'I don't understand. Isn't this part of the plan?'

Then he looked up at her, and his eyes were so fierce and terrible that she couldn't look at them, and she'd turned away, frightened. 'I don't understand.'

'And neither do I.'

Then he had shaken his head, not at her, but at something else, something beyond them, something terrible.

She couldn't see Daniel's expression. He was holding his head in his hands, as though it was too heavy for his neck. 'Daniel,' she said gently. 'We could see the dinosaurs another day.'

It was enough. Daniel jumped down from his rock and began to hurry in the direction of the Kelvingrove galleries. 'Daniel, don't rush,' Sadie chided. 'I am too old to go so fast.' But really she was afraid to see him overexert himself.

They entered the grounds of the gallery through a narrow driveway opening out on to Kelvin Way and approached the building from the back. Before entering the gallery, Sadie stopped to admire the grandeur of the gothic architecture. It reminded her of something her father had told her.

'Do you know, this is not the back of the building at all, but the front,' she said.

'How's that?' He stared up at the façade shaking his head slightly. 'This can't be the front. The road's on the other side.'

Sadie smiled. 'But it is.' She pointed behind them across the steep valley. 'This gallery was built to commemorate the new century.'

His forehead screwed up in disbelief. 'But that's not for ages.'

Sadie laughed. 'The beginning of *this* century.'

'Did you see it being built?'

'I am not quite that old, Daniel. No, my father told me about it. There were three buildings. The other two were on the far bank. But they've gone now.' She gazed over the valley a little wistfully. 'This gallery was built to face them.'

Daniel considered this information doubtfully for a few moments then concluded, 'Mibbe they just had the plans upside down.'

The exhibition was entitled, FROM TRIASSIC TO CRETACEOUS, THE MYSTERY OF THE MESOZOIC, and was housed in a room off the main hall. Outside, stood a dour attendant, dressed as a lizard in a suit of drab orange acrylic, somewhat threadbare towards the tail. They handed their tickets to him, and after holding them up to his eyeholes for some moments, he ripped them in half and returned the stumps. Sadie opened her mouth to ask a question, but he moved nimbly to one side, and drawing back a curtain of black felt, announced in a muffled voice, 'Elcome to the Methothoic.'

Stepping through, they found themselves at the far end of a darkened room. Sadie felt an immediate chill, and looking down, found that her feet were lost in a curling mist of dry ice rising from the floor. She peered myopically through the gloom and could just make out dark silhouettes emerging gigantically out of the murk, their heads lost in fronds of gently swaying plastic leaves.

Glad that she hadn't unbuttoned her coat, she pulled her beret a little more tightly over her ears and took a nervous step forward. Immediately a sonorous, metallic, voice boomed overhead.

'Time travellers, welcome to the Triassic period. Enter the world, as it was more than two hundred million years ago.' There was a sudden, loud and tinny screech from one of the giant shadows at the back of the room, and it lurched forward, turning its head towards her. Terrorised, she glanced wildly round trying to locate Daniel. And, after a panicked moment, discovered him standing beside her, his eyes shining in the darkness, like tiny stars. 'That was a Staurikosaurus,' he explained breathlessly. He pointed to an even larger monster standing next to the Staurikosaurus. 'And that one is a Coleophysis, I think. They ate their own young.' He grinned and his teeth shone white. 'Amazing.'

Sadie, who was impressed to hear such large words coming out of the mouth of such a small boy, was about to ask a question, when there was another bloodthirsty shriek and the booming voice instructed them, to walk forward through the Time Portal to the Jurassic period. Dimly, Sadie could make out an archway made of polystyrene boulders and through it even larger shapes than those of the terrifying Staurikosaurus and Coleophysis. She took hold of Daniel's hand, relieved to find that, under cover of primeval darkness, such intimacies were permitted, and gingerly, they made their way towards it. As they walked beneath the polystyrene arch, she noticed, with a shudder, that it was entitled, THE GIANT KILLERS, CARNIVOROUS DINOSAURS.

Almost immediately, she decided, that by comparison, the Triassic world seemed a warmer, more inviting place. Confidently informed by Daniel, she found herself edging past the huge Daspletosaurus and the even larger Allosaurus as they fought over the remains of an armoured ceratopid.

'Such teeth,' Sadie exclaimed, transfixed by the reptilian stare of a gargantuan monster that towered over everything else.

'That's a Tyrannosaurus,' Daniel whispered. 'He could eat you just like that.' And he made several convincing crunching noises.

'Perhaps we should go on,' Sadie said nervously and she began to edge towards a portal with the comforting title, THE GENTLE GIANTS, HERBIVOROUS DINOSAURS. But Daniel wasn't ready, and he pulled her back into the murk, crying, 'Look, there's a Corythosaurus. We don't want to miss that.'

More than an hour later she emerged behind Daniel from the portal, marked MAN AND BEYOND? knowing more about dinosaurs than she had ever thought there was to know, or indeed had wanted to know. Her legs felt decidedly shaky and her ears still rang with the booming voice that had guided them from one terror to the next. I am a madwoman, she thought. Crazy in the head. But looking at Daniel's face, flushed and pink, his eyes sparkling with the memory, she knew it had all been worthwhile. And, if dinosaurs could make a sick, little boy so happy, perhaps they weren't as bad as they seemed. Then she remembered Velociraptor digging its bony claws into the chest of its writhing victim, and shuddered.

'Are we going back to your house?' Daniel asked. His legs were splayed and he was imitating the ungainly walk of a Tyrannosaur. Sadie watched him, trying to make up her mind. The thought of returning to the tranquil autumnal sunlight outside was tempting, but her legs were tired, and she had no doubt that Daniel's enthusiasm would soon wear off, leaving him pale and exhausted long before they were even in reach of the park. He was watching her anxiously, afraid she was going to say it was time for him to go home, but she pointed at a small, modern tea room on the far side of the hall. 'Why don't we get a cup of tea before we go,' she suggested.

The tea was expensive, stewed and served in small, plastic cups too thin to insulate the fingers from the burning liquid inside. They took their purchases to a flimsy table and perched uncomfortably on the edge of chairs that seemed designed neither for comfort or aesthetic appeal. But it was good to take the weight off the feet and to listen to Daniel chatter on about Centrosaurus and Saurolophus and Anchiceratops and goodness knows how many others. She wondered how he could remember them all. In the middle of a particularly graphic depiction of a meat-eating dinosaur, named Deinonychus, he paused, suddenly thoughtful.

'What is it Daniel?' she asked, hoping to divert him from such blood thirsty topics.

He looked at her earnestly, and pushing away his half-eaten chocolate biscuit, explained, 'I was just thinking I wish we had dinosaurs today.'

'Indeed!' Sadie's eyebrows rose. 'Surely you wouldn't want one for a pet?'

'No.' Daniel laughed at such a ridiculous suggestion. 'No.' He glanced from side to side to make sure no-one was listening, then lowering his voice, hissed, 'I was thinking it would be very easy for you to get eaten by one, then we could add it to our list.'

Our list. Sadie shivered at the sound of that. *Our list* transformed her from witness to accomplice. Unbearable. But what could she do? And I talked to him about dishonesty, she thought miserably. She glanced at him sharply, wondering if her anguish was written on her face, but he had a dreamy, far off expression in his eyes and she wondered what he was thinking about.

Sadie opened her mouth to ask, but Daniel pushed his chair back and got to his feet. 'Let's go now,' he said, and he seemed so agitated, Sadie did not like to pursue the matter further.

As they retraced their steps along Kelvin Way, he was unnaturally silent, walking slowly at her side, but now and again stopping to kick viciously at little heaps of leaves swept up by the wind. Has something upset him, she wondered, but she could think of no way to find out. And they remained silent until, at last, Daniel asked, without looking up, 'If I asked you a question, you wouldn't laugh, would you?'

She was so relieved that she promised at once. 'Of course I would not laugh.'

He seemed reassured, but he kept his head down, seeming to address his question more to the leaves underfoot. 'When you die?' he began then stopped.

Sadie felt a pang of unease, but her conscience pricked at her. 'Go on,' she prompted, hoping her own reluctance wasn't evident.

He dug the toe of his shoe into the leaves, breaking their brittle bodies. When he spoke again, it was in a very soft voice and she had to strain to hear him. 'When you die, you don't wake up again d'ye?'

Sadie didn't answer for a long time, and Daniel studied her face anxiously, looking for that secret smile adults never seem to expect children to see. Eventually she said in a small, abrupt voice. 'No. You do not wake up again.'

Daniel gazed up at her a little longer then sighing began to kick his way through the leaves again. 'I didn't think so,' he said.

Chapter 22

OUTSIDE Ewan's office, Mags stood, trying to work up the courage to go in. She had gone too far this time. No doubt about it. A mistress should be obscene and not heard. She had seen that once, written on a lavatory wall in the library and felt a pang that was part amusement part unease when she'd read it. But now she had broken the golden rule. She had made contact, passed between two worlds, a ghost from Ewan's world come to haunt Helen's.

She lifted her fist to knock then dropped it. It was over. She'd blown it. Just when she needed him most. What am I going to do? She closed her eyes and let her fingers go limp. Better to get it over with. Wait silently through the recriminations. Visit her tutor after class. Talk about changing her course. There would be questions. But she'd say nothing then either. The lesson of silence. Why hadn't she learned it sooner?

'He's not in.'

For a split second the words made no impression then she swung her head round in their direction, as though jerked forward by their force. A girl with tangled auburn hair was standing nearby. Audrey? Yes. Simpering, superior, sexy, superb Audrey.

She was staring at Mags with a puzzled expression that pouted her lips slightly. 'Are you looking for Dr MacLeod?'

Mags managed a nod.

'He's not there,' she repeated. 'I was looking for him myself.'

'Were you?' There was an accusation in Mag's voice that she couldn't prevent from inflecting the question, and Audrey frowned, as though Mags had given her a piece of a puzzle and she was trying to fit it to an unknown picture. Mags forced a smile. 'Do you know when he's coming back?'

Audrey's face relaxed. 'No. I asked the secretary. But she said he hadn't been in today.'

'O.' The smile on Mags' face stiffened into a thin line. There was an awkward silence with both women smiling vaguely at some spot past the other's head. Then Mags started to say,

'I've got to go.'

At the same time, Audrey said,

'I thought that point you made the other day was very interesting.'

'What?' said Mags. 'What did you say?'

She suspected that she was being mocked in some clever, subtle way and the accusatory tone came back in her voice. Audrey looked uncomfortable and repeated, 'I thought what you said about freedom was very interesting.'

'I wasn't trying to be interesting,' Mags said coldly. 'I was just saying what I believe.'

Audrey's frown returned. 'Why shouldn't what you believe be interesting?'

It was such an obvious question that it made Mags feel even smaller and stupider than before.

'Look, I really have to be going,' she said curtly, and turning her back on Audrey, fled down the stairs.

'Do you want me to give Dr MacLeod a message if I run into him?' Audrey called after her, but Mags pretended she hadn't heard.

On the bus home Daniel began to feel unwell again. But, for a long time the thought of the towering giants of the Mesozoic filled him with such a thrill of adventure, that he didn't notice the signs until the bus drew up at his stop. Slowly, painfully, he got up from his seat and made his way to the front. It seemed a long way, longer than it had been when he'd got on, and he had to stop several times before he reached the door.

'Come oan, son,' the driver called impatiently. 'I havnae got all day.' But when Daniel approached, his face ashen, little beads of perspiration standing out on his forehead, he asked not unkindly, 'You okay, wee man?'

With no breath for a reply, Daniel nodded and eased himself off the platform on to the pavement. The bus sat there longer than it should, as though waiting to see what he would do, but when he began to make his way down the street, it wheezed into gasping life and headed in the other direction.

It took him a long time to reach home. There was a group of boys kicking a ball against the wall of the tenement. He passed them, head down, and they stopped kicking and stood in a silent rank, watching him until he disappeared inside the close. As he struggled up the stairs he heard the faint thud of the ball begin again.

He waited outside his front door until he had got his breath back then opened it nervously, certain of his mother's wrath and not sure that his anger with her would sustain him through it. But she was strangely preoccupied, and barely looked up as he came in. 'Tea's on the table,' she said, nodding in the direction of the coffee table.

He went over and sat down on the sofa, positioning his buttocks in the hollow in the centre of the cushions, and lifted a plate of sandwiches from the table, laying it carefully across his knees. He watched Mags working. She was curiously agitated, lifting her pen up then putting it down and he noticed that she wasn't reading any of the books she had laid out before her. He wondered when she was going to ask him about his day, and he was torn between his desire to share his excitement and the worry that she would accuse him of asking Sadie to take him.

But she didn't ask. She just sat there, lifting her pen and putting it down. He sat very quietly, pushing his sandwiches round his plate with one finger, and gradually he began to feel a little better. His chest didn't feel so tight and it stopped hurting when he breathed. But he was tired, so very tired. And, gradually, his eyes began to close.

He didn't even wake up when the front door bell sounded.

The sound shook Mags from her reverie and she checked her watch automatically. Seven forty. Too late for surprise visitors. She glanced over at Daniel, but he was fast asleep on the sofa. A pang of conscience stabbed at her. She should have noticed. The fire was off. He'd be cold. She stood, torn between the desire to fetch a blanket to cover him and the thought of a second ring from the bell waking him up. But he'd slept so far, so she hurried across the room, and slipping the chain into its groove, opened the door a crack.

'Ewan.'

'I forgot my keys.'

The bulb had gone in the landing and she couldn't see his face. Tell him you're busy, a voice in her head raved. Tell him to come back later. Let him cool down. Maybe you can fix things if you give it time. But, while her mind ranted on in silly circles, she was drawing the chain back along the groove and opening the door.

Ewan took a couple of paces into the room then stopped, his back to her.

'It's chilly in here.'

'Yes.' She spoke with difficulty, her voice scraping against her throat, like unoiled gears. 'I was just going to put the fire on.'

Relieved to have something to occupy her, she hurried over to mantelpiece and lifted a box of matches. 'Take a seat,' she said without looking round. Then a thought struck her. 'Be careful, mind. Daniel's sleeping on the sofa.' She heard Ewan check his step then the scrape of the chair at her desk as he sat heavily down. She turned the gas valve open, then bending as close as she dared, struck the match and held its flaming head next to the grill. For a moment, there was nothing but the steady hiss of gas, and the match burned down almost to her fingers. Then, as she turned to see if Ewan was watching, the gas ignited and a cold ball of flame engulfed her arm. Shrieking more in fright than pain, she leapt up clutching her hand. She saw Daniel stir in his sleep, but he didn't waken, and she gave a thin, high laugh of embarrassment and fright and relief. It took her a moment to realise that Ewan was smiling back at her.

Her laughter died, and she asked awkwardly, 'What brings you here?'

His smile also faded. 'I was worried.'

'O.' She stared at him, her tongue choked on questions she couldn't bring herself to ask.

He was still sitting at her desk, his sad eyes studying her. 'When you phoned. I thought … ' He spread his hands, as though suddenly superstitious of voicing his mind. 'I thought Daniel was ill again.'

'No.' Her hand flew to her chest. 'No. Nothing like that.'

His face relaxed then tensed again. 'Then why did you call?'

'I … I just … ' She floundered desperately trying to explain how she had needed to tell him about her conversation with Daniel's consultant. How she had needed his authority to override the treacherous words the consultant had spoken, to tell her that she shouldn't worry so and that Daniel would be fine and they'd soon be a family at long last. But now he was here, waiting patiently for her explanation, she found she wasn't so sure that he would reassure her. What if he agreed with Mr Wilson, academic to academic, ganging up on her? 'I wanted to talk to you about the book,' she finished lamely.

A frown drew his brows together. 'Mags. It's not a good idea. When Helen took the call, she insisted on phoning *call back*. She was hysterical, accusing me of all sorts of nonsense. It took me all night to convince her it was just a wrong number and she was unwell all day. I've only just managed to slip away.'

'I'm sorry,' she said stiffly. 'It won't happen again.'

He stood up and came over to her. 'You're angry.'

'No.' But she turned away when he tried to put his hand on her shoulder.

'Mags. I know this must be very hard for you.'

She shrugged him off. 'I have to put Daniel to bed.'

'Here. Let me.' He bent down and gently scooped Daniel into his arms. Mags watched him, torn between jealousy and a poignant ache of tenderness to see how Daniel didn't stir in the unfamiliar arms.

Perhaps it's meant to be, she thought.

When Ewan had placed Daniel in his bed and Mags had tucked him in, making sure the duvet reached right up to his chin, they stood silently in the darkness, staring down in the shadowy stillness, each lost to his own thoughts.

At last Ewan said in a choked sort of voice. 'Mags?'

'Yes.'

'I don't treat you very well do I?'

She shivered and reached out to take his hand. 'You've got other commitments. I understand.'

They stood in silence a while longer then he bent towards her and whispered, 'Let's go to bed.'

It was late and it was cold. She knew she shouldn't be sitting up so late, not even dressed for bed, but she couldn't sleep. She'd found it in her pocket as soon as she'd reached for her key. Daniel must have slipped it in before they'd gone their separate ways at the top of Bank Street. A small blue envelope with her name printed in adult handwriting in the centre. Despite the chill air, she'd opened it on the back step, and plucked a folded sheet of paper with the same blue trim from its innards.

It was Daniel's writing on the sheet, and it read:

Dear Sadie

I am having a wee tea for my birthday. Please come at six o clock. Not later because you will miss the cake. It is on the 27th. I will be nine and there will be balloons.

Love

Daniel. XXXXXXX

But she couldn't go. How could she go? The address, Cliftondale Street. She'd never heard of it. It wasn't nearby, that was for certain. Had Daniel been deliberately fooling her all this time, making her think he was a local child? But then, she reflected, she had never actually asked him where he lived. She'd just assumed. Assumptions. She'd made too many of those. 'Assumptions are a sure way to learn nothing,' that's what Isaac would have said. And Sammy would have agreed with him. 'Think with your head, ma, not your heart.' But it was too late for that.

Perhaps she should go to the party. Make a clean breast of it to Daniel's mother. Explain her mistake. Ask her to see how easily it could happen. Why it could happen to anyone. Anyone could misread a situation. Could make a promise they couldn't keep. But such a promise? Could anyone promise to take a dying child to heaven? Sadie let her head fall on her hands. 'What can I do?' she moaned. 'What can I do?'

It was only at the second ring of the doorbell that the sound penetrated and she got to her feet. She glanced at the clock. It was past nine o clock. No-one comes to a person's house at this hour. She stared round wildly, trying to detect intruders lurking by the back door. I won't answer it. They'll think nobody's home. But what if that's what they want? She stood perfectly still, listening. There was nothing to be heard except the sound of her heart beating out a frantic tattoo against her ribs. Then, just when she made up her mind that they'd gone, the bell rang again.

Her heart leapt then seemed to stop in her throat. Did they know she was in? Were they toying with her? If only they would go away and leave her alone. Leave her? To what? Her eyes fell on the invitation lying on the kitchen table, its corners crumpled and damp where her nervous fingers had worried them. Perhaps it was better to face the terrors of the unknown than to stay with the accusation of the familiar.

Very slowly, she picked up her invitation and crumpled it into her pocket, then began to make her way towards the front door.

Chapter 23

AT her bedroom door, Mags had hesitated. 'Are you sure?'

He smiled, his eyes already on the open door. 'It's fine. Helen took one of her pills. She'll be out till morning.'

He saw the look of pain that flashed across Mags' face, and reached down to catch her hands in his.

'Mags. I'm a clumsy fool. Please forgive me.'

She smiled, trying not to show that it hurt, and placed a finger on his lips. 'Shh. Don't talk.' In silence their bodies could bridge the gap their minds could not.

She didn't put the light on. A sallow, sliver of moon lifted the darkness into soft shadows hiding everything but the pale gleam of exposed flesh and the glassy reflection of their eyes. She tried to find forgetfulness in him. To seek out a place where 'M' still stood for Mags and not for Mother. And he seemed to recognise her need and was especially gentle, seeking out the folds in her body with delicate urgency, but never rough, never brutish.

She began to feel herself uncurling, bit by bit, like a knot cleverly unravelled by nimble fingers, and when he whispered. 'I love you, Mags.' She responded more to the gentle susurration of his lips against her cheek than to the words themselves.

'Mags! What is it?'

She was sitting up, pulling the sheets around her.

'Daniel's calling me.'

Ewan sat up too. 'Are you sure? I don't hear anything.'

She shrugged, as though too weary to enter an argument then, pulling on a dressing gown, made her way across the shadows and out of the door.

Since she'd pulled the curtains, Daniel's room was darker, and it took a moment for her eyes to adjust. When he saw her, he switched on the torch he always kept beneath his pillow, and a pallid circle of yellow light surrounded him, like an aura.

'Mum.' His face was very pale and the rims of his eyes were red. Without speaking, she hurried to the dresser and fetched his medication. Then she sat on the edge of the bed, supporting his back with one arm and holding a glass to his lips with the other.

When he'd finished, she placed the glass back on the dresser and let him fall back on the pillows. His eyes were like dark hollows in the paleness of his face and she couldn't see their expression. 'Have you been awake long?' she asked anxiously. Had she been too loud? Had he heard something?

He nodded then pointed at a book lying open at the side of the bed. 'I was reading.'

She glanced down and saw the tattered covers of a child's copy of the Arthurian legends. It had been hers, and she picked it up fondly, running her finger down the cracked spine.

'Mum.'

'Don't try to talk.'

'But I want to ask you something.'

His voice was pleading and she relented. 'Just one question.'

'When the maidens took Arthur to Avalon, was that the same as heaven?'

Mags froze, glad that she was standing beyond the perimeter of the light. 'That's a funny question to ask.

'Was it the same?' he persisted.

'Mibbe,' she said hesitantly.

'Exactly the same?'

'Yes. No. Not exactly.' She was floundering.

'How not exactly?'

There were goose bumps along her arms and an acidic taste on her tongue. 'I don't know "how not exactly"' she said sharply.

'Why not?'

'Because I don't.' She sounded angry to cover her fear. 'Never mind all these questions. You should be asleep.'

'Can't sleep.' His eyes filled with tears.

'Why not?' Her voice was gruff.

'My tummy hurts.' He pulled back the bedcovers to display the striped bottoms of his pyjamas. They had bunched around his waist giving the impression of a well-fed, rounded tummy. The tummy of a healthy child. Mags knew better. Anger forgotten, she sat down on the edge of the bed and laid her hands on his abdomen. 'Here. I'll make it better.' His stomach felt like a taut hollow nestling between the bones of his pelvis and she began to stroke it letting her imagination lull her with sweet fairytales of the healing touch of a mother's fingers.

After a while, Daniel asked sleepily, 'D'ye get on a boat, like King Arthur, when you go to heaven?'

'You might,' she said carefully.

'But what if you don't know where to find the boat?'

She heard the anxiety in his voice and thought, Ewan's right. The more I talk the more I tangle myself up in lies. I'm a fool. A stupid, useless fool. What kind of person lies to a … But she couldn't finish the thought and said hastily, 'Don't worry about finding the boat. It's all taken care of.' She chucked him under the chin, and though he didn't respond went on cheerfully, 'Anyway, I don't know what you're so worried about. You're not going to die for a long time.'

She carried on stroking him and murmuring meaningless little phrases of comfort, there there, it's all right, shh shh now. But he'd turned his head away and was staring at the window.

'Sammy?' Her voice was so small that she wasn't even certain she had spoken.

'Ma, what's the matter?' Mimicking her look of concern, he dropped his suitcase and put a reassuring hand on her shoulder. 'I'm sorry. I've frightened you.' His expression softened. 'I tried to call from the airport, but no-one was home.'

'I was in the kitchen,' she explained, then added confusedly, 'You know I can't hear the phone unless the door is open.'

Sammy nodded. 'Next time I'll phone first to see if you've opened the door.'

But instead of smiling, she only nodded absently, saying, 'Come in. Why are you standing outside? Is it your death you want to catch?'

He followed her into the kitchen his dark eyes narrowed with concern. 'Ma, is something wrong?'

But she had recovered a little and gave a little laugh as she went to fill the kettle. 'My son turns up like a ghost in the night and he asks *me* what is wrong?'

'I'm sorry,' Sammy said again. 'I did try to call.'

She was busy laying out a plate and fetching the remains of the latest chocolate cake. 'You called from America.'

Her back was to him and she didn't see the shadow that passed over his face. 'No. I didn't call. There wasn't time.' He began unbuttoning his jacket. 'It was a spur of the moment kind of thing.'

Something in his voice made her turn towards him. 'Sammy, something has happened?'

He was putting his coat over the back of the chair. 'No. No. Nothing's wrong.' He turned back, his smile wide. 'I just took on board what you said about needing a rest.' He pushed his chair back and rested his heels on the edge of the table. 'You're right. I work too hard.'

'Not so hard that you forget how to behave in a person's house,' Sadie said disapprovingly. His grin increased and he removed his feet from the table.

She cut a large slice of cake and placed it on a plate then carried it to the table. 'How is … is …'

'Jamie,' he finished for her. 'She's fine. She sends her love.' His grin was broader than ever.

'You look thinner,' Sadie said reprovingly, laying the plate in front of him.

'Chocolate cake?' He sounded surprised then disapproving. 'What happened to the diet?'

Sadie felt the thrill of the morally superior. 'I do not make it for myself. It is for Daniel.'

'Daniel?' For a moment, Sammy's eyes were blank then they widened in disbelief. 'The kid you met in the park?'

Sadie nodded, then seeing her son's look of disapproval, added, 'You were wrong about him. He is a sweet boy.'

'Who has you making chocolate cake for him whenever he pleases.' Sammy was frowning. 'What other little things has he wheedled out of you?'

Sadie thought it best not to mention the trip to the dinosaurs. 'He is no more greedy than another little boy I once knew.'

Sammy chose to ignore the remark. 'I still think you are playing with fire. You know nothing about this boy, where he comes from, who his family is.'

'There you are wrong,' she said triumphantly and laid the invitation on the table before him. 'I know quite a bit about his family.'

Sammy's dark brows had pulled even closer together. 'Cliftondale street? Where is that?'

Sadie coloured and she hurried over to fetch the teapot to cover her confusion. 'Always you ask so many questions. Even as a little boy you were always asking. I thought by the time you were a man you would be tired of it.'

Sammy's frown disappeared to be replaced by a knowing expression that raised his brows and quirked the corners of his mouth. 'You don't know where it is?'

'You see,' Sadie said, thumping down the teapot. 'Just as I said. Not a minute in the door, but already questions, questions.'

Sammy fingered the edge of the invitation, noting how crumpled it was. 'Would you like me to find out where it is?'

Sadie lifted the teapot and began to fill one of the cups. In a casual, almost disinterested manner, she asked, 'This you can do?'

Wednesday was a bad choice for Daniel's birthday, Mags decided as she ran down University Avenue after her last lecture had finished. I shouldn't have spent so long with Ewan, she chided herself. But somehow the day had seemed longer and more leisurely in the early hours of the afternoon. She had a tutorial with him, and though she'd been dreading it, having not seen him since their abortive attempt to make love, he'd seemed so touched and delighted by her presence, that she felt as though there was no other motive for her being there expect their need to be together. They'd sat together at the worn tutorial table, and he'd leaned back listening to her, his head resting on one hand, his eyes upon her, as though everything she had to say was of special importance to him and he did not want to miss a word.

She had been shy at first, not wanting to sound critical, but his smile had given her courage, and she began hesitantly. 'It's Sergei's story.'

He frowned. 'Remind me.'

Mags was shocked. How could he have forgotten? 'On the face of it,' she began uncertainly, 'the story is about Sergei Jacobi's escape from arrest. But I think there's more to it.'

'Ah yes,' he interrupted. 'It was the one about Aaron Vasiliev's struggles in the communist movement, wasn't it?'

'I think the story is more about Aaron Vasiliev's struggle to free himself from his communism. He turned his back on the Party to help Sergei escape to the West.'

Ewan shook his head, as though trying to loosen a memory. 'He was prominent in the youth movement after the revolution?'

'He was very young,' she answered.

'Full of that fanatical zeal that appeals so much to youthful minds,' Ewan agreed. 'The author, Sergei Jacobi, he was one of his followers.'

'Not one, *the* follower,' Mags corrected. 'It was to Sergei he chose to express his doubts about the communist regime.'

Ewan's eyes were narrowed. 'There's something about the author. Something I ought to remember.' He shook his head. 'It'll come back to me. What appeals to you about this particular story then?'

How can he not know? How can he not see it? 'It stands head and shoulders over the rest of the book.'

His expression told her that he didn't believe her. 'In what way?'

She felt he was testing her. Would her arguments stand up? 'It's a love story.'

She hadn't thought that she'd have the courage to say it. But now that she had voiced it she knew that she couldn't take it back.

'You see a homosexual aspect to it?' he said doubtfully.

'No.' He hadn't understood. 'No.' Her brow creased as she tried to find the words. 'A love that goes beyond the sexes.' She spread her hands. 'Like David and Solomon. Like Plato and Socrates. It doesn't matter that they were two men. They could have been two women. Even a man and woman. It's the love itself that counts.'

He was smiling, and she couldn't help but feel he was laughing at her. 'I'd never have taken you for a romantic,' he teased.

'That's not the point.' She was angry now. He wasn't taking her seriously. 'You think your book is just about revolution, about people struggling against material and political forces. But you're wrong.' She ran a hand through her hair in agitation. 'Terribly wrong. This is deeper than all those other things. It goes beyond them.' She glanced at him to see if he was still paying attention, and was gratified to see that he was leaning towards her now, resting his chin on both hands. 'Go on.'

She took a deep breath. 'This isn't just the story of a man, who throws away his communist ideologies to save his friend. It's about Aaron Vasiliev's discovery that the individual is always going to be more important than the system he lives in.'

Ewan made a moue with his lips. 'And you believe that he truly left his communist ideals behind to help his friend escape to the West?'

Mags nodded emphatically. 'He gave his life for it.' She leaned across the table and took Ewan's hands in her own, too overcome by her enthusiasm to notice how strange and bold a gesture she was making. 'Aaron Vasiliev died to help Sergei Jacobi live when all his ideology and great principles should have had him hot tailing it to the authorities at the first possible chance. Aaron saw that the system was strangling what was good in Sergei and he wanted to save him.' Her eyes had grown very bright and intense. 'Sergei's story isn't about Sergei at all. It's about Aaron Vasiliev's revelation that freedom is the most important gift one individual can give another.'

The corner of Ewan's mouth quirked. 'Love conquers all?'

He was mocking her. She pulled her hands back sharply and stood up. 'You're laughing at me.'

Ewan stood up, towering over her, his face suddenly serious. 'No. I'm not laughing at you.'

'You just think I'm wrong.'

'I didn't say that.' He shook his head sadly. 'Mags, you have to have a little more faith in yourself. If you give up on an idea every time someone else doesn't agree, you'll end up without a thought in your head.'

She didn't answer, uncertain whether she'd been insulted or complimented.

'You've given me food for thought,' he acceded. 'If your interpretation is correct, I should be giving this story a more significant role in the book.'

Embarrassed, she shrugged off his praise. 'I don't know. Maybe I'm wrong. I get too wound up about things. See things that aren't there.'

He placed a finger on her lips to stop her. 'You're a clever girl, Mags,' he said softly. 'You just have to learn to believe it.'

He took his finger away and she opened her mouth to protest. And this time he silenced her with his lips.

But now it was almost half past three and she hadn't even picked up the cake.

'Mrs Gallagher,' the assistant read from a tag of paper attached to a cardboard box. 'A small ice with "Happy Birthday Daniel, Nine Today" printed on it.'

'That's right,' Mags said and reached for the box.

'I'll open it and let you take a look,' the assistant insisted.

Mags shook her head. 'I haven't time. Just give it to me.'

'It won't take a minute,' the assistant said, already untying the strings. 'I'm not allowed to let a cake leave the premises unless a customer has seen it.'

'Okay.' Mags fidgeted while the assistant laboriously untied the string.

'There.' The assistant pushed the cake forward. 'Blue icing and the candles and holders are in the box.'

Mags face fell when she inspected the box's contents. The icing looked more grey than blue and instead of a sugar drawing of a Spitfire there was a small plastic plane of unidentifiable type wedged into the icing. 'It's very small,' she said at last.

'It was a *small* ice that you ordered,' the assistant said in an injured tone. 'I can check your order if you wish.'

Mags sighed. 'No. Just tell me how much I owe.'

She had better luck in *Woolworths*. The airfix model was not only there but had been further reduced by another pound fifty. It was still too expensive, but it was so perfect. Just what he would have wanted. Mags reached into her purse. As she watched the box being wrapped her mind wandered and images of previous birthdays assailed her. Last year the presents had been small, the cake bought ready made from a local shop. Why was she going to all this trouble this year? Why was this year so special? Was she afraid there wouldn't be another? With an effort, Mags forced these nagging thoughts away and all but snatched the box from the assistant's hand and fled the shop.

Outside, the autumn sunlight had given way to the chilly darkness of early night. Shivering, Mags started up Byres Road towards the bus stop. The large boxes bumped uncomfortably against her legs, but she didn't mind. She could picture Daniel's face when he opened them, his excitement, his pleasure. And that made it all worthwhile. Any half decent mother understood how important birthdays were to a small boy. And that, of course, was the reason she was going to such trouble this year. She felt some of the warm glow of the earlier part of the day return to her. She was doing okay. Everything was going to be fine. She knew it.

Back at the flat, Mags was disappointed to find Daniel home ahead of her. She had hoped to have the decorations up to surprise him. But he looked so excited, trying to peek round her back at the parcels she was concealing that he almost seemed to have a pink tinge to his skin, and the sight of it dissolved any traces of her disappointment. Sending him off for a bath, Mags bustled round the kitchen trying to get everything ready. She realised too late that she should have done more the day before. Once certain that Daniel was in the bath, she hid the cake and the present in one of the cupboards beneath the sink, then hurriedly laid a packet of frozen sausage rolls on a tray and slipped them into the oven.

She looked round trying to decide what to do next and then it struck her how much there was to be done. Her palms began to sweat as she realised the long list of tasks that needed completed and it was already twenty past four. 'Daniel,' she yelled suddenly annoyed that he was splashing about in the bath when she was in the middle of a crisis. 'Get in here and give me a hand.'

She began gathering up handfuls of clothes, from where they'd been drying on the backs of chairs, and throwing them in the wash basket in amongst the dirty clothes waiting to be washed. She plumped up the cushions, placing them strategically to hide the more worn parts of the sofa, then ran her dilapidated carpet sweeper across the floor, trying to convince herself that the carpet looked cleaner.

Daniel emerged from the shower wearing his faded trousers and school shirt and she yelled at him for not putting on his best clothes, then when he went to fetch them, she called him back and said there was no point on putting on his best clothes if he was going to help her. His hurt expression was not lost to her, but it only served to panic her more. She handed him the carpet sweeper and told him to pay special attention to the bit in front of the door.

'That's the bit people always look at anyway,' she said trying to inject a little levity into her mood.

But Daniel didn't smile. 'I shouldn't be doing housework on my birthday,' he muttered.

This was more than Mags could take. 'Well you wanted a party,' she yelled. 'You can damn well help get ready for it.'

She saw his lip tremble as he turned away and after a moment he sniffed a little as he pushed the carpet sweeper ineffectively back and forth. Mags stopped in the middle of clearing her books away and said guiltily, 'That'll do, Danny. It never picks up anything anyway.'

He kept his back to her, but he stopped pushing the sweeper across the carpet.

'Why don't you put the decorations up,' she suggested.

He looked at her suspiciously. 'I thought you wanted to do them.'

She was on the verge of getting angry again and pointing out that she didn't have time, when she checked herself and said, 'But you make such a lovely job of them.'

He still looked hesitant. 'Go on,' she coaxed, hoping her voice didn't convey how desperate she felt.

With great dignity, so that she shouldn't see that he was secretly mollified, Daniel fetched the box of decorations from their box behind Mags' wardrobe and began to put them up.

'Don't put up the ones that are too Christmassy,' Mags warned and was rewarded with a withering look and the information that at nine years old he knew exactly which decorations you used for birthdays and which for Christmas.

Chided, Mags began spreading A plastic table cloth across her desk. She had picked it up in *Oxfam* for fifty pence the day before, and in the dim light it had seemed quite acceptable. But now, it looked crumpled and she saw that some of the patterning had worn off near the top. She drew that side towards her chair and hurried over to the kitchen to make the sandwiches. But the butter was too hard and it kept tearing the bread. She cursed under her breath, or so she thought, until Daniel turned towards her and said in shocked tones, 'Mum, you're using really bad words.'

She gave up on the sandwiches and began to fill a couple of plastic bowls with crisps.

'Mum, look,' Daniel announced. 'I've finished.'

'Very good, pet,' she said without looking up. 'Now go and get changed. Why are you not in your good clothes yet!'

While Daniel was changing, she carried the bowls of crisps and the untidy heap of sandwiches over to the table. Then, having arranged them to take up as much room as possible, stood, staring sadly down at her handiwork. Even with the crepe bows Daniel had added to each chair, it wasn't at all how she'd imagined, seeing in her mind's eye those perfect parties that leapt out the pages of glossy magazines. God knows, she'd leafed through enough of them in doctor's waiting rooms. Parties where grinning children all sat round fairy-tale landscapes of pink sugar icing and shimmering jellies.

She'd meant to do more. Little marshmallows topped with chocolate beans, cup-cakes, puff pastry mice with sugar noses and tails. It had all been in her plan when she thought about it late at night unable to get back to sleep after comforting Daniel. But there was always something lacking, time, money, a little luck even. As she watched, one of the sandwiches fell off the top of the clumsy pile, unravelling itself across the table towards her, like an accusation.

The doorbell rang startling Mags out of her reverie. They're early, she thought. But glancing at her watch she realised that it was already five past five. She groaned and ran a hand through her hair. Not even enough time to change. The doorbell rang again and she hurried towards it.

Chapter 24

SAMMY had insisted on taking her. Sadie had tried to protest, but he'd refused to take no for an answer. 'I still have the hire car for a couple of days. It's a waste to leave it out in the road.' And he looked so like his father, dark eyes, quirked mouth, the expression that mocked and challenged at the same time, that she couldn't refuse.

It was already dark by the time they left, but the city was well lit and Sammy insisted he could find the way without her help. 'Ma, it's no good giving directions when you always hold the map upside down.'

She had feigned a hurt silence, but was secretly relieved to have the leisure to stare out of the window. How long had she lived in this city and yet there were still vast stretches which she knew nothing about? A real Glaswegian after all, she chuckled to herself. Never moving out of my territory. Despite the dark she enjoyed the journey, hardly able to suppress little tremors of excitement. It had been so long since she'd been out on a social occasion. How long was it? She couldn't remember.

After they crossed the broad bridge spanning the Clyde, she sensed more than saw the change in her surroundings. The tenements grew somehow darker and meaner, their entrances devoid of decoration save for the shadowy forms of rubbish that found refuge there. The strangeness of it all sent memories rippling through her, sweet, foetid, like rotting fruit.

Running through the muddy streets. Short hair matted with rain. Her hat lost somewhere along the way. People turning towards her, seeing their own fears on her face then turning quickly away. Blind terror driving her on, forcing her up the stairs, through the gaping yawn of the door, past the upravdom with his disgruntled, Hey, comrade Shamilyevich is not to be disturbed. Banging on his door as though they were after her, as though it was her life they were taking. Then, Piotr opening the door, eyes alarmed and alert. A sea of frightened faces behind him. Falling to her knees, the words barely audible between her gasping breaths. 'Mother. They have arrested my mother.'

Traumatised, Sadie turned to Sammy intending to tell him to turn back, to get her away from this place back to the safety of her home. But Sammy pulled the car over to the kerb, saying, 'This is it.'

She followed his grim expression to the black entrance of a close. There was no security door and it gaped obscenely at her, like an open mouth. Sammy saw her horrified expression and offered, 'I could take you home, ma. We can always phone and say you weren't well.'

Yes, she could do that. Pretend to be ill, while a little boy, who was really ill, waited for her to come to his birthday party. She undid her seatbelt. 'Don't forget to pick me up.'

'Ma!' Sammy was startled by this sudden change in manner. 'Why don't you let me come up with you.'

'You have an invite?' she asked stubbornly.

'I'll just see you to the door.'

'No.' She opened the car door and swung her legs stiffly on to the pavement. And to Sammy's plaintive expression she said dismissively, 'It's a child's party not an assault on the Winter palace.' Then her courage wavered a little and she added, 'Don't forget to come back for me.'

Sammy looked as though he would argue, but then he sighed and took hold of the handbrake. 'Be careful,' he warned.

A good boy Sammy. Always thinking of his mother. She managed to wave to him quite cheerily as she entered the close and felt his eyes on her even as she disappeared into the darkness.

No-one had said anything for more than a minute. Daniel was busy playing with his new *Batman* car struggling with the tiny remote control box to make it do his bidding. Mags' mother sat on one end of the sofa, her father on the other. They had tight, fixed smiles and both looked vacantly into the room neither meeting Mags' eye or each other's. 'Can I get anyone a drink?' Mags asked. Her voice was brittle and cheerful, and tinged with an edge of strain she couldn't control.

'Aye.' Her father responded first. 'I brought some beer with me.' He stood up and began routing around inside a large paper carrier that had been lying at his feet.

'I've got beer,' Mags said.

'Aye. Aye,' he agreed. 'But I know what I like.'

'Maw, d'ye want a drink?' Mags asked again.

Mrs Gallagher considered the matter. 'Have ye any port? I like a wee bit of port with lemon.'

'No,' said Mags. 'I've got wine. Red or white.'

'Or what about some gin? I wouldnae mind a gin.'

'I've only got wine,' Mags said, her mouth set in a firm line. 'White or red?'

Mrs Gallagher glanced at her husband. 'I told ye I should have brought something.'

The lines around Mags' mouth grew tighter and she opened her mouth to say something, but the doorbell rang again.

'I'll get it,' Daniel said, but Mags was already heading for the door relieved to have a diversion. At the door, she hesitated, forcing the corners of her mouth upwards then reached for the handle.

For a moment, she stared in confusion at the old lady in the expensive tweed suit clutching an enormous shopping bag. There was something familiar about her, though she couldn't place her. Both women stared at the other, warily.

'Sadie,' said the woman a little hesitantly, and Mags understood. Smiling, she glanced over this grandmother's shoulder for the little girl who had been escorted to the party. But when she found no-one there, she turned puzzled eyes back to the woman. For a second it seemed that neither of them would speak, but suddenly Daniel bounded across the room and took the old lady's hand. 'Sadie. I knew you would come.'

Mags held the door open in shocked silence as Daniel led the old lady over to one of the worn arm chairs. 'This is my gran and granda,' he explained, waving a hand in their direction. 'And this is Sadie, my friend,' he added when they didn't respond.

'Pleased to meet you,' Sadie said shyly.

'Aye. Aye,' Mr Gallagher said in a dazed fashion. 'Very nice to meet you.'

'Yes,' his wife added then pressed her lips together in a tight line. 'Very nice.'

Mags said nothing. She was standing behind the kitchen counter staring at Sadie as though she thought that she might be some elaborate form of fancy dress and a little girl would step at any moment from the wrinkled folds. At last Daniel remembered his manners. 'D'ye want a drink?' he asked.

'Thank you.' Sadie smiled with relief to be able to break the silence. She was about to request a brandy when she changed her mind, asking, 'What do you have?'

'Wine,' Mags responded mechanically. 'Red or white. Or soft drinks.'

'White please,' Sadie said.

'I'll have one too,' Mrs Gallagher added. 'I think I need one.'

As Mags poured out two glasses of white and a generous glass of red for herself, the adults sat in silence. Her parents had gone back to staring at phantoms, while Sadie sat fidgeting on the edge of her chair. It was quite hot in the room and she wondered whether to take her jacket off. She'd dressed carefully before leaving that evening, changing her mind about what she would wear several times. In the end, she'd chosen a light tweed suit with a green and lilac grain. And beneath it, she wore a lilac blouse ornamented by a large amethyst studded brooch that Isaac had given her on their last anniversary. But looking round at the shabby room with its plainly dressed inhabitants, Sadie felt uncomfortable and out of place.

Mags handed her the wine in a glass different from the one she handed her mother. Sadie noted this as she noted the cheap prints on the walls and the one or two items of clothing tossed into the darker recesses of the corners. A poor home, poorer than she'd imagined. She shouldn't have come. Gratefully she took several long sips of the wine and tried not to think how long it was before Sammy came to pick her up.

Something bumped against her foot and she looked down to see a black plastic car reversing away from her shoe. 'Gran and granda gave me that,' Daniel informed her proudly.

'A very fine present indeed,' Sadie said, watching it disappear behind the table legs. She thought of complimenting him on his appearance but remembered that little boys don't like to be reminded that they've been forced to be smart. Instead she rummaged around in her bag and pulled out two colourfully wrapped parcels, one large, one small. Daniel's eyes lit up and he quickly put the control box down and rushed to her side.

'I don't think these can compete with such a fine present,' Sadie said smiling. 'But I hope you will enjoy them anyway.'

Daniel almost snatched them out of her hands and began unwrapping the largest one. 'Oh mum, look,' he breathed when he had the paper only half way off. Mags came closer and saw the glossy cover of a thick hardback book. A monstrous head peeped from the folds. 'It's a book about dinosaurs,' Daniel explained. 'It's the biggest book I've ever seen.'

'And you can build your own dinosaur. The man who sold me it, explained it to me,' Sadie added encouraged by his enthusiasm. 'The pieces are in the back.'

'So they are,' Daniel said, as he turned to the last page with almost reverential awe. For the first time that evening a genuine smile formed on Mags' lips. 'That's a good present,' she agreed.

'Aren't ye going to open the other one,' Mr Gallagher interrupted. There was something of a small boy's excitement in his tone and Daniel laughed and said, 'Hold on a minute, granda.'

He unwrapped the oddly-shaped parcel with difficulty. It was small and there was almost more sellotape than paper. But at last he had it open and held the contents up. 'A Swiss army knife.' He leapt into the air and did a sort of war dance up and down on the spot, whooping with delight.

'It is not new, Daniel,' Sadie said quickly. 'It belonged to my little boy and he thought it is something you would like.'

'It's smashing,' Daniel said, then words failing him, he threw his arms around Sadie's neck. Mags watched the embrace her face quite expressionless, and as though sensing his mother's eyes upon him, Daniel let Sadie go and turned towards her. 'When am I getting my present form you?' he asked.

The smile left Mags lips and she glanced at the door. Ewan should have arrived by now. She had wanted him to see Daniel open his presents and to impress him with her self-reliance. *Mags, however do you manage so well on your budget.* It would show she could cope, and assuage the pangs of guilt that made her feel that people thought she was after his money.

She considered going over to the window and having a look for this car, but, from the corner of her eye, she caught the sight of her mother pursing her lips and she forced herself to attend her guests. 'I'll get your present now, Danny,' she said and turned towards the kitchen. In doing so she missed Daniel's puzzled stare. His mother always smiled when she called him Danny.

His face lit up as soon as he saw the large box and he gave her a beaming smile. Mags recovered some of her composure while he tore the wrappings off, and asked if she could refill anyone's drink. Everyone was happy as they were. She waited for his cry of excitement. It didn't come.

'A model kit,' he said.

'You still like making them?' she asked anxiously.

He caught her tone, and she saw him force a smile. 'Of course I do. I really like it' He got to his feet and gave her a brief peck on the cheek. 'It's great, mum.'

'When are we going to eat?' Mr Gallagher wanted to know.

'We can do it now,' Mags said dully. She turned to check the oven, but not quickly enough to miss Daniel explaining to Sadie, 'I made a lot of models last year, when I was younger.'

'But model making is not just for children,' Sadie chided him. She turned to the Gallagher's for support. 'Many grownups like it, no?'

'Aye,' Mr Gallagher agreed. 'That's right.' He nudged his wife. 'Isn't that right?'

'Yes,' Mrs Gallagher said grudgingly. 'If they've nothing better to do with their time.'

A groan from Mags turned everyone's attention towards the kitchen. 'The oven's gone cold,' she explained. 'The sausage rolls are ruined.'

'Did ye feed the meter?' Mrs Gallagher wanted to know.

'Of course I fed the meter,' Mags snapped.

'Sorry I spoke,' Mrs Gallagher responded her mouth drawing into a thin line again.

'Now Mags. Your maw's just trying tae help,' Mr Gallagher said.

Sadie watched this exchange with increasing embarrassment before interjecting, 'I have some things for the table. I should give them now, yes.'

Mags turned in Sadie's direction, but her expression grew no less heated. 'What did ye say?'

Sadie got to her feet, and picking up her bag, hesitantly offered it to Mags. 'I made some food for the party.' And when Mags continued to stare angrily at her without offering to take the bag, Sadie went over to the table and began to unpack it. 'Sammy, my son, said I would offend you,' she explained uncertainly. 'But I tell him, always I have brought something to a party and I cannot stop now.'

'What did you bring?' Daniel demanded, tugging at her sleeve. He turned to his mother. 'Look! An apple pie. I told you Sadie makes brilliant cakes. And what's that?' He pointed at a plate filled with objects that resembled Cornish pasties. 'These are *piroshki*,' Sadie said. 'And here are some of those honey cakes you liked.'

Daniel beamed at Mags. 'I told you she was good at cooking.'

'Your friend didn't seem to think there would be any food at the party,' Mags said tightly.

Sadie recognised the tone and turned apologetically. 'I have offended you.'

Mags felt an immediate pang of guilt. *She's only trying to help. And it certainly doesn't look like anyone else is going to bother.* Forcing a smile, she said, 'No. Not at all. You've saved the day.'

'Can we eat now, mum?' Daniel asked, already climbing on to his chair. 'I'm starving.'

'It is a hungry business opening so many presents,' Sadie suggested. He laughed and pulled the chair next to him back for her. As she took it the smile left Mags lips. She turned hastily to her parents. 'Looks like we're eating then.'

Despite the good food and the glasses of wine and beer that Mags continually topped up, the atmosphere around the table was tense. The adults said little and avoided each other's eye. Only Daniel seemed unaffected, and mistaking the silence for attention, poured out stories that Sadie had shared about her childhood. Sadie was surprised how well and accurately he retold them, and she watched him with a proud, almost maternal look, quite oblivious to the hostile stare from Mags. The Gallagher's said nothing, except once Mrs Gallagher commented in a disapproving tone, 'Ye seem tae have lived a very interesting life.'

'Yes,' said Sadie contemplatively. 'I suppose I have.'

'The war must have been very hard for ye,' Mr Gallagher said. 'My father was with the Desert Rats in North Africa. He said he saw sights there he'd never forget.'

Mags saw the dark shadow that passed over Sadie's eyes. 'It was a hard time,' she agreed. 'To leave Russia before the war was my plan. But I only made it as far as a village in Latvia.' She spread her hands. 'It is hard to explain. Getting out. It was so difficult. I stayed near the border for a long time. Years. I used to pray every night that I make it back one day to Scotland.'

Not to be outdone, Mrs Gallagher added, 'We pray for your people.'

Sadie turned puzzled eyes towards her. 'Pray?' she repeated.

'At my church,' Mrs Gallagher explained, and ignoring Mags warning look added, 'We pray for the Jews.'

Sadie stared for a moment. Then Mags caught the corner of her mouth quirk up ever so slightly as she replied, 'That is very thoughtful of you.'

When Daniel paused between stories, Mags asked again if anyone would like another drink. Sadie saw a kind of desperation in her eyes and realised how much the tension between the adults was affecting her. Hoping to change the subject away from herself, she turned to Mags. 'Tell me, did you also live abroad at some time?'

Mags eyebrows knit together in a puzzled frown. 'No. Never. Not even for a holiday.'

'I see,' Sadie said nodding thoughtfully. Mr Gallagher held out the plate of sandwiches to her and Sadie examined them greedily before reaching out to take another. 'I shouldn't really,' she explained. 'My appetite, it is not what it used to be.' She chose a cheese one, narrowly avoiding the one next to it that looked like ham. Not that she was strict, not really. But old habits die hard.

Mr Gallagher was finishing a second slice of Sadie's apple pie. He held up his empty plate towards Sadie in mock toast. 'Delicious,' he said, mouth still full. 'Never tasted better.'

Sadie smiled at him warmly. It was nice to have an appreciative audience. Just like having Isaac back.

'It'll be a Kosher recipe then,' Mrs Gallagher commented. She was looking at Sadie, but her words seemed to hold some kind of warning for her husband.

Sadie stared at her, her face blank, and Mrs Gallagher repeated. 'The cake, that'll be a Kosher recipe, will it?'

There was a short silence then Sadie said, 'No. It is not Kosher.' Then she blushed a little before confessing, 'I tore it from a magazine when I went to make a visit to the dentist.'

Mags asked suddenly, 'What made you think I'd lived abroad?'

'O,' Sadie had half-forgotten she'd mentioned it. She thought for a moment, then said, 'It is the way you speak. It is different from your mother and father. Daniel too, he speaks like you.'

'How is it different?' Daniel wanted to know.

Sadie put down her sandwich and struggled to explain, 'Sometimes it is difficult for me to hear what you are saying.' She nodded over at the

Gallagher's. 'But when Daniel or your daughter speak, it seems clearer to me.' Then seeing the frozen expression of annoyance on Mrs Gallagher's face, she went on a little lamely. 'Of course, perhaps it is only me who hears a difference.'

'No, no,' Mrs Gallagher agreed icily. 'That'll be her university voice.'

'Now, Ellen,' Mr Gallagher said, but was ignored.

Mrs Gallagher threw a cold glance in her daughter's direction. Mags sat with her shoulders hunched staring at her wine glass, but said nothing, and encouraged Mrs Gallagher continued. 'She likes to talk like her university friends. She'll soon no be able to understand us. Isn't that right?' She glared at Mr Gallagher and he twisted the top of his bottle and grunted something below his breath.

Sadie opened her mouth to say something more, but catching the look of rage and pain in Mags' troubled eyes, she closed it again. The doorbell rang, and all heads turned towards it.

'I'll get it,' Daniel said slipping down from his seat, and Mags nodded, relieved, yet nervous. Ewan's presence could act as both as panacea and irritant. She glanced at her mother, who was staring at the door, an expectant, triumphant expression playing about her lips.

Daniel opened the door to a dark-eyed man of middle height, wearing an expensive wool overcoat, who bent down towards him and held out his hand. 'Daniel Gallagher?' he enquired.

Chapter 25

'DANIEL Gallagher?' the stranger asked again.

Startled, Daniel stepped back nodding dumbly. Mags got to her feet. 'Can I help you?' Her voice was a mixture of politeness and unease.

'Mrs Gallagher,' the man said, advancing across the threshold. 'I'm Samuel Gordon. I've come to collect my mother.'

Mags turned to Sadie seeing at once the resemblance in the dark, hooded eyes. She turned back to the stranger. 'Come in please, Mr Gordon.'

'Sammy,' the man said. He walked quickly over to Sadie and kissed her affectionately on the cheek. 'I'm a little early,' he apologised. 'But I know how tired you get these days.'

Sadie beamed. Such a thoughtful boy. But Daniel was tugging at her arm. 'Sadie, you can't go yet. We haven't had my cake yet.'

Sammy looked as though he was about to make an excuse, but seeing Daniel's pleading eyes, she quickly nodded, saying, 'You are right, Daniel. A birthday party is not complete without a cake.'

A small frown creased Sammy's brow, but was quickly replaced by a more genial expression. 'It seems I am here to stay,' he said. Then turning to Mags, added, 'If that is all right with you.'

Mags shrugged. 'Yes, of course it is,' she said gruffly. 'Let me take your coat.'

'Thank you.' He smiled at her while he unbuttoned his coat and Mags smiled back, a nervous, unblinking smile. There was something about him that made her uneasy. Although his eyes had never left hers, she had the feeling that he had taken in the whole room and the people in it, and come to a quiet and accurate judgement of his own. As she took the jacket and turned away, the stupidity of such thoughts struck her at once. Like some silly peasant, she thought contemptuously, frightened by strangers. She glanced at her parents, saw their narrowed, suspicious eyes, and shivered.

But when she returned from the bedroom, she discovered that Sammy had worked a kind of magic. He was already sitting between her parents, one long leg folded over the other, a bottle of beer nestled in one hand. He was listening to an animated description of a darts match as explained by Mr Gallagher.

'Wheest Andy, the boy doesn't want to hear about that,' Mrs Gallagher said disapprovingly.

But Sammy turned his black eyes towards her, and smiling broadly to show two sets of white, even teeth, said, 'Not at all, Mrs Gallagher. While it's true that I'm no player, your husband has a most entertaining way of telling a story.'

Mags saw her father puff up a little in a way she realised she hadn't seen for years, and even Mrs Gallagher gave a grudging smile.

While Mr Gallagher entertained Sammy with a surprisingly large collection of anecdotes relating to the world of darts, Sadie expounded the virtues of her caring son to Mrs Gallagher. It seemed that on this mutual maternal ground they could meet and were soon in an animated discussion of the respective virtues of their sons. Busy lighting the cake from behind the kitchen counter, Mags tried not to mind that her name had not been mentioned.

As she slipped across the room, ready to put the light out, she heard her mother explaining. 'Of course, Gary couldnae be here tonight. He had to work overtime.' She nodded in a satisfied way. 'He'll go far that lad. He's got a good head on him.'

'And you must be very proud of your daughter too,' Sadie added thoughtfully. 'To go to university while looking after a child alone is a marvellous thing.'

'Yes,' Mrs Gallagher agreed doubtfully. 'But in my day a woman put her child first.'

Bristling with anger, Mags snapped the light switch off sending the whole room into startled exclamations of 'O!' Then she ran behind the counter and brought out the birthday cake skilfully turning the 'O!'s to 'Ahs!'. In the dim candlelight, a rousing chorus of *Happy Birthday To You* was sung and Daniel's face glowed as much with the thrill of it as with the hot candles he was hovering over. And once the candles were blown out and the wish made, Mags snapped the light back on blinking along with the rest of them and listening to the exclamations of what a fine cake it was.

Sammy leaned down and lifted the plastic plane out of the icing. 'An F16 I believe,' he said.

'No,' Daniel was emphatic. 'It's a F15.'

'Never. The wings are too short.'

'But look at the nose.' Daniel pointed triumphantly and Sammy nodded his assent, as though beaten by a superior intellect. 'You seem to know a lot about planes,' he said.

Daniel beamed at him. 'My dad used to fly them.'

'Indeed.' Sammy was about to ask more, but he caught exchanged glances between the Gallaghers, and Mags said quickly, 'Daniel is going to be a pilot when he grows up, aren't you Daniel?'

But Daniel only shrugged, his eyes on the plastic plane.

'Daniel's a star pupil at his school,' Mags said to no-one in particular. Then, she went on a little desperately, 'No wonder he can't make up his mind. Miles of time to decide, though.' She smiled brightly at the back of Daniel's head. 'Who'd like a slice of cake?'

There were no refusals, though Sadie's eyes stayed on Mags' back as she took the cake over to the table to cut it. She saw, with sudden clarity, what was going on. *She thinks he's going to grow up. All that talk of time to decide.* Sadie's hand clutched at the amethyst at her throat. *Dear God. She doesn't know. She hasn't realised.* Immediately, her eyes sought out Daniel. He had hold of the plane now and was demonstrating a kind of swooping land on to Sammy's knee. *Poor, little lamb,* she thought. *You know what is going to happen. Is that why you came to me?*

Mags returned to hand out the cake to an enthusiastic audience, interrupted only by Sadie's protest that the size of her slice was much too large.

'My appetite. It is like a bird's now,' she explained.

'Only if we're talking about vultures, ma,' Sammy said through a mouthful of crumbs.

'Sammy!' Sadie was hurt.

But Mags noticed the way one side of his mouth quirked up in a grin and saw the hurt on Sadie's face replaced with tenderness. She was surprised to find herself a little moved by the exchange and quickly turned away to pick up the empty plates from the table.

Somehow Daniel and Sammy had gotten on to the subject of dinosaurs. 'The T-Rex is the biggest dinosaur ever found,' Daniel announced with authority. 'I learned that when we done dinosaurs at school.'

Mags opened her mouth to correct him, caught her mother's narrowed, threatening gaze, and shut her mouth again.

'Nonsense,' Sammy was saying. 'There's the Giganotosaurus It was much bigger.'

Daniel studied the man's face unsure whether he was serious. But Sammy's dark eyes stared intently back and Daniel dropped his gaze to the floor. 'How big was it?' he asked grudgingly.

'About twenty-one and a half feet high,' Sammy said. 'At least that's what the book at home says.'

Daniel looked up, his eyes shining. 'Could I see your book?'

Sammy's serious expression broke into a smile. 'Of course. I'll look it out next time you call.'

As though hearing her cue, Mrs Gallagher suddenly asked, 'D'ye see our Danny often then?'

Caught off guard, Sadie stammered, 'Yes. And I am always very pleased to do so. So few people visit me these days.'

Mrs Gallagher gave a sympathetic nod of quite undisguised insincerity, and asked, 'How did ye meet our Daniel?'

Mags, who had been piling dirty dishes up on the table suddenly froze, her hands hovering above the remains of the sandwich plate.

'I found Daniel in my garden,' Sadie explained, smiling at the memory. Then seeing Daniel's anguished look, added, 'You had lost your way, had you not. The Botanic Gardens is such a large park.'

'The Botanic gardens!'

Everyone turned in Mags direction. She had turned to face them and was standing there, face white, hands balled into fists at her side. 'Did you say the Botanic gardens?' she asked when no-one replied to her exclamation. 'It is where I live,' Sadie answered meekly, not knowing what she had done wrong.

Mags stared from Sadie to Sammy and back again. Suddenly they didn't seem so cosy. They were strangers, strangers in her home. Sammy's hand resting on Daniel's shoulder now seemed sinister and she had to force herself from the urge to stride across the room to force them apart. And this wizened, old woman, who had lured her son half way across the city? It was disgusting. Surely it had to be. These people were wealthy. Strangers. What did they want with her son? Her eyes focused on Daniel. He'd slunk on to the floor and was busy staring at the dinosaur book. 'Have you been going around during the week?' she accused.

His back was to her and he shrugged, deliberately turning one of the pages, as though the question was of too little consequence to merit more.

'Have you?' Her voice had risen, and she saw Sammy exchange a puzzled glance with Sadie.

'Mibbe.' The word was barely audible, but it was enough. Mags rounded on Sadie. 'You've encouraged my wee boy to play truant to come paying court to you.'

Sadie shook her head, baffled. 'No. I didn't ...' She looked helplessly at the hostile faces. 'At least I did not mean ...'

Sammy got to his feet. 'I think it's time I took you home, ma.' He turned to Mags, his eyes black and unfathomable, stilling the angry retort in her throat. 'Perhaps you would fetch my coat.'

She opened her mouth to reply, then, when he did not avert his gaze, snapped it shut again and went to find it. When she returned, she saw that Sadie and her parents were on their feet. Mrs Gallagher had a protective arm around Daniel's shoulder. He stood limply in it, staring at the floor. Sammy took the coat from her without a word and draped it over one arm, with the other he took hold of his mother's shoulder. 'Come on now. We should be leaving.'

Mags stood, stiff as a sentry as Sadie stiffly made her way across the room. Despite her anger, Mags saw that Sadie was older than she'd first realised. Deprived of her cheeriness the years suddenly became evident, her back was stooped, and she shuffled on the arm of her son, rather than walked. At the door, she hesitated and turned back towards Daniel. 'Daniel,' she called softly, but he didn't look up. 'Thank you for inviting me to your party.'

He made an incoherent sound that might have been a sniff, and she added hastily. 'I hope you'll come and see me soon when your mother lets you.'

He didn't reply and Sadie turned a nervous glance towards Mags. 'Thank you for such a nice party,' she said.

'You're welcome,' Mags replied stonily. She opened the door and mother and son disappeared out into the darkness without saying goodbye.

As soon as they were gone, Mags shut the door and leaned heavily against it. Her eyes fell on Daniel. 'You've got some explaining to do.'

But Daniel wriggled free of his grandmother's grasp, and grabbing up his Swiss army knife, ran from the room. 'I hate you,' he called over his shoulder as he slammed the door. 'I hate you forever.'

Mags closed her eyes for a long moment and drew a hand down the side of her face. When she opened them, Mrs Gallagher was staring directly at her, her lips pursed in a disapproving fashion. 'I certainly wouldnae let any wean of mine talk to me like that,' she said.

'Now, Ellen,' Mr Gallagher began, but was silenced by a look. 'If either you or Gary had spoken to me like that, you'd have known what for,' Mrs Gallaher continued. 'A boy has to have some fear of his mother, especially when there's no father around.'

'We do fine,' Mags said. Her voice was a dangerous growl, but Mrs Gallagher didn't appear to notice.

'Well I wouldnae have thought playing truant half way across town with some frustrated auld granny was fine,' she spat. 'It's dangerous.' She took a step towards Mags, her eyes accusing. 'I didn't like the look of those two from the moment they walked in. There was something funny about them.'

'Like being Jewish?' Mags asked.

Her mother coloured. 'Don't get smart with me.' She advanced closer to Mags so that their faces were only inches apart. 'I'm no like that as well you know. But ye have to be careful with that kind of person. They have different ways from us. Ye can't trust a wee boy with them.'

Mags took a step back then opened the door, holding it pointedly ajar. 'You needn't worry,' she said coldly. 'Daniel won't be seeing that woman again.'

Chapter 26

S HE was dead. She was quite sure of it because she couldn't feel anything. Her face was scratched and raw, and her hands and feet were
swollen with the cold and the grazes and the lack of food, but she
couldn't feel them at all. Keep going! The snow was up to her knees. True
snow. Not white, but blue. It must be freezing her, but she couldn't feel it.
Don't look back. There was no sound from the others. Perhaps they were dead
too.

In the distance, she could hear the soldiers crashing through the
undergrowth, their dogs baying with the heat of the chase, and her heart
began to thud so maybe she was alive after all. But she didn't feel it. A while
ago she had been running, breathless and terrified, scattering like the others,
frightened rabbits scenting the farmer. But now she only walked because she
had no breath left and she didn't know where she was or where she was going.
Only that she must keep going. Keep on.

The sharp crack of a gunshot rang out and she froze in her tracks, staring
around trying to gauge its direction. Had it come from in front or behind?
There were no landmarks. The skeletal trees waved the same bony fingers in
every direction she looked. And a horrible thought occurred to her. What if
she was running towards the soldiers instead of away?

She whirled round. There were tracks in the snow going in every
direction. Hers? There was another gunshot. Closer and yet still strangely
elusive. Which way to go? If only Piotr was here. He would know what to do.
She nodded vaguely to herself. Then a thought struck her. Something she had
done. Something terrible. But, no. she couldn't think about that now. Not in
the confusion and the cold and the white blue snow. No. She wanted him to
be with her. Wanted him here to hold her hand, to tell her what to do. If only
he would come now, if only in spirit, just one more time to show her what she
must do.

In her memory, she began walking again, but later she always wondered
if she had, or whether she'd simply stood there, gazing up at the swirling sky
waiting for them to come. And when the bullet burrowed gently into her
back, she fell forward without a sound.

They had her hands dragging her through the snow, and she fought them
off weakly trying to free herself from their grip. They were saying something

and only vaguely could she make it out.

'Ma. You're dreaming. Wake up.'

Her eyes fluttered and the black form that had taken hold of her resolved itself into Sammy's face. He had hold of her wrists and she was still trying feebly to escape. When he saw she recognised him, he let her go and stood up. 'I brought you a cup of tea,' he explained, waving a hand in the direction of a rose-patterned cup balanced on the side table. 'When you didn't answer my knock, I came in. I thought you'd overslept.'

'I was dreaming.' She would have liked to have said more, but the images were already fading from her mind.

'You were calling out in Russian,' Sammy told her. She could tell he was concerned and hastened to reassure him. 'You don't forget a language you spoke for over thirty years,' she said. 'Sometimes it comes back.'

Sammy looked like he was about to say more, then changing his mind, reached out and handed her the teacup. 'Drink some tea. You'll feel better.'

She accepted it gratefully and looked round hopefully for some sugar, but there was none. Sammy raised a knowing eyebrow. 'I didn't bring any. I remembered about your appetite being like a bird's these days.'

She threw him a rueful glance, but began to sip the tea. It was bitter without sugar but it calmed the nerves. Sammy sat on the end of the bed watching her. 'How do you feel?'

She smiled at him. So thoughtful. 'Fine now, darling,' she assured him. 'It was only a bad dream.'

Sammy frowned. 'I didn't mean the dream.'

She stared at him blankly.

'I was wondering if you were upset about last night.'

Sadie considered the matter. 'No I am not upset.'

She saw a worried look crease his forehead. 'Ma,' he began slowly. 'I know you're very fond of Daniel.'

'He's a fine boy.'

Sammy nodded. 'I'm not disagreeing. But after last night, you realise you might not see him again.' He studied her face. 'You understand that, don't you, ma?'

Sadie smiled fondly at him. So concerned. What other mother had a son as considerate as Sammy? She reached across the coverlet and took his hand. 'Daniel will come back. I know he will.'

Sammy opened his mouth to protest. 'But what about the mother? Even if the boy wants to come back, she may stop him.'

Sadie let go his hands and looked calmly into his troubled eyes. 'I do not think so,' she said firmly. 'She is a clever girl. She will come around. But even if she does not,' Sadie's eyes seemed to be looking beyond Sammy now. 'Daniel will find a way. He must.'

A furry, grey caterpillar of ash had formed along the edge of her saucer, but Mags had done nothing to move it. She was staring into the murky blackness of her coffee watching a faint film of grease rotate slowly on top. It had all gone wrong. Everything she'd planned, the food, the presents, the guests. Nothing had worked out the way she had wanted it to. And now he hates me, she thought wearily.

Daniel had gone to bed by the time she had finished clearing up, and later that night, when she hurried into his room after hearing him cough, he had lain cold and inert, pretending to sleep until she had been forced to return to her room. She had lain on her unmade bed, staring sleeplessly up at the ceiling well into the early hours of the morning. I'm right, she thought. I know I'm right. But a nagging voice at the back of her head kept asking, *how can you be so sure?*

Light had just begun to crack the winter morning when she finally fell asleep, and so she slept on until nearly ten o clock when a crash from outside startled her back to consciousness. She'd stumbled towards Daniel's room calling for him to get up, but when she got there he was gone. Something in the sight of his cold, empty bed chilled her and she slumped down on to it hugging the pillow to her stomach. There was a stale smell of Daniel about it and she let her head rest against it, remembering a saying of her mother's that went along the lines of a person never being truly dead until their smell left the house. When she began to grow cold, she got to her feet and headed out to the university.

She had missed her first lecture and sat through the next neither hearing it nor taking down notes. She scribbled in her margin, *heartfelt, heart ache, heart warmed, heart's content, heart's desire, heart break.* When the lecture ended, she went to the men's union and ordered a cup of coffee, which she didn't drink and lit a cigarette, which she didn't smoke.

'Mags.' The voice was so soft that for a moment she didn't react. And it wasn't until he was sitting opposite her that she fully acknowledged he was there. 'Ewan.' She said the word in no particular tone hoping that would be more hurtful than anger. She was gratified to see the pain of her indifference pucker his brow.

'Mags, I've been trying to get hold of you all night.'

'Bearsden must be further away than I thought,' she said, taking a sip of her coffee forgetting it was cold.

He sighed and leaned back in his chair. Out the corner of her eye she could see his long legs barring her escape on one side of the chair. There was something possessive in the gesture and it irritated her.

'I know you must be angry with me.'

She feigned surprise. 'I'm not angry. What have I to be angry about?'

Ewan looked almost amused at her indifference, and she forced herself to take another sip of cold coffee to prevent her anger bubbling over. He expects me to throw things, she thought. And now he doesn't know what to do. She wasn't entirely sure what she expected him to do either, but she waited in stony silence refusing to make the next move. At last he said, 'How did the party go?'

'It went fine,' she lied. Then as she had lied once added, 'Daniel missed you being there.'

Ewan looked surprised and not altogether convinced. 'I wanted to be there,' he said humbly. 'But the damn car broke down on the Kingston Bridge last night. And I didn't have the mobile on me. It took hours just to get someone to tow me away. Some kind of strike they said.'

'Were the phone boxes on strike too?' Mags asked. She didn't look at him but stirred her coffee with cold, efficient strokes.

Ewan studied her for some moments then, as if restraining himself, said in a quiet controlled voice, 'As a matter of fact they were in a way. I walked miles to find one that wasn't vandalised or nine calls only, only to find that your phone isn't working.'

On the point of dismissing this as nonsense, it occurred to Mags that she hadn't heard it ring for several days. As almost no-one phoned and she rarely used it herself, she had thought nothing of it. But then she remembered a bill, a red reminder that she'd put away in a drawer telling herself that she'd deal with when she got a chance. But she'd been so busy that she'd forgotten. When had she got that bill? A week ago? No. fortnight at least. Abashed, she looked into Ewan's face. 'I think I forgot to pay the bill.'

It was his turn to look angry. 'In heaven's name, why?'

Mags looked away, tracing the edge of a scratch along the Formica surface of the table. 'I didn't have enough money.'

'But I pay for the telephone,' Ewan protested, then realising he had raised his voice said more softly, 'Why didn't you come to me?'

Mags shrugged. He doesn't understand, she thought miserably. How could he? Being poor to him means not going abroad for a holiday in the summer. He couldn't see what money meant to her, freedom, independence, a way out for Daniel and her. 'I'm sorry,' she said at last. 'It slipped my mind.'

He reached out a hand. 'Am I forgiven?'

She looked at it for a moment, seeing the slim, tapered fingers, the neatly filed nails. A scholar's hand. She reached out for it. 'Aye, maybe this once.'

As they walked back to the office, he asked, 'What was the party really like?' And she blushed and gave him an edited version of events. He seemed amused by her description of the old lady, especially when she described the inscrutable expression on Sadie's face as she thanked Mrs Gallagher for praying for her people. And Mags felt it would be hard to explain her sense of outrage to him. As she had this thought, a little voice in the back of her mind asked whether she could explain her sense of outrage to herself. She didn't say much about Sammy either and she wasn't sure why, but some sixth sense made her keep quiet on the subject.

Once in his office, he closed the door and embraced her. She smelled the warm tweed and expensive aftershave and wanted to stay there for a long time, like a little girl seeking comfort in her father's arms. But he pushed her away. 'I haven't got long,' he apologised. 'I just wanted to give you this.' He fumbled about in the drawers of his desk and found a pale blue envelope with neither address nor stamp on it. He held it out to her. 'It's for Daniel,' he explained. 'Just vouchers I'm afraid. I'm rather out of touch with the desires of small boys these days.'

'Thanks.' Mags took it and dropped it into her bag. She knew without looking that it would be too generous and it would have embarrassed her to open it.

There was a brief, almost awkward silence, and Mags had the feeling she'd overstepped her welcome. She didn't want to lose the feeling of well-being bumping into Ewan had instilled, so she picked her bag up, saying, 'I should be going.'

Ewan's disappointment at this announcement seemed genuine and she immediately felt better. At the door, he stopped her. 'There is just one other thing.'

She turned puzzled eyes towards him and saw, to her surprise, that he looked a little shy. He coughed slightly and said, 'I don't know if I mentioned it or not, but my book has gone through the final acceptance stages.'

'You didn't. No.'

He looked so proud, and was so obviously trying not to show it, that she felt a rush of affection that made her want to reach out and gather him into her arms.

'The launch is in three weeks' time,' he went on quickly.

She held her breath, not daring to hope. But he carried on. 'I was hoping you'd be able to attend. It's in the evening at the university bookstore.'

She couldn't keep the smile from spreading across her lips. Acknowledgement at last. Margaret Gallagher no longer in the background, subject of curious stares and hostile questions, but out in the open where she belonged, by Ewan's side.

'You will come?' he asked, concerned by her silence.

'Couldn't keep me away,' she beamed.

Chapter 27

THE fragile aura of happiness cocooned Mags all the way home until she reached her door. Her key turned uselessly against the mortice lock meaning that Daniel had unlocked it and was already inside. She turned the Yale and entered, calling out, 'Danny, I'm home, son.'

There was no reply, and at first, she assumed he was in his room. But, as she took off her jacket, she saw him sitting on the sofa reading his dinosaur book the knife on the cushion beside him.

'Daniel.' Mags went over and sat down beside him. He didn't look up. She picked up the knife and regarded it worriedly. 'You didn't take this to school, did you?'

He turned a page deliberately. 'I'm no a child, you know,' he said.

'But you could get into trouble,' she protested. 'Or worse, you could get seriously hurt.'

'I didn't take it.'

'O.' She was relieved.

They were silent for a while, then Mags said slowly, 'Daniel, we need to talk about last night.'

He shrugged and turned another page. Mags reached out to stroke his hair, but he flinched away. 'How often have you been going around there?'

He shook his head non-committally. 'A few times.' Then he added angrily. 'She makes good cakes.'

'I see.' Mags tried to keep her voice level. 'But surely there must be someone nearer by for you to play with.'

He shook his head again. 'I like Sadie.'

Mags took a deep breath, and said carefully, 'It isn't that I don't want you to have friends.'

He turned towards her then, and his eyes were cold. 'Is it because they're Jewish?'

'Daniel!' She was shocked.

'Well, is it?' he demanded.

'You know perfectly well it isn't,' she said angrily. But the words sounded hollow. She hadn't believed her mother when she'd denied it. Why should Daniel believe her? 'Danny,' she spoke more gently. 'It isn't about Sadie. She seems like a very nice person.'

His eyes narrowed suspiciously but he let her continue. 'It's just that you can't be running away from your school work.'

'Can I see her on Saturdays?' he asked.

Mags drew her top lip across her teeth. 'I don't think it's a good idea. A boy of your age should be playing with friends of his own age.'

'I don't want friends of my own age,' Daniel cried jumping to his feet. Anger had put two pink spots in his cheeks and he stared angrily down at Mags. 'I like Sadie.' He arced a hand around the room. 'Sadie's house is always clean. And it's warm. And she's always home when I go to see her.'

This was too much for Mags. 'And I suppose she always welcomes you with open arms whenever you barge in,' she countered.

'Aye she does,' Daniel said contemptuously. He turned towards his room then stopped to fling a final rejoinder over his shoulder. 'And if you won't let me see her I'll find a way to talk to her.'

Mags was on her feet too now. 'You can talk to me,' she all but yelled. 'I'm your mother. If you've got something to say, you can say it to me. What's so special about this woman that …'

But she got no further. The expression on Daniel's face wounded her into silence. 'She tells the truth,' he announced coldly. And before Mags could say another word, he turned and walked from the room, slamming the door behind him.

When he had gone, the air felt strangely charged. Mags took a step after him, then changing her mind, sat down on the sofa, staring at the closed door to his room.

As she hadn't taken the route through the park, it had taken Mags longer than she'd expected to find the house. The air was crisp and she could feel it crackling against her face and bare hands. For an instant, she had thrust her hands into the pockets of her jacket, but the posture made her hunch over and she felt less confident that way, so she braved the cold instead.

Once she had rounded the tree lined corner she'd come upon the house at once, unmistakable in its lonely grandeur at the top of the park. But instead of going in, she stood outside the gate trying to work up the courage to walk up the gravel path. One glance at Sadie and her son had been enough to tell her that they were well off, but she hadn't realised to what extent. The house was huge, a sprawling Victorian villa fronted with mature bushes of holly and rowan to either side of the door. It seemed far too big for one family, and she half expected a gardener to appear from behind a bush and order her to take the tradesman's entrance.

Suddenly all the care she'd taken in dressing that morning seemed to have been for nothing. Her only skirt, pink cotton, a little out of fashion but still good quality, teamed with a blouse of grey satin and black shoes, a little tight at the toes suddenly seemed cheap and inappropriate. Should have stuck to jeans, she thought. Stupid pretending to be something I'm not. Better to stick to what I am. But then a cold, sad, little voice asked, *but what am I?*

For a moment, she considered turning back. Glancing up and down the street she could see no-one. The place was deserted. She could run and no-one would know. No. That would be stupid. She'd come to do something and it would be better to get it over with. Reluctantly she opened the gate.

Her tentative ring was not answered immediately, and she was filled with a mixture of relief and regret, but then she heard a male voice shout. 'I'll get it,' and the door swung open, revealing Samuel Gordon. He looked down at her with a puzzled, curious expression on his face. 'Can I help you?'

He was dressed in jeans and a plaid shirt and somehow, he seemed less intimidating than when she'd last seen him. Nevertheless, her smile was forced. 'Is your mother at home?'

He nodded. 'Who shall I say is calling?'

She felt embarrassed to be forgotten so readily and stammered. 'Margaret Gallagher. Mags. Daniel's mother.'

He stared at her for a moment, then recovering himself held the door wide for her to enter. 'Forgive me. I didn't recognise you.' He studied her trying to work out what was different. 'Your hair. It's different?' he asked.

Surprised, Mags nodded.

'You were wearing it back at Daniel's party.'

Mags nodded again. For a moment, she thought he was about to make a comment, some polite remark about it suiting her, but he simply stood there, studying her for a further moment, then leaned down and opened the door to one of the rooms. 'Please come in. My mother is in the kitchen at the moment. I'll let her know that you're here.'

Trying to appear at ease, Mags walked through the open door and into a large, dimly lit room. She stood uncertainly near the entrance surveying elegant, expensive furniture, almost buried beneath lace doilies and embroidered cushions. Heavy drapes and antique lace hid most of the light from the large bay window at the end of the room, and beneath an assortment of rugs she glimpsed a densely-patterned carpet. Without meaning to, she turned questioningly to Sammy, who smiled and said simply, 'My mother's tastes are somewhat eclectic.'

Embarrassed that she might be thought to be criticising, Mags looked away and made out a dim figure lost in the mounds of cushions piled on the sofa. It was peering at Mags, and before she could react, asked in a shrill, hostile voice, 'So, you're going to introduce me or am I going to sit here like a *shmatte?*'

Sammy smiled. 'Etta, this is Margaret Gallagher a friend of ma's.'

Even in the dim light, Mags saw the grey eyebrows raised. Sammy touched her shoulder lightly. 'And this is Etta, Mags,' he said, his mouth twisting up at one corner. 'A character from my childhood come back to haunt me.'

'Pah,' Etta said contemptuously. 'Don't listen to him, sweetheart. He's such a big man these days, he doesn't have time for his old auntie Etta.' She patted the sofa cushion beside her. 'Come. Sit next to me so I can see you. My eyes aren't what they used to be. The doctors say it could be a sign of something serious, you know.'

With the stiffness of embarrassment Mags made her way awkwardly through the dim light and settled herself next to the tiny woman. The sofa cushions were large and she sank deeply into them, making her feel uncomfortably off-balance. Etta's sharp features loomed close and she studied Mags with a disapproving frown. 'You're very thin,' she commented. 'In my day, such thinness was a sign of consumption. But now,' she sighed regretfully, 'I suppose it's just a fashion with you young girls.'

Not knowing how to respond, Mags glanced helplessly towards the door, and was relieved to see Sammy following Sadie into the room. Sammy was carrying a large, lace-covered tray piled with scones and cakes. Four cups were balanced precariously on a pile of saucers and a steaming silver teapot sat resplendent in the centre. Sammy was saying something she couldn't hear, but she caught Sadie's reply. 'But they are for the guests. You know I hardly eat a thing.'

'I hope you're hungry,' Sammy said, his strange, lopsided smile aimed at Mags. 'This isn't a household to be anorexic in.'

He was about to place the tray on the covered coffee table when Sadie gave a little shriek. Sammy paused, tray held in mid-air. He turned a questioning look towards his mother. Sadie was lifting several placemats from a sideboard drawer. She hurried over and arranged them on the table. 'There,' she said imperiously. 'The tray can rest on them.' She glanced at Mags and Etta, and shook her head. 'Men never know the value of things. In America, he tells me, they never cover anything. But I can't believe it.'

Etta shuddered at the mere thought and recalled an uncle who'd died of septicaemia after getting a very nasty splinter from a rough wooden table. While she related this anecdote, Mags stared hard at the floor and tried to mutter something that could be interpreted as a yes or a no depending on how you wanted to take it. When eventually, she dared to look up she could see Sammy staring at her, his dark eyes liquid with amusement.

As Sadie poured out the tea, Etta suddenly asked. 'So how is it you know

Margaret?'

Referred to in the third person Mags didn't immediately recognise herself, and it wasn't until Sadie replied, 'It is Mags' son who comes to visit me sometimes,' that Mags realised that they were talking about her.

'A son,' Etta said sadly. 'It's a nice thing to have children.' She patted her stomach tenderly. 'Me? Only one girl. I wanted more, but the doctors said I didn't work right inside.' And before Mags could comment she continued. 'A good boy is he, your son?'

'A wonderful boy,' Sadie answered. She placed a large scone on her plate, ignoring the frown from Sammy. 'He helps me with the baking and he's a good, quiet boy. Not like some children today.'

Etta turned towards Sammy. 'A grandchild is what your mother wants,' she said with authority. 'How long are you going to leave it?'

'Until I'm ready,' Sammy replied. He wasn't smiling any more.

'You see,' Etta continued, as though his words had confirmed her own. 'Look at the age of him and no child. Not like in our day, eh?' She shook her head sadly at Sadie, who mirrored the gesture. 'In my day,' Etta added, 'There had to be something wrong with you if you didn't have children.'

Sammy gave a small, exasperated sigh. 'Maybe I'm just getting too old,' he suggested.

'Old?' Etta shrieked the word indignantly. 'Look at him. Not turned forty and now he's old.' She leaned forward, nearly tipping off the sofa, and patted his knee. 'I'll tell you what old is. Old is when you bend down to tie your shoe lace and wonder if that's it. You're going to spend the rest of your life looking at your toes.' With a satisfied smile, she sat back.

Sammy could evidently take no more. Getting to his feet, he announced in a calm, even voice, 'I'm afraid I have a couple of errands to run, so if you'll excuse me ladies.' He glanced towards the door, but his escape was not to be so simple. 'Good, good,' Etta said, also standing up. 'You can walk me to the top of Byres road.

'You have to go so soon?' Sadie said, and Mags detected a faint tinge of relief belying the words. Etta was oblivious. 'Yes. I'll go now,' she insisted. 'It's better not to walk alone these days.' She turned to Mags, her expression grave. 'Even in daylight.' But before she could launch into another morbid recollection, Sammy took hold of her arm and gallantly led her from the room. 'I won't be long, ma,' he called.

With Etta gone, the room seemed suddenly empty, and Mags felt some of her initial unease returning. She sipped her coffee awkwardly, not touching the scone Sadie had slipped on to her plate. Eventually, before the silence numbed her throat entirely, she said awkwardly, 'I suppose you're wondering why I've come.'

Sadie gave a small nod of assent. She was studying Mags with grey, hooded eyes, unblinking, like a bird's. There was no expression in them, and for the life of her, Mags could not see what attracted her son to this woman. That made it harder. If she'd understood, she'd have felt more in control. At last she said in a rush, 'I don't want you getting the wrong idea about me.'

Sadie said nothing, but her eyes narrowed a little, as though she was struggling to understand. But Mags had begun and she couldn't stop now. 'I know what you must be thinking. Seeing a wee boy running around on his own when he should be in school.'

Sadie was wise enough not to deny it, and Mags continued, uninterrupted. 'I know what someone of your …,' she hesitated, glancing around the room. She'd been on the point of saying 'wealth' when it occurred to her that Sadie, like Ewan, probably never considered herself wealthy. 'Someone of your generation thinks of someone like me,' she ended lamely. And when Sadie still didn't respond, she added defensively. 'No-one chooses this sort of life, you know. Single mother isn't normally listed in the top ten career opportunities for women.' She paused, uncertain how to go on, and seeing her defiant, helpless look, Sadie said gently, 'You haven't told me why you came.'

Mags blinked, as though she'd forgotten the reason herself then sighed. 'I want you to understand that I work very hard for my future and that of my son,' she began.

'Daniel is a very sick boy,' Sadie ventured and Mags looked up sharply. 'What did he tell you?'

The hostility in her voice surprised Sadie, and she answered guardedly, 'Only that he has trouble with his heart.'

'He has been ill,' Mags agreed. 'Seriously ill. And we're not out of the woods yet. But he's getting better.'

She hesitated a moment, and in that moment the two women looked into each other's eyes, saw the lie there, the terrible, black mass at the heart of what Mags was saying, and neither of them could face it. Together they looked away, and Mags continued in a small voice. 'I don't want you thinking that he comes here because he lacks anything at home.'

'Mags,' Sadie interrupted and Mags fell silent. 'I think you have a very fine son. And a boy does not grow into a fine son if there is something lacking at home.'

Mags smiled gratefully. 'Thank you.' She stood up, and placed the tea cup carefully back on the tray. 'Daniel thinks a lot of you,' she admitted, and Sadie understood how much that confession had cost. 'I think a great deal of him,' she said.

Mags smiled and they headed towards the front door. On the threshold, Mags stopped. 'I'd like Daniel to be able to visit,' she said a little awkwardly. 'If you'd still like to have him.'

Sadie beamed. 'I would be delighted.'

The door was open but Mags found she had difficulty crossing it. There was something holding her back. Something scrupulous in her make up held her until she had completed her task. Sadie saw her conflict and waited curiously. With an effort, Mags opened her mouth to speak then let her eyes drop to the floor. She studied the pattern of the carpet for several long moments then said all in a rush, 'I'm sorry if I behaved badly at Daniel's party.' She looked pleadingly into Sadie's face. 'You weren't what I was expecting and I … I suppose I overreacted a bit.'

The grey of Sadie's eyes cleared, like a parting mist. 'Not at all, my dear,' she said. 'You did not behave badly. You are just as I was once. Caught between two worlds.'

Chapter 28

'NOT studying?' The voice was contemptuous, mocking, sexy. Mags closed the book with a snap, and looked up into the laughing, curious eyes of the girl with the auburn tangle of hair.

'Audrey,' she said awkwardly. 'I didn't hear you.'

Without waiting to be asked, Audrey bent down and lifted the open book from Mags' lap. 'Paediatric Cardiology?' she said wrinkling her nose. 'Thinking of medicine now?' When Mags didn't answer, she went on, 'Not at all the type of book we thought you read.'

'O?' Mags' face betrayed nothing.

'We had a bet on that it would be terribly esoteric.' Her hands swept into the air and the silver bracelets on her wrists tinkled. 'Something highbrow about freedom and truth and all that.'

'Sorry to disappoint you.'

If Audrey heard the irony in Mags' tone, she showed no sign of it. 'Come and join us.' She pointed vaguely in the direction of the door, and following her gesture, Mags saw the sullen boy and the mouse from her tutorial group sitting languidly over a cup of coffee. They didn't look over, but their turned backs seemed somehow contrived, as though they were deliberately ignoring her. Mags felt something in her stomach churn over and she glanced apprehensively up into Audrey's face. *Were they talking about me? Is that why she came across?*

But Audrey had grown bored. 'Come on. You can't sit by yourself all day.'

Her tone was so authoritative that Mags began putting her book in her bag before she checked herself. *Sit amongst them? To talk about what? Music? Parties? Boyfriends? Waiting until I say something stupid to amuse them.* She put her bag down. 'I can't. I … I've remembered something I have to do.' The words sounded horribly inadequate even to her own ears, and Audrey's dubious expression told her the worst.

'Surely you can spare us some of your time.'

Mags wasn't sure if she was being cajoled or accused. 'No, I—'

But Audrey cut her short. 'We're really not that bad, you know. We're having a bit of a laugh about some book old MacLeod is bringing out. Julie's dad is in the publishing business, and has all the gory details.'

'MacLeod?' Mags' echoed, not quite understanding.

Audrey nodded. 'Something stuffy about the Russian revolution. The word is, that we'll only have to be able to quote from it to pass the degree exam.'

She was so angry that she was speaking before she knew it. 'Dr MacLeod is a brilliant man. Personally, I find his lectures fascinating, and I'm sure any book he might have written will be more important than just a means of passing exams.'

Audrey's eyes were narrowed and her mouth unsmiling, but she gave her simpering laugh. 'Yes. We had a bet that you felt that way.'

'But my family lives in only one room.'

The man with soiled red kerchief and the expensive leather jacket seemed unimpressed. He wasn't much older than Sadie, but his eyes were already cloudy with power. 'But before the revolution your family owned land?'

'A little. My grandfather was a doctor.'

'A doctor? And did he treat any of our brave comrades during the revolution?'

'He treated anyone who was sick.'

The cloudy eyes clearly did not believe her. 'And you say you want this job?'

'I need to work.'

'And you have the necessary qualifications?'

Sadie dared to raise hopeful eyes. 'I can type and I can file and …'

'Are you a member of a Trade Union?'

'No. I haven't had the opportunity …'

'And you are no longer a party member.'

'No.' Sadie's face had become hard and expressionless as marble. 'My social origins were deemed inappropriate.'

'They kicked you out.'

She nodded dully as she had nodded a hundred times before.

'So why should we give you a job?'

'I have no money.'

'So? You think we think we should support you when thousands of deserving proletarians are out of work?'

'I didn't say that.'

'No? And what about your boyfriend? Don't gape, citizen. There is not much that escapes us. Can't he find you something?'

'Comrade Shamilyevich would never abuse his position.'

'Then comrade Shamilyevich has more sense than you.'

A hand touched her shoulder. 'Ma, what are you doing?'

She jumped. 'Sammy, always you have to be sneaking up behind a person?'

'That sounds guilty.'

'What nonsense,' she said guiltily. She waved a hand at the sheet of paper covered in Cyrillic text. 'Something for the archive. That is all.'

Sammy looked pleased. 'But this is great news. I thought you'd given up on it. Will you ask that chap over at the university to do the translation?'

Sadie nodded. 'It is better when I write it in the language I remember it in. I see things how they were.'

'I understand.' He bent down and kissed her cheek. 'I'll leave you to it. I have to pop out. Don't work too hard.'

She waited until he had left the room before she lifted the paper from the table and examined it. There were less than a dozen lines. Disjointed fragments of the scene that had played so lucidly in her head. She stared at the blank spaces between the snarled loops of her handwriting. Is the past trying to hide itself, she wondered.

Daniel's eyes narrowed and he shook his head slowly from side to side. 'No,' he said decisively. 'It looks dirty.'

Mags, resplendent in a cocktail dress of turquoise crepe, her jeans bunched about her calves, opened her mouth to protest then turned back to the dressing cubicle mirror. The light was poor, overlaying everything with the same dingy cast, but even peering through the dimness she could tell he was right. The dress was cheap, the style out of date. She remembered the words of an acquaintance who had worked for a large clothing chain; *if people would pay money for it, it wouldn't be on the sale rack.* But put another way, who would go to the sale rack if they had money to spend?

She looked down at her previous attempts, now lying crumpled on the cubicle floor, too tight, too large, too garish, too cheap. Nothing was right for the woman who was to stand next to Dr Ewan MacLeod. She saw her reflection blink and turn cringingly away as she thought of the stares, the whispers behind hands, the nudges in the ribs. *Not quite his type. No, not at all. Not what we expected.*

'I'll get dressed,' she said gloomily and swept the cubicle curtain across the rail. From behind it, Daniel said, 'We could try another shop.' But what was the point? The last shop had been the same and the one before that. And what if she found the perfect dress in her limited budget? She had no accessories, no jewellery, nothing to distract the eye from the plain, hard woman at the centre. Like a lump of coal set in a cluster of diamonds, she thought bitterly.

As she began to pick up the discarded dresses and haul them roughly on to their hangers, she took the decision not to attend the party. I'll tell him I can't get a sitter for Daniel. Why not? It's happened before. But it sounded so lame. I'll tell him Daniel's ill, she decided. But she couldn't do that. Not gamble with Daniel's health. Not even in falsehood. Mags pulled the last dress over its hanger. Rationalist or no, it didn't do to tempt the fates.

With a swift, jerky motion, she pulled back the curtain, her ready smile painted on her lips. Daniel had found a couple of buttons and was playing a sort of solitary tiddlywinks in the middle of the floor. He looked up when he heard the sound of the curtain, but didn't return her smile, and she noticed, with alarm, how pale he was. *Bad mother. Indulging herself at the expense of her child. Doesn't deserve a healthy child.*

Mag's face grew paler while her grin grew wider. 'How about tea and cakes at *The Jenny*?'

Daniel stared at her in surprise. 'What about your dress?' he asked uncertainly, but there was an unmistakable glint of hope behind the concern.

Mags shrugged. 'I don't like anything here. We can look another day.'

'All right.' His agreement came readily, but he got to his feet slowly, a little, old man in a child's body.

'Come on then,' Mags said, holding the door open. She was still grinning, her mouth a gaudy slash distorting her face.

It was raining when they got outside, a soft grey mizzle too light to be felt, yet heavy enough to leave their clothes hanging in damp folds and their hair plastered against their scalps. They walked, heads down, blinking the spray from their eyes, their mouths firmly shut against the dank air. Mags was thinking about Sergei's story again. What does it take for one person to let go of all they believe to give another person their freedom? Ewan has to understand that this is what his whole book is about. He's too close to it now. He can't see it. But then, and she gave a little shudder of pleasure, wasn't that her role? It was to her he'd turned with the manuscript. He wanted more from her than just a decorative wife, who knew which forks to put out. He wanted someone to challenge him mentally. And perhaps the manuscript was his challenge to her. Mags smiled into the rain. He'd find her ready.

When the stranger bumped into her, she shouldered her way past him, barely mumbling an apology.

'Mags?'

They froze, turning narrowed, suspicious eyes towards him. 'Sammy.' The pleasure in Daniel's voice was unmistakable, though his voice was little more than a hoarse wheeze. Mags saw a frown darken Samuel Gordon's face for a moment, as though he too heard the unnatural breathlessness, and she opened her mouth to distract him. But, before she could speak, a wide smile replaced his frown, warm and welcoming, and she was grateful for the shelter of it.

'Where are you going?' he asked.

'For tea and cakes,' Daniel explained. He pointed up the paved street. 'At *The Jenny.*'

'O.' Sammy's frown returned. 'You can't. I've just passed it, and everyone's standing outside. Fire alarm I think.'

Daniel's face fell. And suddenly the spark seemed to go out of him. Mags watched with mounting horror as he took on the aspect of an old man once more, his head drooping, his shoulders hunched. Sammy saw it too, and he bent towards him. 'It's lucky our meeting like this.'

Daniel's eyes were doubtful. 'Why?'

'Why?' Sammy feigned astonishment at the question. 'Because I want you to see my dinosaur book so I could prove Giganotosaurus was the biggest monster that ever roamed the earth.'

'You mean go back to your house?' Daniel asked.

'O, I don't think that's a good idea,' Mags began. But Daniel had already moved closer to Sammy and they had turned in the direction of the taxi rank. 'Come on, mum,' Daniel threw over his shoulder as they began to walk away, and Mags, suddenly feeling like the forgotten playmate, had to hurry to catch up with them.

They had to wait a long time for a taxi, the queue snaked back around the corner of Central station, a cold, damp crowd of disgruntled shoppers, driven home by the rain. As Mags and the others drew closer to the dwindling line of black cabs the queue grew unruly, spilling out on to the road, making it hard to tell who was in front and who was behind.

They inched forward and Mags noted that Sammy didn't cringe against the rain like the rest of them, but stood tall, watching the movements of the crowd, like a commander surveying an opposing rabble. He didn't speak and she felt the need to fill the silence. 'Is it as bad as this in America?' she asked.

He seemed surprised by the sound of her voice and bent towards her. 'What did you say?'

'I asked if getting a taxi was as bad as this in the US.' She felt suddenly a little foolish. Her question seemed so trite. But he laughed and shook his head. 'No, it's worse.' His smile broadened. 'And at least they don't shoot you here.'

A taxi drew away and the crowd surged forward. An old woman, no taller than a child pushed past, her umbrella catching Mags just below the eye. For a terrible moment, she was blinded and lost in the swirling, chaos of the crowd.

She felt the ground tilting up beneath her and called out in panic, 'Daniel!' He was too small. He'll be swept away. But a strong arm took her by the shoulders and held her upright, and Sammy's voice sounded close against her ear. 'It's all right. I have him.'

She blinked, fighting to see again, and made out a shivering image of Daniel clinging to Sammy's arm. There was the sound of a moving engine and the crowd roared forward again. Sammy didn't let either of them go, but steered them purposefully forward and into the open door of the last standing cab. As he leaned over to the glass partition to give their destination, Mags suddenly realised that his arm was no longer around her. She felt strangely aware of its absence, as though something that belonged to her had been taken away.

Sadie's face was a mirror of Daniel's when she opened the door to find them standing dripping on the front step. She returned Daniel's hug without even noticing the wet patch it made on her dress. Despite herself, Mags felt her expression darken and she turned away to hide it. In doing so, she saw Sammy watching her thoughtfully. He didn't comment as she expected him to, but turned to Sadie. 'Put the boy down for heaven's sake, ma. You'll squeeze the life out of him.'

Sadie let Daniel go a little guiltily. 'Why, you are soaked through,' she exclaimed, as though realising it for the first time. 'You can't stand in wet clothes. That is how you catch your death.' She turned to Sammy, as though she held him personally responsible. 'What do you stand there for? Take their coats. Fetch towels. I will put on the kettle.'

Ten minutes later they sat around the big oak table in the kitchen, each holding a steaming mug of tea. Daniel had been disappointed to discover that there were no cakes, but was quickly mollified by a large selection box of biscuits provided by Etta on her last visit. As he reached for his third one, Mags gave a warning glance and his hand stopped mid-air. He turned pleading eyes towards Sadie. Mags' warning glance grew more dangerous, but Sadie said mildly. 'It is such a joy to see a little boy with a healthy appetite.' And Mags suddenly slumped in her seat and waved a hand at the biscuit tin. Overjoyed, Daniel reached in and took two just to be on the safe side.

'It was a lucky coincidence that I bumped into Mags and Daniel while I was in town,' Sammy said, evidently feeling the need to distract Mags from the marshmallow carnage taking place across the table.

'Yes. We were going for tea and cake,' Mags explained. 'But the tea-room was closed.'

'No, we didn't,' Daniel said through a mouthful of crumbs. 'We were going to get mum a new dress.' He either didn't see the warning look this time or chose to ignore it. Swallowing the last mouthful of biscuit regretfully, he added. 'But all the dresses we could afford were clatty.'

'Daniel!' This was too much for Mags. 'They were not *clatty*.' She fought to find a more appropriate adjective. 'They were … they were …' She looked round helplessly then a slow smile formed on her lips and she dropped her head self-consciously. 'I suppose they were clatty.'

'The dress, it is for a formal occasion?' Sadie asked, interested.

'Yes.' Mags didn't look up. 'For a party.'

'Ah,' Sadie nodded sympathetically. 'Finding something suitable is always a problem.'

Sammy raised his eyebrows. 'Ma, you have more dresses than wardrobe space.'

'Yes, yes.' Sadie dismissed this comment with a wave of her hand. 'But Mags is young. I am talking of when I was young. In Russia, there was never enough of anything. And clothing was one of the hardest things to find.'

'Uh oh,' Sammy said, getting to his feet. 'This sounds like girl talk to me.' He beckoned to Daniel. 'Let's go see these dinosaurs.' He held the door open. 'Come on. I'll show you my room. It hasn't been changed since I was eleven years old.'

Daniel jumped down from his chair and ran to join him. Sadie waited until the door was shut before commenting to Mags. 'He is the one that hasn't changed since he was eleven years old.'

But Mags appreciated the way Sadie could talk to her son without talking down to him. It was a trait she wished Ewan had. For a wild moment, she considered the possibility of introducing the two men. They were both lively, intelligent individuals, and Ewan could learn a lot about relating to Daniel from Sammy's easy manner. That would be necessary when they were finally together as a family. But no, it probably wasn't a good idea, and she put the thought from her mind.

For a while they sat in silence, and Mags, feeling she should break the ice, finally said, 'You're English is very good.'

Sadie's mouth broadened into a wide smile. 'That is because it is my first language.' Then she laughed aloud at Mags' incredulity. 'You did not think I am a Glasgow woman by birth.'

Mags shook her head. 'You sound … you sound …' She broke off, unable to think of a way to avoid hurting the old lady.

'So bad?' Sadie finished for her. She sobered somewhat and her expression darkened. 'I left Glasgow to go to Russia as a little girl. After my father died.'

'Why Russia?'

'My mother was Russian. She had no family here. And after my father was dead, no money. It was a sensible thing it seemed, to go back.'

Mags raised an eyebrow. 'But you didn't think so?'

Sadie considered the question for a few moments then shook her head. 'No. I did not really ever fit in.'

Mags looked wistfully down into the dregs of her tea. 'It's strange. They say that the young can adapt to anything.'

'Perhaps,' Sadie agreed. 'But perhaps it is not always the thing that adults expect them to adapt to.'

Intrigued, Mags was on the point of asking another question, when Daniel came bursting into the room. 'Mum,' he yelled. 'Look at this. Giganotosaurus was the biggest dinosaur ever. It says so here.' He thrust a glossy book into her hands. 'It could eat whole velociraptor with just one snap of its jaws.' He snatched the book out of Mags' hands and headed for the door again. 'I have to go back up. Sammy says he has a book about prehistoric penguins, and one was bigger than I am.' He hesitated, considering his last statement. 'But I don't really believe him. Besides,' he added carelessly, 'I don't suppose a penguin could really eat anyone, no matter how big he was.'

Mags smiled, shaking her head after his retreating back, and Sadie noticed how different she looked when she smiled at her son, the hard lines in her face softened and her eyes seemed to light up. The mysterious luminescence of motherhood.

'Little boys are so morbid,' Mags remarked, and suddenly feeling relaxed helped herself to a bourbon cream. Sadie set down her tea, and avoiding Mags' eye, said carefully. 'Daniel seems particularly occupied with thoughts of death.' The smile left Mags' lips, but she hurried on. 'I have often heard him talk of it during our conversations.'

Mags was watching her, a hunted, suspicious expression holding the muscles in her face rigid. Sadie saw the expression and it frightened her, but she kept going. 'I thought perhaps his illness bothers him.'

A nerve danced in hollow of Mags' cheek and Sadie was certain that she had gone too far, but Mags suddenly nodded and her shoulders slumped forward. She looked smaller then, worn down. 'He's had a hard time,' she said slowly then turned sharply towards Sadie. 'Has he ever told you about his stay in hospital?'

Sadie shook her head and Mags nodded grimly, as though it was no more than she expected. 'He never talks about it directly. But Daniel was born with a serious defect in his heart.' For a moment, she covered her eyes with her hands, as though, she too, found it too hard to talk about, but then she gave a little shiver, as though mentally shaking herself and continued. 'It was a hard time. I was just a young girl. No experience. No sense. And they told me my baby wasn't going to live. Daniel's father couldn't hack it. He ran away.'

Something bitter twisted the corner of Mags' mouth. 'Fathers can do that.'

Sadie made no comment, but her eyes grew dark with understanding. And, encouraged, Mags continued. 'He had his first operation as a baby. A temporary thing they said. Until he was older and could survive a more complicated procedure.'

'But this is not the operation of which you were speaking,' Sadie said.

'No.' Mags shuddered suddenly and pulled her shirt tighter around her body. 'No that came later. He'd just turned four.' She was looking over at Sadie, but her eyes were smeared with memory. Shaking her head, she tried to dislodge the images, but her lips went on describing what she saw. 'He was so wee. A tiny wee thing holding my hand as we went up to the ward. So trusting, even though I'd tried to tell him what was going to happen.' She looked over pleadingly at Sadie. 'When they took him away he waved to me. And I waved back. Then the nurses took me aside and told me there was always hope. They told me there was hope and all the time I knew the lying bitches didn't believe a word of it.'

Sadie saw Mags' right hand begin to scratch at the wrist of the left. 'But Daniel proved them wrong.'

'Yes.' Mags' head came up defiantly. 'We showed them. For all their medical knowledge and their theories. We showed them.'

Sadie's eyes, never leaving Mags' face, saw how her jaw had locked and her brows drawn down over eyes glassy with tears. 'Mags,' she began carefully. 'If you don't want to talk of this.' But Mags shook her head. 'I've started so I'll finish.' And Sadie, not understanding the reference, nodded her on.

'It took him a long time to recover. A tiny child doesn't get over an operation like that in one go.' She smiled suddenly. 'But he was so strong. You wouldn't have believed it.' She ran a finger under one eye, as though surprised to find it was wet. 'I learned a lot about determination from that wee boy. And he was brave.' Her smile deepened. 'Everyone loved Danny. Complete strangers used to abandon their own patients just to come and talk to him. Can you believe it?'

Sadie nodded to show that it was incredible.

'Everyone loved Danny,' Mags went on, and the smile faded. 'But Danny only loved the big boy in the bed next to him.' She gave a mirthless laugh. 'Big boy. He was ten. Rory was his name. He went up for his operation the week before Daniel. His mother got the same speech as me. Only ...' She stopped scratching her wrist and laid her hands flat on the table. 'Only they were right about him. Complications set in and he had to go back and that time he didn't come back.' Mags stopped speaking and stared at the table.

'Daniel must have taken that very hard,' Sadie said softly.

'He didn't even know what to die was he was so wee,' Mags said, and it was obvious that the words pained her. 'But the other children told him. Told him Rory was dead. Gone to heaven. And he kept asking me if he was going to go. And he seemed so ill, so fragile. And I was afraid that something would happen and he would be scared, so I told him. I made him understand. Because … because …' Words failing her, her eyes turned back on Sadie. 'Because I thought it was the only way to protect him. And I didn't know that when he came out, he'd never give up asking me about heaven and dying and what was involved. And I couldn't go back on what I'd said, could I?' Mags' head slumped forward on to her balled fists and she sat there, a statue of melting snow, weeping for its own demise.

'Mags,' said Sadie carefully. 'There is something I must tell you.'

Mags slowly raised her head, her eyes masked and unreadable, and Sadie's heart began to pound. My God, she knows. She's always known. Her mouth felt dry and she reached for her teacup only to find it empty. 'Mags,' she began, her voice dry and papery. 'I …'

But the door flew open and Sammy was standing there, his face pale and tense. 'Mags, it's Daniel. He's unwell.'

Mags was out of her seat and across the room before Sadie could replace her teacup on the saucer. 'Wait,' she called. 'I will come too.' But the others were already heading up the stairs. Forcing her stiff limbs across the floor, she tried to hurry after them. But it was no use. She was an old puppet, rusted joints and decaying bones. And by the time she reached Sammy's room, they had been there at least a minute ahead of her. She heard Mags saying, 'No. Not as bad as it looks. But still I'd better get him home.'

And Sammy saying. 'You're sure you don't need a doctor. I can call one in a minute.'

'No. Just call me a taxi. He needs rest. My fault for dragging him round town like that.'

She heaved herself in the door, and stood there, panting, her eyes, the only mobile part of her, searching out Daniel. He was lying on Sammy's bed. Such a tiny figure. The familiar bluish tinge around his lips and nose. He seemed to sense her presence and opened his eyes to smile at her wanly. 'Daniel?' She thought her heart would burst. 'You are all right now?'

He nodded weakly and held out a hand, so small and so frail and yet it drew her towards him as surely as steel cables tied about her waist. She sat down on the bed's edge, oblivious to the ache in her unsupported spine and took his hand in hers. It fluttered slightly then was still, the damp fingers reaching into her gnarled flesh.

Mags was standing at the bottom of the bed, watching them her face covetous and pained. Sadie saw her look and hastened, 'Mags, please sit down here.'

'No.' Mags' voice was stony. 'I need to call a taxi. Better if I get him home quick.' She reached out and tweaked Daniel's foot. He didn't respond.

'Let me show you where the phone is,' Sammy offered. 'I think there are some taxi numbers on the table next to it.'

Mags gave a curt, unsmiling nod and followed him from the room. At the door, she hesitated, and looking at Daniel, said lightly. 'Don't go to sleep now. I don't want to have to carry you downstairs.'

He blinked slowly and rewarded her with a faint upcurl of his lips.

Their footsteps quickly receded on the soft carpet and for several minutes there was no sound in the room save for the ragged, shallow breaths that Daniel tore from the air. Sadie closed her eyes and found that her voice was louder in her head than it was in her throat, and that it was calling out into the void in a way it hadn't done in many, many years. Perhaps she was praying, she wasn't sure, but she was calling to God to change the way things were destined to be, and knowing that she had to keep calling louder and louder to drown out the certainty that nothing would change.

'Sadie.'

She opened her eyes and Daniel was looking up at her, his bruised eyelids already drooping with the weight of keeping awake.

'Don't talk, Daniel,' she chided him. 'Rest now. We can talk later.'

But he shook his head, or at least the curls on his forehead trembled a little in negation. 'No, Sadie.'

His voice was very weak and she had to lean very close to his mouth to hear him. 'We have to think of a new plan.'

She blinked. 'Plan?'

'Yes.' He frowned at her, a child's frown at the disingenuousness of adults. 'You haven't forgotten your promise.'

If only she could. 'No, Daniel,' she said contritely. 'I haven't forgotten.'

He sighed and coughed a little, distracting her for a blissful moment from what he was about to say. When he did speak, his voice was so low that she almost heard nothing above the rattle in his chest. She strained and did not make out his words. 'Why must we have a new plan, Daniel?'

He sighed again and this time his eyelids fluttered against the last vestiges of wakefulness then gave up the fight altogether and closed against firmly against consciousness. But his lips were still moving, and she felt him brush her cheek with words that scored her flesh and pierced her heart.

'There isn't much time left.'

Chapter 29

THERE was a dry crispness in the air as Mags hurried through the park gates, a chill of winter crackling the pathways and frosting the leaves. It made Mags shiver and pull the cheap scarf, purchased from a charity shop, tighter around her neck. She dragged the long ends down below her denim jacket, before forcing her hands deep into the ripped lining of the pockets. But it was a bright chill, crisp and full of promise, and it covered the skeletal trees in a lustrous sheath of white that made them seem less bleak and even a little cheering.

She chose the route through the park because Daniel had told her it was quicker. But it was also for the chance to be alone with her thoughts and for the sheer freedom of walking through a cold, empty place with no sense of fear at her back and purpose resounding in her footsteps.

Crushed in her ancient holdall, a small bunch of winter violets were sheltering from the cold. She'd paid for them with the last of the money set aside for her dress. The rest had gone on the taxi to spirit Daniel back to the safe haven of his home.

Sammy had come with them, insisted on paying, but she wouldn't let him. And after seeing the fierce, protective fire in her eyes, he had acquiesced with only a rudimentary fight. He'd carried Daniel, still fast asleep, upstairs to the gloomy little flat they called home. And once Mags had opened the door and let the damp smell waft over them, had felt it cling clammy to her skin and seen Sammy's dark glance about the room, only then did it seem less of the haven than she'd thought. She led Sammy through to Daniel's bedroom, making no protest when he switched on the electric convector, glad only that Daniel was not awake to protest that they never put it on. And when Daniel was tucked up in bed, and she expected an awkward silence to fall between them, she found that he was gone. He called to her from the lounge. 'What do you take in your coffee?'

She followed the sound of his voice incredulously. 'Why do you think I want a coffee?'

He had turned at the sound of her voice, coffee jar poised in one hand. 'You haven't any tea.'

Then she'd smiled, the first real, genuine smile in a long time, a smile so broad and so fragile that it threatened to crack under the weight of what it

193

hid. She watched silently while he spooned the last granules out of the jar into two mismatched cups, impressed and disconcerted that he returned the empty jar to the cupboard rather than consigning it to the bin.

He made no comment, gave no meaningful glances, but something in the very richness of his presence seemed to suggest that he found her home distasteful, a shabby excuse of a place to bring up a child. And yet she felt no sense of judgement from him. She was confused and bewildered by him, desirous to be resentful and yet curious to know what he thought. Instinctively, she reached towards her handbag, intending to take out a cigarette, then changed her mind. He didn't smoke. At least she had never seen him smoke. Why should it matter? This is my home. Not his. Unreasonably, she felt angry towards him. But she left the cigarettes, untouched, in her bag.

He joined her on the sofa, carefully avoiding the dip in the centre of the cushion and handed her a steaming mug. 'Not too strong. I guess we have enough adrenalin pumping through us right now.'

'Yes.' Then because she felt she had to say something she began to say, 'I'm very grateful for everything …'

But he shook his head, his eyes so suddenly stern that she fell silent before them. I've offended him, she thought in panic. Why do I only find it easy to speak when I should stay silent? She looked at him helplessly, but he was speaking now, very gently. 'Mags, you should never be grateful for something you have a right to expect.'

'But I haven't any right …' she began then fell silent again, seeing that what he said was true and that, once again, she was using gratitude as a barrier that relieved her from the intimacy of her debt. They fell into mutual silence that was on the point of becoming awkward when he said suddenly, 'I believe you go to my old *alma mater.*'

'Your what?' He'd taken her by surprise.

'My old university. Glasgow.'

'O. Yes. That's right. I'm only in my first year though. I did an entry course last year never thinking I'd make the grade. But one of my tutors, Ewan. Ewan MacLeod. Dr MacLeod, he thought I was ready to go the whole hog.' She was talking too much again, little irrelevancies to fill the air.

'What are you studying?'

Mags almost smiled with relief at the blandness of the question. 'Politics. The history of politics.' She smiled shyly into her coffee. 'My main interest is the Russian revolution at the moment. So I'd be particularly fascinated to hear your mother's story.'

'I think she'd be equally fascinated to hear yours.'

'Mine?' She felt the muscles in her face stiffen. Is he laughing at me?

'I don't think there's anything about me your mother would find very interesting.'

'On the contrary.' He was smiling. 'My mother admires your courage. It must be very hard to cope with a full-time education and such a … ' He paused, and for a furious moment she was certain he was going to say, sick child. Single mother. Sickly child. Did she embarrass him with the cliché of her circumstances? She took a violent sip of her coffee, challenging him with the full force of her glare. But Sammy seemed not to notice. 'Such a bright, little boy,' he finished. 'I expect he makes a lot of demands of you.'

She turned away then, not sure what to say. 'He's very smart,' she admitted gruffly. 'Smarter than I was at his age. He'll go far.' And because her eyes were downcast, she didn't see the doubtful flicker that narrowed his eyes. 'Daniel seems very proud of you,' he said cautiously.

Then Mags' head came up and she laughed. And, braving a glance back in his direction, she saw that his eyes, black as the coffee, were still fixed upon her, open and unwavering as a child's. 'He'll be a lot prouder of me when I can afford to buy him trainers with the right kind of name on them.'

'Is that what you're doing it for. To be able to buy better things for him?'

'No.' It was her turn to look doubtful. 'I do want those things, nice clothes, money in the bank. But it's something more.' She coloured, but kept her eyes fixed upon him. 'I want what you have.'

He frowned. 'What I have?'

'Yes.' She gave an embarrassed, little shrug. 'Not just the big house and the antiques and everything. Something more. Something special.'

He was still frowning, but she didn't feel afraid of his frown. 'You've got the confidence,' she began, then shaking her head, started again. 'You've got the freedom to enjoy these things. You take beautiful things for granted, as if they were your right.'

Sammy's frown had deepened. 'Why should it be different for you?'

'Because,' Mags struggled to put into words thoughts she had never dared express before. 'Because I come from another world. It's hard for me to explain. I come from a good, salt-of-the-earth working class family. We don't ask for much. We certainly don't expect it. And we're very, very suspicious of anyone who's got it.'

'But surely your family wants you to get ahead. Your brother. Hasn't he got a good job?'

Mags' expression darkened. 'Yes. Gary has a good job. But he's never forgotten his roots. Never got above himself.'

'And is that what you want? To forget your roots?'

'No.' She was looking at him without really seeing him. 'Not to forget them. But not to be dragged down by them either. You see to me there are two Glasgows. I see them as though they were superimposed on each other. There's my world where all men are equal and stamped with the same mould. And God help the one who doesn't want their equality. And there's yours. I'm not blind to its flaws. It's harsh and bitter and beautiful. It's dog eat dog and its brutal. But there's a chance. Just a little one that lets a person be who they are without caring about who they've been.' She focused back on Sammy, her eyes wide and unblinking as a child's. 'I want what you have. I want a better life.'

For a moment, she looked like a different person. The lines around her mouth were not so harsh and her eyes were wide and soft, but then she looked up and she saw where the damp had made an ugly stain on the wallpaper, causing it to curl away from the top of the wall, and she dropped her head, suddenly defeated by the weight of it all. 'You probably think I'm very stupid or self-centred,' she said in a small voice.

But he reached out and took her hand, drawing her eyes towards him as effectively as though he'd taken hold of her chin. 'I think neither, Mags,' he said softly. 'I think you're a very remarkable woman.' He smiled, half sad, half teasing. 'You have a very rare quality. A sense of vision.'

'Don't take me too seriously,' she shrugged. 'I don't know what I'm saying half the time.'

He shook his head, negating her words with a simple gesture. 'I don't believe that. I think you're serious almost all of the time.'

Not knowing what to say, she gave a half shrug, half shudder of embarrassment, aware that her burning cheeks were answering for her. 'I suppose I'm afraid I sound daft,' she said at last.

'Why?' He sounded genuinely surprised. 'Is it daft to want a better life. That's the principle my mother nearly died for.'

'Sadie?' She hadn't meant to sound so incredulous, but Sadie, in her beautiful house filled with antiques and sepia memories, seemed so self-contained that she couldn't imagine her in any struggle for a different life.

Sammy took a sip of his coffee then grimaced. 'It's gone cold,' he explained. 'I talk too much.' And for a moment Mags thought he would evade the subject and move on to some more bland topic. Ask for more coffee. She hoped he hadn't forgotten that the jar was now empty. But he was studying her carefully, openly, as though trying to come to a decision then he said, 'I know what you're thinking. Nice Jewish boy thinks the world of his mama, but I'm quite serious.' He looked across the room into the middle distance seeing things that were beyond her. 'I understand how you see her, how Daniel sees her. An old lady in the twilight of her life, a funny-sounding voice, eccentric ways.'

Mags opened her mouth to protest, and though he didn't turn to face her, he held up a hand, sensing her objection and silencing it in one gesture.

'The way people see my mother is not the way she is, not really, not the woman inside.' He stole a sly look at her. 'And, from what you say, I think you'll understand that. I think you have a lot in common with my mother.' He turned towards her, his eyes spotlights focusing on her and she had to force herself not to stare down into the dark depths of her coffee because they were easier to bear. 'My mother believed so strongly that we each had a right to live our lives as we choose not as we are forced to, that she nearly died for it.' He spoke softly, almost blandly, as though the emotional charge of his words was too great to allow him to speak them in any other way but simply. 'I know I have hardly known you, Mags, but I feel …' He spread his hands to indicate that this was not a sufficient explanation. 'I sense that you are a person that could gain a great deal out of knowing my mother.'

'O.' Mags lips formed the word, but no sound escaped. And for a moment she was thrown into confusion. Had she thought he would sense something else? Had she wanted him to? But he was speaking, urgently. 'My mother is becoming very frail. Since I've come home I've noticed a great change in her.' A shadow passed over his face, a spectre of his own mortality perhaps. 'Frankly, I don't think she has much time left.'

'But surely—'

The corners of his lips drooped down in a mirthless, phantasm of a smile that silenced her more effectively than words. 'I'm not being dramatic or even overly morbid.' Then he gave her a queer look and added, 'Death isn't such a secret, you can see it on a person if you know where to look.'

She was on her feet before she knew it, cup in hand, snatching up his and heading for the kitchen. 'I should rinse these out,' she threw irrelevantly over her shoulder. 'I hate the way you can't get rid of coffee stains if you leave them too long.'

Now Sammy was on his feet. 'I should be going.'

She knew she should make some protest *O, must you* but she wanted him away. 'I'll show you out.'

She all but ran to the door, her fingers scrabbling clumsily, desperately against the locks. In the face of his kindness, her haste was inexcusable, indecent, but she couldn't help it. He'd touched a nerve and she felt his curiosity probe for its root. He made no comment about her sudden change, nor did he seem to notice the agony in which she waited as he put on his coat and buttoned it. But once at the door, he hesitated, and asked, almost humbly, 'You will come to see my mother, won't you? I think it would mean a great deal to her.'

'Of course.' She smiled a wide, bright smile of falsehood.

He took a step, placing him half outside the door, half still in, and she had to steel herself against slamming the door against him. But he turned and she felt him appraise her desperate expression.

'Mags, let me ask you one more thing.'

'Of course.' Her smile was no longer bright.

'Is Daniel a very great part of your plan for a better life?'

And when she gasped and could not answer, managing only stare up at him, hopeless and exposed, his eyes widened slowly in understanding, and without speaking, he turned away.

Her resolution had held all through the night. And even when Daniel felt better the next day and she no longer had to worry about him, her intentions did not waver. Not until, waking in the crisp, grey light of Monday did Sadie's words come back to her, resoundingly clear, as though spoken into the silence *You are just as I was once. Caught between two worlds.* And then she'd known what she had to do.

There was something strangely intimate about knocking on the back door instead of going around to the front, but Daniel had assured her it was the way Sadie usually entered, and it made her feel less conspicuous to be hidden on all sides by the high garden wall.

'Mags. What a wonderful surprise.' The delight on Sadie's face was so genuine that Mags blushed with guilt at her motives. And, unable to mutter more than a gruff, *hello*, she dug about in her bag then proffered the drooping violets by way of greeting.

'These you brought for me.' Sadie took them with all the pleasure of a child receiving a much-wanted birthday gift. 'Come. Sit down.' She ushered Mags over to the kitchen table. 'I will find a vase. But tell me first how is Daniel?'

'He's fine.' Mags felt her news would be better received than the present. 'He gets these fits from time to time. They're not as bad as they look. You mustn't worry.' To her surprise, Sadie frowned and seemed to be about to argue, then recovering herself, said only, 'That is good news. An answer to our prayers. Now, wait a moment while I find a suitable vase.'

As she rummaged in the cupboards, Mags noticed, to her chagrin, a large bouquet of roses, presumably from Sammy, standing on the dresser. They made her offering seem horribly inadequate, but Sadie fussed over them, as though they were the very flowers she had longed to receive. She put them in a tiny, crystal vase, which she placed in the centre of the table. 'Beautiful,' she said, standing back to admire them. 'A wonderful thing to have flowers in the middle of winter.'

'I suppose our winters almost don't exist next to the ones you had in Russia,' Mags said, seizing her chance clumsily.

Sadie looked a little surprised then nodded. 'It's true. We had some terrible winters there. They are Russia's blessing and her curse.'

'Blessings?'

'Yes.' Sadie nodded absently. 'It is hard for an invader to stand a Russian winter, no?'

Mags nodded. 'And were they a blessing to you?' As soon as she'd asked, Mags regretted it. Sadie's face closed over, her eyes shuttered, her lips sealed. But not before Mags had glimpsed the pain that was hidden there, a raw, aching pain that breathed, like a living thing. It shocked her. I can't do this, she thought. I shouldn't have come. But the question had been asked and couldn't be unasked, and Sadie felt obliged to answer. 'It was a curse for me,' she said simply. 'In winter the body does not fight disease so well. The cold weakens it. It was in winter I lost my mother. She was not a strong woman. They took her away and I never saw her again.' She paused, closing her eyes against the pressure of the memories. 'And it was also in winter I lost other things.'

'I'm sorry,' Mags stuttered uselessly. 'I should never have asked.'

Sadie opened her eyes, as though surprised to find her still there. 'No. You must ask. When questions are no longer asked, we learn to forget.'

'Is it always good to remember?' Mags asked.

And suddenly Sadie knew why she had come. She smiled, a wide, weary, drooping smile of understanding and turned towards the sink. 'Let me fix a pot of tea.'

Mags watched as she shuffled across the tile floor, her head nodding a little to itself, as though answering unspoken questions from the air. She is frail, she thought. Sammy's right. She doesn't have long. And suddenly it seemed vitally important to gain an understanding of this woman, of whom she knew nothing, except that her son loved her. While there was still time. She opened her mouth to ask another question, to lead into the subject more gently, but Sadie was already speaking. 'If when you ask, is it always good to remember, you mean is it always a pleasant thing to remember, then no, it is not.' She switched on the kettle and opened the tea caddy. 'But if you are asking, is it an evil thing to forget the lives of individuals who have lived and suffered by you, to make them no more than the dust we walk on, then yes, to remember is the one good thing we can do.'

All the time she had spoken, her back had been to Mags, her hands clutching the edge of the countertop, her shoulders hunching as the burden of explanation weighed heavily upon her. Then, slowly she turned to Mags, the spoon from the caddy still in her hand. 'We are our past,' she said softly. 'Our future is only a thing of dreams. A very great man told me that once. And he told me that remembering the painful and the terrible is what makes us what we truly are, what makes us human.'

She paused, and not knowing what to say, Mags lowered her head to stare at the tablecloth. A row of embroidered daisies danced blindly along the hem, and without meaning to, Mags put out a finger and began to trace one. Sadie studied the woman's drooped posture and seemed to understand. 'Forgive me. You come to visit me and I give you a lecture.' She brought two cups over to the table and set them down. 'Perhaps you know now why I have so few visitors.'

On the point of politely protesting, Mags glanced up and saw the irony in the old eyes. She gave an embarrassed smile. 'I think you're maybe giving me what I asked for.'

Sadie beamed. 'You are a clever girl. I said that to my Sammy.' She reached out and patted one of Mags hands. 'Do not be harsh with yourself. None of us like to keep alive what hurts. I think of my mother all the time and yet I find it hard to talk of her She looked towards the window, and Mags understood that it was not the grey sky of today she was seeing. 'Ach, even now, I find it hard.' She wiped the corner of her eye with the back of her hand, a child's gesture to wash away the past. 'You know, that is when I lost all my English. I knew they had taken her for having lived abroad. And somehow, in my mind, I thought it was because she spoke English.' She gave a slight, bemused shake of her head. 'After that day, I would not speak it for a very long time. And it never came back to me. Not properly.' Her voice changed, a forced conversational tone intended to distract. 'Sammy has been making me put everything down in an archive.'

'It must be fascinating,' Mags said, her interest piqued.

Sadie shrugged. 'This I am not so sure about. To Sammy tragedy is romantic.' She nodded confidentially towards Mags, mother to mother. 'But he's young. What does he know?'

Mags had a ridiculous, overwhelming urge to laugh just for the sheer relief of it, but, instead, she nodded and drew a connecting finger between the embroidered daisies.

She wondered how to ask Sadie more about her life. Would she let her peep inside the archive? But before she had a chance, Sadie slapped the table with the palm of her hand and got to her feet. 'What am I thinking of. I am forgetting why I asked you here.'

Mags stared at her in astonishment. Was Sadie confusing intention with coincidence? Sammy had described her manner as eccentric, but Mags had never actually witnessed it before. It threw her off balance and made her uneasy. She glanced at the door. Perhaps she should leave. As though in answer to her prayers, the door swung open and Sammy entered. His cheeks were red with the cold and he was blowing on his gloveless hands with all the fury of a young scout trying to start a fire. He grinned when he saw Mags, perhaps a little smugly she felt. She had told him too much. And she returned his, hello, with a cool nod.

'Sammy, shut the door before Mags catches her death,' Sadie admonished him. She turned to Mags again. 'Such weather to be letting into the house.'

'How's Daniel?'

'Daniel is fine.' Sadie spared her the necessity of an ungracious answer.

'That's good news.' Sammy was unbuttoning his coat and he bent down to kiss his mother on the cheek. And feeling she was intruding, Mags looked away.

'Have you told her about the dress?' Sammy asked.

Mags stared. 'What dress? I didn't come about a dress.' She had the vertiginous feeling of entering Wonderland where people knew in advance that she was arriving and garments appeared before her marked *wear me*. Sammy's grin widened at her distress and he was on the point of answering when the phone rang. 'I'll get it,' he said springing up and bounding from the room. Mags' eyes followed him, thinking how like a little boy he could be, and understanding how Sadie had never really thought of him as any bigger than Daniel. She wondered if she would be the same when Daniel grew up.

'I am sorry Mags,' Sadie was saying. 'You must think Sammy and I quite mad.'

'No. Not at all,' Mags protested unconvincingly. But Sadie held up a hand. 'It was after you left. I was so worried about Daniel I was not really thinking about anything at all.'

For some reason this confession irked Mags and she was hard pressed to keep the smile from leaving her face. Appearing not to notice, Sadie went on. 'Anyway, I got to thinking that perhaps your trip into town had over tired him when I remembered what you had been saying about finding a dress.' She gave the table a light tap. 'Then I think, Sadie, you old fool. You have a wardrobe of dresses upstairs you never use. Mags will surely take one.'

'O, but I couldn't,' Mags protested more out of panic than politeness. 'They'd be … they'd be …' She looked round helplessly for a way of refusing, but Sadie dismissed her protests with a wave of her hand. 'I know what you are thinking,' she said. 'My dresses will not fit you. But I am a competent seamstress and I am sure we can make it work.'

'But,' Mags began feebly. But Sadie was already leading the way. 'Come, we can look now.'

Slowly, Mags got to her feet. Where's the harm in looking? I don't have to wear it. But still her footsteps crossed the tiles reluctantly, Cinderella discovering she has Groucho Marx for a godmother.

Out in the hall, Sammy was still on the phone. He glanced up as she passed, his grin wide. He's laughing at me, she thought and she could not help the petulant glare that formed on her face. His grin disappeared and she felt a moment of satisfaction before hearing him say into the receiver, 'No. We agreed this was the best way.' There was a rumbling on the other side then he said, 'We've been over that. Besides, it was your idea in the first place.'

There was something in his tone that made Mags want to stop on the stairs and listen, but Sadie had already reached the landing and was opening one of the panelled doors. 'Mags. Come please.'

Mags hurried up the stairs then stood hesitantly at the threshold of Sadie's room. She was too shy to enter, intimidated by the dark splendour of the furniture and the fragile grace of the white, Bruges lace bedspread. Sadie had already thrown open the mirrored door of the tall wardrobe and was busily rummaging through its densely-packed contents. When she realised that Mags was still standing in the hallway, she turned and beckoned to her. 'Please come. You can see nothing where you stand.'

Smiling shyly, like a little girl suddenly invited into the world of adults, Mags crossed the threshold and stood awkwardly in the middle of the room, trying to find a pose that did not betray her discomfort. She put her hands in her pockets, then finding that slovenly took them out again and tried leaning back on one leg, as though relaxed against an invisible support. Sadie seemed oblivious to this posturing and began lifting down hangers and throwing them carelessly on the bed.

A sidelong glance at the tweeds and ruffles had Mags heart sinking. Lines, which appeared classical to one generation, must surely seem horribly antiquated to the next. How could she convince Sadie of her gratitude? A wicked, little voice in her head whispered, *Lie. You find it so easy.* She tried to shut it out, but it persisted. *Hypocrite. If you can lie to your own son, why not to please an old lady?* She swallowed hard then lifted the sleeve of a satin blouse gingerly in one hand. 'It's beautiful,' she said. Surprised, Sadie turned towards her. 'These old things?' She dismissed them with a wave of her hand. 'I think you would have to have a few more grey hairs before you wore these, hmmm?'

Mags blushed. 'But I thought …'

Sadie's eyes widened. 'You want to dress like an old lady?'

'No, but—'

Sadie had turned back to the wardrobe and was struggling to free the last of the hangers. 'Come. Help me,' she said hoarsely, and Mags could see that her face was flushed with the exertion.

'Here. Let me.' Mags helped Sadie over to the stool by the dresser then turned to complete the task. Sadie watched her, breathing noisily and rubbing a hand across her breast. 'Ah, age is a terrible thing,' she commented. But

Mags wasn't listening. She had discovered the wardrobe's secret. Behind the rail of clothing Sadie had been emptying, lay a second rail. The dresses on this rail were fewer, less than half a dozen, and each was wrapped in soft tissue and clear plastic, protecting them from time's decaying touch. She turned wondering eyes towards Sadie, who smiled, and finding it too hard to speak, waved a hand of consent for Mags to remove them.

Mags drew the first one out, wrinkling her nose at a sudden waft of camphor.

'Moths,' Sadie wheezed. 'You can never be too careful.'

Mags was about to unwrap the plastic, but Sadie shook her head. 'No. Not that one. The one on the end. Nearest the door.' There was a rattling below Sadie's breath that frightened Mags. 'Let me get you a glass of water,' she suggested. But Sadie shook her head. 'No. I am fine. Truly. Now fetch the dress.'

Reluctantly, Mags turned back to wardrobe. But in doing so, she caught her hand on the edge of the dressing table and knocked over a small jewellery box. Rings and brooches scattered across the floor, and horrified Mags watched them, a kind of dream paralysis preventing her from catching them. 'I'm sorry,' she blurted helplessly. 'I didn't mean...'

Sadie raised a hand to silence her protests. 'An accident. That is all. Besides,' she said, looking down at the swollen joints of her fingers, 'it is not so much the days for wearing jewellery any more.'

Mags was on the floor, scrabbling beneath the bed, filling her hands full of gold, like a modern-day member of the forty thieves. 'It won't take a minute.'

Sadie watched Mags in her strangely plaintive position, rear presented, head beneath the bed, wishing there was something she could do to ease the younger woman's embarrassment. 'Do not worry,' she said. Then, when there was no response, she added a little louder, 'At my age you think of jewellery only in terms of who will want what when you die.'

Mags head reappeared, her face flushed, her hair escaping from its band in dishevelled tendrils. How much younger she looks, Sadie thought. She could see a shadow of Daniel in her features now. Mags began to return the jewellery to the box, but Sadie interrupted her. 'Leave it Mags. Put them on the dresser. I will do it later.'

Mags opened her mouth to protest, but Sadie frowned. 'Mags,' she said a trifle wearily. 'I am old and time is short for me. Do not let us waste time on polite argument.' She gestured firmly towards the wardrobe and Mags turned to it once again, careful to keep her hands by her sides then pulled the last hanger from the rail, as instructed. It felt light in her hand, lighter than the others, and she laid it on the bed with special reverence.

'Open it,' commanded Sadie, seeing her hesitation.

Mags slowly undid the wrappings, afraid to hope, but when she at last tore away the yellowing tissue shroud, she could not keep her exclamation of delight to herself. 'It's beautiful.'

A shift of silk, square-necked, sleeveless, the colour of rich burgundy wine glimmering red from within shadowy depths. The hem was embroidered with tiny beads of jet, little black droplets of rain that shivered when Mags lifted the dress up to examine it. It was a dress for a princess, someone who belonged to the world of capped smiles and expensive wines, where candles were lit for ambience not to save electricity, where men held open doors and women wafted in, like breeze-blown flowers. Not for her. Not her world.

'I can't—' she began, but Sadie was staring forcibly at her, and Mags was surprised to see how formidable she could appear when the soft lines of muddlement left her face.

'Mags, may I ask you something?'

Surprised, Mags gave her assent in a shrug.

'Did you come here of your own free choice or because Sammy asked you to?'

'I...' How could she answer?

Sadie nodded, seeing something in Mags' confusion that she didn't know was there.

'It's not that I wouldn't have wanted to come myself,' Mags began awkwardly. But Sadie shook her head. 'Please, I understand. I am not offended that you should come because of Sammy. He thinks a great deal of you. And my Sammy, he is a smart boy.'

Mags wanted to blurt out, 'What does he think of me?' But she kept her lips pressed tight and stared down at the little, winking beads on the hem. 'He hardly knows me,' she said to them.

Sadie's smile returned. 'Sammy is like me. He does not always say much, but he watches and he listens. He knows when a person is worth something and when he is not.'

Mags began to have that surreal sense again that Sadie was having an entirely different conversation to her own. 'Sammy thinks I could learn from you,' she said tentatively then laughed. 'I'm not sure what though.'

'I think I know,' Sadie began. But, just then, there was a knock at the door. 'Ma, can I come in.'

Both women looked round startled towards the door, and Mags experienced a guilty pang that she could not explain to herself. 'Ma?' Sammy asked again.

And, gathering her wits, Sadie called, 'Of course, you think we are the KGB?'

Sammy entered, grinning ruefully. 'No, ma. But I thought Mags might not be decent.'

'O.' Both women looked at each other then laughed in high, nervous tones that made them seem guiltier still. Sammy looked from one to the other, his eyes narrowed a little, then his eyes fell on the dress. 'Is that the one?' he asked.

'Yes,' Sadie replied confidently. 'It is perfect, yes?'

Sammy reached out a hand and stroked the silk. 'It's a beautiful dress,' he agreed.

He didn't say I would be beautiful in it, Mags noted. Perhaps he thinks it's too good for me. But then she felt foolish and paranoid, and she said quickly, 'Yes. It's a classical style.'

He turned to her, eyebrows raised. 'Is it?'

And she blushed. *What did she know about classical?* 'Well, that is to say, it seems so to me.'

He shrugged. 'I'm afraid I don't know anything about women's fashions. But I like the colour. It's subtle yet it catches the eye.'

She found herself blushing as though the compliment had been directed at her rather than the dress. And it was a relief when she saw that he had turned to speak to Sadie.

'I have to go into town to wire some money to the States,' he was saying. 'Now?'

He glanced at his watch. 'I should do it now. Do you still need a lift?'

Sadie turned disappointed eyes towards Mags. 'I wanted you to try it on for a fitting. It may need taken in.'

'Well.' Mags didn't know what to suggest. She too was disappointed. Not so much about the dress, but about the things she had wanted to ask Sadie. She wasn't sure she had the courage to try again.

'I know this is awkward,' Sammy said apologetically. 'But I really have to deal with this now.' He looked at the crestfallen expressions, and ran an irritated hand through his hair. 'Wouldn't it be possible to do this later?' he asked.

Mags glanced down at her battered watch. 'I have lectures,' she explained. 'And after, Daniel.'

They stared at each other in guilty silence until Sadie said equably 'Perhaps I could come tonight Mags. Sammy can drive me.' Then seeing no response from Mags, added hopefully, 'If it is okay that I should come.'

Mags smiled. 'Of course you can,' then added magnanimously, 'I'd be glad to see you.'

Sadie turned a smile of satisfaction towards Sammy. 'See. It is easy to order your affairs when you think ahead. Maybe you could use me to advise you in the business a little'

Sammy raised his eyebrows but didn't rise to the bait. 'I need to get some things from my room,' he said heading for the door.

Once he was gone, Mags turned to Sadie. She was staring down at the ruby dress, a little wistfully, as though it brought back memories she didn't want to share. Mags watched her feeling a strange, shy affection growing for the woman she knew so little about. But then Sadie looked up and Mags said quickly, 'I should be going. I'll tell Daniel that you're coming tonight. He'll be pleased.'

Sadie nodded absently and Mags suspected that her mind had moved on to other things. She raised a hand in feeble farewell and hurried out of the room. Her disappointment at the interruption was already ebbing. That was her trouble, always trying to rush things. Her questions could wait. Perhaps it was even a deliberate ploy to make her see that. Time would tell.

Sadie waited until she heard the gentle thump of the back door shutting before heaving herself out of her seat and heading downstairs. The archive was where she had left it in the cupboard under the sink. She heaved it on to the table and prised off the lid. The photograph of Piotr was still at the top, face down. She didn't turn it over, but stared down at the age mottled backing recalling another girl who had worn a red dress. It was made from the lining of a pair of velvet curtains. The velvet was moth-eaten, but Piotr had brought her the material and she had stitched together a dress more beautiful than anything she had ever owned just to please him.

Only she wasn't pleased now. She was afraid. Despite her coat, she was shivering. The red dress was too thin. But she couldn't go home. Not now. Piotr held her hand, but she couldn't bear to look into his eyes. He was speaking, asking her something. 'How did you know they were there?'

For a moment she couldn't think, but then a vision came to her. A tiny face appearing out of the darkness as she stepped off the trolley bus. 'Monia, the upravdom's little boy. He came to warn me.'

She dared a glance at Piotr. He was shaking his head slowly from side to side. 'The party can offer you no protection now. It will be the same for Leib and Rivka.'

'I was too afraid to try to reach them.' She tugged at his wrist. 'Russia has no place for me now. I must get away. Soon.' She dared a peek into his face. It was stiff and unyielding, and all she could see in his eyes were two terrified, little reflections of herself.

Sighing, Sadie removed the photograph and laid it, face down, on the table. Beneath it was a letter, with the motto, *Via Veritas Vita*, along the top. She pulled it out and placed it alongside the photograph. Then, one eye still on the mottled underside of the photo, she reached for a fresh block of paper and a pen, and began to write.

Chapter 30

ANIEL was already home when Mags barged clumsily into the flat. She was carrying a couple of bags of shopping, the week's groceries, and one of the plastic handles had snapped. 'Hey,' she said, seeing him bent over an exercise book at her desk. 'What are you up to?'

He turned, startled at the sound of her voice, and regarded her smile suspiciously. 'You're late,' he said, his eyes fixed on hers, while one hand snapped the exercise book shut and flipped it on to its back.

'I was shopping,' Mags explained, gesturing unnecessarily with the carrier bags. The one with the broken handle was not up to the strain and unceremoniously spilled its contents on to the floor. 'Damn.' Mags bent to pick up the escaping groceries. His eyes still fixed on her, Daniel slipped off his seat, exercise book in one hand, and began to head for his bedroom door. He stopped short, a few feet from where Mags was crouched. 'Biscuits?' He retrieved a packet of cream bourbons and held them wonderingly in one hand. Mags grinned at him. 'Guess who's coming over tonight.'

His face darkened. 'Ewan?'

'No.' She held the smile. 'Guess again.'

He shrugged impatiently. 'I don't know.'

'Sadie.' She had expected him to return her smile, but his frown deepened, and he asked in a small, gruff voice, 'Why is she coming here?'

Mags got up from the floor and distributed her shopping untidily across the desk. 'She's bringing me a dress.'

'A dress!'

Mags saw the incredulity on Daniel's face that must surely have been on her own earlier that day. Her smile grew more confident. 'Yes. She had the perfect dress hidden away in the back of her wardrobe. But I didn't have time to try it on, and—'

'You were in Sadie's bedroom,' Daniel interrupted, his face stony.

'Yes.' Mags felt the smile leave her lips. 'What's the matter?'

'Nothing.'

He was staring at her with a stranger's eyes, and suddenly she felt a little afraid. 'Are you feeling all right? You've gone awfully pale.'

He gave a little, one shouldered shrug. 'I'm a bit tired. I think I'll go and finish my homework in my room.' And leaving her with the sense that something wasn't being said, he turned and left the room.

Although the trip into town had been short. Sammy had insisted that it be so, Sadie had felt worn out when they returned. She obstinately refused Sammy's urgings to go upstairs and lie down, but had allowed herself to be cajoled into her favourite armchair, where she sat pretending to knit something until Sammy had left the room, whereupon she had fallen into a deep, dreamless doze.

Sammy had had to wake her, and though they had eaten a light tea, prepared by Sammy while she slept, she still had that disconcerting sense of unreality that dogs the breaker of a deep sleep. Now, both Sammy's strangely preoccupied mood and the darkness beyond the windscreen with it rhythmic flicker of street lights were threatening to lull her back to a blissful oblivion, and she struggled to keep her mind focused.

'Sammy,' she cried out startled. 'The dress. I have forgotten it.'

'Ma, don't clutch at my arm when I'm driving,' he said irritably, then more gently, 'You didn't forget. It's safe on the backseat.'

She tried to crane her head round, but the seatbelt held her too tightly. She would have to believe him then, a matter of faith. They drove on in silence a little longer then she asked quite suddenly, 'Was that Jodie on the phone earlier?'

'Jamie, ma,' he replied tightly. 'And yes, it was.'

He did not elaborate so she suggested timidly, 'She is missing you, no?'

He shrugged. 'Parts of me.'

She frowned. 'Which parts?'

He took his eyes off the road for a moment to glance at her, and there was something of his usual irony in his eyes. 'The parts that sign the cheques.'

'Sammy.' Sadie was shocked. His irreverence made her feel the necessity to defend her daughter in law. 'You should not make light of it. The poor girl hardly hears from you. It's not good for a man to neglect his wife.'

He didn't answer, but she saw the preoccupied look come back into his eyes.

Sadie had expected Daniel to open the door, and was surprised to see Mags, her face strained, little lines of tension around her mouth pulled taut.

'Come in.'

As soon as they were across the threshold, Sadie saw Mrs Gallagher sitting on the sofa talking in hushed tones to Daniel. They turned towards the open door, and Sadie noted that Mrs Gallagher's eyes were expressionless, though her body was hunched forward in anticipation, while there was a guarded look to Daniel's face, as though he was holding the real Daniel from peeping out.

'Good evening everyone,' Sadie said, starting to hand her coat to Mags then almost dropping it in agitation. 'Sammy. The dress.'

'It's here, ma.' Sammy was clutching a delicate parcel of brown paper. He smiled at Mags, not in the way that made her colour and look away, but an absent-minded, vague kind of smile that made her stare at him curiously, certain that he would not notice.

'Where will I put this?' he asked gesturing at the parcel.

She was flustered. He had noticed. 'On my desk,' she said quickly, then when he looked round, puzzled, said hastily, 'I mean the table. I just call it my desk to … to … '

'To impress,' Mrs Gallagher finished for her.

Sadie's eyes that had been studying Daniel's figure as he crouched over a drawing, flicked in the direction of Mrs Gallagher and then to Mags. 'Try the dress on now,' she said. 'I do not know how much work is to be done and it would be better to start now.'

But Mags seemed reluctant to take it. She felt suddenly awkward at the thought of being scrutinised and cast about for an excuse to refuse.

'Well, try it on,' her mother said impatiently. 'Sadie's been good enough to drag half way across town to bring it for you.'

Mags' shoulders stiffened. 'I was going to make some tea,' she said lamely. 'I've got biscuits.'

'I'll deal with that,' Mrs Gallagher said, suddenly business-like and efficient. 'You try on this wonderful dress so we can get a chance to see it.'

'All right.' Mags' shoulders drooped and she held her hands out for it, like a little girl receiving a doll that is only for admiring not for playing with. 'I'll just be a minute.'

With Mags out of the room, the role of the Gordons suddenly seemed uncertain. They looked at one another then over at Mrs Gallagher, who was busy opening cupboards then shutting them again with a dissatisfied shake of her head. Sadie looked to Daniel, who still seemed very busy with his drawing, then uncertainly at Sammy. 'I think we should sit down, ma,' he said, leading her over to the sofa.

As they crossed the room, Daniel gathered up his paper and pens and spread them on the carpet. He continued his drawing on the floor, too absorbed apparently to look up. Sadie studied him for a while then asked hesitantly, 'Daniel, what is this you are drawing?'

He shrugged, as though her interruption was an irritation. 'A space ship.'

'Ah. I see,' Sadie said, leaning a little further forward to inspect it. 'I thought it was planes that you liked.'

'It is planes I like,' Daniel retorted crossly. 'But this ship is going to heaven.'

'O.'

Sammy was surprised to see his mother spring back, as though stung, then hastily look away searching for another topic of conversation. 'Can I help you with the tea?' she asked.

'No. No. There's no problem,' Mrs Gallagher replied. She was already pouring the thickish liquid into three mismatched cups. Her glance fell on Daniel. 'Danny, where does that mother of yours keep her tray.'

'Haven't got one.'

Mrs Gallagher's lips pursed together, like a cork holding down an explosive liquid. 'No tray,' she repeated ominously.

'Allow me.' Sammy was on his feet and crossing the room. But before he reached the kitchen, Mags opened her bedroom door and stepped out. He turned towards her, one eyebrow raised. 'Well, well.'

'Wait,' she said, throwing a hand up in panic. 'I'm not decent.' She struggled to pull the dress up by the shoulders. 'I can't do the hooks and eyes at the back.'

Sammy's expression was cool. 'Let me help you.'

But surely he couldn't expect her just to stand there and let him touch her. Mags backed away, hiding her nakedness and exposing her confusion instead. 'I can manage.'

But he was already at her side. Had she seen him move? 'It's no trouble.'

She was tense before he touched her and therefore all the more amazed at how much tension his touch could induce. Cool fingers brushed against her skin as he fastened each hook, and she had to fight the ridiculous desire to stretch and lean against him, arching her spine like a satisfied cat. Instead, she stood, like a stiff, little tomboy being fitted for a first party dress. She could feel her mother's eyes upon her, watchful, curious, and a blush crept along her jawline and down her neck. Ridiculous, she thought. I don't care what she thinks. Then she stiffened suddenly making Sammy lose his grip on the tiny hooks. What is there to think. Nothing. Nothing to think.

'Nearly there.' Sammy's voice was encouraging. 'Just another two to go.'

'My, but you're awful good with a dress,' Mrs Gallagher remarked.

'I expect he has had plenty of practice with his Jamie,' Sadie said. She smiled over at Sammy, wanting to see his surprise at her getting the name right first time, but his face was hidden and he did not reveal himself.

'Jamie?' Mrs Gallagher asked, her voice had a mild, enquiring tone.

'My wife,' Sammy answered. And this time, the jerk that tensed Mags' spine was visible to all.

'O, I didn't know you were married.' Mrs Gallagher's voice was conversational, but her eyes were on Mags, hard and unblinking. Mags pretended not to see them, staring deliberately ahead, her face as immobile as stone. But her thoughts were racing. Did I know? Was it mentioned before? O, now she'll have a good time. Another fall from grace. But it's not what she thinks. There's nothing to think. Nothing. Nothing at all.

She felt Sammy straighten up behind her. 'There you are.'

But she didn't move.

'Turn around. Let me see you.'

She turned slowly, a mannequin responding to the pull of levers.

'Ah.' It was Sadie who spoke. 'Is she not lovely.'

'Lovely,' Mrs Gallagher agreed flatly. 'Though I wouldn't have thought that was really Mags' colour.'

And Sammy said nothing, but the eyes that studied her were unsmiling and critical. And suddenly she knew what she must look like, a peasant dressed up in a princess' clothes, every line of her hard, harsh face emphasised by the flowing opulence of the silk. He hadn't seen it before. She'd fooled him with her exalted words and grand plans. But now she stood before them, a circus freak, grotesque in her splendour, splendid in her absurdity. But what did his opinion matter? It didn't. Not at all.

'I should take this off now,' she said sharply.

They stared at her in surprise. 'Here, let me help you.' He advanced towards her, but she backed away. 'No. I can manage. Really.'

She was actually running by the time she reached her bedroom and she slammed the door behind her afraid that their censure would follow her in there. Her reflection in the mirror opposite showed a haggard creature overwhelmed by the arterial richness of the burgundy silk, and though she wanted nothing more than to rid herself of it, she sank down on the bed and stared at nothing because that was how she felt herself to be. Nothing.

After a minute, or was it an hour, there was a faint knock on the door. It was so light that it might almost have been Daniel's hand, except that Daniel wouldn't have knocked. She ignored it, but the door swung open tentatively, and after standing half open for a moment, as though unsure of itself, it completed its arc and Sadie peeped around its edge.

'Your mother has gone,' she said timidly. 'She said to tell you she had to get Gary's tea on.'

There was a silence then Mags blurted, as though she hadn't heard what Sadie said, 'This dress … I can't wear it. I'm sorry.'

Sadie's eyebrows rose. 'How is it that you can't?'

Mags made an irritated gesture towards herself. 'Look at me. It's not meant for someone like me.'

'Someone like you?'

Mags shot Sadie a warning glance. 'You know what I mean.'

'No. No, I do not.'

'This dress. It says things, things about the person wearing it. Things that aren't me.'

'And what is you?'

Mags eyes grew wide and her mouth dropped open. A face slapped into recognition. And Sadie, seeing her confusion, nodded, as though it was no more than she had expected. 'Take the dress,' she said firmly. 'It is only a dress. It says much less about you than you can say about yourself.'

She saw Mags open her mouth to protest and went on hastily. 'Please take it, Mags. I would like you to have it. I know you would care for it, and how could you deny an old lady the pleasure of giving something precious to someone who will look after it.'

'But I can't,' Mags argued. 'What about Sammy. Surely it should go to him.'

Sadie raised an eyebrow. 'My dear, strange as my son is, he is not in the habit of wearing evening dresses.'

Mags managed a grin then forced herself to say, 'I meant his wife. Surely he will want to give it to her.'

'Who? Jodie?' Sadie's eyes were wide with disbelief. 'No, no. She is an American and would not be happy in it.' She nodded towards Mags. 'It is for you. A girl who is seeking a better life.'

Mags opened her mouth to protest again then shut it quite firmly. 'Thank you.'

When they emerged from the bedroom, Sammy was sitting on the sofa staring listlessly into the distance. He sprang to his feet when he heard them come in. 'I hope my mother persuaded you to keep the dress,' he said politely. But there was a masked, glassy look to his eyes, and Mags had the feeling he was avoiding looking directly at her. He caught her casting about and said quickly, 'Daniel has gone to bed. He said he was feeling tired.'

Sadie saw Mags' worried glance in the direction of his bedroom. 'We should be going,' she announced. 'Daniel is not the only one who is tired.'

'Of course.' Sammy was still distantly polite. 'I'll get the coats.'

Mags saw them to the door and exchanged the usual courteous goodbyes. Sadie insisted that Mags not be a stranger and Mags felt it incumbent upon herself to return the offer. Sammy stayed silent, eventually interrupting to say, 'Come on now, ma, we mustn't keep Mags from her studies. I'm sure she has a lot to do.'

'Yes,' Mags agreed. 'A lot.' But Sammy had already started to lead his mother down the stairs and Mags had the uncomfortable feeling that, quite without meaning to, she had actually answered an entirely different question.

Daniel was asleep when she entered his room. But his bedside light was still on and in his hands, were a drawing and a felt tip pen. The tip of the pen was resting against the edge of the paper from which a blot of ink was bleeding across the page. Gently Mags eased the pen out of his hands and replaced the lid, then she took the paper and held it close to the lamp to examine it. Some kind of plane? No. A ship. A sky ship, multi-coloured, its sails billowing against the setting sun, it was climbing its graceful way through the heavens. Towards what? There appeared to be something near the top right corner of the page, something Daniel had started but not finished. Mags peered but couldn't make it out. A gate perhaps? But why would there be a gate in the sky? Frowning, she placed it on the bedside table. She could always ask him in the morning. She thought of bending down to kiss him, but that might wake him, so turning off the lamp, she crept from the room.

As soon as the door clicked shut, Daniel reached for the drawing. And without opening his eyes, tore it to shreds.

Chapter 31

MAGS found the reference in the index and looked up the appropriate page. There was not much there, a couple of paragraphs, but it was just what she wanted. Pleased, she copied it into her essay. And when she was finished she paused a moment to look at the red roses Ewan had sent that morning. She hadn't been in when they'd arrived. And she hadn't known about them until she was putting her key in the lock and Mrs McKellor had coming panting up the stairs after her. She shoved the roses into Mags' surprised hands, her face grim and immobile. 'The postman left them with me,' was all she said. And, without waiting for Mags to express confusion or gratitude, she turned and heaved herself back down the stairs.

Mags looked at the roses. They were crushed and badly in need of water. Mrs McKellor's neighbourly duties extended only so far. And there was no card. But who else would have sent them? It was a sign. He wanted the world to see that she was going to be the new Mrs MacLeod. A new beginning. Time to shuck of the old world and try on the new. Was that going too far? Well, why not? What was life without dreams? Wasn't that what Sadie had been trying to tell her?

Unwillingly, she drew herself back to her essay and began to jot down notes on a sheet of foolscap. Keep a grip, Mags, she told herself. But her eyes kept slipping back to the flowers. The doorbell rang and she started up, more startled to find that she had been dreaming than by the noise itself. She glanced at the clock. Two thirty? But then she shrugged. What did it matter? Life was full of surprises. She threw open the door.

Daniel was standing there, his expression sullen, and behind him, was a tall lady dressed in tweeds. She smiled at Mags with a quiet, assumed authority that immediately put Mags on her guard.

'Mrs Lorne,' she said, extending a hand. 'I'm the deputy head at Daniel's school. Could I come in?'

'Of course.' Mags stepped back forgetting to take the woman's hand, her eyes glued on Daniel, who slunk in first, avoiding her glance. He stood in the middle of the floor, eyeing Mrs Lorne uneasily as Mags guided her to a seat.

'Can I get you a cup of tea,' Mags offered.

Mrs Lorne smiled. 'That would be lovely.' She gave a slight, condescending nod as she answered, indicating that she felt quite in charge of the situation.

Mags saw the nod and her shoulders tensed. She glanced over at Daniel, frowning. 'There hasn't been any trouble has there?'

'No. Not at all.' Mrs Lorne seemed quite relaxed, though her eyes darted round the room making obvious mental note of the dirty laundry and the worn patches on the carpet. 'Daniel's just a bit of a sleepyhead these days, aren't you?'

Insulted by the patronising tone, Daniel didn't answer. He shrugged off his jacket and let it fall to the floor.

'Daniel, put that away,' Mags said sharply.

He looked at her in surprise and she coloured in the face of his confusion. Why was she pretending in front of this woman? Mrs Lorne stared politely at the fireplace. After a moment under Mags' glower, Daniel lifted his jacket and flung it over the back of a chair. 'There,' he said sullenly. Mags ignored his tone. She didn't like it, but she couldn't bring herself to do anything about it while the smiling woman sat in the chair watching them.

Mags went back to making the tea. 'I haven't any milk,' she said.

Mrs Lorne's smile widened, as though it was no more than she had expected. 'That's fine. I'm always trying to give it up.' Before Mags could make any comment on this, she turned to Daniel, her smile as broad and unchanging as ever. 'Why don't you go to your room and do me one of those lovely pictures Mrs Ferguson was telling me about, while I have a bit of a talk with mum.'

Daniel's eyes fastened on Mrs Lorne and stayed there until she looked away. He glanced over at Mags. 'I'm going to my room,' he announced, as though the thought had just occurred to him. Mags nodded. She felt strangely excluded, as though she was watching a scene on the television. And though she had poured the tea, she stood watching him leave the room before carrying the cup across to the deputy head.

'Thank you,' Mrs Lorne's gratitude was effusive. Mags ignored it, and taking the chair opposite, took out a cigarette and lit it. She took a long drag. 'What's going on?'

Mrs Lorne's smile faded somewhat under such direct scrutiny, but she recovered herself with admirable speed. She opened her bag and took out a sheaf of notes. Mags could make out Daniel's name in upside down print along the top. She waited, while Mrs Lorne ran an eye down the top page, and took another drag on her cigarette. 'Ah,' said Mrs Lorne. 'Ms Gallagher.' She emphasised the word, *Ms*, so that it sounded clumsy and rather affected. Get on with it, she thought. What are you waiting for? And her fingers on the cigarette squeezed until the filter flattened between them.

Mrs Lorne was smiling again. 'I'm afraid that we're reaching a bit of a problem stage with Daniel now.'

'Is he in trouble?' Mags was suddenly afraid. How many hours did she leave him alone or in the care of others? What use was her striving for a better life, if Daniel was falling into bad company while she was away?

Mrs Lorne saw her panic and shook her head. 'No, no, Ms Gallagher. Nothing like that.' She paused to straighten her skirt across her bumpy knees. 'We appreciate your telling us about Daniel's condition right from the start.'

'He hasn't been trying to join in at games?' Mags interrupted.

'No.' Mrs Lorne said it quite firmly to indicate that she didn't like being interrupted. 'You requested that he be allowed to sit out and the school has taken a very strict line about it.'

Mags took another drag from her cigarette to prevent herself from interrupting again.

'No,' Mrs Lorne was continuing. 'We feel that Daniel is reaching a stage where he requires more help than we have the provisions to provide.'

Mags eyes were like glass. 'I don't understand.'

Mrs Lorne gave a small sigh, as though she'd expected this to be a difficult case. 'Daniel is finding it hard to keep up in class,' she said gently. She was unprepared for the look of anger that flashed across Mags face. 'Daniel's a bright boy,' she said. 'Everyone says so.'

Mrs Lorne held up a placating hand. 'I don't doubt it. Mrs Ferguson is full of praise for him, though she does say he spends a bit too much time drawing.' She nodded conspiratorially at Mags, but Mags wasn't in the mood.

'I don't see where you're coming from.'

Mrs Lorne's face grew serious. 'Daniel's condition is visibly worsening. His class, as you no doubt know, is on the second floor, and Daniel is often breathless before he reaches the first landing.'

'He's always had trouble with stairs,' Mags snapped. What was this woman suggesting? Daniel went up and down the stairs all the time and she hadn't noticed any change. But, then, when was the last time she'd watched him climb the stairs? They'd been coming in and out at different times. No. She shook her head. She was often at home by the time Daniel got home. He hadn't seemed wheezy then, no more than usual at least. But he had looked pale, hadn't he? Was he hiding something from her?

'And it's not just the stairs,' Mrs Lorne continued, as though reading her thoughts. 'Daniel is tired during the day. He often falls asleep during a lesson and Mrs Ferguson hasn't the heart to wake him up. He used to be such a bright little boy, but now he seems to have lost enthusiasm. Everyone's noticed it.'

There was a long finger of ash on the end of Mags' cigarette. She held it so still that it did not fall, but hung in the balance, waiting. 'Is he like this all the time?'

'No,' Mrs Lorne conceded. 'There are days when he seems fine. Well …,' she paused. 'All things considered he seems well.'

'Then it could just be that he's been overdoing things a bit,' Mags suggested.

'I don't really—'

'We've been very busy lately,' Mags went on hurriedly. 'There's been a lot of excitement for a wee boy.' Her hand jerked agitatedly and the ash spilled on the carpet. Mags didn't notice. 'I should have realised that it was going to be a bit much for him. I should have realised.'

Mrs Lorne looked doubtful and she went on hastily, 'He's been getting better. No. Really. You probably can't see it because you're not with him every day.'

A sea of lines between Mrs Lorne's eyes undulated doubtfully. Mags struggled on. 'I know what you're thinking, but he is improving. It's really only the sort of thing that a mother can see.' She forced a laugh. 'I even have difficulty persuading the doctors.'

Mrs Lorne did not laugh. 'Our feeling is that Daniel's condition really has worsened,' she began slowly.

'It hasn't.' Mags' tone brooked no argument. She pulled her lips back in a smile. 'I think Mrs Ferguson is reading too much into the situation.'

Seeing that confrontation was doing her no good, Mrs Lorne tried another angle. 'We feel that Daniel may be happier at home. There would be less stress on him. And you needn't worry about his education. We could arrange for tutors.'

'No.' There was panic on Mags' face. A sick child, lying forlornly in bed while well-intentioned adults forced little flutters of recognition out of him then cooed about their result. That wasn't her child, not her Danny. 'No,' she said, this time more firmly. She stubbed out her cigarette on a dirty saucer by the chair and got to her feet. 'I appreciate your coming here. But I feel the whole thing has been exaggerated.'

Mrs Lorne opened her mouth to protest, but Mags hurried on. 'I can see that Daniel has probably been a bit under the weather recently. That's my fault. I've been expecting too much from him. I'll keep him off for a few days and see how he does. We can take it from there.'

The worried expression was still on Mrs Lorne's face, but Mags' could see that she'd won. Her smile was reassuring. 'I'm sure it's all just been a mistake.'

Mrs Lorne got to her feet. 'Well, I'm certainly willing to give it a chance,' she said, but there was still the doubtful undertone in her voice. 'But if we don't see a considerable improvement, I'm afraid …' She hesitated.

'I understand,' Mags said quickly. 'Here, let me show you to the door.'

When she was gone, Mags went straight to Daniel's room. He was sitting on the floor surrounded by small pieces of grey plastic. He looked up when he heard her come in. 'I've started my model,' he said.

She was surprised and pleased. 'I thought modelling was last year's hobby,' she teased.

He shrugged. 'It's a good plane,' he admitted condescendingly.

Mags sat on the edge of the bed and watched him drawing a tube of glue along one of the edges. A transparent teardrop hung from the nozzle. 'Watch you don't get any of that on the carpet,' she said.

He nodded, still concentrating on the piece. 'I know.'

She swallowed two or three times wondering where to begin, wishing she didn't have to break the tranquillity of the moment. 'Daniel,' she began slowly. 'Do you know why Mrs Lorne brought you home?'

He fitted the glued edge carefully against another piece. 'Because I went to sleep in the class?'

Her heart began to beat wildly. 'Do you do that often, Danny?'

He shrugged. 'Mrs Ferguson's so boring.'

Mags felt a rush of relief so great that she had to struggle to stay stern. 'You can't just go to sleep when you feel like it, you know.'

'I know,' he said. He was searching for the next component.

She didn't like the way his face was hidden from her, but she wanted to keep the conversation relaxed. You can't force the truth out of a child. 'Daniel,' she began again. 'You would tell me if you had any secrets, wouldn't you?'

'Yes, mum.'

She didn't see his eyes flit towards an old, grey covered exercise book. 'You'd tell me if you weren't feeling well.'

'Yes.' He found the missing piece and turned it round trying to fit it in place. 'Mrs Ferguson thinks that you haven't been feeling well.'

He gave a disdainful snort. 'She doesn't know anything.'

'She's your teacher, Daniel,' Mags said with more relief than severity. 'You shouldn't talk about her that way.'

He didn't answer, but continued with his gluing. Feeling a little braver, Mags said, 'I think she's right though. You have been looking tired lately. Maybe a few days off wouldn't do any harm.' She was amused to see how he looked round gleefully before remembering to appear unmoved. Mags smiled to herself. Who knows a child better than its own mother?

Chapter 32

'DANIEL! How long have you been there?' Sadie's voice was shrill even to her own ears. Daniel didn't shift from his position on the backdoor step. He didn't even look round. He was wearing his thin, nylon anorak with the hood pulled up against the light smir falling from the sky. But his bottom must have been wet and cold sitting on the hard stone. Sadie held the door open wide. 'Come in. Have you been there long? I didn't hear the bell. But my ears, not so good these days.'

She kept talking, repeating herself, making no sense at all, while she led Daniel over to a chair and made him sit down. He was silent and she didn't know how to break into that silence. 'You're lucky,' she rambled. 'I have just finished making some cakes. With a bit of luck, they'll still be warm.'

He didn't answer and she felt a cold chill shiver down her spine. This wasn't the Daniel she knew. This sullen, silent child was a stranger. 'Take your anorak off,' she said sharply. A little boy should not be making an old lady feel nervous. 'You won't feel the benefit otherwise.'

He did as she said, and, with a jolt, she saw that he had been protecting the exercise book beneath it. She tried to ignore it, but it lay in his hands accusingly. It had a silencing effect on her, and she stopped rambling and filled a plate of cakes and laid them on the table, without further comment. Daniel didn't take one. He didn't even look in their direction. He sat, pale and silent staring across the kitchen, waiting.

His demeanour at first made her angry then nervous, then finally she gave a sigh and took the chair next to him. 'You're angry with me,' she said. It was not a question. Daniel kept staring ahead, but there was the faintest hint of a nod. Sadie sighed again and nodded to herself. 'You think I have forgotten,' she said quietly.

His head swung round then, eyes blazing. At his sides, his small fists were clenched. 'You don't care,' he hissed. 'You promised,' he spat. 'But you don't care. You think I'm just a little kid who'll forget.'

'No, Daniel.'

But he wouldn't let her finish. 'You like my mum now,' he went on bitterly. 'And she's made you just like her.'

'I don't understand—'

He waved a hand impatiently. 'You want to pretend. To pretend, like her, that I'm going to get better so you don't have to keep your promise.'

Sadie sat back in her seat and studied him carefully. A thousand things sprang to her mind. Don't let him intimidate you. What can he know about dying? His own mother doesn't believe it. Why should I? At last she said, 'I'm sorry.'

The anger went out of him then. And he lowered his head and his shoulders drooped, and it seemed that all the fight had been sucked out of him and he was just a sick child, who'd been let down.

'You don't care,' he said softly.

'No, Daniel.' Sadie reached out and took his hands in her own. They lay there limply, like dead petals. 'I care very much.'

He raised his eyes and they were full of doubt and suspicion. 'You don't believe me.'

Sadie shook her head slowly. 'No, Daniel. I believe you. But I need you to believe me now. Will you do that for me?'

He looked at her curiously. 'What about?'

'I made a promise to you, and I want you to believe that I will keep that promise.'

He was still looking into her eyes. 'How?'

Sadie made a face. 'I … I don't know that bit yet.' His face fell, and she caught his chin and forced it up so that he was looking at her again. 'I asked you if you would believe me.'

His eyes darted across her face, trying to learn if this was another adult trick. 'Okay,' he said gruffly. 'I believe you.'

'Good.' She let go his chin. 'Now, tell me what you are doing here on a school day.'

Much later Sammy found her still sitting at the kitchen table, her chin resting on one hand, the fingers of the other beating a tattoo against the table cloth. In the centre of the table was a plate of uneaten cakes.

'Ma, are you all right?' Sammy asked, pulling up a chair beside her.

She nodded at him vaguely, her thoughts obviously many miles away. 'Yes, of course. Why not?'

Puzzled, he studied her trying to fathom her mood. He opened his mouth to ask something, but before he could speak, she asked quite suddenly. 'Sammy, you don't think we should have secrets between us, do you?'

Taken aback, he blurted, 'No. Of course not. What on earth do you mean?'

She looked up at him then, as though only seeing him for the first time since he'd entered the room. 'I just mean,' she began hesitantly, 'that no matter how bad a thing was, you would always tell me about it.'

Something in her tone made him look away. 'Of course, ma.'

'And it wouldn't matter to me how bad it was,' she went on a little desperately. 'Because no matter how bad it was, I would know that you had your reasons.'

'Yes, ma.' He still wasn't looking at her, and gathering up all her courage, she began, 'Sammy, I …O I need to—'

But he was looking at her now, his black eyes opaque, like stones. 'Ma, I have to tell you something.'

She shook her head; not certain she'd heard correctly. 'Tell me something?' she repeated.

A pink flush spread across his cheeks and he lowered his eyes. 'I should have told you before. I meant to. And now I suppose you've guessed.'

She was shaking her head back and forth in slow arcs of negation, but his eyes were still lowered and he didn't notice. 'Jamie and I are getting a divorce.'

'No!' Her hand flew to her mouth. 'But why?'

He shrugged and she noticed for the first time that there was a weariness under all his *bon homie*. 'I'm not sure that I can give you a reason that you'd understand. Maybe we just grew apart as we grew older. Wanted different things out of life.' He spread his hands and began twisting a thick gold ring, which she only now noticed was not on his wedding finger. 'I've felt things weren't right for a long time. But over the last few months it's just gone from bad to worse. Fights every night. Her spending more money than I could earn.' He stopped twisting the ring and looked into Sadie's face. 'That's why I took that damn job in New York in the first place. I kept thinking if I could earn more money then everything would be all right.' Sighing, he dropped his gaze again. 'But even an old fool has to wake up some time, and I realised that I couldn't hack a young man's job any more.' He quirked the corner of his mouth. 'Well, not when my only motive was to feed a bottomless pit.'

'She was never the girl for you,' Sadie interrupted loyally. 'I never liked her.'

'Ma,' he said reproachfully. 'When you met her, you said that we were meant for each other. You said you could feel it.'

'So, now I am God,' she retorted. 'Now I look at a person and I know their whole future.'

'No, no, ma. It's all right. Calm down.' He raised his hands in front of him to ward off her onslaught. 'Whatever we felt, it's over now. And it's for the best.'

'You really think so?' She felt guilty for her outburst.

He smiled at her, not the old Sammy with his flippant grin, but an older, slightly sadder man. 'Yes,' he said. 'I really think it's for the best. 'When I saw Mags standing there in your dress, I felt something I haven't felt in a long time.'

'Sammy.' Sadie was a little shocked.

He grinned at her and some of the old, ironical Sammy was back. 'Not what you're thinking,' he assured her. 'Yes, there was desire there, but it wasn't just that. It was the first time in a long time that I've desired something that wasn't just a pretty filling for a dress. She has dreams, ma. I don't know if she ever told you, and she made me feel young and old at the same time, if you can understand that, because she reminded me that I used to have dreams too.' He looked away, a little colour darkening his jaw. 'You know, I actually sent her some roses this morning because the colour reminded me of her in that dress.'

Sadie was staring at him, as though a stranger had stepped out of the body of her son. 'But what will you do now?' she asked. 'Are you coming home for good?'

Sammy stretched and put his hands behind his head. 'Why not. You can't live alone in this big house forever. I can make a living free lancing. It can be good money. And if it's not, it'll be enough to get by on. My needs are simple. They had to be after Jamie had cleared out the monthly account. Who knows, maybe I'll get around to writing that book I've always talked about.'

'But why didn't you tell me this?' Sadie cried. 'Why sit there day after day saying nothing.'

Under this chastisement, Sammy let go of his relaxed pose and sat up straight. 'I'm sorry, ma,' he said gently. 'It's just the things that you've written to me about your health and what Dr Farmer has said, that I was afraid to give you a shock. I know you've tried to take more care of your health.' He glanced, askance, at the plate of cakes. 'But let's face it, old girl, you're not getting any younger and I didn't want to give your old ticker a start.'

'Give my ticker a start,' she repeated.

'Yes. Your ticker. Your heart.'

But Sadie didn't need a translation. Not now that she saw things so clearly. All she needed was a strong cup of tea and some time to think.

The broad smile that Mags greeted Ewan with was not returned, and she felt it falling from her lips, like an unfortunate comment. She gave an embarrassed shrug. 'What's wrong?'

He was sitting behind an unusually unruly sprawl of papers and books, his fists clenched on top of one of the piles, as though he was restraining the impulse to sweep it from the desk. He was frowning, and she noticed that he too seemed dishevelled. His hair looked uncombed and his clothes had the crumpled, sagging look of garments worn a day too long. He inclined his head across the desk, not trusting his hands. 'Just these proofs they've sent me. They're full of mistakes.' He snatched up a page and waved it angrily towards her. 'They've spelt Kalegaev three different ways on this page and it isn't even the right name of the character.'

Not knowing what to say, she stood silently, avoiding his eye, as though the errors were her fault. She'd come to him in her new, confident guise as the future Mrs Ewan MacLeod, but he hadn't noticed, and she didn't know how to draw his attention to it.

'I'm sorry, Mags,' he said after a bit. 'It's just with the party tonight, I want everything to be perfect.'

She dared his eyes. 'Ewan, everything I've read has been amazing. I've wanted to go back to it time and again. And I haven't wanted to give it up when I had to put it down to do other things. It's a wonderful book.' Her smile returned, a little shyly. 'I think it's the best book I've ever read.'

He dismissed her grand words with a wave of his hand. 'Yes. Yes. But I have to think about what academia will think about it.' He looked at her pleadingly. 'You don't know what they're like. They'll tear it to bits if they find the tiniest flaw.'

She swallowed the bitter taste of his indifference then said as brightly as she could manage. 'I'm sure these problems can be sorted out. Everyone knows that there are always difficulties with the first draft of anything. Surely, it's the content that really matters. A few spelling errors won't count for much.'

She watched anxiously for his reaction, and was surprised to see him get to his feet and stride across the room to join her. He looked down at her sadly and put a hand on her shoulder 'My dear girl,' he said with gentle irony. 'Your faith is touching, and very much what a man needs at a time like this.' He bent down and kissed her gently on the forehead. 'Now, I'm afraid I must shoo you out. I have to finish reading the final chapters before this evening.'

'Yes, of course.' She was nodding to cover her confusion. 'I just wanted to give you my copy back.' She rummaged clumsily in her bag and pulled out the remaining pages. 'I'll leave them here.'

He was smiling at her, but his eyes were already distant. 'You are coming tonight?'

'Yes. It's all arranged.'

'Good, good.' He was opening the door. 'I'll see you there then.'

She was out the door before she had time to reply with the strange feeling that something had happened that she hadn't quite understood. And it was not until sometime later that the future Mrs Ewan MacLeod began to wonder if her opinion would ever carry more weight than that of a beloved pet.

As soon as they entered, Sadie was aware of three things; a noise so loud and solid that you felt it would knock you over; strange blurred colours moving past, like streaks of paint in the air, and, finally, the sickly, delicious smell of popcorn and spun sugar and winter apples covered in melting toffee. Overpowered, as she was, she might have been content to stand there forever, but Daniel was tugging at her sleeve and shouting something at her that she couldn't make out. She bent down to read his lips, but they seemed to be saying, 'Mega!', and as that made no sense, she yelled. 'What do you want to try first?'

Daniel shook his head, obviously no better equipped to hear over the noise than she was, so she waved a hand in the general direction of the chaos. 'Which one?' she yelled. This time Daniel seemed to understand. He took her sleeve and began leading her over to a ride that was slowing to a standstill. It had long, spider-like arms from which were suspended tiny, rocking carriages and on seeing it Sadie's heart began to jump nervously in her ribcage. Am I mad, she wondered, as she let Daniel lead her through the crowd. Still, it doesn't look as though it goes very high and these machines are very thoroughly checked. But then Isaac would have never got on one. *You can't check for metal fatigue.* Daniel pulled on her sleeve. 'Hurry up. We'll miss it.'

She looked down at his shining eyes and knew what she had to do. After all, it was all for Daniel. All part of her plan.

As the rough-looking man fastened them in and took their money, Sadie took a firm hold of the safety harness. Nothing in the world was going to make her let go of it. But Daniel, barely able to contain himself, was craning his head round and talking excitedly of what he saw. 'This is called the Octopus, I think. It gets really fast and makes you think you're going to crash into other seats.' Then noticing her terrified expression, he added reassuringly. 'But you don't really. And after this we can try the Big Dipper. And then we can get some candy floss and popcorn.'

There was a creak of gears and the faintest whisper of motion, so that she was barely aware that they had begun to move. Daniel leaned against her.

'Here we go.'

Chapter 33

MAGS got home a little after five, cursing herself for not making it earlier. She had meant to be back by four, but she wanted to go through the past paper questions for the last several years before doing her final revision for the Christmas exam, and the queue for the photocopier had been backed up for miles. Then, when she got there, she discovered that someone had ripped the pertinent questions out of two of the booklets and she had to go and find different copies and begin the process all over again.

As she stood in the queue, she'd thought of phoning home to see how Daniel was. But she was afraid of wakening him from a well-earned sleep. It was all he needed really to pep him up. The last few weeks had been a strain. She should have thought of that. She'd been too wrapped up with other things. Once the exams were over she'd have more time to think.

The TV was on when she opened the door, but it was broadcasting some dull gameshow, where the contestants were encouraged to guess the missing letters from words by a bored looking presenter. Not the kind of program a small boy would choose to watch. She crept over to the sofa and rightly guessed that he had fallen asleep, his head pillowed on one of the pages of his dinosaur book. Smiling to herself, she switched off the television and eased the book out from under him. She had been right. Just one day's rest and already there was a healthy flush to his cheeks and his breathing seemed less laboured. A few tell-tale streaks of pink around the corners of his lips suggested that he had eaten the remains of the strawberry jam.

Sadie entered the house timidly and opened the door to the hall. 'Sammy,' she called. Then, realising that her voice was hoarse, she called again more loudly. 'Sammy, are you home?' Even when it became obvious that he wasn't there, she stayed waiting and listening and all around her the house waited and listened with her. There was no sound, so gingerly, with all the exaggerated caution of the novice burglar, she made her way back to the kitchen and fetched out the shopping basket she'd hidden beneath the table.

Carefully, almost reverently, she took out the items one by one: a pint of full cream milk, a pound of butter, a bottle of cooking oil (she'd use that

226

later), a packet of rich, cream-filled puff pastries. With a thrill, akin to sensual pleasure, she turned the packet over and checked the fat content of the cakes once more. The figure was ridiculously, delightfully, deliciously high. Sighing, she laid it on the table in front of her chair and got up to make a pot of tea. As she filled the kettle, she was satisfied to see that her hands were still trembling.

Despite leaving the immerser on for longer than usual, the bath water was still tepid. Mags had used the last of her Christmas bubble bath to scent it, but it wouldn't form bubbles, leaving instead a scummy layer of soap floating on top, which she had to rinse off. Still, she felt better for it. The water had cleansed off some of the frustrations of the day and there would be just enough time to dry her hair in front of the fire before her mother arrived. Guiltily, she had turned it up to the highest setting. It's not for her, she told herself severely. It's for Daniel. It's cold tonight.

It was ten to seven before Mrs Gallagher arrived. Eight minutes late. Mags was ready for her, sheathed in dark silk, feet squeezed into her best shoes, she paced up and down anxiously watching the minutes tick by on the clock. She'd already tried on all her jewellery and discarded each piece as unfitting. It was more chic to leave your arms and neck bare, she told herself, but she still hadn't dared to turn face on to the mirror. She preferred what she caught out the corners of her eye, an attractive woman going out to a party. The woman in the mirror was used to such events. She was vivacious, talked easily to strangers putting them at their ease, and every so often she patted her husband's arm and they looked at each other, as if to say, 'Isn't that right, darling.'

When the sharp note of the doorbell pierced her dreams, she started up and, unused to the precarious balance of high heels, all but fell towards the front door. Her mother was standing there, clutching several plastic carriers to her ample front. 'You took long enough.'

Mags felt some of her good will freeze. 'I'm not used to these shoes.'

Her mother glanced down disapprovingly. 'If this is the first time you've worn them, you'll be sorry.'

Mags gritted her teeth. 'I meant to practice wearing them. I never got around to it.'

'O.' There was an ugly pause while Mrs Gallagher took off her coat and handed it to Mags. 'Where's the wee fellow?'

Mags' smile grew warm again. 'Asleep on the sofa. Mind you don't sit on him.'

'Asleep at this time?' Mrs Gallagher checked her watch. 'Is he all right?'

'He's fine. Just a bit tired.' Mags gestured to the table. 'I've left you some sandwiches. And you know where the coffee and everything is.'

'Aye, that's fine.' Mrs Gallagher was nodding. 'I've brought my knitting with me. If the wee one's asleep I'll get on with that jumper for Gary.'

Mags forced herself to ask, 'How is he?'

Mrs Gallagher's face lit up. 'Och, you know your brother. Always into something. He thinks he's up for head of his department next month. But he's too young. Your dad says he's too young.' She smiled to herself. 'But we'll see. We'll see.'

'That's good news,' Mags said flatly.

'We'll see,' Mrs Gallagher said again and settled herself in the chair nearest the fire. 'Does he not need a blanket?' she asked, her gaze now on Daniel.

'No, it's hot in here,' Mags said then added quickly. 'You can put one on him later if you think he needs it.'

There was another awkward silence then Mrs Gallagher said uncomfortably, 'So this is you all ready then.'

Mags gave a shrill laugh. 'I feel like I'm going to a school party.'

'You look very nice,' Mrs Gallagher said after a moment. 'The dress looks better now I see you in the right shoes.'

Mags gawped, like a little girl, but didn't answer.

'Is *he* coming to pick you up?' Mrs Gallagher suddenly asked.

The sting in the compliment. Mags had been expecting it, but she still felt the blood rush to her cheeks. 'No,' she said carefully. 'He has to be there early. And I needed to be here for Daniel. I don't like to leave him too long.'

'O.' Mrs Gallagher didn't look as though she believed her, but she only asked, 'You're not going to wear that moth eaten, old jacket, are you?'

'I can take it off in the cloakroom,' Mags said stiffly. 'No-one will see it.'

Mrs Gallagher glanced towards the window. 'You'll freeze. There's frost on the ground already.'

'It's fine,' she said unconvincingly. 'I don't feel the cold.'

Instead of answering, Mrs Gallagher pushed forward one of the plastic carriers she had been carrying. 'I brought you mine. The black woollen one. It's nothing special, but it'd be warmer than yours.' She threw a contemptuous glance towards the denim.

Mags bent down and pulled the woollen jacket from the bag. The act of kindness reached into her and frightened her in a way an attack could not have. She pulled it on, face lowered to hide her confusion. 'It's not a bad fit,' she said once she had buttoned it. But Mrs Gallagher was busy with her knitting. 'I thought it would do you. It's a bit tight on me anyway.'

Mags glanced at the clock and was surprised to see that only a few minutes had passed. 'I'd best be going,' she said.

'Aye, you do that.'

Careful not to wake him, Mags bent down and kissed Daniel on the cheek. She was a little disappointed that he hadn't been awake to see her in her finery, but she remembered that he had lost interest in any talk of the party when he'd realised that there would be neither cakes nor games. 'Sleep tight, sleepyhead,' she whispered. 'Who knows. I might have a surprise for you when I get back.'

Glancing up, she caught her mother's curious look, but she too had a secret smile, and wearing it prominently, she headed for the door.

The table was pristine, the tablecloth hanging in crisp folds, the cups and plates cleared away. In fact, it was its very neatness that drew Sammy's eye and made him cross the room to inspect it. And finding nothing, he went over to the sink and inspected the dishes. They too were without blemish. Something wasn't right. But he couldn't put his finger on it.

In the lounge, he found Sadie sound asleep in her chair. There was no sign of her knitting or memorabilia, or any of the other things that she might usually have dozed over. She seemed to have sought refuge in her chair and once there fallen into an immediate, if fitful, sleep. She groaned slightly, as though aware he was standing there. Sammy frowned. Something was going on. He just wasn't sure what.

Very gently, he reached out and touched her shoulder. 'Ma.'

She started into wakefulness the moment he spoke and reached out with both hands, as though trying to find something. Realising the something wasn't there, she stared up at him and blinked several times, trying to get her bearings. 'Sammy?'

'It's me, ma. Are you okay?'

'Yes. Yes.' She nodded vigorously at him. 'I am fine.' Her eyes were very bright and there were too pink spots in the centres of her cheeks.

'You were asleep,' he said a little helplessly. He felt there was something he should be asking, but he didn't know what. She looked at him, askance. 'At my age, you do that.'

His face relaxed. 'Okay, I guess I deserved that. You just looked restless, that's all.' He took the seat opposite her, and stretched his legs. 'So, what have you been up to today? A bit of shopping.'

'Shopping?' Sadie seemed injured. 'You think all I can do is shopping. Why should I have been shopping?'

'All right. All right.' Sammy held up a hand to defend himself. 'It's just that you seem tired. What were you doing today?'

A flash of streaming colour and screaming metal, and her own screams mute against the roar of the crowd, paralysed her throat for a moment, then she saw Sammy's questioning look and said abashed, 'I was shopping.'

Sammy laughed. 'It's not a vice, ma. Just go a little easier on yourself.

You'll tire yourself out, and you've got a busy schedule.' He glanced at his watch. 'Isn't it about time you got ready?'

Mags had taken the underground and walked up University Avenue towards the John McIntyre building. Mrs Gallagher had been right about the weather. It was already a cloudless, freezing night, and, with each step she took, her heels sent tiny constellations of frost sparking off into the darkness. But Mags wasn't cold. A clammy heat, sheened her breast and brow, and she'd long since taken her gloves off, stuffing them into her pockets with feverish contempt.

Tonight's the night, she told herself. This is what she'd waited for, down through the lonely, sleepless hours when she paced up and down eyes fixed on the phone, never daring to reach for it. But when she got close to the entrance, she discovered that she couldn't go in. Instead, she stood in the shadows and watched as expensive cars drove through the arched gateway to the car park, and men and women, tall and angular as Greek columns, made their way across the slippery ground, gliding, like dancers over the ice. She heard their voices, English and alien, cracking through the silence like splinters of glass, and for a moment she was filled with a xenophobic revulsion that made her want to turn tail and run away, putting as much distance between these suave, impossible people and herself as she could. She knew now that she couldn't go over there. She couldn't mix with them. They wouldn't see her as the future Mrs MacLeod, they would see her for what she was, and they would be charmed and puzzled and a little repelled, as if they were witnessing something unnatural, like a talking dog.

When the last couple had entered the building, the door slammed shut, taking the last vestige of yellow light, and leaving her out in the cold and the darkness. Alone. Excluded. A base need for flight turned her in the direction of home, and she had taken half a step when she suddenly remembered Ewan. *You are coming tonight, aren't you?* How could she have missed the obvious plea in his words? He wanted her there, needed her to be at his side. And here she was contemplating running out on him, abandoning him just when he wanted her to be there at his side, part of his big moment. Mags, you're a fool, she reproached herself, and slowly she began to cross the road.

A cloakroom had been set up just outside the book room, and she checked her coat in. Once it was gone, she felt suddenly self-conscious and found herself shivering in the warmth when, outside, she had sweated in the cold. To her right, two elegant, middle-aged women were entering the party, and, timidly, Mags followed behind them, hoping that their quiet self-assurance would rub off on her.

But it seemed they were known, and with hugs and kisses, that never quite met human flesh, they were absorbed into a group, leaving Mags standing, awkwardly by the door. She glanced round rapidly, trying to find a refuge, but everyone seemed to know everyone else and were standing about in laughing groups, impenetrable to the outsider. By the far wall was a table with Ewan's books piled high and a large, cardboard blow-up of the front cover standing slightly to one side, but no sign of the man himself.

'Red or white?'

Mags jumped. 'What … what's that?'

A tired looking waitress was holding up a tray of cheap wine glasses. They were alternately filled with a pale yellow or dark burgundy liquid. 'If you want a soft drink, they're over by the fire escape,' she explained wearily.

'I'll take white,' Mags said hastily. She lifted a glass clumsily, then desperate to prolong the conversation, asked, 'Have you been on long?'

The waitress stared at Mags then shrugged. 'Since half past. It's not a long affair, so I'll be on for the rest of the night.'

'Shame,' said Mags, and as she couldn't think of anything else to say, the waitress moved off, saying to no-one in particular, 'Red or white? Soft drinks by the fire escape.'

Mags watched her, feeling the sheen of sweat begin to gather on her forehead once more. She took a gulp of her wine. It was sharp and warm and bit at the back of her throat, but she didn't care. It gave her something to do. Where is he? She sipped again at her wine, but it was soon gone and she was left holding an empty glass. Glancing round for somewhere to put it down, she spotted another tray of drinks sitting on a counter. She approached it casually, and substituted her empty glass for a full one. She drank more slowly this time, but it still seemed to vanish in the blink of an eye. The alcohol lay heavily at the pit of her empty stomach. It had a giddying yet steadying affect and she quickly took another.

More confident now, she moved slowly through the crowd, trying to look as though she had a purpose. A few paces took her to the book table and she hesitated there, fascinated by the glossy towers. It was hard to believe that this thick volume, with its hard covers and glossy dust jacket, was the dog-eared manuscript that she'd pored over for so many hours. She picked one up and opened it at random, and instantly felt better. What better place for Ewan to find her? Standing, half in shadow, casually examining his book. Him, hurrying through the crowd, seeing the glamorous stranger, and faltering in his path, then realising and rushing over, his cry of delight startling everyone in the room into looking.

'Do you want that autographed?'

Mags whirled round, dropping the book on the table. The voice. Something about it. A woman was standing before Mags. She was considerably older than Mags and taller too, but there was a strange, unexpected delicacy about her, a fragility in her thin limbs and the tapering lines of her face that made her seem like one of those glass wind chimes, connected but not altogether whole. 'An autograph?' the woman repeated. She glanced over her shoulder. 'Ewan is about here somewhere. I saw him just a moment ago.' Then she smiled and gave an attractive, tinkling laugh and held out her hand. 'I'm Helen, Helen MacLeod.'

'Helen, have you seen my notes for—' Ewan's voice sounded just behind Mags' head. He broke off when he saw the two women facing each other. 'Ah,' he said bluffly, 'I see you two have found each other.'

Both women turned puzzled eyes towards him. Ewan's smile did not waver. 'Helen,' he said, putting a protective arm on his wife's shoulder. 'This is Mags, my star pupil.'

'Mags?' Helen sucked on the name, as though it had a familiar taste. 'O, you're the one with the sick, little boy.' She put a long-fingered hand to her breast. 'Ewan's told me all about it. Tragic.'

Mags said nothing. She wasn't even looking at Helen. Her eyes, large and bewildered, were staring up at Ewan, while her thoughts ran crazily round her head looking for a way out. He hasn't noticed my dress, she thought stupidly. Sadie will be disappointed if I tell her. How can he not notice? It's such a beautiful dress.

'Ahem.' Ewan was clearing his throat. 'I'll need my glasses in a minute. Now, where the devil, did I put them?'

'They're over by the bags, dear,' Helen said. 'I'll get them for you.' Her eyes were on Mags once more and they lingered there a little longer than necessary. 'So nice meeting you.'

Mags stared after her, and even when Ewan whispered in her ear, 'I didn't know she was coming. She only made her mind up this evening.' She didn't look up, but pushed him away with the unconscious carelessness of someone brushing away a fly.

'Mags,' he said urgently into her ear, but she seemed not to hear him, and just then, a young man in a turtle-neck sweater and round, thick-lensed glasses, appeared at their side. 'Dr MacLeod, I'm afraid she hasn't turned up yet, but we really need to begin soon,' he said. 'I tried calling again, but there's no answer, so she may be on her way.'

Ewan nodded then turned back to Mags, but she was walking away, heading towards the waitress with the tray of drinks.

The young man in the round spectacles rapped several times on the side of an empty wine glass with a pencil and a hush fell over the crowd. 'Thank you for joining us in this celebration of *The Shadow In Our Wake*. I'm sure that you are every bit as excited, at its publication, as we are.' He paused to allow the inevitable murmurs of approval and raisings of glass. Mags didn't raise her glass to Ewan. She raised it to her lips and took a long, defiant swallow. She was standing quite apart from the chummy cliques around her. It didn't matter that she was alone, because no amount of human contact could have reached her then.

She saw Mrs MacLeod, the real, the only Mrs MacLeod, sidle up beside Ewan and hand him his glasses. She saw her whisper something to him and him smile and nod, as though they were sharing a joke. Then Ewan began to speak, but she didn't hear what he was saying. She saw only a couple, who were married, and a man, who had no intention of changing things. Vaguely, she was aware of him thanking the contributors to the book, and at one point, it seemed that everyone turned to look at her, but she stood there, encased in silence, a wax image without thoughts or senses until a familiar voice said,

'O, Mags, good. Look after Sammy for me please.'

The wax cracked a little and Mags turned to look at Sadie. 'What are you—' she began and then it was suddenly all so clear, so very obvious that she should have seen it from the start, that she burst out laughing. 'I should have known,' she spluttered. 'I really should have known.' She was aware that Ewan had stopped talking, and that a shocked silence had fallen over the room, but she didn't care. 'I am a fool, Sadie,' she said loudly, then looking over at Ewan, repeated, 'I'm a fool, Dr MacLeod, a complete and utter fool.'

Sammy had his hand on her shoulder, pulling her back, and Sadie had hurried forward into the spotlight, taking hold of Ewan's hands and exclaiming loudly, 'Dr MacLeod, so good of you to wait for an old woman. There is still time for me to speak, no?'

Ewan gave a frozen smile. He seemed relieved to pass the focus of everyone's attention on to someone else. 'Ladies and gentleman, I would like to introduce you to Mrs Sadie Gordon, or rather, as those of you who have read the draft versions, to Sergei Jacobi.' There were murmurs of interest and all eyes fell on Sadie. She had several crumpled sheets of paper in her hand, the translation of her speech, already committed to memory, but accompanying her as a prop should her courage fail. Noticing them, Ewan continued more confidently. 'Sadie was one of those, who asked for her true identity to be concealed in the book, but she recently came to me to suggest that she would like to take this opportunity of revealing who she is and of saying a few words.' There was a polite patter of applause. Mags did not join in. She was leaning heavily against Sammy, her eyes, wondering and concerned, on Sadie.

When the applause had trickled away, there was a long silence, and even through her haze, Mags could see that Sadie was plainly terrified. She took an involuntary step towards her, but Sammy squeezed her shoulder, perhaps in restraint, perhaps to show he understood. She waited, strangely finding Sadie's embarrassment more excruciating than her own. But then, she hadn't had time to think about her own humiliation. Time enough for that when this dreadful evening was over.

Feet had begun to shuffle and Ewan was staring desperately at Sadie, as though trying to find a way of controlling her remotely, when suddenly she began to speak. 'Thank you everyone for taking the time to listen to an old lady,' she began slowly. The room was hushed in a reverent silence, as though afraid of breaking her concentration by making a sound. Sadie glanced over at the trays of soft drinks, wished she had one to whet her throat, and continued in as loud a voice as she could manage. 'Many of you here today perhaps have read my story. Many of you think maybe that you understand why I did not want my name revealed.' She was talking to the crowd, but her eyes were fixed on Mags. 'But you will be wrong.' For a moment, she broke contact with Mags eyes and stared down at the floor. She seemed almost to say something to herself, and when she lifted her head again her eyes were filled with determination. 'You are wrong,' she repeated. 'The reason I wished my name concealed is because part of my story is a lie.'

There had been silence, but now a wave of shock rippled through the crowd. Heads turned to each other, shook back and forth in disbelief then turned to look back at Sadie. She stood there, a tiny, lonely figure, waiting for the confusion to die down. At one point, she turned to Ewan and said something, and a moment later a chair was fetched so that she could sit down.

'Please,' she said, and her voice was so hoarse that she had to repeat herself. 'Please understand that most of my story is true. Sergei and Aaron existed, or as we truly were Sadie and Piotr, just in the same way that you do. The difference is in the end, and is in the way people understand themselves and those around them.' She paused briefly and sighed before going on. 'To some people, we are singular, alone. We come into the world on our own and we leave it that way. That is the essence of who we are and where our freedom lies' She looked round to see if anyone understood, but their faces were blank. Only Mags was nodding slowly.

'But to others we are not free, not gods to ourselves. We are only part of a greater whole and the individual is nothing but a cog or a wheel in the great mechanism that drives us. To such men, life is not sacred, not precious. But something which can be sacrificed towards the greater good. Such a man was my Aaron. Or Piotr, which, as I said, was his real name. You should know that.' Sadie stopped again, and even at a distance, Mags could see tears in her eyes.

'The Piotr that you will read about in Dr MacLeod's book came to see that a single human life is worth much more than an empty idea that denies life.

The real Piotr, my Piotr, did not.'

There was no sound in the room, no sound at all. There was only the emptiness that follows a gasp.

Sadie shifted a little in her chair and her voice dropped so that it could only just be heard by the straining audience. 'On that last night, when all our compatriots fled into the forest and I alone went back to warn Piotr. I found him. But not a changed man, not a man who finally saw that the part is so much greater than the whole. No.' she shook her head sadly. 'A great man cannot change his ideals. Even if those ideals are wrong.'

The grip on Mags' shoulder tightened and she knew that Sadie was coming to the climax of her speech.

'My Piotr was going to betray us to his Party. To him it meant more than any one of us, more than life, more than love itself. And in a way, when I found him on the phone calling the GPU, my Piotr died there and then.'

'What did you do?' an excited voice in the crowd suddenly cried out and was hushed by those surrounding it.

'What did I do?' Sadie repeated, her eyes still on Mags. 'Me, who believed in the right to be oneself before any other moral precept. What did I do?' She took a deep breath and seemed to be struggling to exhale it. Her cheeks turned red and her eyes bulged. 'What did I do?' She grimaced, spitting the final words out between clenched teeth. 'I did the only thing I could do. I shot him.'

There was a stunned silence in the room, exactly as though a real gun had been fired. There was no sound, not the tiniest tinkle of glass or the slightest rustle of clothing. Then a small voice asked incredulously, You killed him? And a riptide of questions spewed forth as though the recoil of their curiosity suddenly swept them back into life.

'How?'

'Why?'

'Did the others know?'

'Have you kept this secret all this time?'

'Why now?'

Helpless and terrified, Sadie was buffeted against their questions unable to speak a single monosyllable. She had done what she had come to do and now her courage failed her. The clamour of their voices reached her only as a shrill, harsh babble, the shriek of wild animals, appalling and meaningless. She looked desperately towards Mags, but she wasn't there any more. The space she had occupied was now fought over by two predatory men, who tried to jostle closer to her, mouths wide with words she couldn't hear. A strong hand took her by the shoulder and she might have flinched if her maternal instinct had not forewarned her.

'Come on, ma' said Sammy in her ear. 'Time to get you out of here before you start a riot.'

Sadie obeyed with involuntary, marionette-like movements, her startled eyes still on the place where Mags had been standing.

She found Mags ten minutes later, sitting on a bench in that sliver of Kelvingrove Park that extends behind the university quadrangles. She was sitting perfectly still, her eyes fixed on the black water of the Kelvin, her mouth in a narrow, expressionless line. And, had it not been for the thin trail of breath escaping from her lips into the cold night air, she might not have been a living being at all. She made no sign of hearing Sadie's clumsy approach down the steep bank behind her, but just as Sadie reached the bench, she said in a hard, flat voice, 'Why did you tell me that story?'

Numbed by her confession and her escape and her frantic search in the darkness, Sadie could only find it within herself to slump down on the opposite end of the bench from Mags, her breath coming in ragged, freezing clouds. 'You shouldn't be out here without a coat,' she said irrelevantly. 'Sammy has gone to get it. But I think he went to see if you were anywhere in the building first.'

'But you knew I'd be here,' Mags said softly. 'You know quite a bit about me, don't you, Sadie?'

Sadie glanced at Mags sharply, but she was still looking at the water, her eyes as black as their depths.

'All that talk about the individual, the rights of the person. I thought you were trying to tell me something about me. But that's not it, is it?' Mags suddenly turned towards Sadie and her eyes had two white lights in them, the reflection of a distant street lamp, hard and penetrating as twin stars. 'What's it all about? Why did you tell me that story?'

Sadie sighed, and afraid of those eyes that looked at her so fiercely and pleadingly, she let her own glance stray over the water. When she spoke, her voice was very soft, a ripple of sound on the still, night air. 'I wanted you to know that not all stories have a happy ending.'

She had expected an exclamation or at least a gasp, the first-born cry of new insight. But there was nothing. Mags made not the smallest sound. When at last she dared to take a peep, she found Mags' face closed and shuttered, an oval of stone on a granite body. Sadie felt a rush of remorse. She had gone too far, pushed this woman beyond what anyone should have to face. 'O Mags, please believe I—' she began, but Mags' face turned towards her and she could not go on in the light of what she saw there. The granite lips parted painfully and Mags said in a frightened voice, 'Don't say anything more. It's best that we don't say anything more.'

Sadie's open mouth shut, like a door closed fast on a room full of secrets, and when Sammy eventually found them, they were sitting together in silence before the black stillness of the water, close as lovers, distant as stars.

Chapter 34

It was early when Mags woke the next day. Darkness had not yet lifted and the street lamps still cast their cadmium haze through the thin curtains. She lay for a little watching the shadows on the ceiling, feeling strangely refreshed.

Last night, when she got in, having refused Sammy's generous offer of a ride home, she had fended off Mrs Gallagher's suspicious curiosity with numbed ease, even managing to smile and assure her that everything had gone perfectly as she helped her on with her coat and saw her to the door. Even once her mother had gone there was no passionate outburst, no storms of emotion tearing her apart. She felt quite calm, an enduring rock in a turbulent sea.

Daniel was in bed by the time she'd arrived.

'Wee soul barely woke up,' Mrs Gallagher had said. 'He practically slept walked his way to bed. You'd think he'd been out running in the marathon.'

So she'd crept into his room and stood in the darkness, straight and silent, longing to cradle him in her arms, afraid that it might disturb him. She stood, feeling that something had broken, something she had thought to be very precious. But now that it was gone, she realised that it had never really been hers in the first place. At last, when the ache of her bones and the protests of her muscles reached her brain, she dared to reach out and touch his cheek. 'Just you and me then,' she whispered.

By the time Daniel made his groggy way into the lounge the next morning, she had already showered, drunk two cups of strong coffee, and was engrossed in taking notes from one of her large, musty-smelling books. She looked up as Daniel entered the room and smiled. 'Morning, sleepyhead.'

He grunted and yawned, then suddenly remembering asked, 'Was it a good party?'

Mags shook her head and her smile shrank just a little. 'No. No games, no cakes.'

'Told you.' He headed off to the kitchen to pour out some cereal, and she found herself watching him furtively from the corners of her eyes. Was he thinner? The bony elbows, the triangular shoulder blades, were they more pronounced?

'How are you feeling?' she asked. And then, because her tongue had been papery and stuck to the roof of her mouth, she coughed and asked the question again. 'Daniel, how are you doing?'

He glanced over at her, surprised. 'I'm fine, mum.' Then an anxious thought furrowed his brow and he added, 'Well maybe not fine.' He clutched his stomach. 'I feel a bit sick … sometimes.'

She arched an eyebrow. 'It's all right. I told Mrs Lorne you'd be off for a few days.'

He brightened visibly, and wanting to keep that light in his face, Mags took the plunge. 'Daniel, it … it wouldn't bother you too much if we didn't see so much of Ewan any more, would it?'

Daniel's eyes grew round and astonished, but she was touched to see that he fought to control his delight. 'No,' he said casually. 'Not much.'

'Good.' She smiled and was about to add something more when he said suddenly, 'Maybe we could see more of Sammy.'

She bit her lip. His fondness extended beyond Sadie. She should have seen that. 'I don't think Sammy's wife would like that,' she said gently.

He shrugged this information away dismissively. 'O her. She doesn't care. They're getting a divorce.'

'Danny!' Mags was shocked. 'How do you know that? Sammy didn't tell you.'

'No.' His contempt for this suggestion was evident. 'I heard him speaking on the upstairs phone last time I was there.'

'What were you doing upstairs?'

He sighed impatiently. 'I had to go to the toilet.'

'But what about the one under the stairs?' she asked stupidly.

'I like the one upstairs better.'

'Why?'

'The towels are warm.'

She stared at him, not knowing whether to laugh or cry. Eventually, she asked guiltily, 'How do you know he's getting a divorce?'

Daniel screwed up his forehead trying to remember. 'He said he'd spoken to his lawyer and she'd got everything she was going to and there wasn't much of anything anyway.'

'Even so,' Mags said doubtfully, but Daniel wasn't finished.

'He said that it hadn't been so much of a marriage as a shopping expedition, and as soon as he got something … ' Daniel rubbed his left temple trying to recall the term. It came to him and he grinned at Mags triumphantly. 'As soon as he got his nice degree it would be all over.'

'His *Decree Nisi*?' Mags suggested.

Daniel shrugged, a little injured at the correction. 'Anyway, he said it would be all over.' He watched her closely. She was nodding to herself, a thoughtful, faraway look in her eyes. And realising that it was important to say something positive about Sammy without appearing to be too interested himself, he said, 'He knows all about dinosaurs.'

Mags blinked, as though starting awake. 'You haven't told him that you listened to what he was saying?'

'Course not.' Daniel was hurt.

'Good,' Mags was looking stern. 'See that you don't.'

Daniel shrugged and rubbed a toe along the carpet. 'Wasn't going to anyway,' he muttered disgustedly. 'I'm not stupid.' And with that he swept from the room, carrying an overflowing bowl of *Coco Pops* with him.

He was mildly surprised to find that Mags made no attempt to chide him for his rudeness.

Sitting with the tutorial group, awaiting Ewan's arrival, Mags began to feel the palms of her hand begin to sweat. She was angry with herself for the feeling because she felt that she was calmer than that. It was over. And in her heart, she was glad, but her heart still beat too hard when she heard his footsteps approaching.

She wasn't sure what she'd expected him to do. Gasp to find her sitting calmly with the others? Order her out? Something. She expected some event to mark the change between them. But, when Ewan entered the room, he seemed as composed and self-assured as ever. He smiled politely and took his place at the head of the table, rustling through his notes with such quiet concentration that Mags found herself trembling, as though in equal and opposite reaction to it.

'Right, let's get started.' Ewan looked up, and somehow his gaze encompassed everyone except Mags, effectively excluding her as precisely as though she'd been cut out with a scalpel's precision. For a brief moment, she felt angry. So, this was how it was going to be. Two people who had never known one another. Just for a few seconds, Mags felt a rush of sadness for what might have been. But then some wise, new part of her brain told her that those things were never to have been. It had been her dream, not his.

And she felt Sadie had been trying to tell her this during her confession. A shared future must have a shared dream. And now seeing him, thumbing through papers, his glasses perched on the end of his nose, the thumb of his right hand inky with marking, she knew for the first time that this man could never share her dreams. She sat up suddenly, straightening her back and startling the mousy girl opposite with her sudden smile.

The mouse was talking, her voice small and stuttering as she read passages from her essay to back up her argument. Mags was a little surprised to hear that she was talking about historical freedom. Hadn't they left that subject weeks ago? But, then again, perhaps they hadn't. Perhaps she had merely made up her mind. The mouse was reading her essay, carefully referencing her disconnected thoughts to the recommended reading in a desperate effort not to be held responsible for an original idea. 'We can never act in true freedom. We want to act freely, but our inner potential will always be limited by external forces which prevent us from realising it. That's from Spinoza.' She glanced at Ewan, who was staring at her, a bored, contemptuous smile quirking one side of his lips. 'Go on,' he said. 'I'd like to hear more about your opinions on the progression of freedom.'

And for no apparent reason at all, Mags suddenly realised that whenever he smiled, he pulled his lips down, whereas Sammy's always curled up.

The mouse rustled her papers and nibbled nervously at the end of her pen. 'As … as Hegel tells us,' she began uncertainly. 'History is the advancement of humanity towards an increasing self-consciousness which is … which is freedom itself.' She could not bear to meet Ewan's eye. 'That's what Hegel says,' she ended lamely.

Ewan sighed. 'Would anyone like to add to that?' Again, his glance went around the table, but somehow exempted Mags.

Craig began to speak in his low, sardonic tone without waiting for acknowledgement from Ewan. 'I think what … ' He plainly couldn't remember her name. 'I think that what you are … trying to say, is that the advancement of history is the progression of man, of individuals reaching for a common good.'

'Yes.' Audrey was plainly excited. 'Freedom in a historical context is the progression of the common man.'

'No, it isn't.'

All eyes swung towards Mags. Even Ewan was looking at her, perhaps with the deliberate intention of intimidating her. But he couldn't do that anymore. She took a deep breath and began to speak. 'Freedom isn't about the common man. He has nothing to do with it. He doesn't even think about it.'

They were staring at her with shocked, disbelieving faces, but she went on. 'The common man doesn't want freedom. He wants food on his table and a roof over his head and for history to leave him alone.'

'Don't you consider yourself to be one of the common people?' Audrey asked. There was a note of incredulity in her voice, as though she was asking if Mags considered whether she had ten fingers and ten toes.

Mags didn't answer for a moment and when she did her voice was very soft but very level. 'I don't really know what's meant by the common people,' she admitted. 'If you mean people who work nine till five then drink in a pub till bedtime and get up in the morning and do it all again, no I don't consider myself one.'

'So where does freedom lie for you, Mags?'

Ewan had spoken and she met his eyes without pain, without regret. 'It lies in the heart of the individual. In the uncommon man.' She smiled self-consciously. 'Or woman. It doesn't lie with the common man, whether he is part of the herd because he goes down the social or the bingo or the pub, or whether because he has a fat bank balance and stocks and shares and he goes to the theatre and the opera. It lies with those who have a vision of a better life and who need to change things. Not because they can or because they should. But because they must.' Her speech came to an end and she was surprised to find that she had risen to her feet and that her eyes were on Ewan alone.

There was a silence then he coughed uncomfortably. 'That's certainly a very original way of putting it,' he said carefully. 'Would anyone like to add to what Ms Gallagher has said?'

There was a shuffling of feet and a restless rustling of bags and papers. Someone offered a comment. Someone else countered it. Mags wasn't listening. She was standing in a calm space that separated her from the rest of the room, relieved that she did not have to find the words to say goodbye to Ewan. Her speech had divided them more powerfully than any words of law for putting man and woman asunder.

Later, outside in the quad, she looked up at the sky, half expecting to see some symbol of her freedom, a bird soaring overhead, the rays of the sun breaking through. But the sky remained grey, the clouds, like shadows over the world.

Sadie spread a thick layer of butter on her toast then looked round for the jam platter. It was empty and she regarded it with wide, surprised eyes. Hadn't it been full when she'd sat down?

'It's your fifth slice,' Sammy said from behind his newspaper.

'No. I'm sure I have not eaten more than two.'

Sammy put down his paper.

'Maybe three,' she admitted.

'Five. Six if you had any before I came down.'

Downcast, she looked at the unjammed toast on her plate until Sammy softened. 'It isn't good for you. Fat does terrible things to your arteries.'

'At my time of life, I should want to be a keep fit fanatic,' she said irritably and took a defiant bite of toast.

He watched her for a moment then offered. 'I could go and get the dress back for you. She isn't the type to steal it. She's probably just embarrassed.'

Sadie turned miserable eyes towards him. She'd failed. How could she explain that to him? She'd tried to reach Mags through the only medium she knew how and she had failed. He was watching her expectantly and she waved her hand irritably. 'What do I need a dress to fit a knitting needle? You think I will be going out on a date, maybe?'

Sammy opened his mouth to protest, but the phone rang, startling them both out of their hostility. 'I'll get it,' Sammy said, getting to his feet. A moment later he was back, a strange look on his face. 'It's Mags,' he said. 'For you.'

'Right,' said Sadie adopting his tone of indifference. 'Just give me a moment to get there.'

Out in the hall, she hesitated before the receiver, only daring to pick it up when she heard the crackling from the mouthpiece that sounded like a voice calling, hello. She held it to her ear. 'Mags?'

'Yes.' The voice came distantly and a little shyly over the line. 'How are you?'

'Fine, and you.'

'O fine, fine.'

'How is Daniel.'

'O, he's fine too. His teacher was a bit worried about him, but there doesn't seem to be anything the matter.'

There was a silence, and Sadie was wondering if she was expected to say something, and if she was, what that something might be, when Mags suddenly blurted, 'I'm sorry about last night. I think I had too much to drink and I probably said things I shouldn't have.'

'Mags.' Sadie's relief fuelled her compassion. 'There is nothing to be sorry about. Truly. I was just afraid I had upset you.'

'No. Not at all.' It was Mags turn to be compassionate. 'Just the drink talking.' There was a short silence then she said hurriedly. 'I'll bring your dress round next dry day.'

'O, I had forgotten all about it,' Sadie lied. 'Bring it any time. No rush.'

'I'll do that.' There was another awkward silence and Sadie was suddenly afraid that Mags was about to hang up. 'Would you like to go to a balloon show?' she asked.

Chapter 35

LOOKING back, the balloon show was one of the most perfect days of Mags' life. It was one of those strange, magical times, which seem to have been crafted from finer sentiments than the grey wash of ordinary days. Sammy hired a car and drove them down through the angry tangle of countryside to the little holiday town of Largs. All the way there, the adults threw wild bantering remarks at each other, as though the gift of the laughter was too precious and dangerous a thing to hold, and had to be tossed to the next person, like a live grenade. And Daniel sat on the back seat behind Sammy, silent and wondering and pleased.

They were late arriving. The narrow road along the coast had been blocked by roadworks, and they'd passed the time listening to Sammy singing an obscene song about camels until Sadie managed to piece together enough of a translation to tell him to stop.

Once the car was precariously and illegally parked, they piled out and headed towards the beach. They walked slowly, and Mags was happy to do this because Sadie could not have gone any faster. Besides she enjoyed watching Daniel's excitement, seeing him straining against his anticipation, like a puppy on the leash. He turned to her at one point, saying, Mum, come on, in such pleading tones that, for a moment, she could believe that it was her own slowness that held them back.

They rounded a corner and there they were. Majestic as towers, diaphanous as clouds, balloons rising, like magnificent sprites straining against their puny earthbound chains to reach the blue arch of the heavens. Sammy waved a hand towards them, the grin on his face as proud as though he were personally responsible for their beauty.

'What do you think, Daniel?'

'Amazing,' Daniel replied, awed. 'Just like great big clowns' bums.'

Mags stared at him then glanced sharply up at Sammy, then she was laughing, huge, great gulps of mirth that made her hold her sides then Sammy's arm was there to keep from falling over. And he was laughing with her because he understood, then Daniel and Sadie began to laugh too, because they didn't. She went on laughing until there were tears in her eyes and the whole world was washed away in it. And even years later, when she thought of this day, the laughter would come back to her, bitter-sweet, like the call of ravens.

They had to wait in a long queue, and as they neared, Sadie began to see how flimsy the structures were that she intended to entrust her life to. What if it was to collapse under the weight of three adults? And she thought guiltily of that extra slice of toast she'd had that morning. Glancing anxiously up at Sammy, she hissed. 'Maybe it would be better if only Daniel and I go. You and Mags could watch us from the ground. Wave even,' she added by way of encouragement.

Sammy's eyes narrowed. 'Ma, as you're the one who's petrified of heights, shouldn't you stay on the ground?'

He spoke loud enough for Mags to hear, and she turned around, concerned. 'You're afraid of heights?' she asked, puzzled.

'Afraid of heights?' Sadie gave a careless laugh. 'Why would I ask you to a balloon show if I was afraid of heights.'

'But—' Mags began, looking to Sammy for help. But Sadie dismissed his opinion with a wave of her hand. 'He thinks he is God that he can see into my mind now.'

Mags was still looking at Sammy, but he raised his eyebrows and shrugged. 'We'll all go together,' he said firmly.

Getting into the basket proved by far the worst obstacle. Mags and Daniel clambered in easily, Daniel glowering at the man, who dared refer to him as 'the little un'. Then Sammy swung his long legs over the side with comparable ease. But Sadie had gone rigid with fright and could not manage the tiny, mobile staircase. No amount of coaxing could persuade her to take a step and yet she was adamant that she must go. And, in the end, she was hoisted, without ceremony, up the side of the basket by two of the men, obviously more used to hoisting hay bales, and dropped into Sammy's arms, quite intact with only a stocking and her dignity shredded.

Fumbling to get upright, she grasped the side of the basket and regarded the others through wild eyes. 'We are having fun, no?' she whispered hoarsely and nodded vigorously in the hope of reassuring them.

'It's okay, ma.' Sammy put a reassuring hand on her shoulder.

'I thought Daniel might be frightened,' she said weakly. But Daniel's smile was so broad that his whole face was almost lost behind two rows of pearly teeth. 'It's ace, Sadie,' he called. 'Really ace.'

Then there was a shout by one of the men and there was a rush of air. Beneath them, the earth fell away and they were rising, through the ice blue atmosphere. It was all too much for Sadie and she closed her eyes. But she heard distinctly Daniel shouting, '. Look at me, Sadie. Look I'm flying.'

It was raining the next day, a bleak, steady downpour, depressing and grey, but Sadie didn't notice. She wasn't wearing her gloves, and her hat was on more from habit than weatherproofing. She stood quietly, waiting for a small funeral party to leave. They were on the East side of the graveyard, and had shown no sign of even noticing the small, stooped woman standing patiently before one of the graves, let alone being curious about her. But, still, there are certain things a person needs total privacy for.

When the gate had clanged shut and she was certain she was alone, she took a deep breath, and said in a calm, clear voice, 'Isaac, we need to talk.'

There was no response, and after waiting a polite length of time, she shrugged and glanced skywards. 'That's okay. You don't have to say anything. It's me that needs to talk.' The rain was too heavy to allow her to keep looking up so she concentrated on the headstone instead. 'Sammy's well,' she began hesitantly. 'He doesn't send his love because he doesn't know I'm here, but I know he would if he did. I didn't tell him I was coming because he was already angry with me for not having my pills in the car yesterday. But he'll understand when he finds out. He's a good boy.' There was a rustle of wind, like a sigh and Sadie grimaced guiltily. 'I know. I know. Get to the point, Sadie. Well, Isaac, I've done it. He's laid to rest and gone.' There was nothing but the sound of falling rain, but she nodded faintly, as though in answer to a question. 'Yes, yes I know. I should have done it years ago, but sometimes you need a reason to let someone go.' Her eyes fell on some moss that had begun to grow in curving letters of his name. Had it been there the last time? Things change so fast.

'She's trying to pretend that she doesn't understand, that she doesn't see what I'm trying to tell her. But she does. I am certain she does. And she'll understand later too. I hope you understand. I can't think of a better way, and it is time. I'm sure of that.' She straightened and paused a moment, checking her pulse in the way Dr Farmer had shown her. It throbbed steadily under her wrist, like the tick of a well-oiled mechanism. Sadie looked back up at the sky, blinking the rain from her eyes 'Trouble is, I never felt better in my life.'

Mags ran up the concrete steps to the library, her mind full of the morning's events. She had sat for a long time with her tutor pretending to listen to all the arguments against changing a subject mid-term. He had made a number of hints that such things were not acceptable and refused to commit himself. 'It really is a most unusual request. I'll have to look into it.'

And, she in turn, had refused to give her reasons for wanting to change, merely hinting that there were some things better overlooked.

But, secretly, she knew that she was going to change no matter what, so she looked past him at the view of a brick wall outside the dim little office and thought of the balloon show.

The journey back had impressed itself most on her mind. Daniel had been so fatigued by the whole event that he'd fallen asleep in the car, still chattering about how wonderful it had all been. Even, as his head began to nod, he'd reached out to her, letting her cushion him on her lap and place her arm over him, like a baby. It was a long time since he'd allowed such intimacy and she held on to it with all the passion and terror of new love. She let the warmth of him make her drowsy, and her head nodded gently forward closer to the soft, exposed hollow of his neck.

He'd been overexcited by the day, rushing around after Sammy, haring back to her with questions about hot dogs and whether he liked mustard, and an afterthought about, was it all right to have popcorn as well when he'd obviously already accepted the offer. He didn't smell too good now, an acrid, little boy smell, too sour to smell like a baby, too milky to smell like a man. It was the most wonderful smell in the world.

'Mags.'

The voice startled her out of her thoughts. 'Sammy?' She stared up at him, surprised. 'What are you doing here?' She was standing in the entrance to the library with no memory of how she got there.

He was leaning into against a corner, hands in pockets, obviously trying to keep out of the watchful stare of the porter. 'I came to find you.'

She shook her head blankly. 'How did you know I'd be here?'

'I didn't.' He looked uncomfortably. 'But your phone's off.' —She had cancelled it just after the book party. It was Ewan's gift, and she had no right to it now.— I thought of driving over, but I had to give the car back yesterday, and, besides, I don't like leaving ma.'

Mags was alarmed. 'Is Sadie okay?'

'No. Yes.' Sammy brushed a hand through his hair. 'It's just that she's been acting so peculiarly these last few days.' He glanced away from her through the glass doors. 'Look, could we sit down somewhere.' He pointed at the building opposite. 'We could get a coffee in the Ref'. You can't drink it, but it would be an excuse to sit down.'

Over a coffee, which was every bit as undrinkable as they'd expected, he explained. 'All my life, ma's been like a rock to me.' He stirred the liquid in his cup with a sliver of plastic. 'Don't get me wrong, my father was a fine man. But ma was always the one everyone went to, if you understand what I mean.'

Mags didn't, but she nodded and dared a sip of her drink.

Sammy went on stirring his, and Mags had the impression that he was talking more to himself than her. 'Lately, she's been so strange. Self-absorbed. Not quite here, as if there are other things on her mind.'

'She is getting on a bit,' Mags ventured.

Sammy didn't look up. 'I know. I know,' he said dismissively. 'But it isn't like that.' His brows wrinkled with the effort of explaining. 'It's not like an old person getting confused.'

Mags leaned forward on her hands trying to understand. 'Does she seem sick?'

'No.' Sammy looked back at her with helpless, puzzled eyes. 'If anything, she seems healthier than ever.'

Mags struggled to find something to say. 'Has she lost interest in things. Some old people get very—'

But he cut her off. 'No. She's taken to doing things she would never have dreamt of before.'

An image of Sadie's terror came back to Mags. 'Like the ballooning.'

'Like the ballooning,' Sammy agreed. 'And other things too. I found ticket stubs to the carnival in the bottom of her shopper a few days ago.'

Mags shrugged and tried to suppress a smile. 'Well, maybe she feels like she's missed out a bit.'

Sammy shook his head. 'No, it's more than that. She's eating all the things the doctor told her to avoid. I don't know what's got into her.'

A half-remembered memory slipped into Mags' mind. 'In the car,' she began excitedly. 'Something about pills? I was half asleep.'

Sammy slapped the table. 'Exactly. She had such a fright over the balloon flight that I told her to take one of her heart pills.' He opened his arms in a gesture of bafflement. 'She wasn't carrying them.'

'She forgot?'

'No.' Sammy was adamant. 'No. Something's going on.' He looked at Mags pleadingly. 'I hoped she might have said something to you.'

'To me?' Mags was startled. 'Why me?'

Sammy frowned. 'Isn't it obvious? She thinks a great deal of you.'

Mags gave a slight shake of her head to dismiss the remark, but Sammy's expression was so intense that she was afraid that he would bring up the party. She scrambled to her feet. 'I really have to be going,' she said quickly. Then, feeling bad, added, 'I'm sorry, Sammy, but she really hasn't confided anything in me. I'd tell you if I knew.'

She left him staring into his coffee, stirring it with the sliver of plastic.

She had meant to go back to the library. She needed to do a lot of research if she was to change subject half way through the term. There was no reason not to go. She had no classes that afternoon, and the day was grey and unpromising. It was the perfect time to hole up in the library and catch up on some reading. There was no reason not to go. No reason at all. She turned briskly, and headed for the bus stop.

The house was quiet when she entered. So silent and still that she was aware of her own footsteps falling on the thin carpet. 'Daniel.' She shouldn't call him. He might be asleep. But she did it again. 'Daniel.' Her voice was thin, not penetrating the thick air. No wonder he couldn't hear.

She crossed the living room, checking the sofa as she passed, though she knew he wasn't there. 'Daniel.' She whispered it now, softly opening the door to his room. It was dark inside. The curtains were still drawn, but a steely light filtered through the gaps where they didn't meet. Daniel was sleeping, his arm thrown carelessly over his head, the fingers dangling, delicately in mid-air. Mags stood in the doorway letting the breath slowly out of her lungs. Asleep. He was just sleeping. She stood there, transfixed. He was so beautiful in sleep. She'd never really realised until the car journey when he'd lain in her arms. Sleep in children is so poignant to mothers because it marks a place they cannot go. They must let their children cross into the dark alone, unable to warn of danger, unable to catch them when they fall.

Mags stood in the doorway, silent and afraid. The daylight made the shadows in the room seem lighter than black. She could see how they tinged the pallor of his skin a pale blue. But it was just the shadows. Only the shadows.

Chapter 36

SADIE had almost never been in a hospital in her life. Sammy had been born at home. Isaac had died at work. And she had never been ill, not seriously ill. So, apart from the odd visit to a recovering friend, she had never actually been inside one. It was strange, therefore, to feel such hatred for them. And yet she did. The antiseptic smell, clawing at the back of her throat. Covering, what? The endless maze of corridors, the menacing doors, marked, Authorised Personnel Only. It all added up to a frightening whole that couldn't be seen or heard or pointed at, but that crept under her skin making her scalp crawl.

They got lost twice and had to ask directions three times. 'God help they should have an emergency,' Sadie sniffed disdainfully, then turned frightened eyes to meet Sammy's. 'I didn't mean ...'

But he squeezed her arm. 'It's okay, ma. I know what you meant.'

The nurse that greeted them was not young, but she had a fresh, scrubbed look about her that made her seem kindly. 'Are you family?' she enquired.

'Yes,' said Sammy as Sadie replied, 'No.' They gasped, appalled, then contradicted each other again once then twice more before looking sheepishly at the nurse. She was frowning, but seeing their anxious faces, she relented, pointing out a small room off the main ward. 'Through there. But, don't stay too long,' she warned. 'He's only meant to have two visitors.'

They approached it reverently, not knowing what they would find. The door was half open, and Sammy pushed it wide, sensing that the harsh percussion of a knock was inappropriate. Sadie entered first then stopped, blocking Sammy's way. At first, she couldn't see Daniel. There was a hospital bed, stark white tucked into chrome. And round the bed, hard, threatening machines. Machines of all kinds, they blinked their LCD eyes at her, repeating their dismal tasks over and over, indifferently. Wires ran out of the machines and converged on a single spot on the bed. An area, so tiny that it hardly disturbed the flat expanse of the bedcover. Daniel.

'Daniel.' Her lips moved without her knowing it. A figure, by the bed, she hadn't noticed suddenly lifted its head from its hands and looked up. 'Sadie?' It got out of its chair and shuffled towards them, arms outstretched, like a dazed, old woman. 'So nice of you to come. Thanks for coming. So nice.'

'We heard from a neighbour,' Sammy explained. 'I went round to your house to see you. The neighbour said there had been an ambulance.' His voice trailed off.

'Yes.' Mags was nodding vaguely. 'Nice of you to come. So nice.'

'How … is he?' Sadie asked, daring to take a step closer. The figure in the bed was motionless, unreal, a waxen doll. Only the machines around him groaned and chattered with metallic life. Mags didn't look at the bed. She seemed to look at anything but the bed. 'He's sedated just now. But the doctor said he'll be awake in a couple of hours. It's good of you to come,' she added vaguely.

'Mags, I think you should sit down,' Sammy said, leading her back to her chair. 'Here, ma, you take this one.' He pulled out a straight-backed chair for Sadie.

'Mags,' Sadie began timidly. 'What did the doctor say about his … whether he will … ' She could not finish the question. But Mags seemed not to hear her. 'Do you know how near Christmas it is?' she asked suddenly. Sammy and Sadie exchanged glances. 'No,' said Sammy. 'But not long, I suppose.'

'Ten days.' She stared at them wonderingly. 'Can you believe that. I had no idea. The shops are full of tinsel and plastic snowmen. They must have been for months. You know what they're like. But I didn't notice.'

'You have had a lot on your mind,' Sadie ventured.

But, still, Mags was not listening. 'I should have made sure that Daniel saw Santa. Daniel loves Christmas. And I should have gotten his presents by now.' She shook her head and went on in baffled tones, 'But I didn't think it was so late. How could it have gotten to be so late?'

There was a rap on the door and the fresh-faced nurse looked in. 'Not too long now,' she said.

Sammy nodded. 'We're just leaving.' He turned to Mags. 'Are you able to get here all right? I could get another car.'

She shook her head and pointed in the direction of a battered Z-bed. 'They let me stay here. My mother and father have brought me most of the things I need. Gary has a car. He brings them.'

Sammy nodded. 'If you're sure.' He turned to Sadie. 'I think we should be going.'

Painfully, Sadie got to her feet. Her shoulders heaved a little because she was trying not to cry. 'I … I'm sorry, Mags,' she said softly.

'That's all right.' Mags' voice was as brittle as bone. 'It was nice of you to come.'

'May I come back?' Sadie pleaded. She was so afraid of the answer that she barely heard Mags reply, 'Yes. Danny would like that. Come tomorrow. My parents are coming this evening and I don't want to tire him.'

Outside in the corridor, Sadie said nothing, but she walked very determinedly towards a young man in a white coat. 'You are the doctor?' she demanded.

He was obviously a junior, but he answered carefully, 'I am Dr Allen.'

'Good.' Sadie needed to talk to someone in authority. 'The little boy in room B, his condition is serious, no?'

Dr Allen nodded. 'Children don't arrive on this ward unless their condition is critical.

'Can you give us some indication of how critical Daniel Gallagher's condition is?' Sammy interrupted.

'Are you family?'

Sammy glanced at Sadie. 'No,' he admitted.

'We're good friends,' Sadie added hopefully.

The doctor shook his head. 'I'm sorry. I can only release that kind of information to relatives.'

They're faces fell, and not yet being hardened to such distress, Dr Allen shifted uncomfortably on the spot, not knowing how to end the conversation. He had just decided to remember an urgent duty when the old lady looked up at him, the unblinking stare of her eyes startling the excuse out of his head.

'Would a person be right in thinking that Daniel is dying?'

'I'm afraid I can't answer that,' Dr Allen, newly graduated with distinction from Glasgow's distinguished medical school, replied. But Sadie had seen the pain in his face, the doctor's fear of failure.

'Thank you,' she said quietly. 'That is all I wanted to know.'

The hours passed in a kind of daze for Mags. Daniel took longer to come around from the sedation than the doctors had predicted, and when he did he was groggy and confused. She sat, holding his hand, whispering, 'You're a brave soldier, Danny. You're a brave soldier.' Then the room seemed filled with people. Her parents were there, her mother's arm around her shoulders, though she couldn't feel it. Her father kept starting sentences then stopping them. Eventually, he left the room and came back some minutes later with a comic for Daniel and his eyes rimmed with red.

A doctor entered and asked Mags for a moment. She followed him out and nodded to whatever he was saying, but none of it made sense. Words blew against her, like leaves, soon … be prepared … so sorry …, but she shook them off and went back into the room, still murmuring, 'You're a brave soldier, Danny. You're a brave soldier.'

She sat awake the whole night, sitting on the edge of the large, fold-down chair that was her mother's right, trying to hold on to him by willpower alone. Don't sleep, she screamed inside. If I go to sleep it'll get him. But she was too afraid to put a name to *it*.

Near dawn her eyelids drooped, and the chin, she had held up so defiantly in the face of death, slumped on to her chest. She struggled briefly against the weight of it then let it lure her down into its dark folds.

When she opened her eyes, Daniel was staring at her, his eyes huge and calm over the top of his oxygen mask. The sight of his lucid curiosity startled her into wakefulness and she sprang from her seat, as though caught enacting a crime. 'Danny, how are you, pet? Do you feel better? No, don't talk. Wait till I get a doctor.'

The doctor came. He smiled in front of Daniel, but his voice was grave. Mags didn't listen. She was elated. They had gotten through the night. They had beaten *it*. She knew. Daniel was going to defy them all again. What did the doctor know? He hadn't been there, hadn't consecrated Daniel's life with an offering of pain, hadn't witnessed the miracle. But she had. She knew.

And the miracle grew. By lunchtime, Daniel could take the oxygen mask off for brief periods, and even to eat a little soup. She was feeding him it with all the eagerness of the devotee, when he suddenly said something that frightened her. 'Mum.'

'Yes?'

'Can I have Rumble Bear here?'

The hand that was holding the soupspoon started to shake, so she dipped it back in the bowl, pretending to stir. Rumble Bear was a baby toy, discarded disdainfully long ago. He was old and worn and his growl had diminished to a throaty rattling, hence his name.

'Rumble Bear? Do you want me to bring anything else?'

'No.' He was propped up on pillows, and he slumped back into them. There were blue smudges under his eyes and he looked tired. 'I don't want to eat anything else now.'

'That's all right.' She adjusted the oxygen mask over his face again. 'You just sleep now. You're a brave soldier.'

He woke up again in the afternoon, his breathing sounded raspier and the blue smudges beneath his eyes were deeper despite the rest. 'Did you get Rumble Bear yet?' he asked.

'Not yet.' Mags was contrite. 'I didn't want to leave you alone.'

His face crumpled in a way she hadn't seen since babyhood and her own heart squeezed up inside her until she thought that it would choke the breath out of her. 'I'll get him as soon as your next visitors arrive,' she promised. 'You can wait that long, can't you?'

He nodded, but the look of doubt on his face sent terror piercing through her and she had to make a show of folding his clean pyjamas away in order to hide her face from him. She picked up one of the comics that her father had bought. 'Shall I read you some of this?' she began. But, just then, the door opened and Sadie put her head round. 'It is okay to come in now?'

Mags leapt up, her grin too wide. 'Sadie, come in. Look who it is Daniel.'

Sadie came into the room shyly. She had a large Tupperware box under one arm, which she handed a little guiltily to Mags. 'Sammy said not to, but hospital food is so bad. It's not much, just a few bits and pieces.'

'Thank you.'

'Maybe you don't feel so hungry now, but later, yes.' Sadie studied Mags' face anxiously, needing to ask questions, unable to bring herself to do so.

'Thanks,' Mags said again. She laid the box next to the folded pyjamas.

Sadie turned to Daniel. 'You are awake to see me this time,' she smiled.

Daniel returned her smile, wanly.

Sadie studied his face for a moment longer then said grandly. 'But it is not me I want you to see. I have brought you a visitor. A special visitor.' She glanced at the door, and when nothing happened, she repeated in louder tones, 'A special visitor.'

'Ho, ho, ho,' came a muffled voice, then Father Christmas entered the room. He was a little thinner than his portraits might have suggested, but his coat was of a brilliant red and he sported a fluffy white beard, reaching almost to his waist. He drew a sack from his shoulders and placed it beside Daniel's bed.

'Ho, ho, ho,' he said again.

Daniel regarded the sack for a moment then turned his attention back to the spirit of Christmas. 'Hello Sammy,' he said.

Santa seemed a little put out by this reaction, but then he threw back his hood and pulled down the beard. 'No fooling you, then.'

Daniel's eyes had shifted from Santa. 'What's in the sack?'

'Just a second,' Mags interrupted. 'I have to nip back to pick some things up. Maybe Sammy and Sadie could stay with you while I'm gone.'

Sammy began unbuttoning the Santa suit. 'Let me drive you. I've hired another car.'

'O, I can catch the bus,' Mags said quickly. 'I don't want to spoil your surprise.'

Sammy smiled. 'That's all right.' He glanced over at Sadie then winked at Daniel. 'We'll let Rudolph open them. She picked most of them anyway.'

Mags opened her mouth to protest then found she didn't have the energy. She picked up her coat. 'I'll be back soon.'

The car journey was lost to her. Vaguely, she could recall Sammy asking tactful questions about Daniel's condition and her own voice answering them, as if from a long way away. Then Sammy was shaking her shoulder, and saying very gently, 'Wake up. We're here.'

She blinked guiltily at him. 'I must have dozed off.'

'People do that when they're exhausted.'

She tried to smile at him and found that even the muscles in her face were too tired to rise. He shook his head. 'Stay here. Let me get whatever it is you need.'

'No.' She struggled with her seatbelt. 'I know where everything is. It'll be quicker if I go.'

But when she got in, she discovered she didn't know. She'd flung on a clean pair of jeans and her last clean sweater then hurried into Daniel's room. The emptiness of it caught her breath and she stood for a moment at the centre, lost and a little frightened. There was a sense of absence about it that seemed stronger than in the other rooms. As though the owner had permanently relinquished tenancy. The vacuum threatened to consume her, and she forced herself to hiss, 'Stop it, Mags. You're wasting time.'

Her legs jerked forward and from somewhere she found the strength to search through Daniel's drawers until she found an extra pair of cleanish pair of pyjamas. She tossed them on to the bed and went in search of Rumble Bear. But he was nowhere to be found. She tore out the contents of drawers and emptied the shallow wardrobe. Nothing. In panic she began to wonder if she might have given him away or, worse, thrown him out. She looked about desperately searching for a clue. Where would a discarded toy be hiding?

'Is something wrong?' Sammy was watching her from the door.

She looked up at him, frantically. 'I can't find a toy Daniel wants me to bring.'

'Have you tried under the bed?'

The bed. It was so obvious. She was a fool. Without even taking the time to thank him, she threw herself on all fours and reached an arm under the narrow gap below the bed. A great many things had found a resting place there, and she pulled out toy cars with no wheels and boxed games missing their counters. Eventually, her hand touched something soft, and, with a cry of relief, she dragged out a battered bear by the tip of an ear and held it aloft. 'I've got it.'

'Good. Let's go then.' He walked back into the living room and she turned to follow him when her foot nudged something she'd dislodged from under the bed. She stooped to pick it up, and seeing it was only an old exercise book, she almost threw it on the bed, when her eyes read the words, PRIVIT, HIGHLY CONFDENSHAL, and under them a skull and cross bones and something that might have been a radiation symbol.

Chapter 37

MAGS was silent on the journey back to the ward, and even as they approached Daniel's room, she ignored Sammy's questioning glances, and walked determinedly ahead, her fingers pressed deep into the guts of Rumble Bear. As they approached, Mags could hear Sadie's voice rising, as though in answer to a question. 'In heaven, time works differently. So you might only be there a few minutes before your mother arrives.'

Sadie glanced round guiltily at the sound of the door opening. 'You were quicker than I thought,' she said uncomfortably.

Mags ignored her and went straight to Danny. 'Here you are. Take good care of him, now.' He accepted the bear without embarrassment and tucked it in beside him.

'Did you get good presents?'

He nodded sleepily. 'But we couldn't get one to work. The remote-control car. It won't start.'

'Sammy will be able to fix that.'

He nodded again. 'That's what Sadie said.' His eyes were closing.

Mags turned briskly to Sammy. 'Would you mind staying with him for a little longer.'

Sammy frowned. 'Of course, but—'

Mags turned to Sadie. 'I think we should talk.'

Her eyes on the exercise book, Sadie gave a frightened nod and followed Mags from the room.

They went to the cafeteria, and ignoring Sadie's suggestion that they get a cup of tea, Mags steered them to a secluded table near a window and sat heavily down. She didn't speak for a long time, but sat with the exercise book open at the first page. Sadie watched her with frightened eyes, and just when she thought that perhaps she was waiting for her to speak first, Mags snapped the book shut, as though she'd read something obscene and looked Sadie full in the face. 'Why?'

Sadie opened her mouth to explain then, knowing that she couldn't, shut it again.

'You think he's dying,' Mags said accusingly. 'You've thought that all along.'

'Mags, I—'

But Mags wasn't listening.

'That's what all that rubbish about wanting me to realise not all stories have a happy ending was about, wasn't it?' Her eyes burned holes through Sadie's defences and the older woman nodded miserably. 'Yes.'

'You've been telling him you'll go to heaven with him.'

It wasn't a question, but Sadie nodded again.

'It's obscene.' Mags slapped the table making the exercise book jump in the air, and the one or two inhabitants of the cafeteria glance in their direction. Mags' voice dropped, but her tone grew uglier. 'Congratulations Mrs Gordon. You've invented a new form of child abuse.'

Sadie's eyes filled with tears and she shook her head trying to make Mags stop. But Mags wasn't ready to stop. 'Do you know what my son's one chance of survival was? Do you?' She didn't wait for an answer, but went on hysterically, 'It was the belief that he was going to live.' She leaned aggressively across the table. 'The belief that he was not going to die.' She emphasised each word separately. 'And you.' Her finger stabbed at Sadie. 'You couldn't stand the thought of meeting your maker on your own, could you? You've had your life, but you wanted my son's as well.'

'Mags please—' Sadie began, but Mags had heard enough. 'Stay away from Daniel,' she said, getting to her feet. She was swaying slightly as though intoxicated. She turned to go, then something occurred to her and she turned back. 'Sammy thinks that we're so alike. Did you know that?' She laughed scornfully. 'Do you know what the difference between us is? Do you?'

Sadie shook her head.

Mag's lip curled back. 'The difference is, I love Daniel. You only pretended to. I believe in him. Do you hear?' She clutched the edge of the table to steady herself. 'I believe *in* him. That's the difference.' She shook her head suddenly, as though just remembering something, and turning her back fled the room. Her mind was so filled with Daniel that she didn't hear Sadie say softly, 'But I believe him.'

Her own hanky was quite soaked through by the time a large, male handkerchief was proffered before her. 'Come on, ma. Tell me what's happened.'

Sammy listened while Sadie recounted everything, right back to her first meeting with Daniel. He offered no comment, but his eyes grew wider and he shook his head from time to time, as though not quite believing what he was hearing. When she had finished, he stared at her open-mouthed for some time, before saying incredulously, 'Why did you do it, ma?'

She sniffed and wiped her nose in his hanky. 'I made a promise. I didn't know how to get out of it.'

'But, ma. He's not even Jewish.'

She stared at him, surprised. 'I didn't think that would make a difference.'

He ran a hand through his hair. 'You've never heard of the chosen people?'

She frowned and dabbed at her eyes. 'You know I agreed with Golda Meir on that,' she said. 'I think we were just the first to be chosen. God is there for everyone.'

Sammy was rubbing his temples. 'A lot of schools of thought might disagree with you.'

'Pah.' She waved a hand. 'What have I to do with schools of thought. They're all run by men with more time on their hands than sense.'

'This from the woman who promised to take a child to heaven with her.'

Sadie's face crumpled again and Sammy was sorry for his words. 'But, how on earth did you think you were going to do it?' he asked. An unpleasant thought occurred to him. 'You weren't considering suicide.'

'No.' She blew her nose. 'I went to see Rabbi Karpf, but he said it was out of the question.'

Sammy rolled his eyes. 'We should be thankful for small mercies. So how were you going to perform this miracle of babysitting?'

Sadie frowned to show that she didn't like his tone. 'It was your idea,' she said crossly.

'My idea?'

'Yes. You said my old ticker couldn't take too much strain.'

Sammy saw the light. 'So you've been trying to scare yourself to death with all these visits to carnivals and balloon rides.'

Sadie nodded sorrowfully. 'I thought if it just happened I wouldn't be doing anything wrong and I could maybe wait for Daniel.'

Sammy covered his eyes, not knowing whether to laugh or cry. 'So you thought you'd tempt fate into taking charge.'

'Yes. I've done everything I'm not supposed to.' Sadie's eyes filled with tears again. 'But I never felt better in my life.' She covered her eyes. 'I'm a foolish, old woman,' she sobbed.

Sammy put an arm round her. 'No, ma. No.' He patted her shoulder. 'You're better than all of us.'

When Sammy put his head round the door, he couldn't see Mags' face. Her hair had come out its band and hid her profile. She was back, sitting at the bedside, Daniel's hand clasped in hers. Daniel was very still, a waxen image again. On the side table were all the toys he and Sadie had brought.

He let himself in and said very softly, 'Mags.'

She jumped, as though he'd screamed at her. He was taken aback to see the look on her face. He'd expected anger, coldness at least, but there was nothing. Her face was empty, lost to a pain that he could never touch. He dropped his eyes. 'My mother ... she didn't mean any harm.'

He dared to look up and found Mags' empty eyes on him. 'I understand,' she said tonelessly.

Sammy shoved his hands in his pockets. Maybe anger would have been preferable. 'She's outside,' he explained awkwardly. 'Can she … would you let her say goodbye?'

Mags nodded dully. 'All right.'

On Sammy's command, Sadie crept into the room. She had intended to say something to Mags, to beg for forgiveness, or at least understanding, but seeing her wretched, blank expression, she only took the seat on the other side of the bed and took Daniel's free hand. It was so light and colourless that she could scarcely feel it at all. 'Daniel,' she whispered. 'About the promise. 'I am so sorry.'

She felt the faintest pressure on her hand. Or had she imagined it? She was afraid to disturb him again.

Mags was silent for a very long time, then she said quite unexpectedly. 'What am I going to do? How will I learn to live with myself?'

Sadie wasn't sure she was speaking to her, but she answered anyway. 'You'll learn because Daniel is giving you a great gift.'

'A gift?' Mags' blind eyes sought Sadie out. 'What kind of gift is this?'

Sadie's eyes were so brim-full of tears that she wasn't sure she could speak, but she forced herself to explain. 'He is giving you his childhood.'

Mags shook her head and Sadie went painfully on, 'He is the child that all we mothers secretly long for, the eternal child that will never leave you. He's your little angel, who'll never make that ultimate betrayal of loving another woman. He's yours, Mags, and only yours, now and for ever.' Sadie stopped, unable to continue.

'You were better to him than I was,' Mags said sadly. 'You understood when I never did. You saw he was a person. I only ever saw a child.'

'You are his mother,' Sadie said firmly. 'You are not meant to see these things.'

But Mags wouldn't let it go. 'You wanted to tell me, didn't you?' she said slowly. 'You've been trying to tell me about Daniel since we first met. Trying to tell me to let him go.'

Sadie didn't deny it, but before she could speak, there was a faint tremor in Daniel's body and his grip on both women suddenly tightened. 'Mags' eyes grew frightened and she stared wildly at Sadie, as though expecting her to do something. 'It's not too late,' Sadie said. 'Let him go.'

Mags turned to Daniel, staring down at him, as though seeing him for the first time in a long while. His skin had become strangely translucent, more like stone than flesh and there was a tinge of blue about his lips. 'Danny,' Mags began then bit her lip. She swallowed hard, and, Sadie watching her, suspected that she was remonstrating with herself. 'Danny,' she began again in a more confident tone. 'Mummy loves you. You know I love you. But I think it might be time to go and see what colour heaven is. Don't be afraid. Remember what Sadie said. Time's different there. I'll be there before you know it.' She glanced at Sadie and Sadie nodded, encouraging her to go on. 'It's all right, Danny. Everything's going to be fine. Mummy's here and I love you. Don't be afraid to go. Heaven's a wonderful place for little boys.' There was no response, not even the faintest pressure on her hand. But he seemed more peaceful than before and his breathing was no longer laboured, but low and shallow.

Mags looked at Sadie and they turned together to look at Daniel. Watching. Waiting.

There was the slightest sound, like a sigh, and one of the machines began to give out a piercing wail of alarm. Then the room was filled with medical staff. Efficient, calm, they swept Sadie and Mags aside trying to turn back the course of nature. Mags stood in a corner of the room, her hands stiff beside her sides, like a soldier awaiting orders. She made no attempt to interfere in the frantic exertions around her. She felt quite remote from anything they were doing. She knew he was gone.

They let her sit with him and she took her seat quite calmly, not even touching him, happy just to see him at rest. It was very quiet. Someone had turned off all the machines. Sammy entered the room and stood beside her. He didn't attempt to touch her, understanding that bereavement has its own boundaries, frontiers that the unbereaved cannot cross.

After a while, she said irrelevantly, 'You never think your child will go before you. But it's all right. I can see that now. And it's all right.'

'I'm so sorry,' he said helplessly. 'For everything.'

'That's okay.' She surprised herself at how calm she sounded. The real grief would take a while to hit home. 'Sadie only wanted to help. And she did. I think she was really able to help Daniel more than anyone.'

Sammy drew the back of his hand over his eyes, and Mags was surprised to find that she couldn't cry yet. She extended a hand. 'I hope we can stay friends.'

He nodded vigorously. 'I'd like that.' He glanced round. 'I should take ma home now.'

Mags shook her head. 'Isn't she outside?'

'No. She never came out.'

They exchanged a look that said more than words, then panic set in and they began to search. It didn't take long. She was sitting on one of the visitor's chairs on the far side of the room, hidden by a large piece of equipment that had been shoved aside in the fight for Daniel's life. She was quite erect, though her eyes were closed, as if in sleep.

As they approached, they knew, but Sammy couldn't help but whisper, 'Ma?'

He was about to go forward, but Mags restrained him. 'No, don't.'

He looked down, disbelieving. Pleadingly. 'What is it?'

Mags' eyes were filled with tears and she reached out to take his hand. Together, they turned towards Sadie's peaceful figure, and this time Sammy understood. 'Has she … ? She hasn't … has she?'

Mags squeezed his hand. 'It's all right. She's keeping her promise.'

SIMON'S WIFE

Jerusalem, September, 70 CE

THE sun, a blinding orb, threw flames across the sky above the ancient city. But its scorching light revealed an uncertain landscape. Seared stone walls, fallen archways, colonnades with their roofs smashed, their shattered pillars littering the cracked and dislodged paving stones that had once lined the streets. And in between the pyramids of rubble and the charred, broken beams the city was peopled by figures stranger than the landscape itself. Mostly they lay on the ground, their twig-like limbs held stiffly, their heads rolling back, as though Death had come amongst them and persuaded them to dance a macabre jig. Those whose bodies had not been torn apart by starving dogs, that is.

Not all Jerusalem's inhabitants were inanimate. Here and there the sunlight caught the crown of a dented helmet or the surface of a cuirass turned rust-coloured with blood. The men who wore these were dressed in tunics the colour of mercuric sulphide. They had sallow, vicious faces, and the hard, well-fed figures of soldiers. In their hands they wielded the deadly *gladius* of Rome, and they marched steadily through Jerusalem, tearing her apart.

Sometimes screams pierced the air or a building crashed to the ground with a rolling sound, like a tremor in the earth. Rarely, other inhabitants of the city were exposed. Bands of stringy Jerusalemites, moving quickly past, glancing everywhere with the haunted faces of wolves. And shortly afterwards the screaming would begin again.

In the midst of this chaos a woman and a small boy, barely out of babyhood, were running for their lives. They were not running to safety. There was no safety to be had. Torn from where they had been hiding in the tunnels and sewers under the city, they were as helpless in the sudden light as the first creatures of creation struggling out of the earth. Nor were they running in the hope of evading their captors, because they were already captured, and making them run was simply the way the legionaries had of making sport.

The woman's name was Shelamzion bat Judah. She was nineteen years old. And until a few days ago she had been the most important woman in the whole of Jerusalem. Now she was nothing. A faceless captive in a defeated city. Holding on to her child, dragging him behind her. A gash on her inner thigh oozing blood down her leg. Daggers of breath tearing at her breast. Hopeless. Nowhere to go. Everything gone. Jerusalem in flaming ruins about her. The mighty temple destroyed.

'Simon!'

She called out his name, knowing it was useless, knowing that the End of Days was upon them. Still clinging to that last vision of him being dragged away on the orders of the Roman commander. Pleading with God, who must surely come now, to spare him.

Her shins collided with hard stone—the ruins of a pillar—and she stumbled, almost letting go the precious fingers that clung to hers.

'*Imma!*' Mother.

She did not answer. Her eyes had found the smoking remnants of the Sanctuary. And she looked up towards that place, where millions had come to pray. To be near the inner sanctum, that holy of holies where the spirit of the deity dwelt, seeing only crumbling stone and charred rafters, and a huge, blank emptiness, a colossus of nothing that went on and on, reaching all the way to the sky and beyond. And she understood then, more than any of them, that the dream was over. The Jews were no more. God had abandoned them …

Two Months Later

Rome, November, 70 CE

Abandoned, yes. The flaring image of the Temple wavered then collapsed behind Shelamzion's fluttering eyelids, and was replaced by a yawning maw of blackness, so thick it seemed to press against her eyes. The stench of it crawled over her skin, confusing her senses for a moment, so that time wound backwards and she thought herself still in the ruins of the Temple Mount. At once she reached out for her son. But the chain around her wrist cut the movement short, drawing her widening eyes towards what she could not see. Then instantly all the horror welled up again. Rome. They had brought her here in the last days of the war. When everything was lost. Half mad with grief and terror they had brought her. Because she was Simon's wife, and her death was a morsel to be savoured.

Later, her jailor, who was known as the *custos*, fastened the chains about her wrists. Ghastly as a grinning skull in the torchlight, his was the last face she saw. Then it was the spiralling darkness for company, except for those rare, unguessable moments when her water bowl was refilled or a morsel of food was pushed alongside it.

Gradually, as the days passed and horror grew over her, like a numbing scab, she began to wonder what had happened to the other prisoners. Those with luck on their side had probably been sold as slaves. The unlucky ones would already have met their deaths in the arenas and theatres. Or was it the other way round? She shuddered and drew her knees close in to her chest. What a world to live in, where the dead were more fortunate than the living.

The mist rolling up from the Tiber had an evil smell about it. Along the walls of the basilica ragged beggars huddled against the dank archways, while soothsayers and penniless prophets hissed out words of doom into the yellow air. Late in the morning a hired litter passed them by, moving laboriously along the *Clivus Capitolinus*, before finally setting down in front of a low, uninspiring building, known to the citizenry of Rome as the Carcer; the state prison. After a few moments the elderly occupant of the litter made his exit with more than the usual degree of stiffness, and stood self-consciously in the middle of the road, his head turning slowly to look back the way he had come. He seemed undecided.

Above him the sun appeared briefly, imprisoned behind the curtain of dense vapours and blank-faced as an uninscribed coin. The same sun that had beaten down, like a relentless harpie, on the legionaries' heads all through the long war in Judea. Hard to believe it of this pallid disk. And, for a brief moment, he wondered if the prisoner might not be thinking the same thoughts. Then he smiled at his foolishness. Given where they were holding her, there wasn't much chance that Shelamzion bat Judah was looking at the sun.

The fog was lifting his skin in a patina of tiny bumps. It made his bones ache. He had slept poorly, as old men do, kept awake by pains in his legs and thoughts of the prisoner. She would surely be in chains; the mighty bandit queen brought low. And he found the thought did not displease him. He took a step towards the Carcer. As her interrogator it was fitting that she should be humbled before him. But he had not come here, as if on Nike's wings, for vengeance. It was a story that had drawn him. If he was right, she held within her a tale, like a searing flame, Homeric in breadth, alive with battle and bloodshed, the cries of soldiers over sun-blackened landscapes, hubris, lust, and the dreadful, harrowing echo of a toppled god. *Anthropos versus Theos.* The clash of the mortal with the divine.

He drew a deep, shuddering breath. To hear such a tale would be to remember it forever. And for weeks now it had existed right under the long noses of the literati, there for the taking, yet he alone, Fabius Cornelius

Grammaticus, a humble schoolmaster, had been graced with the wit to see it.

At once a great contentment washed over him, and he forgot the evil in the air. Indeed, so certain was he of the gods' favour that he could almost feel it, like a warm breath upon the back of his neck. Boldly he mounted the steps and beat out a commanding tattoo on the Carcer's door, all the while thinking, Only let the muse of Hellas linger on my tongue. And they will hear me sing more sweetly than Theocritus. The door opened and he stepped inside.

The *custos*, a small, wizened individual, with an incongruous pot belly, was waiting for Cornelius. They stared at each other for a moment and Cornelius was forced to ask, 'Do you know who I am?'

'Fabius Cornelius Grammaticus, your honour. Our new assistant governor,' the *custos* answered. He gave a bow, which was obsequious enough, though Cornelius noticed that it was somewhat shorter than decorum demanded.

'You may have heard of me,' he suggested.

'Indeed, sir.'

Cornelius bestowed upon him a small smile. And, encouraged, the man continued, 'You are the cousin of our esteemed governor, Fabius Quintus.'

Cornelius' smile vanished and his voice became icy. 'It is my humble opinion that I am an *historicus*.' And when the *custos* stared up at him with filmy, uncomprehending eyes, he added wearily, 'I am a writer of histories, a scholar of … some reputation.' He heard the self-doubt in his voice and wondered if the *custos* had heard it too. But the man only shuffled from foot to foot, then scratched his arse. Cornelius sighed. 'You understand your orders?'

'Yes, sir.'

Nonetheless he repeated them. 'As Fabius Quintus' assistant, I will be taking his place on the weekly visitations. Understand, it is not my intention to make these visits on a regular day or time, or to provide you with warning of my arrival.' He paused, raising an eyebrow to see if the *custos* took his meaning, and the man nodded and bowed again. Cornelius continued. 'I may also decide to inspect a particular prisoner from time to time, or even to conduct interviews with them. If this is the case, I am not to be disturbed except on matters of the utmost importance.' Again he paused and the *custos* twisted his hands into an ingratiating knot.

'Yes, sir.' He ran his tongue over rotten teeth. 'Fabius Quintus gave me to understand that you would be speaking with the prisoners. And that you had a most particular interest in our new arrival.' Cornelius stiffened, but the *custos* did not seem to notice. He cocked his head over his shoulder towards the dark passage behind him. 'Been keeping her nice for you. Though I'm afraid, sir, she's been got at. Legionaries most likely. They're good lads, but rough.' He glanced up unexpectedly and something in his leering expression made the colour in Cornelius' face drain away then rush back in, like an angry tide.

'I will see her now,' he said sharply.

The *custos* seemed on the point of saying more then changed his mind. He gave a soft chuckle, and took a limping step into the passage.

'This way, sir. This way.'

With the aid of a smoking lamp, he led Cornelius to the end of the corridor, and then down a flight of filthy steps. 'Mind where you step, sir. Prisoners aren't too mindful of what they leave behind.'

Cornelius followed silently, appalled as any spirit entering the underworld.

Only let her be beautiful, he thought. It was said that Bouddica had been beautiful. But then they'd said the same thing about Cleopatra, quite in contradiction with those who had known her. Perhaps it didn't matter. The nobility of her spirit would transcend any earthly shortcomings. As he followed the *custos* down the narrowing passageway it occurred to him that he had, in fact, made that very point to his cousin Quintus when he had agreed to take on the role of assistant governor. Naturally Quintus had laughed, pointing out in his usual languid manner that an enemy is never more virtuous than when he lies dead at one's feet. Did not Scipio weep for Carthage just after he'd sown its ruins with salt?

The *custos* had stopped before a low door and was beckoning to him. He flinched and did not move. The *custos* nodded, as though he sympathized. 'Only I need you to hold the light, sir. Easier to pull the bolt back with two hands.' Understanding, Cornelius jerked to life, and took the lamp. The *custos* released the bolt, and with the moan of ages, the door began to swing open slowly under its own weight. Cornelius looked to the *custos* for instruction, but already the man was gazing back the way they had come. 'I'll leave you the lamp, sir. Know this place like the back of my hand, I do.' And when Cornelius still hesitated, he added, 'She's chained, sir. Can't cause you no mischief.' Then looking for all the world like old Charon returning to the gates of hell, he limped past the new assistant governor of the Carcer and was lost in the thickening darkness.

Cornelius felt a number of emotions looking at the bandit queen, the primary one being disappointment. He had hoped for beauty, been prepared for ugliness, but somehow he had not considered how very, very ordinary a legend would appear in the flesh. He stared wonderingly at this wild-haired woman, amazed that no touch of the divine tinged her drabness. And while there was pity in his thoughts, there was also distaste, and a powerful feeling of justice well done at the sight of her degradation. She might have been part of a tableau by Skopa or Veio depicting Psyche's humiliation in the wilderness, entitled 'Defiance Conquered'.

'Stand up.' He spoke to her in the clipped Latin of his class, which, at first, she did not seem to understand. Then, with difficulty, she got to her feet and stood before him, hands clasped, eyes downcast. He moved closer, covering his nose and mouth to protect them from the stench. After careful deliberation he chose not to speak, partly to demonstrate his power over her, partly because all the grand speeches and clever epigrams he had composed in Greek did not seem fitting in this place of filth. Not what I expected, he thought. No, not at all. Yet what did I expect? The flame-haired queen of the Iceni, bare-breasted, her loins girded in the skulls of men, or the venomous sensuality of a Cleopatra? She was none of these. Young, yes. But well past the first, coltish bloom of youth. Her features were too strong for any classical dimensions of beauty. She seemed to be all darkness and tension, poised like a young hind, nostrils quivering, ready for flight. But there was something broken there too. There were marks of suffering upon her, a few silver threads of hair woven through the black, and a livid scar below her temple, which wound its way towards her ear. Without thinking, Cornelius reached out to touch it. She held very still, but her mouth opened in a gasp, and he saw the ragged edge of a broken tooth towards the back.

Her gasp broke the spell and he let his hand fall. At once he saw his mistake in coming here. This was no Arsinoë to be paraded through Rome in chains, beautiful and sad. He had been promised a queen, the remnant of a long and noble line, around whom he would weave his story. *Bellum Romanae*. His magnificent history of the Roman war in Judea. After all, had he not said to Quintus that too many accounts of great individuals were written after their death, pieced together by self-seekers and enemies alike? This was an opportunity to reach out and touch the living flesh of history. And make his name too, though he hadn't said that. And Quintus had agreed, even flattered him on his insight. How typical. He would have said anything to get out of his duties as governor. The man had no scruples.

Well, he had gone too far this time. This ragged, dirty little Jewess was more urchin than queen. So he would tell Quintus when he resigned first thing tomorrow. For the moment there was nothing to be done but to complete the duties of the day as quickly as possible. Coldly, he asked, 'Do you know why you are here?'

She answered without looking up. 'To die.'

He made an irritated sound at the back of his throat. 'Of course.' Only a fool would think otherwise. He closed his eyes for a moment then continued in the weary, deliberate tones he reserved for the slow-witted. 'To be made an example of. You should now consider your life a warning to those who harbour revolt in their hearts. And, you may be assured, your death will merely strengthen the glories of this empire yet further.'

He paused, hoping for a reaction in that narrow, downcast face, but it was immobile. And, knowing of great men who balked at the first mention of their mortality, he softened his tone somewhat as he continued. 'When your husband returns in Titus' entourage, you will be witness to—'

'Simon! Then … he lives?'

Cornelius dropped the hand he had been discretely raising to his nose. He was taken aback. Had she not known? Yet it was possible. She had been shipped back to Rome while Titus set off on his victorious tour of the East. So in keeping with the man's character not to miss a chance to rub his enemies' noses in it. Not much of the poet in that one, it was clear. Cornelius avoided her eyes, which were now turned upwards, beseeching him to answer.

'You … will be witness to the justice Rome bestows on traitors and renegades.' He was faltering despite himself, and he grasped at cruelty. 'Judgement has already been passed. Simon bar Gioras will be thrown from the Tarpeian Rock at the end of the Triumph to mark the return of the Emperor's son.'

He expected her to flinch then, to scream, to fall to her knees. She did none of these things. But two tears, plump as pomegranates, budded at the corners of her eyes and rolled down her cheeks. And Cornelius stood rigid before her, surprised by the vividness of his captive's pain. Quite at odds with the dogged inflexibility of his classical upbringing. True, there had been pity when his wife died. Had she not combined the best virtues of her class, modesty and austerity? And he missed her presence in much the same way he missed a beautiful Corinthian vase he had once owned. But this woman seemed to draw her pain from a deeper, more tragic source, then form it into an arrow, which she aimed straight at his breast. He did not know yet that this was her gift, the ability to pierce men's souls. And he felt only the sudden violation of her intrusion. He took a step back, more to emphasise her humiliation than to distance himself, asking, 'Do you know who I am?'

She looked steadily into his eyes and he looked back, oddly experiencing none of that mixture of pity and loathing the freeborn feel instinctively for the captive, but rather one of those strange moments of perfect communication, which he had read of in Plato's *Respublica*, but had always assumed only existed between men. For an instant he felt perfectly understood, and he whispered again, 'You know who I am?'

She cocked her head to one side, studying him, then nodded, and whispered back, 'A very lonely man.'

Her comment struck him like a slap—what had she seen?—and his jaw fell open under its impact. A huge anger seized him and it was only his need to demonstrate the uniquely civilized cast of his nature that made him rain down words instead of blows. 'You will know me,' he spat over numbed lips. 'I am your gaoler. Every crumb of bread, every drop of water you receive in these last days of your life is dependent upon me. If you do not wish your husband's last view of you to be a crawling skeleton, remember that.' He drew breath and had the satisfaction of spying a slight quivering of her chin. What had disturbed her when the thought of death left her unmoved? The husband? Yes. There was the Achilles' heel. He drove the point home. 'Perhaps you regret the day you allied yourself with a bandit, whose sole intention was the destruction of the finest civilization on earth.'

She had lowered her lids at his first assault. Now she looked up, eyes flashing with unearthly lights. 'What do you see, Roman? A blind woman? A heap of ashes?' She took a step towards him and her chains groaned to restrain her. 'Look again.'

Cornelius blinked. Perhaps it was the guttering light that made the shadows shiver back, like the raising of a curtain. Or perhaps it was the lowering of that soft voice almost to a growl that suddenly made Shelamzion bat Judah something more than a piteous heap of rags crushed into submission in the stinking bowels of Rome. She was tall and gaunt in the half-light, the stamp of her nobility unmistakable. Here was the queen he had come looking for. And how she despised him.

Her lips curled back. 'Look again, Roman. Did you think me a child, following my husband in deed and thought without question? How little you understand. Aye, my husband was the enemy of Rome. Would that you had seen how the legions trembled before him. Their name for him was *Excisio*. Destruction. And I was his bride.'

Cornelius stood transfixed. Did those who sought the cavernous secrets of the Sybil feel this strange loss of power? He gaped at the bandit queen. And suddenly all the pride went out of her and her head slumped forwards. 'Have you got what you came for, Roman?' Her voice was quite different now, small and empty, like a child who has known nothing but pain. Cornelius shook his head.

'This is not why I came.'

She barely lifted her eyes. 'Then … why? Has all Rome not done goading me?'

'That is not why I am here.'

She turned away as far as the chains would allow, and hunched her shoulders against all the weight of her sorrows. He thought she would not speak again. Her eyes were closed. But she shivered suddenly, as though the ghost of her thoughts walked through her, and asked, 'What do you want of me?'

'I want—' He paused, not knowing how to go on. Some instinct warned him to go no further. In a breath of clarity, he had seen her as she was, touched by a source magnificent and terrible. And to get too close would be to burn. *Cave quem di diligent.* Beware whom the gods love.

'I—' he started again, reaching out to her even as he made the sign against evil. She opened her eyes and his hand fell.

'I want you to live forever.'

Further reading

Sparsile Fiction

Simon's Wife

A secret history

L. M. Affrossman

Three decades have passed since the death of Jesus of Nazareth on a Roman cross, and Judea is teetering on the brink of apocalypse. Caught up in the horror that will inspire the Book of Revelation, a young woman is fighting for survival.

In the dark days that follow the Roman devastation of Jerusalem in AD 70, nineteen-year-old Shelamzion bat Judah finds herself captured and awaiting both her own execution and that of her husband, former rebel-leader Simon bar Gioras. Alone and forgotten, there seems little reason to go on living, yet a strange friendship begins to grow between Shelamzion and her austere, old Roman jailor, Fabius Cornelius Grammaticus.

With his pretensions to be recognized as an historian in the style of Livy, it is to her he turns to record the true version of events behind the insurrection in Judea that led to the destruction of her country. Time is running out, however, and unknowingly history is being rewritten by a traitor's hand.

Comics and Columbine

An outcast look at comics, bigotry
and school shootings

Tom Campbell

THE SCHOOL SHOOTER WHO DIDN'T SHOOT.

Growing up an autistic loner Thomas Campbell's schooldays were a living nightmare of bullying and abuse that saw him in psychiatric care by age 8.

The target of entire classrooms, he developed a lifelong hatred of all things educational. This hatred – the shared thinking of the school shooter – has gifted him with a unique insight into the slaughter we are witnessing in our schools now.

For the first time a book is written from the perspective of the classroom avenger, one that explores their distorted thinking and reveals the 'socially acceptable' evils that provoke such a lethal response.

Science for Heretics

Why so much of science is wrong

Barrie Condon

SCIENCE IS BROKEN.

Throughout history, philosophers and scientists have warned about the fundamental flaws lying at the heart of all aspects of science.
The possible extinction level risks that mankind runs by ignoring these warnings have generally been forgotten.
This book, written by an established scientist, looks at the hollow foundations on which our maths, physics, biology and medicine are built and describes better ways to navigate the hidden dangers of the universe. It aims to be accessible to the general reader who lacks a scientific background.